SO FELL ARE THE FAE

A ROMANTIC FAE FANTASY

THROUGH THE WALL
BOOK ONE

KAT KEENAN

TWISTED
ROOTS
MEDIA

To everyone who has felt like they don't fit in.

Fell Fae, Fell Fae, catch me if you can. Fell Fae, Fell
Fae, come get me while you can.

— AN EASTLANDS URBAN MYTH

CHAPTER I
ꓕNNARA

Blood steamed in the snow, bright red and carving dents in the pristine white. I pulled my jacket tight, my breath little puffs of frost. The electric heaters in the greenhouse would have to wait. Mom would be upset, but she'd understand. As the healer who taught me everything I knew, she'd likely be the only person who would. We never stayed in one place long enough for anyone to get to know me, never long enough for me to attend school or college, never even long enough for me to learn how to use city-tech or drive a car.

But I had Nolan now, and I was twenty-two, old enough to make my own decisions. I could decide to stop running. My stomach roiled at the thought. Not running would get us killed. Witchery was a death sentence. But if I couldn't reliably use my magic, I could stop trying, stop running, and be with Nolan, him no wiser that he lay with a witch.

The tracks were likely deer. It was hard to tell in snow this deep. The cold crept around me, wrapping around my legs which weren't nearly as insulated as my torso. The blood splatter wasn't so much, hopefully I could get there in time. The trail turned westward, and I chewed my lip. Not many things went toward the Wall. It was as if the animals knew the area was unnatural.

The Wall separated the humans in the Eastlands from the Fell Fae. And even though my mom chose for us to live this close to it, I never wanted to be too near. She said it was the perfect place to hide, but it unnerved me. There was something about it. They said the fae would suck out your life, bewitch you, control you. Yet every time I was near enough to it, something in me taunted me to reach out, to let a tendril of my magic in, to see what would happen.

The animals had it right. It was unnatural. There were tales of fae beasts coming across and wreaking havoc in our lands. That was ages ago. Money from the neon-lit cities funded an entire garrison of Wall Walkers, men and women who walked the Wall to protect us from anything fae. As far as I knew, the job was boring, yet someone felt they needed to be here despite all the talk of disbanding them.

The snow thickened, and my boots sank deep, wet-cold sliding under the leather. I cursed myself for not having the foresight to put on my snowshoes. The blood trail went right up to one of the stone cairns marking the Wall. The stacked rocks sat there with not a single snowflake on them, the sight always disconcerted me. But one wouldn't know the Wall was there otherwise. To the human eye it looked as if the forest, thick with pines, continued. Some said that if they got too close that they felt the need to turn around. Others said they ran smack into it. But I was the only one who felt beckoned to continue through.

Even now, being this close, I felt its pull. Did Mom feel it? Was it a witch thing? I never asked, didn't plan to. It was bad enough that I couldn't control my magic, feeling an attraction to the Wall was even worse.

The blood trail followed along the Wall, and there was the doe, limping through the snow. Its head turned, ears twitching. I braced myself for it to dart, as well as it could, back into the forest, but it didn't. Instead, it lowered down into the snow, letting out a sad bleat. Requesting help or surrendering, I didn't know.

I itched to bolt toward it, but the healer in me kept my movements slow, not wanting to spook it. Once near, I lowered myself down, gently petting between her ears. Her breath labored. Having introduced myself, I spoke in a low, soothing voice. My hands ran down her back, over her flanks. Her breath wasn't labored. She *was* in labor. It was spring after all, even if all this snow would fool anyone even in these parts, making them think we were still in the grips of winter.

The blood came from her leg. Something — a trap, maybe — had shredded her skin and muscles. She pulled her limb away as I got closer to it, and she let out another low bleat.

I sat back on my heels. I could heal her, fix her leg, make sure the fawn was ok and be on my way. No one was in this forest. The closest house was our own, so Mom might feel me. It would get me an earful alright to use my magic out in the open. She kept our house, barn, and greenhouse all warded. If we performed magic in them, no one else would be the wiser. But out here, my magic could be felt.

I sighed. Who was I kidding? If she felt me use my magic, we'd be packing by the afternoon. She'd make us leave. Again. The threat of Trapper's coming after us was too much.

The doe let out a snuffle. She'd never walk on that leg again, but she could survive. If I used my magic, she could do more than survive. One thing, however, was certain. If I couldn't grasp the magic, I would know my only choice was to get my medical kit. Oh, what would I give for a hospital-standard one with skin-glue or even a suture kit and definitely high-grade antibiotics, and not the herbs and drugstore one I had cobbled together with a sewing kit. I closed my eyes and began to search for the life magic all around me. Green outlines formed.

"What are you doing, Innara?"

I screamed, my heart in my throat. Nolan stood behind me, his Wall Walker rifle slung across his lean chest. His wavy, dark blond hair was pulled back and secured at the back, but strands had already fallen out.

So much for being alone in this forest. That was too close.

"How do you do that?"

"Stay so stealthy?" Nolan grinned. It was his smile that had done me in a few weeks ago. It lit up his otherwise stern face. "It's a gift. Can't catch any fae beasties if we go rampaging around the Wall."

He closed the distance as I stood up, brushing the snow off me. His hand ran up my back, clasping around my neck as he leaned over to kiss me. The necklace he always wore swung away from his skin.

Every time we were together, I couldn't believe it. That he chose me. Before him, no one had ever shown interest.

A few weeks ago, he'd arrived in our small village from somewhere in the south and joined the Wall Walkers. He brought news that they wanted to make sure all garrisons were well manned. We had run into each other at the weekly market. And somehow, he decided I was the one he wanted to get to know.

My cheeks warmed at the memory of how I'd stumbled over my words at that first meeting, but he'd showed up at my doorstep a few days later with an injured Wall Walker and asked if he could come by some time.

He brought his other hand up, touching my face, deepening our kiss. "Is there a night your mom will be out?" he murmured as he trailed kisses along my cheek to just below my ear. His hands dropped to hold mine. His index finger slipped between our clasped hands, and he stroked my palm. I shivered.

I had all but forgotten the doe until she groaned, yanking my attention back to her. I broke the kiss, torn between how my body ached for him and the injured animal beside us.

"She never goes anywhere at night," I said as I sank back down into the snow beside the doe.

Nolan grunted. "Well, I can't take you to the barracks. Maybe we can meet at the old witch hut." His lips curled and his eyes crinkled, pulling at the scar near his right eye.

My stomach flipped. It always did whenever anyone even mentioned witch-anything around me. To everyone else, the hut was a meetup. A place for the younger crowd to have a party, and I was sure plenty of nighttime escapades, which apparently I was now considering.

The doe made another grunt and tried to move her leg.

"Were you going to heal the deer? Is that why you're here?" he asked as he knelt to get a better look at her.

"I saw the blood and followed it." There was no way I could heal her with my magic with Nolan here, and definitely not with my adrenaline still rushing. Panic meant my witchery was well out of my grasp. Besides, I couldn't wind up fleeing again. "Will you stay with her? I'm going to go back and get my kit. I can at least put something on her leg." How had I not grabbed my kit to begin with? I turned and trudged through the snow, not waiting for an answer. My nerves after being snuck up on and then his mention of the witch house could use the space. I could hurry home, get the kit, and be back within fifteen minutes.

A rifle shot cracked and echoed through the forest, and I froze.

I turned back to Nolan as he swung his rifle back onto his back and made his way to me.

My mouth dropped open. "What did you do?" I hissed out. He'd killed her. Fury made my limbs tremble.

"She wasn't going to be able to use the leg again. I put her out of her misery." He stopped a foot away. "You didn't seriously think you could help her?"

"She was in labor," I shouted. "And yes, she may not have been able to walk on that leg, but she could have survived. I've seen it before."

"Don't be naive. She may have healed, and then the doe and her fawn would have been eaten by some predator. I spared them. If you had healed them, you would have been setting them up to be a meal." He crossed his arms. "Let's stop arguing." He reached out, sliding warm fingers into my hair and around the back of my head.

I jerked away. "How dare you! I could have...I could have..."

"You could have what?" Nolan cut me off from saying something I knew I should never say to anyone. "No amount of ointment would have healed her shattered bones." He arched a brow at me, and that beautiful, angular face of his turned smug. I wanted to smack it right off him.

I had to shake myself. Striking people was not something I did. I was a healer, for Wall's sake. Tears stung my eyes, and I didn't want him to see it. He'd already called me out for what I feared I truly was. Naive.

Anger, embarrassment, and something else I couldn't name swirled in an unpleasant mix. I whirled and stormed off.

From behind me, he called out "Don't be ridiculous! It was just a deer! A mercy kill."

I ignored him and made my way home not caring about the amount of snow pouring into my boots or how I'd have to hang up all my warm clothes to dry and suffer with my older, ratty items for the rest of the day.

Inside me was a volcano. Never had I experienced this before. Anger, yes. Embarrassment, yes. But now I questioned why I hadn't healed the doe before Nolan had arrived. If I had, none of that would have happened. This was something more. A questioning. A doubt. But of course, there was no telling if I could have grasped the life magic all around me in any case. Why couldn't I? What kind of witch was I? Living in fear of being found out, yet unable to actually *be* a witch. Helpless. Clueless.

Naive. I scooped up some snow and crushed it between my palms before hurling it at a nearby tree. The snowball poofed into a million bits on impact. And somehow, in that moment, that felt like I had something in common with it.

The back door loomed in front of me. Nolan hadn't followed, and I was glad for that. In my state who knew what I would have screamed at him. I had already been entirely too close to saying exactly what I had been considering before he arrived.

I flung the door open, and the wood door clattered, not used to such treatment.

Mom was in the kitchen. She jumped with a hand on her heart. "What in the Wall?"

I ignored her too and stomped up the back stairs, slamming my bedroom door behind me.

I had about ten minutes before Mom was up here asking me what was wrong. Ten minutes to figure out what I should tell her. The truth?

The truth would earn me a lecture even at twenty-two. Nolan's accusation echoed in my mind. I picked up the hand mirror that sat on my dresser with the intention of hurling it at my wall, but that would only alert Mom even more. This was the one item in my room that she told me I had to pack whenever we ran, some sort of family heirloom. It didn't matter that I didn't like it, didn't use it. I had to be sure to pack it. My finger ran over the filigree at the top and around the bend of the mirror.

Now my heart broke. For the doe. For Nolan. For me. He wasn't who I thought he was. I'd been so happy with him too, but now? Would I be able to look him in the eye after that? It wasn't so much that he'd killed that doe. Mercy killing was common, necessary in many cases. And he certainly had a point with that deer. But he didn't even discuss it with me. It was as if my opinion and ability with common medicine didn't matter.

True to form, Mom knocked softly on the door, and I placed the mirror back down.

"Come in." I sank down onto the edge of my bed.

Mom cracked the door open. She wore black leggings and an oversized sweater. Her graying hair was braided and hanging over her shoulder. Her weight on my bed rocked me, and we bumped shoulders. "What happened? Was it Nolan?"

I nodded and with a sniff looked away from her. "We had a fight."

"I see. Over what?" Her voice was soft and calming, similar to how I had approached the doe. It threatened the dam on my tears.

"He shot a deer. A deer that was in labor." I swiped at the wetness on my cheek.

She remained silent. Damn her for that trick that always meant I would fill the empty space with my words.

"She could have lived, at least long enough to birth the fawn and feed it. But he didn't even consider what I wanted. He just shot it as soon as I turned my back to get my kit."

Mom didn't respond right away, but I refused to say more. She got as much of the truth as I was willing to give. "Were you going to try and heal it?" My spine stiffened. The way she emphasized "heal" meant with my witchery. "Because otherwise he did the doe and us a favor. We can't afford to take care of a doe and her fawn with our money or our time. And we certainly can't afford a stray use of magic."

I stood from the bed and focused on the mirror, running a finger along the braided handle while my back was to her. "I didn't try and use my magic to heal it."

"But you considered it? I thought I felt something earlier."

Heat flushed through my body. Everything was still too close to the surface for me to keep it all at bay. I spun around facing her. "And what if I did? What if I considered using my magic? In the end, I didn't. Isn't that what matters? I came to the correct decision."

Mom stood. "I wish you wouldn't even consider it. You know there have been times when the mere thought of using your magic resulted in your grasping the life energy around you. You can't control it. It's not your fault, but you can't be reckless with our livelihood. Our safety."

"What if we decided to stop running and just faced it?"

Mom's face went from her concerned-parent look to slack. "Have I taught you nothing? This is not something we turn our cheek and bear. Your father would come for us, and burning at the stake might be the least of our worries."

"But what does he do? All you ever give me is vague threats of him."

Mom sat back down, shoulders slumping.

"I'm twenty-two and hardly experienced life. No friends. First boyfriend, who"—I shrugged— "clearly is not right for me. I can't even choose people well because I don't know. Why are we running? What does he want?"

"He wants you." Her voice was a whisper, so soft I could barely hear her. But I did hear her, and my heart skipped. "He hunts you. Me? He'd burn me at the stake unless he wanted me as leverage. You? I don't know what he would do with you. Use you? Force you to do unspeakable things? Strip you of your magic? What I do know is that you would wish you were dead."

"Why me?"

"It is safer for you if you do not know."

I crossed my arms, leaning back into the dresser behind me. "You don't think I deserve to know."

"What you deserve and what keeps you safe can and are separate things." She stood, brushing a hair behind my ear. "What you are is my beloved daughter. I can't risk you." Her eyes drifted to my wrist where the heirloom bracelet she told me to always wear rested.

"What if something happens to you? What then?"

"You continue as we do now. Practice medicine. My wards will disappear over time, so best not to use your magic. If you don't use your magic, you could live a normal life. Marry without your husband ever being the wiser to your magic." Then she breathed in, considering, "Stay near the Wall. If you are ever in that great of danger, go to it."

I couldn't speak for a second, my heart raced at the thought of the pull, the beckoning, I always felt. "Go to the Wall?"

Mom looked me dead in the eye. "Yes, touch it. You will be safe that way."

CHAPTER 2
INNARA

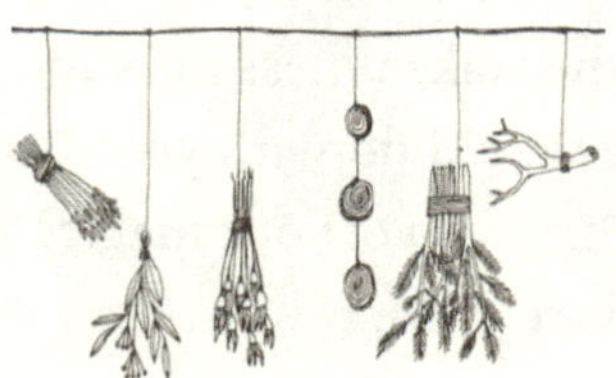

The doorbell rang.

"I'll go see what this is," Mom said as she lightly patted my cheek.

"Let me know if you need me," I said as she moved down the hallway toward the stairs. I sunk down onto my bed.

Go to the Wall?

My heart thrummed. Why did she tell me this now? I rolled over and grabbed my tablet and with a finger swipe the screen lit up. Not everyone had one of these, but if they did then logging on to the wire was free. What better way for my father to brainwash the masses? I had found the sites that as much as he tried to shut them down, had a way of lingering or popping back up. But today, I wanted to see what he was up to. What he was making sure everyone saw.

"Innara!" My mom yelled from downstairs. "I need you now!"

I dropped the tablet beside me and ran downstairs. This must be no minor sickness or injury that showed up on our doorstep.

I was already re-braiding my long hair by the time I hit the bottom step. Mom ushered in two men carrying a third who dripped blood on to the wood floor.

"In here," Mom waved them into our examination room. She was already pulling off her cardigan, revealing her thin but muscled form and grabbing her smock. Our work as healers demanded a lot from our bodies.

I skirted around the blood splatter, donning my smock as I entered the room. The man on the table was William. One of our neighbors. His hands were bleeding, but so was his leg. Not to mention signs of frostbite.

"What happened?"

One of the men turned toward me. They were Wall Walkers. "We were on patrol and came upon him. He was caught in a trap. With his hands..." the man ran a hand through his hair. "I don't know exactly what happened, but he'd been there awhile."

I swallowed down bile. My money was on William had freed the doe and then gotten mauled by the same trap.

Mom shooed the men out of the room. "We'll take good care of him. Let his wife know. Innara will run over when we have news."

I was already cutting away clothes to get a better look at his wounds. "This is bad."

He needed a hospital.

Mom was next to me with the men gone, pouring saline over William's wounds after I revealed them. She wasn't saying anything, so I knew she came to the same conclusion I did.

"He can't afford a hospital, and Betty can't afford to lose him." Mom pressed a sterile cloth to his leg as she moved to assess his hands.

I dropped the scissors in an empty pot for sterilizing later before I washed up again, thinking. She could heal him. Our house was warded. But I hesitated from saying anything.

Mom pressed the back of her wrist to her forehead, bloodied fingers kept away from her skin. "We'll bandage him up as best we can, and then we'll call for transport."

I snatched the saline from my mom to clean William's other

hand. If we used our poultices and bandages, he may or may not have great use of his hands after this.

"Why don't we heal him?"

"You bite your tongue." Mom's eyes darted to me. She gave a pointed look at William.

I rolled my eyes. He was unconscious. "You know as well as I do what will happen to him and Betty if you send him to the hospital."

The cost of transport and treatment would ruin them. They'd be forced to move into the city and serve my father, likely in one of his witch-hunting gangs. How messed up was that? We wouldn't heal him, so he'd then wind up hunting us.

"And you know if we heal him, those Wall Walkers will wonder how we did such a miraculous job. They know as well as we do that he needs a hospital. We can't risk it." She bustled around, grabbing the suture kit and a tray. "We will stitch him up and bandage him. I have some antibiotics we can give him for transport to ward off infection. But after that, he isn't our problem."

"This is wrong, Mom. You know it."

She glared at me. "I do, but this is the world we live in. And..."

"And?" I prompted.

Mom shook her head as if clearing her mind as she prepped to sew up the biggest gash in William's leg. "I heard a rumor your father's men were in the area."

I froze and then stepped away from the table. "And you're telling me this now?"

She kept her head bowed, focused on the wound. "It was a bad decision. I see that now. I didn't want you to worry, but you're not a little girl anymore."

No. I was an adult, and I no longer accidentally wielded my witchery. As much as I loved her, I was tired of her controlling so much of my life. I fisted my hands on either side of me.

"Now isn't the time." She glanced up, her braid slipping over her shoulder. "We can talk later."

I knew a dismissal when I heard it, and I wasn't ever more thankful for one. I turned and stormed out of the room, ripping off my smock and tossing it in the corner as I went.

Rows and rows of greenery greeted me along with an earthy, humid scent when I entered the greenhouse full of herbs and veggies. It was my reprieve. We had been lucky to find this place with a greenhouse half dug into the ground. The lit heaters fooled the townsfolk, who always exclaimed at how abundant our plants were.

They certainly helped, especially on these unusually cold days and nights. But other things helped too. I dug my fingers into the soil, closed my eyes, and breathed deep, loosening the tightness in my shoulders, relishing the warm moisture of the air. I was still roiling from Nolan, Mom, and William. The earthen smell comforted me.

I dug my fingers in deeper, letting the dark, moist soil cover my hands. Secure in the warded safety of the greenhouse, I reached out. The life energy around me pulsed green. Even the worms wriggling in the soil lit up. This daily task helped center me, prove to myself I could harness my witchery. I focused on the roots in the soil, checking each plant. No disease. Catching it early was better for the plants, really better for any living thing. But healing it also took much less out of us. It didn't do well for Mom or me to be laid up in bed for a day or two because we'd expended all our energy on healing our crops, especially if a townsperson needed help.

Mom told me that life witches tended to choose healing people, while others took up farming. Maybe, if I'd been given a choice, I would have chosen this. Plants expected nothing of you. They didn't pressure you. The death of one was a responsibility I could bear.

I released my magic with a sigh. Even though I could almost

always summon it here, Mom didn't like me to hold it longer than necessary. Wards protected us within the greenhouse and our home. But the what-if hung out there. I pulled my hands out of the soil, brushing the dirt off.

I wasn't going back inside. Not yet. This entire morning had me reeling. First Nolan, then Mom telling me the Wall will keep me safe, followed by our argument. I wasn't ready to face her again. She'd hidden too much from me. Kept me like a child, ignorant of so much. I slipped a finger along the heirloom bracelet.

Soon, I'd need to figure something out. I couldn't continue this way.

Once outside, the trail of blood was in front of me again. I sighed and looked in the direction the doe lay. I couldn't heal her then or now, but I could make sure she and her baby rested in peace. It would give me something to do and let me work out the spidery tingles moving along my limbs. With a shovel that had leaned against the greenhouse side, I made my way through the snow again, using my footprints from earlier as a guide.

Many would be appalled at burying the deer, so I needed to get this done soon. Even Mom might argue that we should butcher and share the meat with others, but I couldn't bear it. I should've saved her, but I was too chickenshit to really try. Benefiting from the death felt wrong. I gripped the shovel tight and marched on.

The trees parted, and there was Nolan, dragging the doe through the snow.

I threw down the shovel.

"What do you think you're doing?" I shouted. We were done.

His head jerked, and he stood, releasing the deer. "Burying her. I figured that is what you would want."

I paused in my stormy march toward him. The red ball of anger I had felt moments ago deflated. Maybe he realized how wrong he had been.

"I was coming out here to do that." I approached and now could see the deep hole he had dug. He must have been digging the rest of the morning to do all that. Indeed, the remnants of several campfires off to the side attested. Something I hadn't even considered. "Thank you. I couldn't bear to think of her being butchered or feasted upon by a predator."

Nolan took a few steps toward me. "I figured as much, especially with the Trappers."

Instinct pricked in my gut. The way he had said Trappers. My stomach pitted out. "What of them?"

He met my steady gaze with a grave one as he ran a hand through his hair. "I found some traps. Not the normal ones. Trappers are in the area. They must be hunting."

"How long have they been around?"

"A few days. Long enough to need to hunt."

I pressed my lips together. "Well, thank you for doing this." I waved my arm to the deer. It truly did take a weight off me, but now that he was doing it, I didn't want to stick around and watch. Having my guilt and shame stare me in the face with cold, dead eyes was something I could deal with alone, not with Nolan as witness.

"Can I see you tonight?" he asked.

My gaze bobbed down to the dead animal before meeting Nolan's eyes. "I don't know."

"Let me make this up to you."

I shifted my weight and put my hands on my hips, trying to muster some courage to tell him. My gaze went back to the deer.

"I'm sorry about the doe," he said, catching on. "I thought I was helping."

His intention had been good. But the Wall to Faerie was paved with good intentions. With a tilt of my head and the barest hint of a shrug, I didn't have to say anything.

"Don't be like that." He stepped toward me and reached out for my hand, which I allowed. "I can make this up to you. You have to know caring for that deer would have been more than you and your mom could handle on top of everything else." He stopped and turned his head. "Why don't we go into town. We could get warm tea and chat."

I slipped my hand from his. He didn't get it. It was never that I thought he was wrong. His face was a question as I opened my mouth to speak.

I had to break this off.

"Well, look what we have here," a man said from behind Nolan, who whirled around with a hand on his sword.

Several other men slinked out from behind trees, weapons drawn, crossbows aimed. My heart leapt into my throat. The emblem on their coats, a cross consumed in flames.

The mark of my father's men.

"What is this?" Nolan asked as he slid his sword out of his scabbard.

The lead man spoke again. "You're free to leave, Wall Walker. We only want the witch."

Nolan turned, his face a stone as he looked upon me with new eyes.

I froze, braced for the hatred. My thoughts raced from him to my mother back at the house. How had this happened? How did they find me? Was that barest of grasps on my witchery this morning enough to alert them? Or the plants in the greenhouse?

I readied for Nolan to walk away and leave me here. A moment ago, I'd wanted to tell him I didn't want to be with him anymore. Now I wanted to beg him to stay with me. Protect me.

How pathetic.

"You'll have to go through me first." Nolan moved to stand next to me and then said under his breath, "Do something. A distraction. Whatever. Then run."

I released a breath in a whoosh.

He was helping.

I reached out for my magic, but nothing came. Not a single blip.

"If you don't step aside, we'll shoot you," the lead man said. "Trapper's business."

"Do something." Nolan hissed through his teeth. "Your Trapper is conducting business on Walker land. Attacking a Walker will be met harshly."

I tried again, gripping the sides of my cloak. I strained outward, willing my magic to answer. I didn't want Nolan to get shot. I didn't—

We were so close to the Wall. I just had to do something and run. Sweat broke out on my forehead. Green burst in my vision as the life magic appeared. I saw each man, a human- shaped blob of green. I didn't know what to do. I used my magic to heal. But all I could think was, *Make them smaller.*

Nolan whooped and grabbed my arm. "Run!"

I didn't even see what I had done, but I ran, snow flying up behind me. I lurched as the deep drifts caught me off guard. But we only had feet to go to the Wall.

It was as if Nolan had known exactly where Mom had told me to go. What to do.

Something zipped by my ear. Whatever I had done didn't delay them long. Their green blobs were still there and moving. *Make them smaller.*

My legs pumped, muscles burning. I hit the Wall like I hadn't seen a glass door. Nolan flipped me around to face him. Embracing me? He couldn't come. I couldn't subject him to the Fell Fae.

"Be safe," I whispered, reaching to caress his cheek.

He only smiled before something pulled me, and then he shoved me. I wasn't prepared, and my feet flew out from under me. I flailed and tried to grab him, but I only found purchase on his necklace, which broke off.

My body pushed back into resistance like a cold slime. Nolan's hand, which had been on me, smoked until it was black as he pulled it away, screaming. It was as if I watched him in slow motion. Was I dying? I'd always imagined dying and watching my life before me would be something like this. Nolan yelled my name, but it was as if I was underwater as I fell farther and farther away from him. He looked at his hand and then reached out behind him.

And that was the last thing I saw until darkness descended and all I could feel was that pull, the inexorable pull I always felt near the Wall. Only now, it felt like going home.

CHAPTER 3

KIR

There was something very wrong with Faerie, and it was only getting worse. If I didn't find a solution, my people would perish.

The icy cold gave way to searing heat, and I fought the urge to strip off my heavy clothes. Instead, I used as little magic as possible to cool myself. These pockets of extremes were new. They'd been happening for the past half century.

"Fuck, this is a bad one," Dain called to me, wiping his brow with the back of his hand. He'd be less prone to using his magic to cool himself, wanting to conserve his power.

I had more. It was my honor. It was my curse.

I smirked at my use of "curse." How many could one fae have? Apparently a lot.

I flicked out a finger, directing some magic to cool Dain. I couldn't have him drowning in his own sweat. It would do neither of us any good. His reaction was immediate: a quick, sharp glare. But I held my finger to my mouth before he could say anything.

We needed quiet. We needed stealth. Our quarry would be all too perceptive. And I was Dain's lord, so he had little choice but to obey.

The chiming rang out before the giggles. Even though magic waned, our fae hearing and senses remained. Both Dain and I swiveled, attuned to the direction of the threat. We both drew our swords from our backs.

"Remember what we are here for," I said.

"No kill hit. I heard you the first ten times, Lord Kir." He drawled out my name.

Typical. I rolled my eyes.

My uncle would never have put up with the insolence. But he was no longer here, was he? It was all my problem now.

Dain tracked the baedour. His sense of smell was always better than mine. His magic amplified it, one of his proficiencies. I positioned myself a slight step behind him, ready to follow in whatever direction he led. His head cocked, and he drew in a deep breath. I knew his eyes would be shut, trusting his other senses over his vision. I tightened my grip on my swords, my leg muscles tensing, readying. He darted, and I plunged after him.

The chiming grew loud and then disappeared. Silence rained down except for our boots crunching in the desiccated dirt.

Keeerr, a slithery, snake-like voice whispered.

I whipped around.

The direction was unknowable, but it had to see me to speak to me like that.

"Dain," I ground out. He needed to locate this thing.

The baedour spoke again. *Cursed One, you do not know what you seek.*

Shit. This thing was in my head.

Dain bolted, and as much as I wanted to focus on my mental shields, I had to follow him. I had to cover his back.

The one you dread will be here soon.

I stumbled. "Who?"

The laughter in my head was coarse and laced with chimes. *Wouldn't you like to know?*

I ground my teeth and spit at the ground. I had no time for its ambiguity.

Your friend can't find me.

Dain was nowhere to be seen, and it had its sights on me. But we had planned this...sort of. Baedour always wanted to go for the most powerful, so I planned to be bait. I only hoped Dain realized it took the bait as fast as it did.

I rotated my wrist, the sword arcing in front of me. Fighter stance. I had to be ready.

The baedour moved fast and was in front of me, its gaping maw open, revealing its many rows of teeth. Poisonous saliva dripped down to the ground.

Dain better be ready.

I sifted to where we had started our dash. The baedour was fast, but sifting was inherently faster.

Dain's attack roar rang out. I darted back, slipping my iron dirk out of its sheath. We'd fought so many fae beasts together that I didn't even need to think on it.

Ahead, Dain whipped his sword back and forth, keeping the baedour at bay. Its gray, mottled skin shifted over a skeletal body. No shapeshifting this time to lure us. Matted hair hung from its head, lashing from side to side as the beast lunged for my friend. Its legs and arms were long, and Dain broke out in a sweat—the baedour had that advantage on him.

I had to get there. My last sift was small enough that I could do it again, but I had better make it worthwhile as it would be the end of my reserve for a few days. I could mind-grip it, but that would take too much power. Too much of a gamble. I couldn't risk getting between it and Dain. I'd either be clawed or stuck through by Dain's sword.

I sifted, appearing right behind the baedour. I moved lightning fast, poking the iron dirk under the baedour's chin. My other arm wrapped around its body, which was surprisingly warm. I wouldn't think on how I touched this thing, nearly hugging it to my own body.

"I demand a reading." To make my point clear, I dug the end of my dirk further into its flabby under-chin. The skin was thick, like leather. But it would feel the iron and know I had it.

The baedour's arms went limp, and it ceased fighting. Its mouth closed and returned to a normal size.

Dain stuck his sword point-down into the dirt and leaned on it. "Bout time."

"What do you want to know, Cursed One?" The baedour spoke out loud this time, its voice gravelly and hoarse like it hadn't spoken for ages.

"How do I restore magic to Cirrelea?"

I'd had my question prepared for months. Honed it so there could be no misinterpretation, no manipulations.

"You will not like the answer."

I waited. Speaking more would give the baedour more to go off of, more to misinterpret or decide I'd asked another question and call the whole thing off. I twisted the dirk ever so slightly.

The creature sucked in a breath, a tremble coursing through its flabby body. "The Wall must come down."

At that, Dain flicked the hilt of his sword to the ground and took a few steps away. "We came here for this?"

But I held tight to the baedour.

"I answered your question," it said. "The bargain says you must let me go."

But my mind spun. The Wall must come down? The Wall that protected us from the rabid humans? The human witches? This was how I was to save my people, by unleashing who knew what on them?

"No, you lie." The waning magic must have allowed the baedour to tell untruths. Wall knew, my tongue was looser than it should have been, allowing me to bend the truth more and more. And he must be lying. Destroying the Wall was preposterous, impossible.

I pushed my dirk into its thick skin. The skin began to give while I latched on to its mind. But it slipped and slid. Black oil slipping between my fingers.

It hissed, and I sensed no lie.

In my mind, it wailed. "You know as well as I do, I can't lie. But the piece of your soul you just bargained will come with me, with us if you don't let me go."

Searing pain whacked me in the face, and I stumbled back, collapsing to the ground. My cheek ached, and I spat out blood.

"I make no demand for a reading. I let you go in peace. Leave now." Dain held his iron dirk to the baedour's throat, shoving it away from him.

"I take one price," the baedour said, voice raspy. It lifted a claw and scraped down Dain's face.

Dain, as flagrant as he could be, was stoic. He didn't scream. Bright red blood welled in a line down his face, from eyebrow to cheek. The baedour bounded away.

Kir, you keep your soul, but we won't be so willing to help you next time. It finished its private message and let out a near mind-shattering chime at the end.

Dain towered over me, black hair hanging down obscuring his bloodied face. "What the fucking Wall was that?"

"He did what?" Rylla's voice was a screech, and her ponytail swung as she swiveled to pin her glare on me.

Dain leaned against the kitchen counter, arms crossed, nodding. It felt like I was being tattled on, but everyone tattled to me now.

I shrugged. "I lost my mind a bit."

"But you don't lose your mind." Rylla swaggered near, peering up at me.

"You try being in a mind-grip of a baedour who tells you that the only way to save our magic is to do the impossible." I put my back to her and opened the fridge, grabbing an apple before crunching into it. "It pissed me off," I said around a mouthful of the juicy sweet fruit.

I hadn't told any of them of the baedour's message before all that. That the one I dreaded was coming. There were a lot of people I dreaded. Pretty much anyone with a new problem for me to solve fit that description. The Wild Hunt, suspiciously absent for months, would be one. Another, Gaelin.

Baedour were notorious for saying things that could have any one of a hundred meanings.

"Kir, you almost lost a piece of your soul to the baedour." Rylla poked my chest.

I stepped away with a stern look. She knew how I felt about that. She knew the danger. "Thankfully, Dain stopped me."

"Always there, protecting my lord." Dain ambled up and nudged Rylla back.

And that was exactly what he had done, protected me. In that instance, from myself. If only I'd been able to protect my sister, done my job as well as Dain did his.

"How can you be so flippant about this?" Rylla asked. "If you lost a piece of your soul, your curse may never be undone."

She needed to let this go.

"I'm not being flippant," I said. "I lost my shit. Dain stopped me. End of story. I get it, okay? I get it."

Rylla threw her hands up and left the room.

"Did you really think the baedour lied?" Dain reached past me to the fridge and pulled out some grapes.

I took another bite of my apple, hitting a rotten spot. I pulled it away. Normal rot, just a bruise. At least that was something. A few weeks ago, every crop we pulled from the ground rotted within a day. Some unfortunate animals that ate them then rotted from within. A grisly death.

"At the time, I did think he was lying," I said. "We've all been able to bend our words more. But now I think he told the truth. I just don't like it."

"But what if destroying the Wall did help?" Dain popped a plump grape into his mouth with a *crunch-pop* as he bit down. It must be a good crop.

"Trust me, it's all I've wondered about." I scrubbed a hand down my face then tossed my apple core. "I'll have to talk with Clove. Have her research the Wall. Too many knowledgeable fae died in the past half century. She'll have to find texts. I need to know how it can be done, and ideally, I'd love to know what it will actually do."

"What if it's impossible?"

I couldn't believe I was considering it. The Wall was impassable. Destroying it was unfathomable. But... "What if it's not?"

This was madness. We'd been looking for this cave for days. If we didn't find it soon, we'd have to head back. Haze kept Clove and me apprised with messages from the others, but from the sounds of it, Rylla and Dain were at each other's throats. They had both protested loudly that I'd taken Clove with me. But she was the one who would know how to find the box or operate it. We didn't know what to expect, which was my point. They would stay in my home—our home—and Clove and I would find the journal pages. We hadn't seen or heard much of Gaelin, which unnerved me, so protecting my home was a priority, especially with the Wild Hunt missing too.

Thousands of enormous icicles spilled down, forming a spiky wall, reminiscent of a frozen waterfall—cold under my hand as I let it drag over the surface, feeling for a break that would mark a cave opening my eyes could not see. I allowed the smallest amount of my magic necessary to protect my bare skin from the damage the ice could do so I didn't have to put on my gloves. Out here, not quite alone, it was one of the few places I could be free of them. But if I didn't find what I was looking for soon, they would have to go on because, if I found the glamoured entrance to the cave and *if* it held a box, who knew how much magic I would have to use to open it. Everything was a balance.

I clamped my other hand in a fist. This rationing of magic was new. Our well of power was something we took for granted. No longer. Day to day, year to year, it was barely noticeable, but sometimes within a day, a few days, we lost a chunk of magic like a part of us atrophied and died. We all lived in fear of those times.

How many more of those episodes did each fae have?

Many had only one left. My friends likely had several remaining if the previous losses were anything to go by. And I...I would be the last true fae standing. Maybe Gaelin too, that bastard.

My only hope was to gather these ancient journal pages, which Clove's research said were near this area. They would lead me to the stone, and the stone could break a hole in the Wall. All of my research corroborated what the baedour had told me: to survive, the Wall had to come down. The very idea made a shiver inch along my spine. I may have spent weeks finding the evidence of its truth and getting used to it, but that didn't mean I liked it. All those humans and their ability to lie, swarming into Cirrelea like the pestilence they were.

But the Wall coming down would restore our power. We'd be able to protect ourselves again.

I wasn't prepared when my hand passed into the cave opening. Lost in my thoughts, I had put more of my weight on it, and I lurched sideways when there was nothing to hold me up, even though it looked like there was.

What a mindfuck.

But I caught myself, reflexes trained in battling the fae beasts and Wild Hunt that Gaelin sent into my territory saved me.

It took a moment to register.

I'd found it. By the Wall, I'd found it! My heart nearly skipped a beat as I stared at the icicles in front of me, appearing solid.

"Clove! It's here. Come quickly," I yelled.

Clove rose from several feet ahead of me. She had been inching along crouched down, feeling lower along the Wall for the entrance. "How did I miss that?"

I pushed my hand in front of me, and it passed right through bluish-white icicle wall. I knew glamours well, how to make them, how to dispel them, but the ones guarding these pages were not fae. I could neither detect them nor dispel them.

I was a tall fae, broad too, so I made sure to find the edges. I turned sideways and bent my neck a bit to fit, but otherwise it wasn't too tight. But there was a large step up, which was probably how Clove had gone right past it. I sidestepped until I could see better and managed to reach the other side of the glamour.

Before me lay an ice tunnel. I turned around. The exit was right there, with the dead trees of my court just beyond. At least we would be able to find our way out.

My hope now was that the box wasn't hidden in some maze of an ice cave. These were notorious for having a labyrinth of passages. A fae could get lost in them permanently. If that was the case, I would have to expend more magic so I could find my way out.

A whisper of a breeze blew past me with a delicious smell. If I didn't know better, I'd say it smelled of human, but I hadn't seen a human in my court for decades. The last one was a witch sent by Gaelin to prey on what he called my "moralistic" values. He knew I wouldn't kill her. He knew my instinct would be to aid her. So, aid her I did until she learned of one of the locations of the Winter Court's villages. She took that knowledge to Gaelin, and the village was no more.

Just thinking about it filled me with rage. How he and I had ever been friends was beyond me. He'd killed my sister. An accident he claimed, but now he walked around with her power adding to his. The very last bit of her that still existed in this world, and that bastard held it.

Rylla and Dain always spoke of vengeance, but my focus had to remain on my people. My duty was to them. Talk of vengeance was easy, but pursuing it could start a bigger war. Besides, tearing down the Wall was the best shot at giving them—all of us—a future. My sister would have wanted that for us.

A muffled gasp sounded, and I slipped on my gloves before grabbing my sword.

Someone was ahead of me.

Vengeance or not, I'd be damned if Gaelin assumed again I would never kill. And I would sacrifice myself to protect Clove. I'd go in alone long before I let a human get to her or any of my people.

I turned to Clove, who had stepped in behind me. "Wait outside until I come get you."

"What is it?" she asked.

"Possibly a witch. I'll take care of it." I pointed a finger at her to make my point and waited until she exited the cave.

I steeled myself for whatever lay ahead. Whatever needed to be done, I would do because those pages were my people's only hope.

CHAPTER 4
INNARA

My eyelids had sand in them, and a pulsing throbbed through my head. My body shuddered, as a bone-chilling cold tore through me. Beneath me felt like ice.

I sat up, sucking in the frigid air. It felt like ice because it *was* ice. The Wall had spit me out into an even colder hell than where I had been.

Shades of blue and white surrounded me. Surreally beautiful but not home.

I jerked to my feet, spinning.

I knew what this was: an ice cave. I'd never seen one before in person, but I'd seen it on some show on our plasmavision. Much further north from where I lived in the Eastlands, these things existed.

Under my foot, something crunched and pressed up into the sole of my shoe. I stopped to examine it. Nolan's necklace. It was a green stone. Someone had taken the time to chisel a hole in it to thread the leather cord.

I palmed the stone, staring at it yet not really seeing it.

I had fallen through the Wall.

The common belief was that no one could cross the Wall, but on the day Mom finally gave me information and told me to feed a bit of my magic into it if I was ever in danger was the same day I went through. Unbelievable.

I shivered at the feel of the cold slime as I'd fallen. A flash of Nolan's hand smoking made me wince. I had to get back. There had been no time to warn my mom. The Trappers had been clear they wanted a witch. Would they find her if they didn't have me? Had running meant I'd sealed my mom's fate? She had mentioned they would use her as leverage. Even this morning, she wasn't nearly as concerned for herself as she was for me. All I could do until I figured out how to go back across was hold the hope that she lived.

I curled my fingers around Nolan's necklace until my knuckles were white.

He'd protected me. He'd learned what I was, and he'd still helped me. I'd never seen him without his necklace. The least I could do was get it back to him.

I repeated that to strengthen my resolve. My body was racked with shivers, and I had to do something or die. Panic stalked me along the edges of my mind, but I had to keep her at bay. She was as bad if not worse than the elements.

Because if I fell through the Wall, then I was in Faerie. And the Fell Fae would lurk just around the corner.

But if I'd crossed that easily, perhaps I could go back.

I spun around to get my bearings. The area was smooth, as if a pool of water had once resided here. The thought made me tremble. I stuffed Nolan's necklace and my hands into the pockets of my cloak. I took a few steps to the back of the cave and placed my hands against it, even as cold as it was, and pushed. Nothing. I slid to the side and pushed again. Nothing but ice. No magical Wall.

I chided myself for thinking it could be that easy. Nothing ever was.

Since that didn't work, I had to find warmth. Start a fire. Something.

I turned toward the opening where the blues were brighter, making me think light and day were not that far away, when my gaze snagged on something off to the side.

A chest sat in the shadows, a simple wooden box.

Ice crunched under my feet. Crouching, I ran my hands along it. Plain wood, no embellishment, no lock. It felt like a trick. I was in Faerie after all. My wits would be my only weapon. It wasn't as if I had an iron dagger stashed in my boot. But I also had magic, and I was in Faerie where magic wasn't just accepted—it was how they lived. At least that was what we believed.

At least, I could *try* to use my magic.

I tried the lid, but something held it to the base. It didn't budge. I could throw it on the ground and bust it open, but Faerie had me wondering how much could be a trick. I could leave it. Walk away.

No, Faerie seemed like a place that would reward me for solving a riddle. And that was when I saw the small, faint etching of a witch sigil: lock.

If I could calm my mind, convince it and my body that we weren't in danger, maybe I could channel. There was likely not much life in an ice cave, but I could draw on my own. With a plan of action, I reached into myself. Drawing on my own life energy had always been easier, but that drained a witch even more than wielding it in general. Still, I only needed a tiny amount.

I breathed in slow and let it out. I latched on, grasping my witchery under duress, and smothered my elation to let a tendril into the box.

Yes, there was magic cast over this box.

It *was* a trap. If I had opened it without checking, something would have shot me from inside. I leaned away, just in case, and let my magic touch the trap and it disintegrated. How odd.

I checked again, and yes, the magic was gone. Everyone in Faerie held magic, so how would that have kept anyone out?

Something shuffled behind me.

I spun around, my heart thundering behind my ribs.

"Who are you?" a man in the passage barked at me. Man. A Fell Fae man.

I flinched. "I...I..."

"You're a witch, speak!" he said as he stalked closer to me.

My breath froze as he neared. His pointed ears pushed out of his wavy brown hair, which framed a ruggedly handsome face. I thought of Nolan and how handsome I thought he was. Nolan was a boy compared to this fae.

The man's eyes surreptitiously dropped to the box in my hands, which had only just popped open to reveal a few pages.

"Speak! Who are you? Why are you here?" He sniffed the air. "Human, but with a hint of fae," he said as his pupils grew larger.

"I fell." I trembled, from cold and from him.

He looked at me like I was something to chew up and spit out.

"I fell through the Wall. I just want to get back home." His gaze kept darting to the box. I held it out like an offering. "Is this yours? Take it. Can I get back across?" Thoughts barely registered before the words poured out of my mouth.

His eyes narrowed. "No one can come through the Wall. And no human will taint those pages." He sneered at the word *human* as if it meant disease.

With a raise of his finger and a curl of his wrist, something wrapped around me, invisible but with the feel of bindings. They tightened, yanking my arms down to my sides, forcing me to drop the wood box. The pages fluttered to the ground, and he lunged forward to grab them.

I'd given him what he wanted. He didn't need to attack. Instead of helping me, he'd bound me up. The binds he had me in were tight enough that I could feel the pressure against my ribs if I attempted too deep of a breath. All the tales were true.

All I could do was sputter, "You Fell Fae disgust me."

He glanced at the pages before they disappeared with a flick of his wrist.

"Sorry, human, but I can't have you running around after me." He turned, and the ice ground under his boots.

Then true panic hit me. I would die here, mere feet inside the Wall.

"I'll freeze to death," I said, then more to myself, "Mom said I would be safe here. I have to go back."

His steps faltered for a short moment, and I barely caught an index finger pointing out. If I didn't know any better, I'd say he warmed something around me because at least the racking shivers that tore through my body subsided.

CHAPTER 5

KIR

Clove jumped up as soon as I exited the cave. "What happened? Do you have it?"

I strode right by her, and she fell in line beside me, walking double-time to keep up. "I have the pages."

"You opened it?" Her voice held those high notes of surprise. "Where's the box?"

We had discussed that the most likely scenario would be that I would have to take the box back to our court, and there we'd figure out how to open it. The risk of incineration of the pages and possibly ourselves was entirely too high. At least the witch had done us a favor.

I glanced back: a solid wall of dripping ice. What a mindfuck. I ran my hand through my hair as my stomach twisted.

Guilt at leaving her in there pricked at me. It was an emotion I was all too familiar with but not when it came to witches. I still held her binds. Leaving her like that, defenseless, wasn't something that appealed to me. It was something Gaelin would have done.

The witch posed a threat to me alone. But that scent. It should have repelled me, but it did the opposite.

Clove knocked my arm. "Hello? Give me something."

We approached the trees that didn't grow right up to the magical Wall.

I stopped, shaking my head, trying to get a grip on my racing thoughts. "There was a witch. She had already opened the box. I took the pages from her and left her in there."

"She opened it? And you just left her in there?" Clove dragged her lips between her teeth as she considered the area where the cave opening was.

The witch's smell still tickled my nose. And that hint of fae. Perhaps she'd told the truth about falling through the Wall and the fae-made Wall left its mark, or perhaps she had recently been sifted to that cave by Gaelin.

He'd done it before.

Heat flashed through my chest at the memory. If he did it again, he must be running out of his bag of tricks.

"She is bound in air right now, but I'll need to let it go soon." I hesitated telling Clove more. She'd see through me, but out of all our companions, she would listen. "The witch claimed to be from the other side, that she fell through the Wall."

Clove's hazel gaze darted from me and back to the cave. "That's impossible." But then her eyes narrowed on me. "What did you sense?"

I tapped a finger on my hip, stalling. "Her smell. It's beguiling to me." She knew the depths of what I admitted by saying that, what danger I could be in. And now I really hesitated, but she knew there was more. "A hint of fae on her."

"You think Gaelin sent her."

"That thought did occur to me, but she reeked of fear."

That could have been a trick. Witches, especially Gaelin's witches, excelled at acting. And some excelled at masking scents.

I fisted my hand at the thought that Violet might have a part in this.

And yet I still found myself wavering beyond the cave entrance, holding the witch's binds, keeping them warm. I couldn't shake that scent of her, jasmine and sage.

I needed to get back to my court. The sooner Clove could get to work on translating these pages, the better. Sifting would get us there instantaneously, but then my powers would be drained for days.

I should leave her. Make the call and get Clove and me both out of the area.

I'd walk and hold the witch's binds until I couldn't. Then she could make her own way, and until then, she wouldn't freeze to death.

Clove halted me with a raised hand. "If she was Gaelin's spy, we could get answers from her. And if she is from the other side, leaving her there to die—that's not who you are."

The longer I stood there with that human's scent near, the harder it was to fight the urge to remain and ensure she survived. And Clove's words were not helping in the slightest.

"You'll hate yourself and self-flagellate for decades." Clove rounded to face me, looking me in the eye. "It'll be your sister all over, the village too."

Damn it, but she knew me too well. If the witch survived and was Gaelin's spy, I would surely see her again. But if she really was from the other side, she very well could die within moments of exiting the cave. She had been nearly blue with cold already.

Wall blast it.

"Go home." I rifted the journal pages into my hand and handed them to Clove. "Get started on the pages. Be prepared for our arrival."

"You mean to bring her back?"

"Like you said, if she is Gaelin's spy, we can turn the tables on him. If she is from the other side or not, I don't think convincing her to come to my court will be hard."

Clove rifted the pages away to keep them safe. "Be careful. I'll prep a tonic."

I nodded. We had none with us, which was why I wanted Clove gone. I'd take this risk, even if the witch posed a greater danger to me.

Before Clove left, she had one last thing to say.

"Rylla's gonna be pissed." Then a smirk spread across her lips.

"Rylla doesn't like a lot of things. She'll get over it." I already knew what Rylla would say: *She's a human, not fae. Just kill her and be done with it.*

Rylla also knew how loathe I was to kill any fae. But for all the differences between fae and human, I didn't think we were all that different. I could point to more things in common than not. But she never really understood that side of me.

Now Dain...he'd be pissed, but he'd turn it into sport.

Clove wandered off, my instructions clear. She'd obey just as the others would after lodging all their complaints. Something to look forward to.

But for now, a crevasse in the ice wall was a perfect spot to wait for the witch and see what she did with her freedom from my air bonds.

CHAPTER 6
INNARA

That blasted fae! The binds were tight. I could breathe, but getting my arms to move even a smidge was impossible. But they warmed me, and I didn't know what to make of that. Maybe their magic was warm. It would be handy in this hellscape.

How was I going to get out of them? Panic again stalked me, breathing down my neck, trailing her icy cold fingers along my arms. Goosebumps prickled, even with the warming bonds.

Breathe in through your nose. Hold. Breathe out through your mouth. Again.

I pushed with all my might and could not budge. A scream tore up through my chest, scratched at my throat, before I released it with my head thrown back.

A slight pulse through the bonds was all that warned me before they were gone, and the bitter cold blasted me. I crumbled to the ground, arms flinging out. Wall, having been warm and then facing this brutal cold was cruel.

The box lay discarded on the ice. I guessed that fae got what he came for. And where did that leave me? Still stuck in Faerie.

The fae man had proved there was an entrance to this cave.

I pulled my cloak around me, trapping in the last vestiges of warmth. How bad could it be? I'd already run into a fae and survived. The fact that he'd bound me up—well, let's just ignore that. It wasn't helping.

I gulped down a steadying breath, straightened my shoulders.

With one foot in front of the other, I followed his path. A tunnel appeared, the blues merging, almost undulating from what I could only believe was the sun at the end. My breath picked up and hitched.

There was no choice. I couldn't stay in an ice cave. I had to go out, even if my heart was in my throat.

The walls narrowed, and my shoulders brushed the ice. The sun streamed in ahead, and with a final deep breath and a hand on the wall, I stepped one foot out of the cave.

A veritable wasteland spread out before me. Gnarled branches, devoid of needles or leaves, reached to the skies as if asking for forgiveness. Snow, if you could call it that, covered the ground, but it wasn't the sparkly white of home. It held a tinge of gray. Muted. Tainted. And mounds of it appeared sporadically. A waft of rot reached me, and I pulled a gloved hand out of my cloak to cover my nose. That was a mistake, letting the cold air in.

I needed to move. Movement would keep me warm. Maybe that fae man left a path. I didn't relish encountering him again, but he had to head where others were. Because I had to face it. I needed help.

My nose crinkled. Who knew what I would have to do or face to find a way home. It didn't matter. I had to find help or die trying.

He didn't kill me. There was that.

I glanced back, the opening to the cave clear. A dark gem, the colors going from white to turquoise to dark blue, on a cliff side bombarded with icicles.

Ahead of me, footprints marked the snow, and I followed them toward the trees. The path skirted around the mounds. I eyed them with suspicion, a bit fearful that a fae beast would burst forth out of one.

Or all of them.

I tightened my cloak, my heart a rapid beat.

It was no good to scare myself. It was just a walk in the woods. Very creepy woods. I let out a shaky breath.

A childlike giggle filtered through the air.

Ignore it. I was imagining things. There were no children out here. I straightened my shoulders and continued.

Another giggle, and I froze, one boot slipping on the icy snow. That giggle came from a different direction. I spun around, trying in vain to keep my breath under control. Nothing was out there. Only gray, snowy mounds and beseeching trees.

Whispers filtered through the air, unintelligible to me.

Something *was* out there. My legs refused to move, even though I needed them to. I could play dead. I had no weapon, nothing to defend myself. My breath was deafening, harsh even to my ears.

"Come here, child. You have nothing to be afraid of," a voice said behind me.

Even though I doubted it, I still turned like I had no choice. A haggard old woman stood between me and the entrance to the ice cave. Her graying black hair was greasy and unkempt. She stood stooped over with a tree branch as a cane so like those witches in those children's stories my father disseminated to scare everyone.

"Come closer, child." The witch cocked her head and offered a bony finger, crooking it, beckoning. A smile showed off rotten teeth.

Everything in my body told me to run, but I was frozen to the spot, my heart hammering. The stench of death floated past.

The witch took a step forward, and her face morphed, growing larger. A horrid maw opened, rimmed with sharp teeth, before she screamed, "Boo!"

I shrieked, and instinct took hold. I pivoted and ran as fast as my legs would move.

Behind me, the witch thing—because that was no witch—cackled. "Run! I like the chase."

And I did, stealing a glance behind me to gauge where she was, but I couldn't see her. Beneath my feet, there was cracking and crunching then clawing. My body lurched as something caught me, but I didn't fall. Snow poured in around my ankles.

I was in one of the mounds.

Behind me, the fae beast laughed with glee.

I thrashed, trying to shake off what held me before it became clear that my boot was caught on something. But as the witch thing stalked closer, I gave an almighty kick, which made me pitch forward and come face to face with a skull of some sort, its white-bleached bony eye sockets in line with mine. What was I in?

Fear squeezed a tourniquet around my heart, and I scrambled. Morphing into a wild beast, I ripped and pulled at anything that snagged me until I was out. My ankle burned as I got to my feet. Behind me, the woman-witch took one slow, limping step toward me at a time, now only a table's length away.

It toyed with me. I was no match for it. But I had to try.

I sprinted forward and collapsed. Shooting pains ran up my leg, so I flipped over to face the beast who shook her finger at me in a *tsk*. My chest heaved as I scrambled backward. The only thing I had was my magic, so I reached out for it.

But it wasn't there.

My heart lunged into my throat as the beast came closer. It froze as a chiming hiss nearly punctured my ears.

Then its head crumpled in on itself before its entire body fell over with a thud.

A gloved hand clamped on my mouth, and another grabbed under my arm, hoisting me up.

"There are more," the fae man said as he panted.

CHAPTER 7

INNARA

That thing had imploded on itself, and he'd caused it. At least it was dead, but that left me now with someone far more terrifying. Had I horribly miscalculated in wanting to seek help from this fae man?

I reached up and grabbed at his hand, prying his fingers. The fingertip of his glove began slipping off his finger, which was fine with me. I'd bite his flesh if I had to.

"Damn it, human, don't touch me!" His hands left my body but were quickly replaced with those bonds of air.

"Get away from me," I growled back at him.

The bonds lifted me, and the pressure came off my ankle. The relief was blissful and at complete odds with the rest of me. My bearings were gone as he floated me back toward the ice wall. The cave entrance was no longer visible. I'd run too far.

"Hush," he hissed at me. "More will come looking. Don't cause a newer distraction than the one I *already* made. It was a damn waste of power with no reading." He stalked, behind me, his gloved finger crooked in front of him. "If I let these bonds go, will you listen to me? The baedour knows something happened to the one back there and exactly where it was. We need to move to a safer spot."

I struggled against the restriction. This fae and that witch thing—baedour, as he called it—were both threats. "You killed it."

"Indeed. It was I kill it or it kills you." He moved toward me, and my heart rate shot up. His head cocked to the side, and his hands slowly rose in a pacifying gesture. "Easy. If I wanted to kill you, I'd already have done it back in that cave." He took another slow step near. "We need to move. Now. I can hear them coming. Can I release you?"

I couldn't stay here and let more of those things come after me. I'd have to deal with one threat at a time. With a sigh, I said, "Yes."

The wrappings of air fell away, and my weight went back on to my ankle. I groaned as a white-hot lick of pain whipped up my leg.

"There's a crevasse right there." He pointed, his hand coming over my shoulder so I could see. "Quick, now. The baedour will find the dead body of its brethren and come looking for us."

The shades of blue and white in front of me changed, outlining an opening hidden behind an outer layer of ice, much like a cave behind a waterfall. It was only a few feet away.

I grabbed the sides of my cloak and sprint-limped as best I could to the wall of ice, hissing each time my foot connected with the ground. Once I was upon it, the crevasse was easily visible, the darkness within a stark change in color. I turned my body and slid inside. There wasn't a lot of room, and once the fae pressed in behind me, it was a tight squeeze.

His large body behind me made me feel small and insecure. I turned, brushing my shoulder against his solid chest. Facing him was better. He inhaled tightly and pressed his back into the ice. Good. Maybe I should press up against him if he was that disgusted by humans. But I didn't want to be touching him either. Fell Fae.

From this new position and proximity, he towered over me. I stared straight at his sternum. His shirt opened in a V, revealing a smattering of hair. I averted my eyes. Why had he come back for me?

My ears popped. The crevasse became eerily silent other than our breath rasping and commingling. The top of my head burned, and I became blisteringly aware that he watched me, studied me. My limbs trembled.

"What was that thing?" I blurted into the silence.

"A baedour. Nasty things. Hive mind. Only thing worse is a sluagh."

I grunted.

"What?" he asked.

I shook my head and stared off toward the entrance.

"You want to say something. Say it." A cold, leather-clad finger tipped my chin up and over. He stared down at me. His eyes were a steely blue-gray, and his lush lips were held in a line. Ice formed on his beard and long lashes.

He said he would've killed me already if he'd wanted to. Was this some Faerie game, gain my trust before killing the silly human?

"Don't be shy. You haven't minced your words yet." He drew in a long breath, his eyes shutting momentarily.

A shiver racked through my body, shifting me against him. Both our breaths hitched. Could he smell fear? Lore said fae had great abilities when it came to the senses. Much greater than humans at least.

I jerked my chin away from his finger. "Isn't everything nasty here, you Fell Fae?"

Every ounce of courage I had left, I poured into glaring back at him and keeping my breath steady. If he could smell fear, I would have to not be fearful. Nolan had called me naive, and that was the last thing I had the luxury of being in this unforgiving world.

His eyes turned colder, the dark ring of blue around his iris morphing to almost black. "I would not call us that if I were you."

No fear. I gave my hair a small shake and continued to hold his gaze.

After a moment, he broke the stalemate. "If you *are* from the other side of the Wall, what is your plan?"

He had me there.

The wind went out of my proverbial sails. "Not die? To go home."

His lips quirked. "Doing well, I see." He cast his gaze toward the entrance, biting a lip before letting it go. "You will come with me."

"Oh, I will, will I?" I kept the attitude, but my original idea had been to follow him anyway. Relief warred with trepidation. I had what I sought, but I wasn't sure how much I really wanted it. Another shiver rocked my body, and the hard truth of it slammed into me.

I wouldn't survive here. Not on my own.

"Do you have a better idea? You almost died within five minutes of being outside that cave. You won't last here. The environment alone will kill you, let alone the beasts. Besides, you intrigue me. You reek of fear, but..." He made a show of looking behind me, down my back, causing me to shift and wrap my cloak around me. "You have a backbone, albeit a weak one."

"You insult me." I didn't know what it was about this fae man, but he had me saying things I never dreamed of saying to anyone else.

He shrugged. "Tit for tat. Isn't that one of your human sayings?"

I ignored his comment. "Will I be safe at your place?"

"Safety is relative. You'll certainly be safer there than here." He cocked his head, his lips quirking up on one side.

I had no patience for silly word games. "Are you going to kill me?"

"Ah. No, I do not plan on killing you. I do have questions for you." He glanced to the side. "But we should get moving. I do not sense the baedour anymore. They have moved on. Something else must have gotten their attention, but they'll be back searching for us."

He paused, waiting for me to move. I weighed my options for a moment. I didn't trust him, but I would have to take him at his word. If I was to survive, he offered me the best chance.

I nodded and slid my way along the rock wall back out into Faerie.

CHAPTER 8

KIR

I needed to get out of this crevasse with the human. It was too close, and her smell was intoxicating, which unnerved and enraged me.

She had come out of the cave like a mewling newborn, all big eyes and wonder, fearful yet excited. Our world had quickly sobered her. The baedour had wasted no time. If she was sent by Gaelin, he had invested in a great actor. But even if she was one of his, I hadn't been able to stomach watching her death. I told myself it was because she needed to be questioned, but I had been moving out of my hiding spot before I'd given it any conscious thought. It had felt like instinct.

And that damned baedour. I could still feel its mind, slipping through my fingers like some sort of gelatinous goo, squeezing it until it nearly exploded between my fingers. Vomit threatened to rise in my throat, but I swallowed it back. Baedour were awful creatures, and its death was deserving. But...

This ability of mine. I was a monster too. And what good did it do my people? Something that could grow crops would be much more useful at the moment.

The human before me held to her tune of coming from the East-lands, but I wouldn't let myself be fully convinced. Her naivete could be a put on. The fear wafting off her would be hard to create, but an adept witch would be capable.

Violet would be capable.

I had this witch where I wanted her. She'd capitulated, which piqued my suspicion. Once at my home, we could question and observe her.

Curious that she didn't request safe harbor, and until she did, I wouldn't reveal it, though there was definitely an argument for it.

When I lifted my hand, an indication for her to move toward the entrance, she got the hint and slid along the wall to keep from touching me. I held my breath. Telling her how I was cursed, that a mere touch from the wrong person could kill me was not the wise thing to do.

Her ankle had turned in the bone mound, a veritable graveyard of various beasts. Only the worst ones remained now. But this would never do. I couldn't have her limping the entire way back to my court.

Once outside the crevasse, she tightened that cloak around her like it was some sort of armor. I doubted she only did it for the cold.

"You're injured," I said.

"Observant of you," she sniffed to the side, while her eyes wouldn't meet mine. If I wanted to play with fire, I'd get closer to her, see her reaction, but I wasn't playing with fire. Rashness was a luxury for others, not me.

"You won't make it the entire way back."

"I apologize if my injury is an inconvenience to you." Her eyes now met mine, and they blazed.

A thrill went down my spine at the fire inside her. "My concern is for your welfare."

"I can heal myself." She bent down toward her ankle.

I leapt backward. I couldn't let her use her witchery.

Instinct took hold, and I wrapped her in air and put her to sleep, her head lolling to the side. She wouldn't perform magic around me. Once we had her back, I'd have Clove whip up some witch hazel tonic. If only I had some with me. It wasn't every day I ran into witches in these parts. In my court, they were allowed, invited in even, but they were to remain in the area and roads allotted to them. Rylla hated that I had made that deal, but it was better than letting all the witches in Cirrelea get scooped up by Gaelin.

This would let me see how much I could trust them. It wasn't as if I didn't have them under surveillance. They wouldn't be in my court and allowed to keep many secrets.

Relative freedom in exchange for security. That was the deal. Not an alliance but a truce.

And this witch, wherever she came from, was not yet to be trusted. Certainly not allowed to perform her magic with me standing right next to her. If she was a life witch, she could kill me in a second, curse or no curse.

CHAPTER 9
INNARA

I woke not knowing where I was, but at least I was no longer cold. Softness surrounded me, a luxurious warmth. I was in a bed. My head, however, throbbed, and a general fog hung at the edges of my mind.

I groaned. A chair creaked, and my eyes shot open.

A woman hovered over me. She was beautiful, with piercing blue eyes and rosy red lips. Fae. Her hair was so white it gleamed, and it was pulled away from her golden face in an intricate braid. Her lush lips drew up in a sneer as she crossed her arms. Beautiful but not friendly.

"Who are you?" she asked.

Her harsh words pierced through my skull, and I brought a hand to my temple in a wince.

"I'm Innara," I whispered. "Where am I?"

"I'm asking the questions here." She placed both hands on the edge of the bed and leaned over. "Did Gaelin send you? What does he want? He must have coached you for a while for you to attempt to fool us into thinking you were from the other side." She rapid-fired the questions at me, and a sick feeling stirred in my belly as she leaned in close and whispered harshly, "But I am no fool."

She stood back up, arms crossed, an elegant, blood-red fingernail tapping her lithe arm.

I struggled to sit up. Lying down felt all too much like I was at her mercy. I clutched my stomach, dread overcoming me. "I don't know who Gaelin is. I don't know where I am. I don't know what you're talking about."

"You expect us to believe that? You just happened to be in that cave, by that chest about to open it, and to top it all off, you act as though you have some sort of amnesia. It's laughable. Gaelin must have trained you extensively, but he's failing at the most obvious."

Her constant chatter ricocheted around my head. I tried to make sense of it while controlling the urge to heave.

But I lurched away from her and vomited all over the floor on the other side of the bed.

A door opened.

"Rylla," a female voice said. "What did you do? I told you to be nice, that she'd be in no state to answer questions when she woke."

I groaned and sat back up. A smaller fae with deep brown skin and red hair stood with her hands on her hips and a frown on her face. The white-haired woman—Rylla—was turned away from me, a sword strapped to her back. In fact, several weapons peppered her body.

"She's the enemy," Rylla said. "I don't understand why Kir brought her here." Rylla turned to look at me. "Pathetic." She snorted and strode to the door. "I'll alert him."

Her departure left me alone with this new fae who I already liked more, since she'd gotten Rylla to leave. She smiled as she came around the side of the bed, revealing a dimple in her cheek.

"We'll get this cleaned up. I told Rylla to let me know when you woke." She bustled around the other side of the bed where Rylla had been. "I should have known better. Rylla can easily fly off the handle." She placed a cold hand on my forehead. "I'm Clove. You're dosed with witch hazel. Have you never been given that before? Usually, only witches never dosed with it get sick like that."

I shook my head. Why would I willingly dose myself with something that made my witchery beyond my reach?

"Interesting," she muttered as she pulled the blankets up by my feet, the faintest touch on my ankle. "You didn't break a bone, but you tore some ligaments. It'll be a few weeks before you really want to exercise it. I sewed up the gash but no healing." She waggled her fingers. "Kir doesn't like us to waste our power. There seems to be no infection, but we'll keep an eye on it."

I drew my leg up to see her work but winced as my muscles tweaked the wrong way.

Clove put her hand on my knee. "Try not to move it much. At least for a day or two."

"I can heal it," I said. If it wasn't for their blasted witch hazel.

Her eyes darted to me. "Is that your specialty?"

Suddenly, I felt as though I should conceal as much as I could, but the cat was already out of the bag. Only life witches could heal. So I nodded.

"Thank you for healing me. Is there something for nausea?"

Clove pursed her lips and shook her head. "That's the witch hazel. Not much I can do about it. It'll get better after a few more doses. You'll get used to it."

My stomach rebelled at the thought. "You're going to keep dosing me?"

She moved toward the door. "Afraid so. We can't have a witch in this house with her witchery available, and unfortunately, that means you'll be healing the strictly human way."

"But I thought...I thought magic was welcomed here."

"You thought wrong." The fae man from before entered the room.

He'd cleaned up. His hair held a touch of dampness and like he had run his hands through it recently, and his beard looked newly trimmed, ice-free. But it was his eyes that struck me. They appeared tired yet alert. A man with ninety-nine problems.

He must be Kir, who Clove had mentioned. He leveled his gaze at her. "Leave us."

Clove dipped her head in acknowledgement, but I wanted to beg her to stay. So far, she was the only one to show kindness.

"I have to get cleaning supplies ready," she said. "How long do you need?"

But Kir ignored her, turning toward me as she left. His nose screwed up. "By the Wall, what is that stench?"

My face flamed. First with embarrassment then with anger.

"I vomited since you had me dosed with witch hazel, and then I woke to your lady friend interrogating me. Why bother healing me, putting me in a bed, saving me, if this is how I am to be treated?" I babbled with righteous fury, but it was babble all the same.

Kir leaned to see the side of the bed and my pile of vomit. "Interesting."

"Why does everyone keep saying that?"

For a moment, his gaze softened, almost contemplative, but then he looked to my bracelet. He motioned to it. "What is that?"

I picked up the stone. "A bracelet. My mother gave it to me."

"Clove tried to remove it. Even under my spell, you fought her tooth and nail."

I tried to hide my shock. Mom had told me to never remove it. She even spelled it to be one continuous cord, too tight to remove. But I never thought I could fight someone while unconscious.

"Do you know what it does?" he asked.

I let the black stone fall back against my wrist.

"It's a family heirloom." That was what Mom told me. She said it would protect me, but she never said how or from what.

He smirked. "Is that all?"

Now it was my turn to cock my head at him. I wouldn't give him more.

"It didn't do a very good job of it today." His voice was low as he slowly walked toward the head of the bed. He paused while I tried to parse his meaning. "Why are you here?"

"I told you already. I fell through the Wall. Why did you knock me out when I agreed to come?"

"You were injured."

"I can heal myself."

"I couldn't allow that, and I had no witch hazel to offer you." His eyes scanned my face, down my neck, my body. It was then I realized I wore a thin gown and dearly hoped it was Clove who'd changed me. Heat bloomed in my cheeks.

He arched a brow, and it lit something inside of me, a firm resolution that I wouldn't allow him to force me off kilter. I raised my chin. "I wouldn't drink it willingly."

"Clearly, you never have before."

"Why would I?"

Kir pressed his lips together and reached behind him to pull the chair Rylla had used closer to the bed. Sitting down, he steepled his hands in front of his mouth. "What were you doing with the chest in the cave? Don't lie to me." Then he leaned back into a pose of complete leisure, but I could tell he was primed to strike. "If I wanted to, I could enter your mind, see everything I wanted to see, then crush it like a grapefruit in my hands."

He reached a gloved hand out and mimicked squeezing something.

I shivered. I knew the veracity of what he described, saw it happen to that baedour. Only a monster could do such things. More witch hazel threatened to come up.

He said no more, merely waited. Calling forth that event had done more to throw me than the casual perusal of my body.

I swallowed down my fear and gathered my thoughts. I had no reason to lie. Not that I had any idea of what lie to tell. I'd started with the truth, and that was what he would get. "As I told you, I fell through the Wall and woke in that cave. I was frozen cold and thought the chest might hold something useful. The wood the chest was made of could have been used to make a fire."

His gaze never left mine. My gut told me that if I was the first to break away that he'd conclude I was lying, but I was sorely tempted to. That stare—it made me feel stripped bare. I wanted to squirm and, Wall help me, preen. What was wrong with me? He was a monster, a Fell Fae already using his tricks to bewitch me.

"You opened it," he said at length. "Was it locked?"

I paused. They knew I was a life witch, and I didn't understand what had happened with that lock, but they could tell me. So I nodded, "I undid the lock."

"There was no lock on it. I saw the box, tested it. Why would you lie about something so easy to discern?"

"No, it was magic. I touched the lock with my witchery." I was about to continue, but it was clear my words had an effect.

He pinched his bottom lip, a thoughtful look in his eyes. "Your witchery? But how?"

"I touched it to the magical trap, and it dissolved away."

His lips twitched before he stood up, the backs of his knees shoving the chair back. Then he left the room.

CHAPTER 10
KIR

"Kir, you have to do something about her." Clove sat across from me at the dining table, slowly turning a mug of tea. "We can't keep her in that room. It's a veritable prison."

I dragged a hand down my face, scratching at my beard, fearing she had a point.

"You know how Rylla and Dain feel," she said. "They're like caged beasts with a witch under our roof, a threat to their lord."

I raised a brow. "And you're not?"

Clove shrugged. People always underestimated her. Small and kind, but she'd have a knife pressed to anyone's throat that threatened her friends. "My gut tells me she is who she says she is."

"And why is that?"

"She's putting on a brave face, but there is always that undercurrent of fear."

Yes, her fear. I could smell it too when I was anywhere near her room. And the hate. It was one reason I hadn't gone in to get any answers. It made me want to soothe her, and Wall if I knew why I'd want to do that.

I'd let the conversation lapse long enough that Clove now stared out the large picture window overlooking the frozen lake. I used to glamour that window to show us the view from before, a beautiful blue frozen lake with giant coniferous trees speckling its shores. It would be too wasteful of my magic today, so now it confronted us with the desolate, windswept gray ice that covered my court.

"Have you finished deciphering the pages?"

Clove's attention returned to me, a small sip of her tea, a hum of acknowledgement. "I've gone through them once, hoping context would make some areas clearer. I'm getting there, but nothing that I feel is definite. If I tell you something but get the nuance wrong, we could be off on a wild pixie chase."

The back door slammed open, and the boisterous banter of Rylla and Dain rang out. They were both decked out in their traveling leathers with swords peeking up from behind their backs. Light and dark, the two of them.

"Why are you both here?" I kept my voice calm. One of us was usually at the village.

Dain nudged Rylla who cleared her throat. "Neither of us liked the idea of you here with the witch. We decided it was best to return. Haze can ferry messages to and from the village."

"Who is in charge there?" This time, I let some of my anger filter into my words.

"Perry," Rylla stated simply.

I held their gaze. The concern of theirs was genuine, but they'd disobeyed my order. "Do you think me too soft to take care of myself? Clove is here."

Rylla and Dain both shifted minutely. One had to pay attention to even know they squirmed.

Dain finally got the balls to speak. "She's been here for four days. If you would let us interrogate the witch, we wouldn't feel the need to be here."

"Shall I bring her to our holding cell and torture her?" I asked, a tightness in my throat that I couldn't explain.

I didn't miss the smirk on Rylla's face. Never in my life had I seen her take such a distaste for someone on sight. Even the witches in our court. Rylla didn't seem bothered by them. At least not in an unusual sense.

"I can bring her down in minutes if that is what you wish," Dain said.

Across the table, Clove let out a whimper, her knuckles white on her empty teacup.

Blast it all.

Leave it to Rylla and Dain to devise this entire thing to force my hand. Under normal circumstances, I'd be pissed as hell at them, but they were right. I'd allowed this bizarre whatever-it-was as an excuse to avoid the witch. At first, I let myself believe we'd lulled her into a false sense of security, that she could trust us, but her fear and clear disgust would never allow that. No, I needed to get to the bottom of this, and the easiest way to do that would be to look into her mind. I detested doing it. Avoided it as much as I did killing. But just the same, sometimes it had to be done.

I slipped my gloves on and rose from the table. "Rylla, you will witness."

Clove would put the witch at ease, but Rylla or Dain had to see.

Rylla trailed me up the stairs. I grounded myself by focusing on the smooth grain of the wooden banister under my hand. I had the witch placed in a room away from mine. Clove's was next to hers. Rylla and Dain both preferred the basement.

At the top of the stairs, I paused. It had to be done. It was causing angst within my ranks, and we needed to know if she told the truth. The last thing I wanted was to cause anxiety for Rylla and Dain. Their duty was to protect their lord, and though they never saw it this way, they were my people as much as anyone else. It was my sworn duty to protect them as well. My honor called for it, even though I had little left.

"It's the right thing to do. It's not even painful," Rylla whispered to me. She casually placed her hand on my arm, and I stiffened.

I always dressed to cover my skin. For a long time, I even

wrapped my face and head, but it was too cumbersome. Too hot. I trusted my companions enough to know the risk of a casual touch on bare skin. But I was on edge today.

Rylla drew her hand away, and I wanted to grab it and put it back. I both longed for and feared the touch of another. My body swayed toward hers. Her sky blue eyes clouded over, so I hastily stepped back.

"Don't," I said. "I appreciate the empathy, but you can't."

With a gloved hand, I grasped her upper arm clad in leather. It was all I could allow and what I could control. Touch was always more comfortable for me if I initiated.

"I have a job to do. Let's get it done." My voice was gruff, hiding the longing I felt.

I chided myself at how Rylla might mistake it for longing for her. And it was somewhat for her. She was my friend. A friend I could not embrace, a friend I could not wrestle with in jest. But she had been clear years ago—years before my curse—that friendship was not what she wanted from me. We both knew she was not my mate and that, even though most fae never found one, it was foretold that I would.

I could see it in her eyes from time to time. That heat, that yearning. And I hated how moments like the one that just passed between us could be interpreted as romantic interest. She was a danger to me more than anyone else. Because she did love me, and it was the touch of someone who loved me that could kill me.

Dain had once tried to convince me that a whore wouldn't love me, so I should take one to bed instead of denying myself. But it was too much like playing with fire. Would the curse include attraction? How many times had I read that love and hate were different sides of the same coin? It was too murky in my mind.

Rylla, oblivious to my inner turmoil, used her hand to push open the witch's door while remaining outside. She pointedly kept her body away from mine, turning her head away to hide the glistening sheen in her eyes.

The witch needed to be dealt with. I'd channel my frustration at her.

I allowed my steps to be loud as I made my way into her room. She stood near the head of her bed, holding her cloak, her hand in one of its pockets. Clad in leggings and a fluffy cream-colored sweater given to her by Clove, she'd been rummaging in the closet, the door wide open.

She yanked her hand out of the cloak and jammed it into the pocket of the sweater.

My eyes narrowed. "What do you have there?"

"Nothing," she said, and her throat bobbed.

I stepped closer, and Rylla breathed in with a hiss. My choice to step near this witch was a slap in the face after what had just happened in the hall, but this witch didn't love me.

I took one small step back on that note and pointed at the side table. "Put it there."

She stared at me, motionless, a muscle ticking in her temple. A splotch of red appeared high in her pale cheeks. It fascinated me, but it did not matter.

"Obeying will earn you niceties," I said. As much as Rylla would squirm behind me, I had to walk the line with physical intimidation and not show how I feared touch. This witch had seen enough of that in the cave, although luckily, she seemed to think that was pure disgust. "Please," came out of me without me even thinking it.

Her hand twitched in her pocket like she was going to do as I asked, but then she stomped her foot and spat at my feet. "Obey? What am I? Some dog?"

The splotches of red in her cheeks deepened, and now some appeared on her neck. My hand itched to push back the chestnut locks of hers that blocked my full view. I shook my hand to kill the urge.

"Rylla." I flicked my hand from her to the witch.

Rylla nodded and came into the room, hand out. It gave me an excuse to put more space between the witch and me. Rylla turned to me and held up a necklace with a green stone.

"Do you sense anything?" I asked.

Rylla shook her head.

"Give it back to her then."

"My lord?" Rylla asked.

Behind her, the witch's head jerked up. She didn't know who I was. Interesting.

"Give it back to her." If it was not of note, giving it back might earn some cooperation.

Rylla tossed it on the bed before going back to her post at the door.

My attention was back on the witch, who snatched it off the bed and tucked it back into her pocket.

"Hiding things only begets suspicion," I said. "Honesty, on the other hand..."

"Honesty gets me nothing but held captive in your house." Her hazel eyes flashed with ire.

I breathed in, took my time. "I can't have a witch running wild in my house." Especially a life witch. A prophecy foretold that a life witch could take fae sources. This witch was a danger for many reasons. "You are safe, healing."

"I am not allowed out of this closet of a room," she said. "Do you have any idea what that does to a person's mental state?"

It was almost too on the nose. Her mental state. It was why I was there after all, and I'd let myself be distracted by this necklace.

"Please sit," I said.

Behind me, Rylla groaned. "Kir, just do it."

I clenched my jaw, turning to Rylla, silently trying to communicate to her to shut the fuck up.

"No," the witch said as her heartbeat spiked.

The muscle in my jaw ticked. *Thanks so much, Rylla.* But here we were.

"Sit, or she will make you sit," I said.

Rylla took a step into the room, and the witch sat on the bed. The acrid stench of fear wafted off her but also the heady smell of anger laced with outrage.

I could tell her what I was going to do, but I didn't want her to resist. The resisting was what could cause pain. Luckily, recent memories were always the easiest to get to. I could skim through them and get my answer.

Touch always helped with this. But that was impossible, so I fixed my gaze on the spot between her eyes. The inner well of magic, my source, pulsed within me, and I dipped down into that and allowed it to reach out and connect to that spot I fixed on.

"What are you doing?" Her voice quavered, and fear gripped her like when I'd wrapped her in air after the baedour. All that backbone and fire I admired disappeared. She trembled in front of me.

I couldn't do it. She thought me a monster, and she was right.

A bitter oil oozed through me, fierce and hot. I dropped my magic and my head.

From the door, Rylla barked, "I suggest you stop moving." She must have noticed my extreme interest in my boots. "Kir? It has to be done."

I wouldn't meet her eyes. Either of their eyes.

It did need to be done. But not like this.

Not like this.

I rested my hands on my hips, chewing my cheek and racking my brain before I looked up to meet the witch's eyes. Revulsion pinched her brow, and her chin drew back. Revulsion in me was something we were both familiar with.

I formed my words with care. A bargain. A fair bargain. "The only way I can know you are who you say you are is to enter your recent memories, back to just before crossing the Wall."

She drew back even farther, her legs drawing up on the bed, tight to her chest. "Enter my mind? Never. You'll kill me like you did that thing."

"I won't kill you. I have no interest in doing that to you." *Not at the moment.* "In exchange—"

"Kir!" Rylla spat in admonishment.

My arm shot out to the side in a cutting motion. I would have Rylla leave before I used magic on her, but she got the message and obeyed.

"In exchange," I said again, "you can move about the house if you have been telling the truth."

The witch pursed her lips, mulling it over. "How do I know you won't kill me?"

I sighed. "Have I not done what I said? I risked myself to save you from that baedour and brought you to my home. We've healed you, fed you, sheltered you."

She pressed her lips together.

"If it helps. I detest my ability. Killing that baedour—" I closed my eyes, letting this witch see as much of my vulnerability as I dared. "I can feel it still. It haunts me, the feeling of its mind. How it screeched and begged up until the second I squeezed tight." I flicked my eyes open. She listened with rapt attention. "But I did it. The baedour is a nasty Faerie beast, sent into my lands. Would you have preferred I let it devour you?"

Her eyes darted from me to Rylla as she picked a thread on her leggings. "What will you see? How much?"

I schooled my face. She came around. "I promise to skim back till just before we met. It's like..." I waved my hand in the air, searching for a description. "Like, cards in a deck flipping by."

"You'll look at nothing else?"

"I promise I will only tick back until I know if you truly did fall through the Wall."

"Run of the house, *and* you help me get back across the Wall." She hitched her chin up a notch.

Rylla gasped but kept her mouth shut. Indeed. The timid witch was full of surprises. Brave, considering how scared she was.

I let out a low chuckle. "I don't think so. I made my offer. If you want my help in addition to keeping you alive in Faerie, you'll have to figure something else out. Feel free to stay inside the four walls of this room." I made a show of looking about. "It *is* cozy."

She didn't need to know I would help her, provided she was who she said she was. It went unsaid that if I found out she was Gaelin's witch, the only getting out of this room would be to go down to our holding cell in the basement. And that was everyone's point. I hadn't put her there to begin with. I didn't know why. Maybe it was the sheer thought of doing that to someone who was innocent. And maybe that was why I couldn't do this without her consent, even if I was coercing her, which I still hated.

But it was a fair bargain, and it was in protection of my people.

Her eyes narrowed. "Fine. You can read that memory and *only* that memory." She placed her legs down, feet on the floor, and sat up straight. "Will it hurt?"

"It only hurts when one resists." I adjusted my stance "Are you ready?"

She rolled her shoulders, drawing my attention to her body in a way I had no business doing. I squeezed my eyes shut and opened them again, focusing on just between her eyes like I had before.

Off to the side, I sensed Rylla shifting her weight.

I blocked everything else out except my focus on the witch's mind. The bedroom around me fell away.

Now I was in a dark, empty room, and in front of me was the witch. She wore her cloak from the other day. The hood was up, and I could barely make out her face. But I knew it was her. The scent was a dead giveaway. Jasmine and sage. I breathed it in.

Sometimes mindscapes were a puzzle, but this was obvious. The cloak was her mental shield. It would be easy enough to do away with. I stepped closer until I was inches away. My heart pulsed, and electricity zinged along my arms. A spark flew from me to her then back again, the gold zips warm and pleasant.

I reached out with gloveless hands to push back the hood. But it was stiff, hard as metal. I pushed, but it wouldn't budge. The clasp at her neck also refused to move.

All of it. All of it was as hard and as immovable as granite.

Never in my life had I seen something like this. Her mind was a veritable fortress. There had to be a way in. Everyone had some way in. Some chink in the armor.

I leaned down to peer into her hood. Earlier, I could make out her face. But this time, darkness greeted me. A wispy rope of illuminated light reached from her to me, and that beguiling scent of hers was nearly overwhelming. I sank to my knees as her name whispered through the air. Fear kicked in as another word formed in my mind.

I jerked my awareness out of that darkness, plummeting back into the witch's room.

Her hazel eyes were huge and round. "See? I told the truth."

But she must have sensed my panic and pulled her legs back up onto the bed.

Rylla was there. "What happened? What did you see?" She positioned herself between the two of us. "You were whimpering."

I couldn't stay here. My breath caught in my chest. It couldn't be.

I strode out of the room.

Behind me came Rylla's light, quick steps before she loomed in front of me. Her face nearly swam in my vision. She grabbed both my upper arms, steadying me. "What did you see?"

For once, I didn't care about the touch. A more dangerous foe sat in that room behind us.

"She's my mate."

CHAPTER II
INNARA

Kir fled my room, his face ashen. Rylla still stood near, her mouth agape. She took one murderous look at me as if I had done something to him and dashed off. Their steps faded down the hallway.

Pain in my wrist flared. What in the Wall? A headache bloomed behind my eyes, but my wrist now had a tattoo. Dainty wildflowers —water lilies, jasmine, and freesia—extended from the back of my hand to the edge of my wrist near the bone.

Faerie.

But that wasn't the oddest thing. Kir had been in my head or near it. I wasn't sure. It was the strangest sensation. He had been gentle, like a cat purring and rubbing against my mind. For one second, I'd relished the touch and wanted to rub back. And then it was gone. My pulse was still calming from the shock of him leaving.

I let my chin fall onto my knees, brushing my cheek against the fabric, but it was a poor substitute for what I'd experienced. Did he see anything? Did he see me with Nolan? I didn't know why, but the thought of it made my cheeks burn. Would he be able to know how Nolan's touch had warmed me, made me ache?

What was I doing? This was part of the tales. Fae bewitched you with their beauty, made you their slave.

He was cunning with his games. First, he threatened and then followed it with the well-played shame and bargaining with me. But he had me there. I had little to bargain with, and if I could get out of this room, it was better than nothing. He was convincing with his self-loathing over the baedour.

I wouldn't fall for it. He'd shown me what he was capable of, and now he lulled me into trusting him. Still, in the end, what choice did I have? Submit or...what? Stay in that room?

I chose what I thought would move me forward.

My hope now was that he'd seen what he needed to. If I had more space to roam, maybe I could piece things together. I had to figure out how to get home and find my mom. Was she okay? Had she survived? The Trappers must have gone after her once I was gone. She was my home—I couldn't abandon her. Doing nothing was not an option.

If I got here, then there was a way back across the Wall. I had to believe that.

I rolled my head against my knees again, working out some tension. The door lay open. I slid my feet to the floor and eased myself off the bed. I was at the doorframe before I considered what I was trying to accomplish. On light feet, I tiptoed into the hall. No one was out here. Was this confirmation that Kir had gotten what he needed, that I'd told the truth? If he hadn't, wouldn't they have sent someone up to close me off again?

The floor was made of wide wood planks. Smooth and rich in color. I turned the corner, where everything opened up. The arched ceiling was speckled with skylights, letting in natural light, though the sky above appeared gray. I found myself at a wood banister, a real branch polished to a high sheen. This area looked over an entryway. Off to the side, a large staircase led to the floor below.

Voices drifted up, and I froze. They were downstairs and out of my sight. Could they hear me? Fae had heightened senses. Kir had smelled that I was a witch. Was that proof of keen hearing though? If I could eavesdrop, that was better than nothing.

Boots clomped on stone, and my pulse picked up, matching their cadence.

But they weren't coming to me.

"What happened? Rylla sent Haze to find me. Damn creature nearly bit my ear off." A man's voice echoed up the stairwell, but it wasn't Kir.

There was a pause and some muttering.

Then that same man's voice again. "You're shitting me."

"There's more." That was definitely Kir, and I found myself gripping the rail and leaning forward.

"More than that?"

There was a *thwack*.

"Shut up, Dain. Let him finish." The snarky white-haired woman. I grimaced.

"Don't hit me," Dain said, "but not much more matters after that. Does she lie?"

"I didn't—" Kir started.

"What do you mean?" Rylla again.

I rolled my eyes. My distaste for her probably equal to her distaste for me.

"Shut up. Both of you," Kir commanded. I could picture him pinching the bridge of his nose. "She was shielded. The likes of which, I have never seen."

"And what does that mean?" It was that Dain character again.

"It means I have no idea if she is lying. But you don't have a shield like that unless you are hiding something. She can't stay."

I wasn't sure if I should be elated or worried.

Then for the first time in this conversation, Clove spoke. "But she's—"

"I know what she is." Kir sounded strangled. "And for that very obvious reason, she can't stay. We have to figure out something to do with her."

"I can take her wherever you want me to." Rylla would have dumped me at the bottom of the ocean given half a chance.

"Hush," Kir said.

The hairs on the back of my neck stood up. I hesitated to move. They'd hear me, but maybe they could already hear my now rapidly accelerating pulse. I should run.

Something down the hallway moved. A cat jumped onto the rail and prowled toward me with no care for falling over the edge.

No, it was an owl.

My brain broke trying to figure out what approached.

It stopped in front of me. A heart-shaped face, white fluffy feathers, sea-green eyes with depths like I have never seen. Cat-like ears poked up, turned directly toward me. The creature fluffed its wings, but a long tail swung up behind it in a shade of brown that covered its wings, and white cat legs poked out beneath. It squawked and purred, trying to bump its head toward me, but I backed up. What was this creature?

"Meet Haze," Kir called up. He stood on the stone floor looking at us, his face an unreadable mask.

"Kir, we should speak." Clove moved into view, paying no mind to me, even though I was just busted for eavesdropping.

"I was going to invite the witch down," Kir said. "I can't read her mind. Perhaps let you all have a go at her."

I shuddered at what that might mean, but I couldn't let go of how he always called me "the witch."

"I have a name," I said, stepping forward to grip the rail. I certainly had a lot of false bravado in this place. But feeling like if I breathed the wrong way at the wrong person, it could end my life or crush my mind—it made me willing to gamble every time I rolled the dice.

Haze, beside me, bumped its head into my arm.

Kir ignored me, something passing between him and Clove. He motioned with his arm, and the two of them proceeded to walk back beneath me.

"I'll be damned, Haze likes her." The man who had to be Dain leaned against a statue off to the side. He was taller than Kir, and his complexion was a smooth, dewy tan. Near-black hair hung below his shoulders. A scar crossed his brow, over his eye, and down his cheek. I'd always thought fae healed too fast for scars. What kind of beasts could do that?

"Everyone is allowed one bad judgement," Kir said from wherever he and Clove disappeared to. "Show her to the library."

And with that, Dain shoved away from the statue, his gaze still trained on me as he made his way up the stairs. He jerked his head at the top of the steps before walking away from the landing. It wasn't in the direction of that tiny room, so I followed.

Kir had said library, and I definitely wanted to see what a fae library looked like. As the repository for all knowledge, it would be the best to search for things I needed to know about, which covered anything fae or regarding the Wall.

As I closed the distance between Dain and me, he drew in a long, deep breath. The tales told of beauty that hurt to look upon, but I wanted to do nothing more than to feast my eyes. Dain was pure sensual predator.

He tilted his head so I could see his profile. A cocky grin quirked the side of his mouth as he used one hand to open a large, ornate door.

"Like what you see?" His eyes gleamed as he indicated the room.

Our gazes met. His double entendre was clear.

Normally, I'd duck my head and ignore his comment. Or pretend I only understood the one meaning. Maybe Faerie was affecting me, but I refused to do what I always did.

I looked Dain in the eye. "I've seen better."

A low chuckle rumbled out of him as I breezed past him and he followed.

A large room with arched ceilings greeted me. Branches rose from the walls and curved along the ceiling, meeting in a pattern of arches and leaves. Books covered the walls, and bookcases formed short rows in front of them. On the far end was a floor-to-ceiling window, which drew me in. In the center, between sets of bookcases, was a cozy set of red couches, perfect to read and enjoy the view.

Dain stood behind me, a silent guard.

"Privacy please?" I asked over my shoulder as I ran a finger along the velvety material of the couch.

"Not a chance." He stood, hands behind his back.

"I did what Kir asked. If I had something to hide, why would I let him invade my mind?"

His sight trained on the view outside, but he slowly turned his attention to me. "You shielded yourself from him, which is not the behavior of someone cooperating."

"I did no such thing."

"You might be shocked, but I'm inclined to believe my lord and not some..." He didn't finish, just let his voice trail off as he gave me a once-over.

I needed more information from him. He wasn't exactly forth-coming. "What exactly am I?"

Dain looked at me blankly.

"I overheard your conversation," I said. "Kir said he knew what I was. What am I?"

He leaned over, his black hair falling forward. "You're a witch. A suspicious one."

I stifled my urge to snap back. Dain stood back with a smirk. These fae were infuriating. If he would give me no more, I'd turn my attention to the books.

The first ones filled me with a sense of home. The picture on the front had a fae girl in a ballgown held in an embrace by a shirtless fae man. Some things were the same no matter where you were. A comfort I didn't expect to find.

Behind me, Dain groaned. I slipped the book under my arm and perused several bookcases. So far, all fiction, but fiction held truths too. And what better way to get in a fae's mind than reading their books?

Footsteps sounded on the wood in the library. Dain passed me to see who it was.

Clove came around the corner. "I'll take it from here."

Dain wandered off without a second look at me. Good riddance.

"What have you found?" Clove moved into the aisle. She lifted her hand toward the book under my arm as if to say, *May I?* She slipped it out, examining the cover. "I loved this one. Do you like romance novels?"

Her eyes twinkled, and her lips quirked. I wasn't sure if she was making fun of me or trying to connect.

Straightening my shoulders, I moved past her. "I do, along with other genres." She didn't need to know I could binge read one of these in a day. "Where is the non-fiction?"

The smile on her face disappeared. "Non-fiction is the other side, but you need your dose of witch hazel. Let's sit."

I sank onto the cushion as Clove poured the tonic. Thankfully, the nausea had faded like she'd said it would, and while there was still brain-fog, that had lessened too.

Clove handed me a small teacup, and I threw the witch hazel back. The faster, the better. She immediately refilled it with tea and a generous helping of honey. Clove may be fae, but she was by far my favorite of the lot, even if I couldn't always read her.

She sat across from me. "So..."

I raised my brows. "So?"

"We're going to need answers. I believe you came from the Eastlands." Clove sat forward, and though she wore a dress, it reminded me of someone utterly comfortable in their skin. No fussing with how the skirt draped over her legs or a telltale crossing of legs to appear at the best angle.

Wishing I had the level of confidence she did, I plucked at my sweater over my stomach.

"You're the only one who believes me." I raised the pitch of my voice at the end, making it a question.

Clove sighed. "I am. But I've made headway in convincing Kir."

"But not Dain and Rylla."

"Dain and Rylla will believe if Kir does." She frowned. "Maybe not Rylla."

"She certainly seems to hate me the most."

"We don't hate you."

I snorted in disbelief.

"Fine. *I* don't hate you. Rylla is complicated." A faraway look crossed Clove's face. "She will fiercely protect those she loves."

I nodded, understanding dawning on me: Rylla and Kir. But I was no threat to them. Rylla had to see that. My only wish was to go back home, not break up a fae romance.

"Then ask," I said, "but I want answers too."

Clove sat back, resting one bare, dark limb on the arm of the couch, her fingers dangling and rubbing each other. "Kir will need to be involved for that. You're asking for a bargain."

I glanced down to the small marking on my wrist. "I already did."

She shrugged, her fingers now tracing a line on the armrest. "I heard. We don't take them lightly. It binds your souls together while the bargain is in existence."

Bound with a fae? I rubbed down my arm where goosebumps now prickled. "And what does that mean? What if we don't fulfill the bargain?"

"If you break your side of the bargain, the bit of your soul tied to Kir would remain with him."

"What does that mean?" It didn't sound good. Having your soul chopped up and owned by others seemed a sure way to die a slow death.

"Souls are funny things. If too many pieces of your soul are sold, you would cease to exist. Your body may continue, but your will—the bit that makes you *you*—would *poof.*" She lifted her hand in a cupping gesture and spread her fingers wide as she blew the air above it. Sparkles flittered all over, reminding me of a child blowing the seeds of a dandelion. Her fingers snapped closed, and the sparkles disappeared. "Sometimes the souls recognize something in the other and form a permanent bond, so even if Kir gave back the pieces of your soul, the two of you could still be tied together."

I swallowed. Being tied to Kir was not something I wanted.

"Kir is our lord. He makes the bargains, and since it's a risk to be tied to a witch, he will be the one to take it." Her full lips puckered. "If you bargain more with Kir, be assured that he will always hold up his end. On the bright side, he'd never ask for a full soul trade."

I swiped a thumb over the marking on my wrist. Our bargain had been to let him see what happened before I was in the ice cave. He hadn't seen it.

The thought was lead in my stomach.

Clove stood. "Come, we should talk with the others, and you must be hungry." Her eyes dropped to my wrist. "He hasn't yet determined that you didn't hold up your end of the bargain."

It helped. A little.

She led me through the library. "Let's get you food, and be careful what you say in your next meeting with Kir."

CHAPTER 12
INNARA

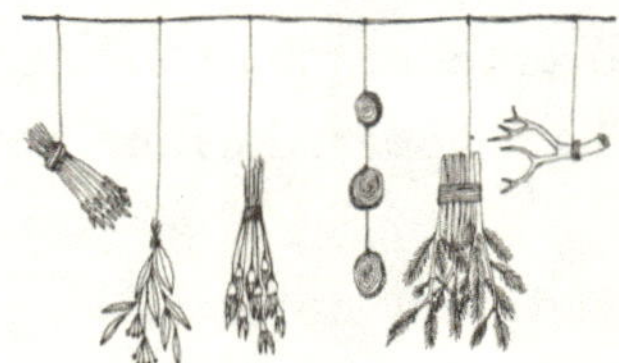

After eating, everyone congregated in the living area where two couches faced each other. They were flanked by a wall of bookcases and a fireplace. Taking my seat, I chose the couch that put my back to the wintry apocalypse. The sight of it unnerved me. It was a reminder of how stuck I was. This house was a cage, and they didn't need bars or magic to keep me here. A fae could withstand whatever happened in this world, but a human could not.

I needed to figure out a way back home. If I gave up hope, I gave up on my mom. As rough as our relationship had been through the years, she protected me. I knew she always did what she did for that reason alone. It chafed having so much of my life controlled.

Haze trotted into the room, followed by Kir. The creature was adorable, and he liked me. As he wove through, rubbing my leg and no one else's, I had to admit the feeling was mutual. Kir leaned against the fireplace. Haze leapt onto the mantel and head butted his shoulder, prompting Kir to raise a lazy hand to stroke him until the creature's eyes slid shut. Rylla and Dain took their seats on the opposite couch. And thankfully Clove, the only one who was friendly, sat down next to me.

I expected Kir to talk, but it was Dain. "Why were you in that cave?"

Not this again. "I fell through the Wall. I'm from the Eastlands."

Dain chortled. "No one passes through the Wall. Try again."

I clenched my fists, and Kir's eyes darted to them. He missed nothing, even with being farther away than the others. It was as if he wanted the others to take the lead so he could observe. Clove's warning rang through my mind.

I took a deep breath. *Be careful with what I say.* Instead of snark, I repeated, "I fell through the Wall."

Dain pressed his lips together as irritation flashed in his dark eyes. The only sound in the room was the crackle of the fire and a blast of frigid air as it pummelled the window. "Let's say I believe you. Why did you come through the Wall?"

Nolan pushing me, me ripping his necklace off, his burnt hand, my mother alone now, and my father's booming voice on the wire. It all flashed through my mind. "I needed to escape."

"Tell us about it," Dain said with a surprising amount of patience.

I glanced to Kir, who seemed to listen but not participate. He took sips from a glass of wine. His posture spoke to not caring how I answered, but something told me the opposite was true.

"My father's men found me. They're witch hunters. He seeks me, and they found me. I had to escape them. My mother told me I could go through the Wall if my need was great enough." I held back on telling them about Nolan. He was mine.

"And your need was great?" Dain asked as he shot Kir a look.

"Would you call half a dozen crossbows pointed at me a great enough threat?"

"Did you do anything when you went through the Wall?" Dain leant forward. "Magic?"

I thought back. Mom said to feed a little magic into it. It was possible I still held onto my magic from defending myself against those men. "I don't think I did."

"How do you not know?" Rylla's voice dripped with disbelief.

I glanced between her and Dain then to Kir. Clove shifted on our couch. I knotted my fingers in my lap until my knuckles turned white.

"I can't always use my magic," I said it more to my hands than to anyone in the room.

"Can't or don't have control?" Rylla asked. Her face was open. For once she didn't snarl.

"My control is good now. In the past—" I blocked out how I had used too much in a game of hide and seek, sending Mom and me on the run. I squeezed my eyes shut. "In the past, my control was bad, but now it is mainly that I need to be calm and relaxed to grasp my magic."

"How did you shield your mind? Are you practiced in mind-shielding?" Clove pushed on.

"I don't know. I've never practiced mind-shielding. I wouldn't even know where to begin."

"Bullshit," Dain grated out. "The witches here are adept at shielding their minds from us, and you're telling me you have never heard of it?"

Heat bloomed in my face and chest as I gathered my thoughts under their weighty silence. If they refused to believe anything I said, what hope of anything did I have? Yet, *I* should be careful what I say. The heat in my chest turned into a boil.

"Let's backtrack to the cave," Rylla said in a shockingly soft tone. "How did you find the cave? A cave with the chest we searched for?"

At this re-questioning, I looked up, my gaze was like a dagger. All my earlier frustration peaked into anger. "I've told you. I fell through the Wall. I had no choice where it spat me out. End of story."

Rylla glanced to Kir, a look full of meaning passing between them.

Clove, in an attempt to defuse the tension in the room, said, "The cave was glamoured. It took us weeks to find it because we couldn't see it. It wasn't fae."

Odd. I remembered looking back and seeing the cave entrance, so I snorted. "Now look who is lying. I saw it after I left."

"We don't lie." It was the first time in the entire discussion that Kir spoke.

Right. "And I'm not a witch."

"See, as you just showed us, you have the ability to lie. We do not." Kir and I locked eyes.

"You expect me to believe that?"

Kir and Clove exchanged a look, but Kir was the one to speak again. "We are incapable. Omitting truths, bending truths, speaking in riddles. All of those we are adept at, but we can't lie. Lying is what humans do. What *you* do."

His words tickled the back of my mind. The trickster faeries with their pretty words. His implication, however, curdled my stomach.

"I may be able to lie," I said, "but coming across the Wall and seeing the cave are not lies."

"I searched for days, going over every inch of that area to find that cave," Kir said. "So imagine how surprised I was to find you there with the chest open. The chest I had been looking for—that no one had found in a millennium."

That sheer amount of time he casually spoke of stunned me, but I seized on what he unwittingly admitted. "You searched that area for days, but you didn't see me enter the cave."

Silence. His lips pressed into a tight line.

I took that as a no. "Yet you don't believe me."

No one answered. I had them.

Across from me, Rylla recrossed her legs, her foot set swinging. I'd definitely made my point.

"How did you open the box?" Clove asked.

I met Kir's eyes before turning my attention to Clove, a smug sense of satisfaction filling me. "I felt the lock. I sent my magic into it, and the entire thing disappeared. Poof."

"But why did you open it? Why were you even looking at it?" Rylla asked with her voice barely disguising her irritation.

"All I had was my cloak. I wanted to see if the box had anything to help me. I had no idea what it held."

Rylla scoffed.

Inside me, a dragon roared, and I stood up. "I had nothing with me. I was in an ice cave, freezing. The box alone could have helped me. Wood for a fire."

Clove placed a hand on my arm and gently urged me to sit. Dain's hand had gone to his boot. I sat, willing my heart to calm. I chanced a glance at Kir. His eyes were keen on me. He didn't move, but I got the sense he knew my heart was racing.

The room was quiet. Wind whistled outside.

"What is it that you want?" Clove asked.

"I want to go home."

Clove glanced to Kir, opened her mouth then shut it. "I think she could be of use to us."

Rylla stood up, arms waving about. "Anyone could be of use to us. She can't stay."

Dain leaned back, manspreading on the couch, but I didn't get the impression much got past him either.

Clove raised a dark, dainty hand. "She opened that lock. Easily. If we want to find the rest, she would be useful."

My gaze ping-ponged around the room. They spoke like I wasn't sitting there. "And what if I don't want to help you?" Clove shot me a side-eye glare, so I adjusted. "What if I offer assistance in exchange for helping me find my way home?"

"Clove, you know what you're asking for," Kir said. Clove gravely nodded. "Why do you think she is needed for the locks?"

"Showing you would be better." Out of thin air, a small, plain wooden box appeared in her palm. "What kind of trap was it?" Clove looked to me for the answer.

I cleared my throat. "Fire."

"I'll lock this box with a fire trap." Clove focused on the box. "There."

She handed me the box.

I cradled it in my palms, too scared I'd set it off. "You want me to open it?"

"Yes, like you did in the cave," she said. "Oh! But you're dosed with witch hazel." Clove reached for my shoulder.

Sword drawn, Rylla shouted. "Hold on!"

"How do you expect her to show us what she did without her magic?" Clove asked, her face the picture of innocence as she gazed up at Rylla.

"Kir, you can't allow this. A life witch—"

"Grant her safe harbor," Clove spoke over Rylla.

Kir remained still, stoic.

Dain on the other hand, the picture of ease on the couch, piped up, "I'm with Rylla."

"Safe harbor would protect all of us," Clove continued.

"It protects her." Rylla with her sword pointed at me, jabbed it.

I jerked back into the couch. Things had gone from me attempting a bargain to dying soon. Never had I more wanted to go home than now, except that baedour incident.

Clove put a hand on my wrist to either hold me there or to soothe. "You're wrong, Rylla. It protects all of us. She knows no harm will come to her under Kir's roof, and if she attempts to harm us, it negates the protection of safe harbor."

"Her *existence* is harmful." Rylla seethed, giving me a look that could flay the skin right off my bones.

"She exists for a reason," Clove said. "Even the tamest of creatures when cornered will bite."

"I don't like it," Rylla said pointedly toward Kir.

"Noted." Kir shifted his stance, placing his wine glass on the mantle. "I grant the witch safe harbor. Clove, show us what you will. Also, I know what you did there."

Clove had manipulated things. She wanted Kir to grant me safe harbor. But I still wasn't sure what it did.

"What is safe harbor?" I asked.

"You are protected under Kir's roof." Rylla, her voice full of impatience. "We can't harm you unless you harm us." She motioned for Clove to go ahead.

But I feared that wasn't all. These were fae, masters of omission. "And nothing else? Is there more?"

Clove in a low, hushed voice. "Safe harbor requires the recipient to remain under the giver's roof until they remove safe harbor."

The wind left my lungs. They effectively captured me here. "And I get no say in this? I'm stuck here until Kir says I can leave?"

Clove grimaced. "It could be used that way. It's an old Faerie tradition that always intended for release if requested. But it was designed so that a recipient couldn't leave the area surreptitiously, effectively negating safe harbor, coming back, and becoming an aggressor." She placed her hand to her chest. "I promise you it is not the intent to keep you here against your will."

Rylla snorted, crossed her legs and arms. "Some of us don't want you here at all."

For the first time, Rylla's snark made me feel mildly better. I didn't like it, but it was done. If it was an issue, I'd figure it out.

Clove shifted, her knees pointing more towards me now. "Back to the box. I'll lift the fog of the witch hazel. I want you to use your magic to open this box just like you did in the cave."

This was my chance to prove myself useful. My chance to bargain for a way home.

No pressure.

Clove placed her hand on my shoulder, and the fog in my head lifted, like being in the dark and entering a brightly lit room.

No one said a word.

I reached out, but the green of life around me wouldn't appear. I tried again. Nothing.

I brought my hands to my temples and massaged. Think of something calm.

"Haze," Kir directed. The creature leapt off the mantle and padded across the rug to me. From there, he leapt onto the couch beside me with a chirrup before he curled up on my lap, a content, purring ball of feathers and fur.

My gaze flew to Kir as I stroked the softness of the animal.

Kir shrugged. "He can be soothing. Try breathing in, hold, now breathe out."

He went through the cycle with me a few times, and the tension melted from my shoulders. I stroked under Haze's chin. His sea-foam eyes closed in pure contentment. I reached out, and the green of life lens flipped into my vision. Kir and all his companions lit up. Haze too.

Switching my focus to the box, I turned it in my hands. Nothing was there.

"What's wrong?" Clove asked.

Rylla, across from us, shifted, her hands gripping her sword.

I kept my focus on the box. Anything else would see me lose my head. I wasn't sure if safe harbor covered me trying to attack them or if the fae had to feel I was a threat. "I don't see the lock."

"Maybe you're still failing," Rylla said.

"Rylla," Kir admonished.

I wouldn't let her get a rise out of me, but I shook my head. "Is this a trick? There is no lock."

"It's locked," Clove said. "Just try a little magic in it."

"Will it incinerate me?" Wouldn't that be a fae thing to do? They can't hurt me but trick me into opening an innocuous box that burns me to a crisp?

Clove laughed. "It'll be a tiny spark if you trigger it. Nothing that can do any real damage to a human."

I took a deep breath and let it out. The only life option to draw from was my own. No way I would risk any of theirs. I thinned a bit out to the thickness of floss and sent it into the box. Around me, someone sucked in their breath. My grasp wavered, and the thread disintegrated. I rolled my neck and tried again. This time, I got the thread farther in and able to explore the interior. Nothing. I let my magic go and met Clove's eyes. "Nothing."

Clove's eyes lit up as she grinned. "Perfect."

Dain growled. "What is this, Clove? What was the point?"

Her hand slipped off my shoulder and the fog set in. Haze, however, stayed in my lap.

"She can't see fae magic. The lock wasn't fae, just like the cave entrance. We wouldn't have been able to undo it." Clove turned to Kir. "You need her."

CHAPTER 13

KIR

I needed her. At one point in my life, I would have been elated. But today, those words struck fear in my fae soul because, as much as I hated to admit it, Clove was right. But I shook my head anyway.

Clove's hopeful face fell. All she ever wanted to do was help. And right now, she thought she'd figured something out.

"Clove, let's speak in another room." I didn't wait for a reply. Sometimes I hated how easily the mantle of rulership rested on my shoulders. It wasn't supposed to have been mine.

I strode into the kitchen. Clove behind me, her light footfalls echoing as she hit the tile. Through the door, I nodded to Dain. He and Rylla needed to stay in there and keep an eye on the witch. I didn't begrudge her the tension that would be in that room.

They guarded my mate. That gave them reason to protect her and reason to kill her. My heart lurched at the thought, and I wanted to check on her.

But why? It would never be.

Clove pulled out a chair and sat down. I reached into my source, which had mostly recovered from the strain of getting Innara here, to put up a sound barrier. The witch couldn't hear what we discussed.

"Just what do you think you are doing?" I chose not to sit. Clove knew what was coming, and she wanted it to be chummy.

"What do you mean? I'm trying to find ways for us to find all the journal pages."

"I know what you did back there with safe harbor."

"You can't tell me you don't feel better knowing she is safe."

"That is neither here nor there." She knew me too well, and she knew if I didn't think they would harm my mate, I would say that. But I couldn't.

She raised a brow, proving exactly that.

I dragged a hand down my face. "Fine. Why are you trying to convince me to use her?"

"Because she can help us." She flung a hand out in one of those *why are you slow on the uptake?* gestures.

"She is a grave danger to me, and you know it."

"No. We don't."

"I beg your pardon?"

"We don't know how big a danger your mate is to you. Gaelin only specified you can't be touched by someone who loved you."

"And you think my mate wouldn't love me?"

"The mate bond is more than love. It's a soul bond. She doesn't just love you. You are one and the same."

"I think you are grasping. She is very much a danger to me, and let us not pretend otherwise."

"You need her. Your people need her. The faster we can get these journal pages and find where the stone is, the sooner we can take down the Wall."

I shook my head, finally caving and pulling out a chair to sink into it. "It's not that simple. She poses a risk to me."

Without me, with no heir, no family remaining, the court would go to the next most powerful fae: Gaelin. All *three* would go to him, making him ruler of Cirrelea.

Sometimes I hated Faerie rules. I was technically the Lord of Autumn and Spring, though I did nothing with their land. It would spread me too thin. I welcomed in the people, those who remained after Gaelin was done. He wanted to rule them all, but Wall help me, that was a bigger reason than I cared to admit as to why I didn't take out Gaelin. The idea of one ruler of Cirrelea was blasphemy.

"But if we don't find those journal pages soon, then what? We search blindly for the stone? Trap every single baedour out there until we get an answer? How long do you think that will take?"

"What makes her so special? Why wouldn't another witch work?"

"If the witches here could see those caves, why would those journal pages still be there after millennia? She detected something else. Something we can't see and something the witches here can't see either. And we'd be stupid not to seize on that."

I couldn't take it anymore. My will to object weakened. I stood up and paced behind the counter.

The witch would speed up the process of finding journal pages, and since I was unwilling to fight Gaelin, speed was the best option.

"Gaelin would seize an opportunity like this," Clove said. "I doubt he'd give it a second thought."

My fingers gripped the counter. "You're manipulating me. Again."

She lifted a shoulder "Is it working?"

"I need a moment alone, but let's be clear, if I agree to this, you will keep her away from me. She is your companion, not mine." Her eyes danced as I said this. "She cannot be mine, and I will not torture myself. You occupy her time, and do not ever tell her the specifics of my curse."

"Understood," she said before standing and leaving.

I put my back to the living room, leaning against the kitchen island.

Perhaps Clove was right. Not using the witch seemed the weak thing to do. The fearful thing to do. Exactly what Gaelin would want and likely the point of his curse.

It was a risk. But wasn't it time to stop living in fear? I'd played everything safely since that fateful day of having to kill my uncle upon his request. I squeezed my eyes shut, trying not to remember the sounds my iron sword made as I sent it into my uncle's chest.

Where had all that playing it safe gotten me? It certainly felt like a losing battle. Our magic draining, Gaelin always on offense, and me always managing to keep him at bay and getting cursed while doing it.

It was time for me to go on the offense for once.

Take the chance, put myself at risk to save my people. And the one thing all that playing it safe would get me now was that Gaelin wouldn't be expecting the change.

I strode into the living room where the tension was thick. Rylla stared down the witch, and I had the momentary urge to tell her to stop. But what use would that be? Rylla already hurt, knowing my mate was here. Dain, on the other hand, pulled out a knife and sharpened it, the rhythmic *thwick thwick* the only sound.

The witch, while not staring back, calmly petted Haze, still in her lap. I snapped my fingers and called him to me. Haze's head shot up before he leapt off her and trotted over. I squatted in front of him. If I was going to do this, we would be leaving soon.

I mentally sent him an image of the Winter Court. From the hidden villages to the encampment of witches to the hermits at the foot of the Suhmmerials, he'd find any gossip or news, especially any pertaining to Gaelin's movements, and bring it back. Haze chirped and sped off.

By the time I stood up, the witch had crossed her arms and stared daggers into the fire. I couldn't blame her. There was no welcome here, except perhaps Clove, and who knew how Rylla or Dain had taunted her while we were in the kitchen.

I took up my position by the mantle. The witch tried to hide it, but she let out a huff of irritation.

No point in me beating around the bush.

"It appears we could both want the same thing. I want the Wall down, and you want to go to the Eastlands. Bringing the Wall down would allow for that. How about we leave tomorrow for those pages." I didn't wait for her response. Instead, I directed my attention to Clove. "You said there was a cave per court, correct?"

Clove nodded affirmative.

I clapped my hands together. "Excellent. Pack your things. We head out tomorrow."

The witch's throat worked, and she squirmed.

But I barrelled on. The less interaction, I had with her the better. "Clove, you'll pack for the witch. Make sure she has what she needs. I can't always hold a shield around us."

"Hold on," the witch interrupted. Good for her, but I still sighed. I had hoped to have her go along with it before she really knew what happened. "You want to tear down the Wall? Are you mad? That would be catastrophic!"

Her frail hands fisted at the edge of the couch.

I smiled. "Those were my sentiments too, but it appears there may be a way to do it safely. The makers built it in. They suspected it may be needed one day and hid a way."

Her eyes were huge, the pupils dilated. Her heart rate trended up. "But the Wall is our protection."

"Protect you from who?" Rylla grinned, all feral teeth. The witch met her eyes and flinched. Rylla pushed on. "Hmm?"

The witch's face morphed. It was fascinating. Her eyes hardened, and she breathed in deep, her shoulders lifting ever so slightly. "From you fae."

Rylla glanced to me with a knowing smile, almost as if to say *See, your mate hates you, hates us.* But she redirected her attention to the witch. "You've been here with us for four days, and you still live."

"I live, but I haven't felt safe."

"Lucky for you to now be under safe harbor."

The witch's eyes narrowed.

"Enough!" I said. "You have seen Faerie now. You see how it dies. We fae lose our power. There is a theory that the Wall is a bottleneck. Magic exists in both worlds. If you are who you say you are, you know this to be true. And something is restricting the balance of magic. The Wall itself, yes, but the Wall alone would not cause this."

"What causes it?" the witch asked.

"I don't know. Something on your side? Perhaps something goes on here that I am unaware of. We will know infinitely more with these journal pages."

"And you need me to open the box they will be in."

I nodded. Hope growing. "The box and finding the caves they are in."

Her arms crossed again, one finger extended and tapping her arm. "I need more."

"Oh?" I said. She was full of surprises.

Rylla growled, and Dain tossed his knife up into the air and caught it by its blade between his fingers. They were not subtle.

The witch bit her lip like she wasn't sure about what she was going to say. "I want a bargain. I help you with these journal pages. You help me find my way home."

"But that is already the deal. No bargain necessary." The last thing I wanted was for our souls to entwine more.

"I need the assurance that, whatever comes of these journal pages, one way or another, you will help me find my way home."

"Do you know what a bargain entails?" Dain asked.

The witch nodded, and I felt Clove's hand in all of this.

"I intend to hold up my end," she said, "so I won't lose a piece of my soul to *him*."

The idea of yet another bargain with the witch bothered me. I needed my own assurance. "I'll make the bargain," I said, "but we will go to the witches in my court and let them tell me who you are."

Dain's mouth dropped, and I believed I caught Clove's attention. It was far past time I saw those witches and made sure they abided our agreement. They'd seen members of my court enough, but they needed to see me from time to time. It would work. Who knew what we would learn. It would be worth the extra day.

The witch gave her head a shake, dark brown locks dancing. The way she could go from so unsure to confident mesmerized me. Every instance of pushback, she mustered up some semblance of courage. But thinking like that did me no good. I kept my face stoic, void of emotion. She either agreed or didn't.

If she didn't, would I capitulate? Likely. Clove was right. We needed her for the pages. But I'd do my best to wrap her end of the bargain with as much elbow room as I could.

"That sounds fine to me. Maybe you'll finally believe me." The witch's eyes flashed with irritation.

I had brought up our doubt in her story again. Irritation led to anger, and anger made one rash. "That easy?"

She nodded but crossed her arms. "I only see a benefit from giving you what you want."

Dain, damn him, nearly choked on himself. He went as far as having to leave the room to get a glass of water. The witch shot him a death glare, a finger tapping on her arm.

Between Dain—albeit unwittingly—and me prodding her sore spot, I had an opportunity to make sure I got a bit more out of this deal to benefit my people. If Clove was convinced the witch could be of use to us, why not? Besides, the easy way to get her back across the Wall would be to take it down. We had the same goal; she just wasn't fully on board yet.

"You will have your bargain," I said. "You help us find the journal pages—"

"I've agreed," the witch said imperiously.

I held out a finger, impressed at her audacity, but her annoyance got the better of her. "And what we need to save my court. You go with us to the witches to determine if you're telling us the truth..."

"Yes, yes," she said waving her hand in the air as if to say *hurry up.*

I tried not to grin as she didn't notice what I sneaked in. "And in return I'll help you find your way home."

With a huff, she uncrossed her leg, let it down with a thud, and stood up. "Agreed."

Then she winced. I felt it too, the etching of our bargain on our skin. My right wrist tingled, but I didn't peek. I knew mine would be exactly like hers. The tattoo from our previous bargain extended, wrapping fully around her wrist.

Peculiar. They typically were new marks, not extensions of other ones.

Fragile flowers extended up the back of her hand, with the other end beginning on her wrist and wrapping around. She turned her hand over to look at the soft underside and gasped. I frowned. Spiky lines. Why would that bother her?

No matter. "Clove will make sure you have what you need," I said. "Eat up. We leave tomorrow for the witches."

CHAPTER 14
INNARA

Another sliver of my soul. I'd bargained away another one, but at least this one held the promise of getting me home.

The horse's body shifted under me, and I gripped the reins tight. I'd never been proficient at riding. And going downhill felt like I could pitch forward at any moment. Our horses trod along, the road somehow devoid of snow and ice. Kir's house stood in a dead forest. Skeletons of trees loomed over everything. Evergreens that lined the lake behind his house either had brown needles or had none.

Last night, the elation of making the bargain had faded into dismay. Had I done the right thing? Did I bargain well enough? I'd been so irritated, which should probably be rule number one in Faerie: no making bargains in anger. But it was finding pages to learn how to tear down the Wall, and in exchange, he would help me find my way home. I should have put a time limit on his end. He could drag out helping me forever. Although he did seem to want me out of his life.

I forced it all out of mind. What was done was done. If an opportunity arose for me to rectify it, I could.

"Relax. Buttercup can sense your nerves." Clove rode beside me. It appeared she was my designated babysitter. She seemed nice, but she was still fae. She'd been winning me over, but it was clear in that conversation yesterday that she was up to things.

I didn't fully trust her. I was a pawn in a fae game with unknown rules.

Not far along the road, a town was nestled below the seat of his court. Traveling through it felt like a funeral. No one breathed a word. The area bristled with deciduous trees, all dead, some rotting. If the trees weren't ominous enough, the abandoned town was worse. All the wood of the buildings was gray with age. Broken windows allowed me to see in: dust- and snow-covered furniture.

But I could see the beauty of what had been.

Maybe it was the stoic faces and bowed heads of the fae I was with, but something had happened here. It remained cared for. The streets were cleared. Glass from broken windows was cleared. The interiors, however, looked to be untouched as if in hope the owners would one day return.

Hours passed, and the barren landscape extended as far as I could see. Rolling hills of nothing but gray snow. The wind picked it up and played with it, tumbling it about, swirling it around us. Kir held a shield to keep the worst of it off. Clove made sure I wore their insulated leathers with a heavy cloak. Her care made me want to trust her. But I couldn't be naive. I could also see it the other way—I had a job to do for them, and they wouldn't want me to die before it was complete. They were protecting their investment.

Ahead of me, Kir rode, flanked by Rylla and Dain.

"Why didn't you sift the two of you to the witches?" Dain's voice carried back to Clove and me, and my ears perked.

"Leave him alone with *her?* We'd have to wait days to have enough power to head out again," Rylla said, tossing her white braid over her shoulder.

I'd love to cut that braid off one day.

"Don't let her get to you. She's not in a good place right now," Clove said as she swayed in her saddle, making it look like second nature.

"Why does she hate me so much?" I asked. None of them seemed to like me, but Rylla clearly hated me. Kir and Dain just acted like I wasn't there.

"I could ask the same of you. Why do you hate us?" Clove asked.

"Aren't humans your playthings?"

"Do you feel like you are our plaything? What exactly would we be doing if we were toying with you?"

"That's just it. I don't know. Are you lulling me into a false sense of security?" I paused, mulling over my words. "I hope these witches convince him I am telling the truth."

"You have to understand." Clove's speech was halting. "Gaelin sent a witch to us, to Kir, before. She incapacitated Kir and brought him to Gaelin to kill. Kir broke free, and he and Gaelin battled. In the end, Kir bargained for his life. As ruler over Winter, Spring, and Autumn, he tried to relinquish them, but the rules of Faerie wouldn't allow it. Instead, Kir allowed Gaelin to curse him. You see, as much as Gaelin wants power, he also likes to toy. Everyone else is a plaything to him. Sometimes, I think he'd prefer having Kir around just to have someone to fight against." She huffed out a dry laugh. "Truly, he wants anything and everything that Kir possesses. Power. Honor. The love of his people. The love of family. The promise of a fated. And the one thing he thinks he has over Kir is a clever mind, which drives him to toy. How fun it is for him to think he is the puppeteer of us." Clove shrugged. "So, you see, you popping up as you did is too eerily similar to what happened before."

Curses and betrayal sounded like what I thought of being a plaything. Bewitching and tricks too. So far, I hadn't felt toyed with so much as I now realized I had been treated in a manner consistent with people highly suspicious due to this Gaelin person.

They had been playthings and didn't wish to be so again.

She'd given a lot of information, but it all felt peripheral. What she left unsaid was that this witch had convinced him to do things. He'd developed feelings for her.

I had so many questions. But the one that popped out was "He's cursed?"

Clove grimaced like a child properly chastised. "It is not my story to tell. Perhaps he will one day."

We lapsed into silence, and I studied Kir riding, as his body shifted with the movement of Ionth, his horse. Rylla sat regally on hers next to him, laughing about something, her chin lifted, eyes sparkling. And the reasons she hated me seemed to make more sense, especially if Kir had previously engaged in a romance with a witch.

After several hours, a village formed within the swirling snow, and Kir slowed our pace. Thatched roofs over circular houses made a rough encampment area. Behind them sat a town similar to the one we had been through outside Kir's house. I wondered if Kir made them build their own houses or if they moved into ones that had already existed.

Mine and Clove's horses pulled closer to the group, and Dain dropped back to my side.

Women milled about, layered in cloaks. In the center, a bonfire roared. One of them maintained it with their magic. The giveaway was the pile of wood and how the flames licked but didn't consume.

Women stopped and stared, their questions written on their faces: *Who are you? Why are you here? What do you want?*

I was familiar with those looks. We received them often as Mom and I ran from town to town, entering new places. But there was something more here. The hairs on the back of my neck stood up.

They knew what I was.

Tendrils of magic danced on my skin, asking me to come out and play.

It was disorienting. Their bodies said, *go away, you are not wanted,* while their magic said, *we see you, we welcome you.*

Kir halted us. To the women gathered, he said, "Where is your matriarch?"

The women didn't speak, but a few heads turned, looking past the bonfire, which blocked the view down the road.

"Lord Kir," a woman's voice sounded. Whoever it was projected it.

Through the flames a womanly silhouette climbed up and grew bigger as she came toward us. Her features became clearer as the fire licked around her yet caused her no harm. Her hair was the same color as the flames and her skin the color of ebony. In her red silk dress, she stalked toward us. There was no welcome on her face.

I swallowed.

"Verna," Kir said.

"What business have you? We've spoken with your lieges recently. Even that *thing* came by yesterday. Have we unknowingly slighted our agreement?" Her tone said more than her words. Even I understood she meant they had kept to their agreement but expected Kir to accuse them of wrongdoing.

"Peace," Kir said. "I am not Gaelin. I come seeking assistance, nothing more."

"You come with a witch." Her gaze fell on me, a knowing look. She had not overlooked me when we came in. Her sparkling green eyes narrowed.

"I do. She is the reason we seek your assistance."

"Assistance comes at a cost."

How I wished I could see Kir's face, but all I could see was a slight tightening of his hands on the reins.

"Do we not offer enough?" he asked. "Safety on my land?"

"How much longer will it be yours?"

Rylla's arm moved to grab her sword. Kir's hand shot out fast to stop her.

A buzz of energy swirled. The witches seized their power, and they wanted us to know. The horses whinnied and stomped their hooves. An irritating static crawled along my skin.

"Let me explain, and we can talk of cost," Kir said.

Verna nodded, and the static crawl dissipated.

"This witch"—Kir jerked his head back toward me—"claims to be from the Eastlands, that she crossed the Wall. I'd like to know if there is truth to that."

Verna's lips pursed before she walked toward us. Without flinching, she made her way between Rylla and Kir's horses, her eyes on me the entire time. A tendril of her magic caressed my arm, warm and feathery. She moved around the horse. Her eyes closed, and she breathed in deep.

Her magic left me, and she walked back to where she had started. "She is not part of our sisterhood."

"Does that mean what she says is true?"

"The cost will be she stays a week with us if you want more."

Rylla's head jerked to Kir, her eyes flaring.

Kir's horse sidestepped, but with a flex of a hand and the slightest tensing of his thighs, he stalled Ionth. "You will not have her for a week."

"She is a witch. She belongs with us." Verna, though standing below, seemed to peer down her nose at him.

Kir turned to me, his saddle creaking. "Why don't you tell them?"

I swallowed, not wanting to be dragged into whatever this was. "I belong to myself, but I have a duty to fulfill with Kir."

Verna snorted. "No lord? My. My. I am shocked, *Lord* Kir." Her eyes flitted to me and back to him. "Since she speaks for herself, I will tell you she is not part of our sisterhood, which is unusual for a witch born in Cirrelea. So unusual it's unheard of but not impossible. If you want more, she stays with us." A feral smile graced her lips. "And believe me, there is more we could tell you."

Kir inclined his head to the witch before he clicked his tongue and turned his horse. Rylla, Dain, and Clove followed his lead. But I could only sit there, watching Verna. Her gaze slid down to my wrist, even though she couldn't see it under the layers of clothes and the cloak I wore.

The markings there tingled a moment before she spoke. "Witch and fae do not mix."

"I don't plan on it," I said as I turned my horse and followed the others.

CHAPTER 15
KIR

"We gonna talk about it?" Dain threw his saddlebag on the floor after coming in from checking on the horses.

A large fire roared in the fireplace next to us, and our things were spread out on the banquet table. We'd cleaned everything up after dinner. Clove, Rylla, and the witch were tucked into their room, and I fought the urge to go see how they were. They were fine. Rylla and Clove were both great fighters if anything happened, and I had wards up all over the place to notify me of any creatures coming close. I didn't need to know how they were.

"About?" I knew damn well what he meant, but poking Dain was a favorite pastime.

Dain grabbed the chair next to me and swivelled it around, sitting down backwards in it. "Fuck off, man. Is she or isn't she from across the Wall?"

I picked up my dagger, which I'd sharpened while he was out, tested the tip on the pad of my finger. A red bead of blood welled up. How long would it take to heal on its own? I sucked the wound and dried it on my pants.

"I'm inclined to believe she tells the truth," I said. Dain nodded like he knew that would be my answer. "What do you think?"

He leaned back, stretching his arms as he held on to the chair back. "I'm inclined as you are. Is it a possibility she could be some long-lost witch that never made it into the sisterhood of witches? Yes, but I think that chance is low. How many witches wouldn't want that protection for their child?"

A peek at my finger showed a small amount of blood. Not healed yet. "So we both think the likelihood of her coming from across the Wall, which is unheard of, is greater than a witch who somehow fell between the cracks and was never initiated?"

Dain scrubbed a hand down his face. "When you say it like that..."

"We sound stupid, don't we?"

"Clove believes her, and the witch sticks to her story. She hasn't wavered, and the things she doesn't know are... How do you not know some of those things if you live in Cirrelea?"

"What does Rylla think?" I busied myself with wiping down my dagger, even though it didn't need it, because I knew the look he would give me. That look that said, *ask her yourself, you pixieshit.*

"Rylla thinks she is Gaelin's plant. Like Violet."

I tossed the dagger down, not sure why I expected Rylla to come around on this one.

We sat for a few moments, the fire crackling behind us. Thoughts of going to see the witch flitted through my mind. Easily rejected. I couldn't show interest in her, mate or not. Even though my gaze was drawn to her all day.

"So what do we do now?" Dain asked.

"The journal pages. As planned."

"Do we trust her?" He drummed his fingers along the back of the chair he straddled.

"I guess we do."

"Should I tell Clove to stop with the witch hazel?" Dain stared me down.

I sighed before I stood and strode to the fireplace. Did I allow her magic? If we believed the witch and wanted her help, it would be best to allow her freedom. But after Violet, the thought nearly froze me. "She'd be more cooperative if we gave her freedom. We've seen how hard it is for her to use magic."

"It's your call."

"And you're an advisor, so advise." My irritation surprised me.

His fingers stopped their drumming. "Technically, she hasn't been under safe harbor since we left."

"Technically, you were always able to do something if you thought she was a threat." I swiped my hand through the dust on the mantel.

"Yes, but I've always found that whatever magic guides the do-you-truly-believe-she-is-a-threat to be somewhat willy-nilly. Now there is nothing holding us back if we remotely think she is a threat."

I nodded. And with our magic fading, one never knew what Faerie would look past. Rules became more lenient as our magic waned, but that left us unsure of how much we could get away with. Now we could take action if we thought we needed to.

"I'll be the one to tell Clove to stop the witch hazel," I said.

"Did I hear my name?" Clove strolled into the banquet hall of the manor we squatted in for the night.

This was Fale Seren, our hidden village for a time. The people occupying the area had to move on, the location compromised by Violet. We picked another one of my villages at random. Random seemed better than trying to outthink Gaelin. We moved our people to the new place, and between Clove and me, we set some deterring wards. I varied my protections as well. Glamour, deterrence wards, attractive wards on other villages. Gaelin's troops and the Wild Hunt would eventually sniff out our decoys, and I'd have to change it up.

Clove stood near the fireplace, wanting to speak to me.

Dain drained his cup and stood. "I'll check the horses and the perimeter."

May as well get this over with. "Tomorrow, we head to the

Autumn Court. I don't want the witch to be given any more witch hazel."

Clove crossed her arms. Surprising since I thought she would want to hear this.

"She has a name, you know," Clove said.

Indeed. I knew it long before anyone told me. Her mind, her heart had whispered it to me. My grip on my cup tightened. "It is easier for me to keep a distance if I don't use it."

Clove's fingers dug into her arms. She bit her tongue. Generally, I encouraged my crew to speak their minds, but on this topic, I'd be happy for her to keep her thoughts to herself.

"Do you agree on the witch hazel? When will it wear off?" I asked.

"I do. I'm glad to see you chose to believe her. It'll wear off an hour or so into our ride if we leave at our usual time."

"Good. Please make her aware. Also, don't tell her that safe harbor no longer applies."

Clove arched a brow at me.

"It's better if she doesn't know." I looked past Clove, into the kitchen and toward where the witch rested.

Clove shifted as if to put herself in my line of sight "For us or for her?"

"Both." I grimaced. The witch didn't need to feel threatened but, also, likewise.

Clove nodded and turned.

It struck me that she had come here on her own accord. "Did you need something else?"

She shook her head, her red curls bouncing. "You answered my question already."

Rylla strode in, and Clove pulled up short, her hands fisted.

"Did you leave her on her own?" Clove asked.

Rylla didn't answer with snark. "No, Dain came by, and I asked him to stay in there with her."

The tightness on Clove's face eased, but she hurried off all the same.

Rylla snorted. "I was shocked she left *me* alone with her."

She didn't like using the witch's name either, I noted.

"Well, it isn't as if she knew Dain stopped by." It was about all I could say without insulting Rylla. When it came down to it, Rylla did her duty.

"So," she drew the word out as she rocked up onto her toes. "What did you two discuss?"

I sighed. I may as well tell Rylla now. Procrastinating as I was wont to do was a weakness. If I worried about these things with my own crew, what kind of leader was I? "We head to the Autumn Court."

"We go after the journal pages? Meaning you believe the witch?" Her eyes narrowed.

"Based on everything we know, I don't see why we shouldn't believe her. Can I say for certain? Of course not. But I think she was curious to the witches. It sways me to believe she is not from Cirrelea."

"Not because she is your mate?"

"Rylla. We've discussed this. That word should not be used when she is near. She can't know."

"Have you thought about what effect that has on you? This is folly. Trusting her is folly."

"Have I thought about it?" I let out a fatalistic laugh. "It consumes nearly half my thoughts." I stood, twisting my blade between my fingers, a pathetic attempt not to meet her eyes. Nearly whispering, I said, "Of course I have considered it. I am not blind to what the bond does." I placed my hands on my hips. "Dain and Clove agree. We trust her. We get the journal pages."

CHAPTER 16

INNARA

I was on a blasted horse again.

"Wall, I've never seen someone look so awkward riding before," Rylla muttered to Dain but loud enough for me to hear. Today, Rylla and Dain rode up front, followed by Clove and me. Kir pulled up the rear.

I shot her a glare. Of course, I'd wind up in Faerie and be forced to ride a horse for days when they could use magic.

This morning, I'd waited for Clove to pour me the cup of witch hazel, but she said Kir had lifted the order. I glanced back at him, my body rocking with the horse as it ascended a rocky slope. He watched me. Our eyes met for a second before he casually looked off to the side of the trail. Why did I keep looking at him?

"Don't you have some sort of magic to travel us somewhere?" I asked Clove.

Clove pulled her horse closer to mine. "It's called sifting, but it takes a large amount of magic. Kir is the only one of us who has enough to go far. It's not worth the risk of depletion."

"Kir mentioned your power faded. Is that what you mean?"

Clove nodded. "Yes, it's why we want to tear down the Wall."

I didn't like the idea, even though I'd agreed to help them find the means to do it. It would benefit me, but the long-term consequence of it—I hesitated to think it would be good for all the unsuspecting humans on the other side.

"Tearing it down will give you back your powers?" I asked. "Restore magic? Restore Cirrelea? And Kir is one of the most powerful?" I glanced back again. Kir still rode behind us. He stared off into the woods. His face was stoic, and his eyes scanned the sides of the road before he let them coast over us and to the other side. All business.

Clove hummed an answer to my questions, an affirmative, but no explanation.

I turned back in my saddle, and Clove watched me, watching Kir. She said nothing, but heat infused my cheeks. Even though fae, he was still nice to look at. "I wonder why he always seems to set himself apart from the rest of you."

Again, Clove hummed as she watched the road. She seemed to have that habit when she didn't want to answer but wanted to let someone know she heard them.

But I did want an answer. "Maybe he thinks he is better than you. Sure seems that way to me. *Lord* Kir."

Rylla twisted in her saddle. "Watch your mouth, human. You speak on something you have no knowledge of."

"Peace, Rylla." Kir appeared on the other side of me. "I don't think I am better than them. There aren't many I do consider myself better than."

I felt a warm smug sense of satisfaction. "And who is that? Me? Humans?"

"Gaelin. For his continued threat on our people, our world, life as we have known it. Humans, until now, have not mattered to us."

My mouth gaped at that.

He waved a hand in the air. "The Wall has separated us other than the covens of witches. But now, it seems, humans may matter quite a lot. But since we're making assumptions about me, allow me to offer one of my own: You are timid. You can't grasp and control your witchery. Why would anyone be after you as you claimed?"

He'd hit me where it hurt. Nolan's words rang out in my head: naive. All those time's we'd kissed, and I wondered how he'd chosen me.

Kir left it unspoken, but the question was right there. *Who would want you?*

I stared at the reins in my hands. My fingers were pink from the cold but not red. Kir kept us warm enough.

"I don't know." And I didn't. I never understood why my father chased me. Why he wanted me. What he wanted from me or to do with me. What made me interesting enough to hunt down?

"You said it was your father's men that chased you into the Wall," Kir said. "Your own father. I didn't get the impression that you believed him a good man. Tell me about him."

Rylla in front of us glared at Kir before she kicked her heels into her horse and set it trotting away from us and out of Kir's protective shield. Yet Kir said nothing, did nothing that I could see.

"You're right," I said. "I don't think he is a good man. He's a tyrant. My father is the leader of the group that makes it their mission to hunt down all witches in the Eastlands. His following grows daily. They believe we should be using all the planet's resources. Witches believe in balance, so they forsake it." Kir remained silent, patiently listening, so I continued. "They've pushed technology so far that our air is clogged with smog, our waters poisonous. The land itself weeps. Where I live the seasons are severe. Winter can last all year. Down south, fires engulf our forests. The people, the humans, suffer. The food supply is failing. The rich have plenty, while the rest of us must try and grow our own, if we can. There are the haves and the have nots."

"And you were a have not out of necessity, out of running." He said the last word like a question.

I hummed an affirmative. "We lived on the outskirts. My mother is a life witch too. We have what other people call a green thumb. We are adept at growing things. We maintain our greenhouse using both technology and our magic, though we try to use precious little of our magic in case someone were to suspect us. But we get by just fine. The townspeople pay nicely for healing and medical care. We are substantially cheaper than the local hospital."

"But none of this tells me why he wants you."

My breath stalled. He'd actually said it this time.

The answer still eluded me, so I gave him the one I always told myself. "His goal is to exterminate all witches, and as his progeny, I am more vile than the rest."

"Do you really think that is the only reason why he would want you?" Kir held my gaze for a second like he had so many things to say to me, to tell me. It warmed my toes, and my stomach flipped.

"There is nothing special about me. I can't grasp and control my magic." My mouth went dry. I forced myself to look at him, even as my eyes grew wet. "Who would want me?"

Kir's lips pressed together. "Sometimes it is the small things, the innocent things, the there-to-just-be-enjoyed things are what is needed most. We all have value."

His cheeks became infused with pink, and my chest warmed. I didn't get a chance to inspect further as he pulled his horse back to the rear again.

These fae were nothing like I expected.

There were moments I liked them and almost enjoyed being around them and then moments where I despised them. I tightened my grip on the reins, bending the leather between my fists. Careful. I needed to be careful. Making friends with fae was not something I should be considering. Maybe instead of dazzling me with their beauty and magic, this group was more into tricking the "timid" human. Make me feel wanted and needed.

I stewed in my thoughts for hours. Clove left me alone for the most part. She handed me food, and we ate while riding. My mental fog lifted, but I still felt exposed with no weapon. Dain, Kir, and Rylla had their double swords strapped to their backs, but I knew knives were hidden all over their bodies. Clove was the only fae with a bow.

Rylla called back to Kir. He trotted past Clove and me. After a few minutes, I could tell the three conversing ahead of us bothered Clove. She leaned forward in her saddle, and her horse pulled away from mine. Even though they had kept me guarded all day, I figured whatever shield Kir had around us likely protected us from fae beasts getting too close. Why else would they all gather ahead of me?

When Clove was far enough ahead that I could see her horse's rear, a childlike giggle chimed through the air.

I jerked around in my saddle, searching the trees. The hairs on the back of my neck rose.

"Hey," I called out.

But no one turned around. Kir's face was stone, and Rylla looked to be imploring him about something. Clove dug her heels in and pulled up to the group of three.

Innara... Something whispered to me. *I see you.*

My pulse jumped as I remembered the creature that spoke like that.

"Kir," I shouted, but again, not one of them turned. Blast it. He'd magicked some sort of barrier when he and Clove spoke in the kitchen after my eavesdropping, and he probably did the same now.

I jammed my heels into my horse's sides, dreading the lurch. The horse took off, and I screamed. Together, horse and I galloped right into Kir's group, and their horses scattered. I lost control as my horse reared, and I fell out of my saddle onto the snow-covered ground. Pain lanced through my back and cold seeped into my bones. I threw my hands over my head, not sure where my horse was.

Feet landed next to me.

It was Kir. "Get up."

I struggled to my feet, fighting against the ache that told me to remain still.

Kir stood in a defensive stance, his two swords drawn. Clove had her bow drawn and arrow nocked, still mounted. Dain and Rylla were nowhere to be seen.

"What was it? What sent you galloping?" Kir asked.

I stepped closer to him. I had no weapon, no protection except him.

And that thing was out there.

But as soon as I moved closer, he stepped away.

"Clove." He sounded nearly panicked.

"Innara, here," she called.

I bristled. I wasn't a dog happy to run when beckoned. She pulled her horse near and extended a hand.

"Get on." She yanked me onto the horse behind her. Her strength was amazing. "What was it? We need to know."

"It was the same thing as outside the ice cave." I shook with fear and cold. Kir must have dropped his shield.

"The baedour," Clove shouted to Kir, and he groaned.

Rylla and Dain burst out of the trees, their horses nowhere to be seen. Dain cursed, swirling his sword in front of him.

The forest was dead silent around us, the only sound the shuffling of feet in the snow as Rylla, Kir, and Dain rotated, covering all directions.

Innara...

I jumped.

"What is it?" Clove whispered.

"Don't you hear it?"

"Shit. Kir, it's close. It has her in a mind-grip."

His face was grim. He looked to Clove, a silent message sent before she nodded once and jammed her heels into her horse's flanks. We took off. I gripped around her stomach, pressing my cheek into her back as the cold wind stung my cheeks.

Shouts erupted behind us. Clove turned to look and dug her heels into the horse again. I hated this. I hated it. My grip on her waist slipped.

"You must hold on," she called to me.

I tried, but a claw-like hand swiped at my shoulder, ripping me off the horse and away from Clove. I was on the cold ground, flat on my back, new and old pain spearing through and across my back, before I knew what happened.

Above me, the baedour loomed, its maw opening.

Fetid, hot breath streamed down on me.

You don't know what you are, do you? The baedour spoke, but this time I was certain I was the only one who could hear it.

I tried to scoot away, digging my heels into the snow and only gaining a few inches. "What am I?"

Kir knows. Ask him. It leaned in. *But I guess you won't be able to. I bet you'll be tasty. I don't get to taste witch often anymore. And a fated one at that.*

Saliva dripped onto my face, hot and burning. I swiped at it and scrambled for purchase.

It pressed in. My hands shot forward to hold it at bay, sinking into the leathery, squishy form.

A foot came out of nowhere, slamming into the side of the creature's jaw. Kir leapt across me, pummelling the baedour with his gloved fists, driving it into the ground as he straddled it. With a viper-fast move he whipped out one of his many daggers. This one was barbed. He held it over the baedour's throat, moving it slightly.

A bead of red welled on the baedour's skin.

"I have you pinned, baedour. I demand a reading," he said.

It chuckled. Dry and raspy.

"Ah-ah-ah. Lord Kir, we told you we wouldn't forget last time. And yet here you are, asking for a reading after almost sacrificing a piece of your soul." Its real voice sounded nothing at all like the whispering child it had used on me.

Kir frowned, and the hand that held the dagger dipped before he came back to his senses and held it tight to the baedour's throat. The baedour grinned, its humanish face morphing eerily to show all those razor-sharp teeth.

Dain, who must have come closer, shouted, "It's baiting you. Don't take it. It wants to waste our time, your power."

Kir's jaw clenched like he was on the crux of making a decision he didn't want to. "You haven't given me a reading yet. Your life is still forfeit."

He pushed harder on the knife, and the baedour screeched as blood dripped down its neck.

"Ask your question fae filth," it spat.

"What do you want with this witch?"

"Gaelin wants her."

Before me, Kir shook, and his skin paled.

"Let me go." The baedour grated out, its words like screeching chalk on a blackboard.

Kir shoved the baedour away. "Leave, or I will trap and kill you, free of any reading. Your entire being is an abomination."

You will pay the price, the baedour said as it scurried off, a lanky hand covering its wounded throat.

Kir stood over me, chest heaving. "Are you okay?"

I nodded and raised a hand, thinking he'd help. He only stared at it before screwing his face up in disgust and turning away.

Clove came back over, leaping off her horse. "We need to get you warm. Kir, she's frozen."

She was right. The cold sunk straight into me, thankfully numbing the pain from the horse and baedour. Only now that the adrenaline had worn off enough, knowing the thing was gone, I shook.

"Kir!" Clove yelled.

"More are coming. That bastard summoned the entire hive mind down on us." He turned, rotating in a circle before pointing. "We go that way! A shelter should be there. We need a fire."

Dain whistled, summoning the horses. He mounted and moved toward us, lifting his hand above and behind us. "Mount up. Stay close to one another."

Rylla led, followed by me flanked by Kir and Clove. Kir's body was rigid in his saddle. He kept his horse well away from mine. Unlike Clove's leg, which kept bumping me.

"Are you okay on the horse? If we have to run?" she asked.

I nodded. The pain from my multiple falls had subsided thanks to the numbing cold. Besides, I felt more secure on my horse as opposed to riding with Clove and trying to cling on for dear life. That was awful. Though the warmth of her body would have been welcome. My teeth chattered, and the snot in my nose froze as crystals formed on my eyelashes.

"It's not too far," Clove said. "Hang on. Dain is covering our scent and tracks."

Kir pressed his heels into the sides of Ionth, and the two shot off in front of us.

"And Kir?" I couldn't help but ask Clove. Did he blame me for the attack, even though I had no way of preventing it?

Clove's eyes darted to me. "He's scouting ahead. He sifted to save you from the baedour. His power is drained."

Snow flung out behind our horses, hitting me in the face, the wet cold not even stinging. My teeth rattled, and my hands lost feeling. I wasn't sure if it was all the cold or how tightly I gripped the reins as I leaned over in my saddle and allowed my horse to be guided by all the others.

I risked a glance behind. Dain had one hand holding his reins and the other stretched behind him. The trail we left smoothed over a few feet behind him, as if we'd never moved through the area.

"I see it," Rylla shouted from ahead.

Thank the Wall.

From the side of me, Clove asked, "Kir, the horses?"

Ahead, a small A-frame cabin appeared, like a mirage in the desert. It had seen better days, but I could feel the fireplace that was surely inside. We raced up to the front. I was so frozen that my fingers were stiff around the reins. Clove darted over and helped me down.

Kir said in a grim voice, "Get all your things. The horses have to run. Hopefully, the baedour are only hungry for us."

Everyone did as asked.

"Ionth, ride home." Kir slapped it on the rear, and Ionth raced away.

I couldn't help but feel like this was an ending.

"Inside." Clove grabbed my things and bustled me into the cabin. Everyone else clamored in after us.

"Now what?" I said through chattering teeth. My body shook violently.

Clove dashed to the fireplace and flicked out a finger and a roaring fire leapt up. "We wait and see if they followed us."

"Won't our scent be all over the horses?"

"I wiped it before they ran off," Dain said. "They're spelled to not leave a trail. It won't last forever but hopefully long enough to be out of the baedour's net."

I stood as close as I possibly could to the fire without being burned. Warmth seeped into my cloak and the pain of thawing out was all over my body.

Clove rummaged in her pack, retrieving a stoppered glass bottle and handed it to me. "Here. For the soreness and —" she motioned to my face where the Baedour saliva had dripped.

I cringed, but downed it anyway, thankful for something that would help even if bitter-tasting.

Innara.

I jolted and whipped around.

"It's speaking to me," I said to the group.

"Shit!" Rylla peeked out a drawn curtain.

Innara. We know you are in there. Come out and play.

"Don't speak to it. Don't acknowledge it," Kir said.

"How? I think I already did."

"How does it get in her mind when you can't, Kir?" Clove said as she paced into the small kitchen area and peeking out that curtain. "I can see one."

Dain stationed at the other front window. "Me too. I think we're surrounded."

The pain began to ebb, and I turned so that my rear now faced the fire.

"I should have left our scent on the horses," Dain said. I didn't miss the glare Kir shot him. "I know you love Ionth, but for fuck's sake, this could mean our lives. And I saved the damn horses."

"Oh, shut up, Dain," Rylla said, and for the first time I wanted to high five her. "There is always a way."

"Oh? And what is your proposal?" He peeked out the window. "Because there's at least three I can see now. Kir's out of power. Mine isn't doing so great either."

The bickering went back and forth. Rylla brought up running out of the house then sifting as far away as she could, hoping to peel off at least a few of them.

My head was finally clear, but the damn baedour continued to talk.

We know you're in there with Lord Kir. Tell him to come out. We only want to talk.

I tried to ignore the voice as much as possible. It paused, whether waiting for my response or reading my thoughts, I didn't know.

As I warmed, I took off my cloak and hung it nearby to dry. I rubbed my fingers into my temples and I sat down. Something dug into my leg. I reached into my pocket and pulled out Nolan's necklace, rolling the gem between my fingers.

"Something agitated them," Rylla said.

Outside, the creatures chimed and screeched.

"I've never seen the like." Dain kept peeking out the curtain, a sword held by his side.

Kir had kept silent. He made me jump when he came near the fireplace. "Is it still talking to you?"

"It's been silent for a few minutes," I said.

"Let me know what it says."

"Earlier it said it wanted you to come out and talk."

"I am sure they do," he said dryly. He squatted down. "Can you do anything? With your witchery."

Since Rylla was in my field of vision, I could see how she whirled around. Kir held a finger up behind him, and her mouth clacked shut. Not a spell, just an order from her lord.

"I don't know if I can even grasp it," I said.

"But the witch hazel has worn off?" he asked. I nodded. "Then try. You might be what stands between us and them. The last wall."

With Nolan's necklace in my hand, I rubbed the stone's surface and closed my eyes. I sought calm. Like before, Kir told me to breathe in and breathe out. His voice soothed. Not too deep but still with a nice male rumble.

"Think about something that made you feel good," he said.

Without warning, I flashed back to him saying we all had value. I thought of Haze purring in my lap. I thought of my mom tucking me in as a little girl. The tension in me eased.

I reached out and found my life magic. Everyone in the room lit up green, even with my eyes closed. Outside smaller bits of green. I focused on those. This winter wasteland made it easy. No roots, no bugs, no small animals running amok. Early on, I'd figured out I could focus on a type of life—roots or a person—to make them more vivid. The rest fell to the background like white noise.

I did that with the fae in the room. I wanted the baedour, but as the green of them grew vivid, a net appeared, surrounding the house as each baedour itself was like an end in the web. They were interconnected, a hive mind.

I tightened my grip on the necklace. What should I do? At the Wall with Nolan, I thought to make the men's life energy smaller. I tried that. I wasn't sure what it had done to them, but it did something. It bought me time.

Make them smaller.

"They're approaching the house, and they looked more pissed than usual," Dain said.

"Try something else," Kir said. "If you're pissing them off, you're on the right track."

My eyes were still shut, but I knew he was still close, still squatting nearby judging by the direction his voice came from. I focused on the web, looking for a weakness.

Then I saw it. One baedour had fewer green lines leading to it.

So, I thought of scissors and cutting those lines.

The green threads recoiled like a wounded tentacle. Gray shadows flew out of the baedour before the green winked out of existence.

An unholy communal chiming shriek erupted. My heart jolted, and I lost the connection to my life magic. My eyes popped open. Kir grabbed his head before falling over backward. Dain was on his knees, while Rylla had managed to fall onto the couch. Clove was prone on the floor. But all of them writhed while gripping their heads.

I had to help them. Dropping the necklace, I slid toward Kir when I was struck by the screech inside my mind. It was unlike any sound I had ever heard. My eyes rolled, and blood trickled out of my nose. My brain felt like it was being split in two.

Then it stopped. Silence rang out.

I panted on the ground next to Kir. Something scraped the inside my skull. Sweat poured off my entire body.

You win this time, soul-releaser, the baedour whispered to me, sounding smaller and tinnier with each word.

CHAPTER 17
INNARA

The baedour's words chilled me. I didn't know what soul-releaser meant. And the fae all lay around the room, their bodies still. Were they alive? Was I alone now in the middle of Faerie?

I reached out for my witchery again.

My heart pounded, but I couldn't grasp my magic. *No. No. No.*

Now was not the time for this to be happening. I'd held it a moment ago. Frustration pooled in my eyes, and I squeezed them tight.

Healers didn't rely only on magic.

I breathed deeply and held it. Humans with no magic could heal, and I knew their methods. I focused on Kir's chest, which rose and fell. He was breathing.

Now for his pulse. I crept closer.

He was so still, like he was asleep, except for the line of pain still on his face. My hand shook as I reached out. I'd gathered that he didn't like to be touched.

My hand paused. I'd try for my magic again. With a deep breath, I closed my eyes, reaching out. He needed me to be able to do this. If something was desperately wrong with him, with any of them, my witchery was my best bet.

I could feel it out there. So close, like a warm fire across the room. The heat reached me, and I craved to be closer. I begged, but it retreated. I always begged for it. Was I a witch, or wasn't I?

I *was* a witch, and I controlled my magic, not the other way around. I straightened my spine. This time I told it to come, to obey. For a moment, nothing happened, and then the warmth enveloped me. Beautiful life-green filled my vision.

Kir's life force was strong, and I heaved a sigh of relief, telling myself it was because he was my chance at getting home.

Outside, the baedour's web was no longer.

In the room, the life forces of the others were there, brilliant with their vigor.

They were alive.

I sat back, breathing heavy, curled on the floor, my back to the couch. Cold air crept in, making me shiver. The fire had gone out. I pressed my palms into my eyes. If they didn't wake soon, I'd be rubbing sticks together.

A sparkle caught my attention. My tattoo. It wrapped around my wrist, and the underside showed the sharp peaks and valleys of a heartbeat. I'd seen them many times on mom's old echo machine, but would Kir know what it meant? When I first saw it etched onto me, I interpreted it as a warning. Heart meant life. Heart could also mean love, but I wasn't going to go there.

The sparkles began at my wrist within a rope-like gray cloud. It was dark and beautiful, light and day. It extended away from my wrist. I had to squint and shift my arm as the light from the windows obscured it. The rope curled back to Kir's wrist.

It connected us. Clove mentioned that bargains connected the two. I swallowed.

His arm lay across his chest, the sleeve of his shirt exposing his wrist while his ever-present glove bunched. His tattoo was made of the same flowers as mine. Since he was fastidious about keeping his skin clothed other than his face, I'd never seen it. I reached out, itching to see if he had the heartbeat pattern too.

He shifted, and I jerked my hand back. His gray eyes opened and focused in on me immediately. He scurried back like I was poison, and I curled my hands into fists.

"Let your powers go," he said with a growl behind his words.

"Why does it scare you?" Where I got the courage to say that, I had no idea. But the way he backed away rubbed me wrong, like I was the monster. I'd made sure he lived, not crushing his mind with ease.

He was the monster, not me. Fae were the monsters.

"Let it go," he repeated.

My witchery was there. It had obeyed me. I didn't want to let it go, but they saw me as a threat, so I relinquished it.

"Did you release it?" he asked.

"Yes." My voice sounded hoarse.

"Do you have any idea what just happened? What did you do?" His eyes were wild, and if I didn't know better, panicked.

"The baedour...they're all connected. I think I cut one out," I said, and his face relaxed at my words. "I was checking to make sure you all lived."

Groaning came from across the room. The others stirred.

"We lost power," he said as he gripped his head before running his hands through his hair. He said it so casually, but it felt like an accusation on the heels of his last statement: *What did you do?*

I shrank back. I hadn't caused that. I'd only touched the baedour. My stomach soured as I glanced at the sparkling gray rope connecting Kir and me. Why could I see that? I'd never seen anything other than life before. Why did I see this now? If it was the bargain, it had been there for days. All of this reminded me of my mother. Her words before we had to run.

What did you do?

My limbs trembled. No.

Kir's eyes narrowed as he got to his feet. "You only cut off the baedour?"

"I had nothing to do with your loss of power." I didn't. If I had, what had I done? It made no sense. I swallowed, the lump in my throat a rock grating against the sides.

Clove rose and checked on Rylla, placing a tender hand on the other woman's forehead before she shifted to check on Dain, who pushed her hands away. Then absently, she flicked a hand toward the fireplace, and flames erupted around the logs.

Warmth spread throughout the room.

"Describe what you saw with the baedour." Kir paced, fingers near his lips.

"The life forces were all connected like a giant spiderweb, but there was one who was off on their own. I could see the threads that connected to it, and I thought *cut* and snipped each line. And that's when they shrieked." I paused. "You all shrieked, but I swear I did nothing more than that. I don't understand how it's related."

"The baedour's pain was in my head," he said, "but that faded before our power fractured."

My heart clenched. "But you were already low."

"I was. That was the first time it happened when I was tapped out. Glad to know it won't kill me." His lips quirked and fell. At least he found something slightly amusing. Right now, I found none of it funny.

Dain rose and clomped around, checking out all the windows, rubbing his temple. "We can't stay here."

"Fuck, that hurt." Rylla sat up and rubbed the back of her neck. "Is it me, or does it hurt more each time? Do any of us have power?"

Dain turned, his eyes fierce, the scar along his eye making him look sinister. "They're going to come back."

"So you'd rather us be out there when they do?" Rylla waved her arm at the window.

"We're sitting ducks here," Dain said, hands on hips. "They know exactly where we are."

For once, I agreed with him, but I kept my opinion to myself.

Kir stopped his pacing. "Calm down. The witch inflicted massive damage to the baedour. It will go lick its wounds. However, Dain is right. It will be back, but we have time to rest."

Clove sat on the couch. "It suffered the power loss too."

"Exactly. We rest. We leave before first light. I'll take first watch."

But I couldn't sleep. It was all I could do to still be in my bedroll. The warmth of the fire was too much for me right now. After Kir's decision, there had been discussions of who would do what protections tomorrow. Clove would hold a small shield around the two of us, and the others would rotate in and out of it. Rylla would cover our scent for the first few hours. Our tracks would have to be left though. Hopefully, the wind and, if we were lucky, a storm would cover them.

I rolled over, putting my back to the fire, but then faced Kir, who sat on the couch. His face glowed from the flames, his features almost softened by the shadows. He watched me like I was something to figure out.

Neither of us looked away.

"You should sleep," he said.

"I can't."

His fingers curled, and he tore his gaze from mine to focus out the window. The movement caused the shadows to now draw sharp contours on his face.

He wasn't beautiful in the way I thought of when it came to fae. Strangely, Nolan fit that bill more. Kir was rugged, bearded, and I knew beneath it was a strong jawline, lush lips. My knowledge proved how often he captured my attention.

I shook my head. That line of thinking needed to stop. I wrapped my fingers around my tattooed wrist and sat up in the thermal shirt and leggings Clove had loaned me. She, along with Rylla and Dain, had taken the loft upstairs to sleep. They said the fire was too hot, but my sense was two of them didn't want to be near the human witch while sleeping.

My bedroll slipped down to my waist. The cooling effect was nice on my flushed skin. Kir's jaw worked as he kept his gaze locked on the view outside the window.

"How far is the Autumn Court?" I asked.

Kir, ever so slowly, turned back to me, and I sensed more than heard a silent, irritated sigh. A weighted pause told me he considered not conversing, but something made him relent. "Less than a day. There was a clue to the location in the pages we have. They should be hidden not far over the border from my court."

"And then?"

"We'll see." His eyes drifted again to the window.

"You don't talk much. You're always off on your own, even amongst your friends here. Why?" Why was I so chatty was the bigger question. Why did I prod at the man who showed zero interest in getting to know me, who treated me with such indifference?

His eyes sliced to me, his jaw working. "Why do you want to know?"

I saw how it was. Question for a question. I'd have to give some answers to get some. "I don't see why someone would purposefully hold themselves off to the side like that when they don't need to."

"And what would you know about that?"

His gaze bore down on me like he saw everything there was to see of me. It was too much. I stared down at my hands, twisted them. "I spent my entire life running with my mom. I had no friends. My mom said it was dangerous for me. For them. We didn't stay long anywhere. Not long enough for me to make a single friend."

I wanted to see his reaction, so I raised my eyes to meet his again to see if he would say anything.

He was like a stone, but he didn't look away.

So I kept going. "It was lonely. Beyond lonely. I used to write in a diary to a friend I made up. Just so I had someone to tell my secrets to." I wasn't sure why I continued. It felt good to say it to someone. "My mom found it and said it could be used against me. I had detailed what I had learned about witches. She threw it in the fire."

Kir flinched. "Your mom sounds...not nice."

My lips quirked in a sad smile. "She was strict, but she did what she thought was right for me. Recording that in a place someone could find it was...not smart, considering."

Kir grunted and looked back out the window.

So far, I had told them nothing of Nolan, but I wanted to see Kir's reaction. Craved it.

"The past few months, she loosened up," I said. "I was dating a Wall Walker. It was the first time I knew what it felt like to have someone else in my life besides my mother."

Kir's nostrils flared as he cut his gaze back to me, and it made my heart race. The side of his lip curled up as he spoke. "I don't need to hear about your boyfriends. I'm not a friend to spill all your secrets to. I'm not your little diary now."

I sat up straight as his words doused me with frigid water.

His eyes gleamed. Waiting.

"I see why you sit aside when you have friends surrounding you. You're too much of an asshole to see what you have. You take their loyalty for granted, Lord Kir."

One of his hands rested on the armrest of the sofa. He curled it into a fist. "I don't take their loyalty for granted. Some naive human girl can't possibly conceive of what we've been through. This conversation is over. Go to sleep."

He flicked a finger.

I didn't fall asleep, but I did feel drowsy. He'd used what little power he had left to shut me up.

CHAPTER 18

KIR

"Why didn't you wake me for watch?" Clove strapped her bedroll to her pack with furious movements. "You're not my mother."

That last comment had been directed at Rylla, who had woken us all before daybreak.

This would be interesting.

I busied myself with my pack, but I welcomed the distraction. It took my mind off the shitshow of my own inner drama. Last night after my watch, I'd tossed and turned, chastising myself about getting sucked into a conversation with the witch. Blast it, I wanted to get to know her. Yet, I knew I shouldn't. All of this would be easier if I kept my distance.

Rylla swung her white braid, flinging it out before it thwacked her back. "Excuse me? Ms. Mother-of-us-all?"

My hands stilled.

Clove's teeth audibly clacked together as she straightened her spine. "Some of you would forget to brush your teeth if you weren't reminded. I should have held a watch last night. We all needed rest."

"You have the most power right now, and I know you were up

late the night before we left, finishing off research. I made a call to let you rest. You're like my little sister." Rylla turned her back to Clove. She pulled the leather cord out of her braid, shook out her hair, and began re-plaiting. It was a move that, at one time, I had found attractive, more than attractive. Now, I found myself glancing at the witch, who sat, seemingly oblivious to the drama in the kitchen, in front of the fire and shoving her few items into a bag.

No, pay her no attention and definitely don't notice how a bewitching line forms between her eyes every time she looks your way.

My concern right now was for Clove. Rylla's tone was patronizing.

Clove didn't notice me watching as she stared at Rylla's back. Her face went from shocked to hurt. In my head, I begged her to drop it. Rylla wasn't ready.

"You make me feel so small sometimes." The ache of hurt oozed into Clove's words.

Rylla didn't turn, but she did pause in her plaiting.

I grimaced. That would sting. I tried not to watch Clove's face as Rylla's non-response sunk in. Rylla bit her tongue, remaining unusually silent, but I wasn't sure if Clove knew that. If she did, it might not be helpful either. Thankfully, Dain had remained in the lofted area. Knowing him, he'd say something utterly daft and make this even worse.

I stepped in. "We agreed on four watches, Rylla. It wasn't your call to make. We should treat each other as equals. You've all earned a spot in my court."

Rylla turned, her mouth pursed. "It's not my call, but we're equals? Or do you mean the rest of us are equals and you're our lord?"

Shit. She always threw my words back in my face. I didn't have much choice in being lord, and there would also be deference there. But I preferred to have us all act as equals. Treat their opinions equally. If they all thought one way and I thought the other, theoretically, I would go with the majority. So far, we'd never had to face an event where that didn't happen.

I pinched the bridge of my nose. "You know what I mean," I ground out. "This whole lord thing isn't me."

Rylla's face softened. "Well, you *are* our lord, whether you want to be or not, so yeah, I do get what you mean."

She turned and took in how closed off Clove now was, arms wrapped around herself. It shook me how a fae who normally had such confidence could make herself so small.

Rylla must have seen that too. "Clove, I'm sorry. I was an ass. I truly thought I was being helpful. You do so much for all of us. I thought you could use the extra rest."

Clove nodded with a little sniff. "I know I met you all when I was a kid, but I'm not one anymore. I pull as much weight as the rest of you do."

"I know you do, but we also look out for one another." Rylla said as she gave Clove a one-armed side-hug.

I breathed a sigh of relief that, even through my ineptness, the two fae women in my life came back together. The witch, for her part, remained silent and kept packing. She held the air of someone not paying any attention, though I doubted that. For being a human with their measly senses, she took in as much as she could.

Hell, she'd proven that last night when she'd called me out in one sentence. No one had ever read me like that before or at least not said it to my face. As much as she inspired the notion of sharing my thoughts with her, she also reminded me that being an asshole was the best way to keep her at arm's length or further.

I had no claim to her. I *should* have no claim on her, and it needed to stay that way.

No more chit chat. And I'd be an asshole if I had to. Though her dislike of fae was clear. It wasn't as if she threw herself at my feet.

I tightened the last straps on my pack and slung it over my shoulder. Even our magical rifts were not much help today. Those were a tiny amount of magic, but we all needed to conserve as much as we could.

The others filed outside. Dain came down and followed Clove and Rylla, while I did my final packing. They knew I'd like to make sure I felt it was as secure as I could make it. This cabin was my getaway after all.

The witch rose from the couch. She was so quiet, and earlier I'd begun purposely filtering out her heartbeat and scent in my attempt to ignore her. But now it was only the two of us in here. I swallowed my irritation with Clove. She must have told the witch to remain inside with me to conserve her magic. Keeping a human warm was a constant tax on us. At least we'd be in the Autumn Court soon.

I stalked to the door as she slipped her arms into her pack. Next, she grabbed her cloak, but she couldn't sling it over her pack. A grin threatened to slip across my lips as she struggled and muttered under her breath.

My hand was on the doorknob to leave. Let her wrestle her cloak or get Clove in here to help her?

"Help." Her face was a picture of frustration and irritation, her hair mussed from the cloak and her struggle to right it. "I also have a bone to pick with you."

"You want to admonish me while I help you?" The words were out of my mouth before I even thought better of engaging with her. Damn it. I quirked my brow and folded my arms over my chest anyway.

"For all your talk of conserving magic, you used yours to knock me out last night." She pulled at the cloak, but all it did was tug her pack. A small growl emitted from her throat, and parts of me that did not need to notice did.

"You annoyed me."

Her eyes widened, and it was as if a fire erupted behind them. "Where I come from, we don't go around putting people to sleep because they irritated us. If that was the case, you'd be in a coma."

"You needed the rest." My lips quirked at the implications that paralleled the earlier conversation, and it took a considerable amount of control to stop them.

"Maybe so." She stalked toward me with a finger up like she was preparing to poke me in the chest with it, so I stepped away from the door and that finger. "But don't use fae magic on me again without my consent." She stopped and took in my retreat "Why do you do that?"

"Do what?"

"That." She motioned at me as she took a step forward. "Do human witches scare you that much?"

I couldn't let on the truth. Layers of clothes covered me. It would be fine. I knew from my friends that touching my clothes was not dangerous. I'd be long dead by now if not. So I stepped forward, pressing my chest into her outstretched finger. Words failed me, literally. There wasn't a phrase at the tip of my tongue, no half-truth. Faerie wouldn't allow it. So I hoped the gesture said what I wished I could say and that she believed it.

Because I couldn't lie. Witches did scare me. And her, the most.

A tingle of awareness ran through me where her finger pressed in.

I held my breath and backed off. "I'll respect your wish if you'll respect mine. Don't touch me."

She eyed me, her gaze flicking from her finger to my chest to my eyes. As she dropped her hand, she inclined her head. It was an acknowledgement, an acceptance of my offer.

HOW DID HUMANS WALK FOR MILES? IT WASN'T THE STRAIN OF THE EXERCISE —it was the fact that, as a species with such short lifespans, they had the hardest way to travel. All that time spent getting from place to place just sucking up the seconds and minutes of their life and yet, here we fae were with our comparatively immortal lifespans and able to sift vast distances.

Were able.

"Are we there yet?" Dain blurted out for the fourth time in as many hours.

The witch laughed, and my gaze darted to her. Clove's shield protected the three women. Rylla had expended half her magic covering our trail for the first few hours. We opted to have her stop and save some. But we all took turns inside the small shield Clove held. She kept the inside air a touch above freezing. But we'd cross over soon, and then I hoped it wouldn't be needed. Where were those pockets of weather disturbance when you needed them?

Clove leaned in to the witch. "What is so funny?"

The witch, whose shoulders still shook, replied, "He sounds like a whiny human child. It's a big joke for us that whenever we travel, the children, fifteen minutes into a four-hour drive, will ask 'are we there yet?'"

Clove nodded as if in understanding, a slight smile on her face. "What's a drive?"

The witch's laugh stopped before it started again. "You know, a car?"

She put her hands up in front of her and moved them back and forth and made odd *vroom vroom* noises. What in the Wall?

Then she waved her hand in the air. "I guess not. Cars are a way to move around faster. They're like a carriage, but instead of horses pulling them, they have an engine, a motor that makes the wheels go."

Clove hummed. I imagined she wanted to write this information down, but she'd have to wait till later.

Something flew towards us, and my hand reached for my sword. A screech tore through the air.

Haze.

I let my sword fall back into its scabbard. He glided in, and I held my arm out for him to land. With my cloak, I barely felt his talons, even though he always took care not to hurt me.

"Hey boy, what's new?" I asked.

He sidestepped until he perched on my shoulder where he leaned down, nibbled my ear, and rubbed the side of his head on mine. He didn't speak words but sent images and sensations. We never really knew if he could do this with anyone or just me. What we did know was he didn't do it with any of my companions. Maybe it was my proficiency in entering minds. It allowed me to be attuned to him.

Haze flashed an image of the witch into my mind. Until a moment ago, I'd studiously ignored her. I hadn't seen how the cold set her cheeks a beguiling shade of rose. Every time I shared the shield with her, I stood on the other side of Clove, and Clove—damn her—constantly maneuvered so I would be by the witch. The entire thing was ridiculous, like some early Winter Court drama. When I thought about it that way, it was easy to see how far the fae had fallen.

And here was Haze, shoving the witch directly into my mind. He was as bad as Clove. I never would have guessed my animal companion would be as invested in my love life as he was. I sent him an image of a fae death shroud to remind him of my curse, and he nipped my ear in response before he paced on my shoulder.

That should shut him up for a bit. He and I had a bond, and lore said many animal companions didn't survive if their fae passed. But it had been so long since any fae besides me had one, similar to fated mates. Both were rare and seemingly rarer now with Faerie dying. Perhaps those elements died as well.

But enough of all this. I needed his help.

I sent him an image of the baedour, followed by the sensation of their shrieking. Haze trembled on my shoulder. After that, I sent him the image of our shelter, my private abode, with the question of where those baedour were now.

He chirruped. I reached into my rift and pulled out one of his favorite treats: dried liver encased in a crunchy, savory cookie that I made when life wasn't hectic. I hadn't been able to make them for a while. Stock was running low, and I rationed them.

It was a message now to him to be careful. This mission held more danger than others.

Haze purred as he gobbled it down before rubbing my cheek again. A tiny pressure down from his legs before he leapt up. Then the minx flew to the witch. Clearly, the idea of my death wasn't impacting him all that much.

I wasn't sure how she knew, but she lifted her arm for him. He landed like he did on me and made his way to her shoulder, where he performed the same ear nibble and head rub.

Then he leapt off into the sky. He'd check my place, where we'd spent the night first. I followed his flight until even my fae sight lost him in the gray. I focused back on the path in front of us and found the witch watching me.

Our eyes met.

She slowed her pace and came out of Clove's protective shield.

"Where did you send him?" Her tone suggested an accusation.

Every time we chatted, she managed to get her witch fingers into me, twisting my emotions, making me want to know more. But I couldn't ignore the question. "He is checking if the baedour have returned to the shelter."

"How did he know to find you?"

"He checks in when he wants. It was fortuitous that he did so just now."

"And you have no qualms, sending him into danger?" Her voice held a note of disapproval. She already cared for my familiar.

"He can take care of himself and did so for decades before he met me. He won't do what he does not want to." Much like me. We did what we wanted, but duty called. The two leached into one another enough that I couldn't discern a difference.

Her lip quivered a second before her shoulders trembled. They already held a blue tinge.

"Get back inside the shield," I said.

Her eyes flared. For someone who seemingly took orders the majority of her life, it rankled her when they came from me.

Good. I could never abide a mate who didn't spar with me.

The thought hit before I could stop it in its tracks.

She hadn't moved. So I did. I picked up my pace and walked over to Dain. Rylla was currently in the shield. I didn't turn to check if the witch joined Clove.

On my next turn inside it, I might pass. I had to remain the stoic asshole to keep the witch at bay. We needed to find these pages and then get Inn—the witch back across the Wall.

It wasn't long before Haze circled overhead, sending me the images of our shelter as we left it. The baedour, so far, had not returned and were not in that area. Haze, knowing the message had been received, took off again. He'd scout for the baedour ahead of us now to make sure they hadn't figured out how to cut off our path.

We would cross into the Autumn Court soon, and the cave, as fortune had it, was closer to the Winter Court than the Spring Court. I could practically taste the victory with those pages in my hand. The location of the stone that much closer, within our grasp.

A scream tore through the air, and my heart stopped.

Innara.

I swept around. I couldn't see her. Rylla was with Clove. Behind them there was a frozen lake. One we had never crossed or seen.

A weather disturbance. I leapt to action, running past Clove and Rylla, Dain on my heels.

My boots hit the ice, and I slid several feet out onto the lake. Innara was nowhere to be found. My heart thrummed.

Dain slid in beside me. "Where is she?"

I fell to my knees, a frantic growl creeping up my throat. If the lake had formed while she stood there, it had swallowed her. The ice below me reflected the forever gray sky.

A shadow drifted by before it rose up.

Fists hit the ice below me, and I lurched into action.

My well of magic was empty, so I drew my sword and slammed it into the ice a foot away from her. But as soon as I raised it to pound again, the ice cracks froze over.

"Rylla!" I screamed. She had magic still. Clove was likely near drained. And it had been clear that Innara needed calm to access her magic.

"She needs to be guided," a voice I didn't recognize said.

I turned and a dark-skinned woman with long, gray hair stood there, clad in heavy robes.

A witch.

"Then guide her." I nearly screamed it. This bond was getting to me. Fear for my mate took over. My heart was in my throat. And I barked orders at a witch I'd never met and who could likely kill me right now.

"No. She needs someone with a connection to her to guide her."

I stood. She didn't mean me. Not the bond connection. I didn't want to use that. What if it strengthened it or made Innara realize how we were bonded? I shook my head. There had to be another way.

"You have to," Clove said. "Kir, she'll die if you don't."

This new witch stood there, seeming to weigh me. And the shadow beneath me stopped hitting her fists into the ice.

Next to me, Dain shifted. "She's your mate. We need her."

Of course they were right. Every fiber of my being sang it, whether she found out the truth or not.

I hung my head. "How do I guide her? I have little power right now."

"She can travel the bond, but she has to see it. The combination of witch and fae magic will allow her to pass."

Right. She has to see the bond, but she has to be made aware of it. Only one way to do that. I closed my eyes and let my mind reach out.

CHAPTER 19
INNARA

I was so cold. My lungs burned. Figures above the ice shifted, their shadows undulating. Why did they not help? A small gap below the ice allowed me to take in sips of air, but the frigid water splashed into my mouth.

Think!

I needed to calm myself. I wasn't a damsel. I had abilities. With my eyes closed, I willed my heart rate to slow as I sipped at the tiniest bubble of air.

My pulse slowed, and I had a brief moment of wondering if hypothermia set in or not. An image of Kir rose in my mind. I shoved it away, but he came right back, walking through the blackness until he was as face to face with me as he could be.

I wasn't sure if I was losing my mind or dying.

"Listen to me," he said.

This was not an unbidden image of him. It *was* him. In my mind. He must have broken through my mental shields.

"You have to get yourself out of this. I can help, but it has to come from you." Lines formed on his brow, and I swore there was a flash of need that he quickly disguised beneath distaste. He wiped a hand on his leathers and extended it to me.

He wore no glove.

"What do I do?" I stared at his hand. Earlier, he had said not to touch him, but he beckoned. I slid my hand into his.

The outer world slipped from my consciousness. A danger unto itself. But the warmth and strength of his hand contrasted with the numb cold seeping into every pore of my being. Something like pain flashed across his face. How he must hate this. He tightened his grip, a thumb grazing the back of my hand, sending shivers through me. He tugged me closer until we nearly touched chest to chest, but then I saw it.

The braided, sparkling rope I had seen earlier. It ran up through the ice.

"Do you see it?" he murmured.

I nodded. What was this? With my free hand, I reached out.

It was solid, something I could grasp. I tightened my hand around it and met Kir's gaze, questioning. He looked up along the line of the cord, and I pulled my hand away. He let it slide out instead of releasing me. My fingers trailed along his palm, and his breath hitched.

I didn't have time to wonder why or revel in how wonderful it felt. I grabbed the rope and hauled myself up, cursing myself for a weak upper body. But it wasn't far. I only had to pull myself a few feet.

My muscles fizzled, and the numbness of being in the water seeped into this alternate reality.

"You have to do this," Kir whispered in my ear.

"I can't. I'm too weak."

His hands came to rest on my hips, supporting me. It was almost enough.

"You're not weak. You've survived this long. One last push and you'll be free from this. This, you can do. I've got you."

Out of everything that had just spilled from him, it was the last bit that got me. When he wasn't a jerk, he was pretty decent. I girded myself for a push. And then I heaved myself upward.

My head slipped through the ice, and it felt oddly like how I remembered moving through the Wall. Hands grasped under my arms and all went black.

But I heard one last thing. "I knew you could do it."

Lips pressed over mine, and I jerked my head to the side and coughed. I couldn't feel my body, and I kept my eyes tightly closed. Pain crept in at the edges, intensifying every second.

"We need to get her warm." That was Kir, but his voice was far away. I had to stomp on the disappointment that filled me. It wasn't his lips on mine.

Warmth surrounded me, and the incessant wind that bit my exposed skin disappeared.

"I can't hold this for long." Clove sounded tense. She was close, practically in my face.

"Follow me" said a voice I didn't recognize. There was a rasp to it that spoke of age and authority.

And then the strangest thing—witchery fluttered against my skin. My body lifted and floated.

"We'll get you fixed up," Clove said close to my ear, but I wanted to hear Kir again.

All around, boots crunched in the snow, followed by the abrupt crinkle of leaves and slide of dirt under boots. Something creaked, and luscious smells pervaded my senses. Smells so much like home. I had a notion that, when Kir said I'd be free, somehow I went home, free from Cirrelea. Maybe I died.

The voice I didn't recognize spoke. "Take her to the back room. Get her out of those wet clothes."

A door shut.

Clove was next to me. "We have to get you out of your things. I need you to help. Can you stand?"

Was I standing, or was I floating? I fought myself to open my eyes. Pain, sharp and piercing stabbed me all over my body. Clove held me up, and I clung to her like a child. An ache opened within me having nothing to do with the cold. No. I sought out Kir, wanted his reassurance, that connection I'd felt with him moments ago, but he wasn't here.

Clove dragged a chair near.

"Hold on to that," she said as she worked my cloak off me. It landed with a soggy plop. Next, she slid my pants down my numb legs and after that my shirt. Finally, she found something warm and dry to slip over my head.

"Come. There's a fire in the next room." She hooked an arm around my back and slung my arm over her shoulder.

My body shivered uncontrollably.

In the other room, everyone stood, the fae looking as if they'd rather bolt. Kir's face was pinched but relaxed as soon as I entered the room. A small, rustic couch sat in front of a blazing fire with a blanket draped across it. Clove sat next to me before she wrapped the blanket around both of us. The pain became greater, which told me the heat was thawing me out. I had been cold before the baedour, but this was much worse.

"Once you get warm enough, we'll get some food in you," Clove said.

A woman I didn't recognize hung a pot in the fire. She was a bit round in the middle and moved with the slow start of someone of age. She turned and fixed her gaze on me, clasping her hands in front of her. "Feeling better, hmm?"

She was a witch and a strong one at that if what I felt earlier had come from her alone. I wondered how the fae felt about two witches now in their presence.

But the focus remained on me. Feeding me, warming me. Making sure I suffered no long-term ill effect from the icy water.

Once I was taken care of, a tense silence settled over the room. The fae shifted restlessly. Kir had shown me that he wasn't that afraid of witches the other day, but this one was powerful. They had to know it as much as I did.

No one spoke, and the witch, seated in a wooden chair, raised an ironic brow at me. Her deep brown eyes seemed amused.

"Who are you?" I asked.

"My name is Muriel."

"I owe you my gratitude."

"I will always aid a fellow witch." What she left unsaid, *who* she left unsaid, hung there. Rylla muttered something to Dain, and Muriel's eyes flicked to her with a flash of irritation before they came back to rest on me. "How interesting it was for me to come upon the Cursed One today with a witch in tow."

"I don't know what you mean," I said to keep her talking. It was clear that witch and fae didn't mix, as Vera had said.

"You hide many things." She smiled and approached me. I shrank back as she peeled away the blanket, exposing my arm. She gave a small *tsk,* so I allowed her to run a finger over the stone of my bracelet.

"How can we repay you for your aid?" Kir broke her examination.

"As I said before, I will always aid a witch." She fixed him with a stare like she wore glasses at the end of her nose. "But it appears you all are welcome here too. She is in good health, and I believe, you all acted on her wellbeing, which is most interesting."

Next, she pushed back my bracelet and exposed the skin underneath. She turned it over, taking in my tattoo. Her gaze flicked from me to Kir.

"You hide things too," she said to him.

A flicker of unease crossed his face, but he asked, "Can we ask one more thing of you?"

"You may ask. I may not grant."

"We've reached an agreement with the—with Innara. She claims to be from the other side of the Wall. Can you confirm that for us?"

He used my name.

Our eyes met, and something passed between us.

Muriel's gaze swung back to me. "We should speak alone."

But I was still too stunned to respond.

Dain and Rylla spoke at the same time, "I think not."

Muriel turned to Kir. "You are in my home. I do not ask permission. You want an answer. This is my cost. Consider this your repayment." She didn't wait. She flicked her hand up, and with a swirl, my ears popped. Silence reigned. "There. They can't hear us. Now tell me, are you from the other side of the Wall?"

"You can't tell?"

She chuckled. "No. I can't tell a witch from this side of the Wall from any other. But your bracelet is odd. I've never seen the likes of it."

I picked up the item in question. It was a rock on a leather string. How was it all that unusual? "My mother gave it to me."

Muriel cocked her head to the side. "You did not create this?"

I shook my head. "It's a family heirloom, passed down through generations."

"And your mother is where now?"

I shrugged. "I hope she is safe. I need to get back across the Wall to help her if she needs it."

"I don't sense any lies from you. These fae can get very touchy with humans and our penchant to bend the truth. You have willingly entered this bargain?" She tapped my wrist.

"I did. I intend to hold up my end of it." I curled my wrist back to my chest and slipped it inside the blanket, my body finally cozy.

"Very well." She lifted her hand again like she caught a thread floating in the air and flicked it.

My ears didn't pop this time, but it was jarring to now hear all the little noises like the fire crackling and the wind outside.

Muriel spoke first. "I sense no lie. She is from the other side. But what I also sense is that you still feel as if she is a danger to you. Am I wrong?"

The question was for Kir. That part was clear, and he nodded, not daring a glance towards me.

"Yet you have made a bargain with her, so you must need something only she can give you." No one responded, so Muriel skirted around the sofa I sat on to move in front of Kir. "You seek something, and if the Summer Court witches showing up at my doorstep a few days ago is any clue, then you must seek the same thing."

Muriel raised a finger under Kir's chin, and he jerked his head away, eyes flashing. "What does Gaelin seek?" he asked. Muriel smiled, earning a sneer from Kir. "What is it that you want? Be clear. I don't want any games."

"That's rich coming from a fae," Muriel said dryly. She came back near me, placing a hand on my shoulder. "I want Innara to come back to see me. She will know when, and it will be before your bargain is fulfilled. There will come a time when she needs a witch she can trust."

"Why can she trust you?" Kir asked.

My eyes widened. The question was practically protective.

"Because I am a witch with a coven but outside it and not beholden to any bargains."

I squished up my face. Why would that make me trust her? But like how she sensed I wasn't lying, I sensed the same from her. She felt like an old relative.

Kir's gaze met mine as if he wanted to be sure I was okay with the request. I nodded. "Fine," he said. "We will come to see you when Innara feels it is time."

To that, Muriel raised a brow. I didn't miss it either. He would join me rather than send me alone.

"Gaelin seeks the stone," Muriel said. "You can find it in the Delves unless he gets there first."

There was an intake of breath. Then Rylla spoke. "We don't need the witch now?"

"Innara is her name," Muriel said as if admonishing a child. If I hadn't trusted her before, I did now. "And *this witch* will be able to guide you to the stone. Gaelin won't have that benefit."

"Why?" Dain asked.

"I am willing to bet Gaelin will be too paranoid to bring a witch with him. He will go in on his own," Muriel said.

"The Delves though? That is insane." Rylla said it to Kir more than anyone else in the room.

However, Kir asked, "And how do you know the location of the stone?"

"A well-kept secret among witches. Passed down mother to daughter for generations."

"So why tell us now?" He shifted, drawing closer to her.

Muriel looked into her cup of tea, chuckling. "Gaelin is a blight upon this world. He uses the sisterhood of witches against us. But it was fate that had you arriving at my doorstep today. Witches and fae have a long history." She paused, her eyes with a faraway look. "A very long history. It's interesting how well that history passed down through us witches, hmm? But I digress. Gaelin"—and she spoke his name with venom—"must be stopped. If he is to rule over all Cirre-lea, it is likely an end to this entire planet."

"Why?" I asked, unsure where I found the nerve. But I'd heard this Gaelin name so many times but with no real information.

She turned to me. "He only cares for his own interests." Then her attention went back to Kir. "The witches do not want to ally with fae, but there will come a time when they have no choice. And when that time comes, I believe they will choose you." She held up a finger. "But fates twist and turn. Strings are cut. New colors are woven in. Your choices will determine what happens."

CHAPTER 20

KIR

Muriel offered to let us stay with her. As shocking as that was, we politely declined. I couldn't put my crew at the mercy of *two* witches. I chose to believe that Innara was who she said she was and not Gaelin's agent. But Muriel? She was an unknown.

I had heard of her. Fae tended to hear of witches who were exiled. Yet, I knew little else. She was either one to trust wholeheartedly or not at all.

So which one of those should I choose? She helped us save Innara. Would I have been able to save her without Muriel's input?

I would never know.

Muriel gave us the heads-up on Gaelin and the stone. But she could also be lying or sending us on a wild pixie chase. She had confirmed Innara was from the other side. And a lying human could, well...lie.

I had to go with my gut. Generally, it led true.

Except for Violet. I didn't see her coming. And Violet colored my view of Innara. It was the fear and humiliation of Gaelin's spy that led me to believe all the wrong things of Innara.

We continued to hike for two days after Muriel's. We overshot where the cave was supposed to be, but I knew of a shelter we could use and that the wards on it were likely still active. And those wards kept out things like the baedour. We could stay there for a few days. Let our power come back to whatever full now looked like. I hated that it meant wasting time before going into the Delves. Beating Gaelin to it was imperative, but going in low on power was asking for trouble.

Few things were in my control. And one of those things not in my control walked in front of me, letting her beguiling human scent drift by.

I gritted my teeth. The thought of being closed up with her for a few days had me on edge. She hadn't said anything about how she'd gotten out of that frozen lake. Maybe she wouldn't.

Still, I'd need to get creative to avoid her. The place wasn't big, but at least it was bigger than my hideaway in the Winter Court.

Soon we were on the dirt trail that led to it. With the sun setting, it looked haunted. Spindly trees and crunchy dead leaves spun in tornadoes here and there. The wind was almost as brutal as in the Winter Court, but with the temperature being survivable, the amount of power needed to shield us was minimal. And every now and again, there was a respite from the battering, which meant Clove could drop it entirely.

Innara lifted a hand to a branch where a leaf bud sprouted. "Look! It's growing a leaf."

"Keep watching," Clove said solemnly as she moved up alongside her.

Innara gave her a questioning look but withdrew her hand and waited. I hated seeing it, but it was good for her to understand. Since Winter was a time of death, we didn't see this sort of thing in my court.

The bud grew, the tip pointed at first, and vibrant green. It felt like forever until it unfurled, so full of life. Within another few minutes, we observed it change colors from the verdant green to yellow to brown. The leaf dropped off the branch and floated to the ground.

By the time Innara leaned down to pick it up, it was already crisp. She twirled the stem between her fingers before letting it drop.

Her eyes were glassy when she looked up. "How long has it been like that?"

"A while," said Clove, hooking her arm into Innara's to lead her away. "It used to happen much more quickly and all over the trees when all this first began. Now it's like that, a leaf here and there, going through the cycle, albeit slowly."

"What does it mean?"

We neared the cabin, and I pushed passed them to get a view on it. "It means we need to get the Wall down."

A SMALL DISTURBANCE POCKET HAD TAKEN OVER THE BEDROOMS, MUCH TO my dismay. We walked in to find gargantuan trees growing out of the walls and beds. Vines grew and withered, an endless cycle. Detritus littered the floors. We shut the doors and decided it had to be safe enough. From what we had seen of the weather disturbances, they didn't grow at an unusual rate. We'd be fine for a few days.

Now we sat in the living room where we would all sleep. Everyone was settled and fed. I scrubbed a hand down my face. My plan of avoiding the witch did not look good. There was one little room off to the side with a desk and couch. I considered sleeping in there, but Clove said not to even think about it. She saw this like some sort of sleepover party for all of us.

Dain lifted a hand, and a bottle of winterberry wine appeared. Because what else would he have in his rift?

"I kept this for a special occasion. I had hopes that it would be for a celebration, but I think we could use it now." Dain grinned as he peeled the wax off and pulled the cork with a little bit of magical help.

Clove was in the kitchen and pulled a corkscrew out of the drawer. "You could have used this."

"Nah. It's much more impressive for the human if I do it this way." He winked at Innara. My blood boiled. Dain took one look at my face and cackled.

I stood. "I'll grab some glasses."

My gloves were on, so I gave Dain a good finger flick to the head as I passed him.

Innara, for her part, took it in stride. She curled up on the couch closest to the fireplace, wrapped in a blanket, and her nose in a book.

I fetched the glasses and laid them on the counter. Dain poured the wine. The winterberry bushes were needed for food now, and there were so few of them. "How many bottles are left after this?"

"I didn't count but only a few on the shelf that I remember," Dain said. "At least they are large bottles."

I snorted. But it weighed on me. We had led such an extravagant lifestyle compared to now. Endless food, endless wine, sifting where we wanted. This felt like punishment. And maybe we deserved it.

Dain handed a glass to Innara, and she sipped, her eyes rolling back at the exquisite taste. When she licked her bottom lip, my mouth went dry. Our gazes met, and I hastily gulped my glass. It went down wrong, making me sputter.

Dain saw the whole thing and clapped me on the back. "You okay, bud?"

Mischief was written all over his face. Still coughing, I flicked him off. By the time I recovered, Innara was chatting with Clove next to her, the book laid off to the side. No concern for me.

I sighed. The moment was a bit of normalcy, but I had to burst the bubble.

"We need to discuss the Delves," I said. "Do we trust Muriel and what she told us? Do we dare enter them and risk Macachera attacking?" We'd had a long walk. Plenty of time for us all to think on it. I'd specifically asked them all not to discuss it until we got here. Everyone needed to form an opinion of their own. "Rylla, I'd like your thoughts first."

She shifted in her seat. "It's an insane idea."

My heart fell. I hoped we wouldn't be at odds on this one.

But then Rylla grinned like Haze when he got a favorite treat. "I love it. It feels like we need a big win right now, and this could be it. The pages lead us to the stone. Somehow, they led us to Muriel instead, and she gave us the location. Imagine stealing it right from under Gaelin's nose." She lifted her hand and snatched at an imaginary item. Her laugh rang out like bells.

"I agree," said Clove. "We have the upper hand. Those witches that were at Muriel's have to travel back to Gaelin to get him the information. I don't think she was lying."

"Or she is trying to off both fae leaders at once. Witches win," Dain said, taking a sip of his wine before sliding down on the couch, legs spread wide.

"So you didn't believe her?" I pointed my question at Dain.

"Why would I?" he asked.

"She helped with Innara," I said from behind the counter in the kitchen, playing with the cast-off bottle cork.

"She helped a fellow witch. She did not help us." Dain turned from his seat on the couch to address me.

Clove leaned forward. "She welcomed us into her home. Fed us. Invited us to stay."

"It could all be a ruse." He shook his head.

Innara rolled her eyes. "Yes, she helped me. Muriel was earnest. I believe she has her loyalties. Who doesn't? But I think she meant what she said."

Dain's upper lip curled. "A witch trusting a witch. Imagine that."

"Yes, and we decided we would trust this witch." I emphasized it by pointing at Innara. What had gotten into him?

"I have a name," the witch in question drawled. Somehow, it had turned into an inside joke, which did something to me. My fingers trembled around my glass.

"Fine," Dain said. "It's the fucking Delves. You seriously want us to go in there and face that-that *thing*?"

"So you're past not trusting Muriel?" I asked as I made my way into the living area.

He threw his head back to rest on the couch. "I don't know if we should believe her. A part of me wants to be like Rylla and say, 'Fuck it. Delves. Woo!' But another part of me wonders if I really want to die in the Delves? Because it's a real possibility."

"What are the Delves, and why are they so bad?" Innara asked, her voice quiet, serious.

I settled on the couch next to Rylla, across from Clove and Innara. "I am not sure how to explain in human terms. They are a maze in another dimension. They are ancient, much like the Wall. Ages ago, we could use them to quickly travel. Opening a gate took less power than sifting. There was a guide, a guardian, in them: Macachera. We believe during a good portion of our lives he morphed. We never saw him. Perhaps the loneliness got to him, the isolation. He became obstinate, refusing to help, then became a prankster, then an obstacle to fae wanting to travel. But the last bit happened at the same time we began losing our power."

"That doesn't sound horrible," Innara said. "What kind of obstacles does he use?"

"He is the obstacle. He can move lightning fast. His swords are venomous. All of that on top of not getting lost. The breakdown of power has led to a shifting maze. Some of us used to know various paths, but now we must rely on the ancient symbology to guide us. And no one knows if Macachera has altered them. So if you don't run into him, which is unlikely, you run the maze and hope you find the way out that plops you out somewhere you want to be."

"So we could die, or it could be a gigantic waste of time and we leave to find ourselves farther from the cave?" Innara asked.

"Yes."

She pursed her lips lost in thought.

Clove touched her hand. "But Muriel felt you would be able to read the symbology."

She shrugged. "I know witch sigils."

"I know the ancient fae symbols. If we go in, we could find the stone, and we could be so much closer to our goal." Clove cast a hopeful look about the room.

"If we go in the Delves, we lose the baedour," I said. I liked this way of looking at what could happen if we did it and succeeded.

"Or we go in and die and make a nice meal for Macachera," Dain said.

We all remained silent, taking sips on our glasses.

"We vote then, and we do what the group decides," I said. "All in favor?" I raised my hand.

Rylla and Clove raised theirs. Innara and Dain's hands remained by their sides.

"All against?"

Neither of them raised their hand.

"You have to vote." My gaze darted between them.

Innara looked startled. "Me? I get a vote?"

I swallowed back my embarrassment and nodded. She really thought little of me, and it roiled. "I don't expect you to put yourself in a life-threatening situation with no say."

Even though I'd been an asshole and was now reaping what I'd sowed.

"In that case, I'm in favor," she said. "I've survived this long, and not taking risks won't get me home faster, so..."

All eyes were on Dain.

"C'mon," Rylla crooned. "Where's my buddy who's always up for stupid shit?"

Dain crossed his arms. "Not wanting to die."

"We won't die. I'll protect you," she said as she snuggled up next to him. This was new. Clove stiffened.

"What is it that's bugging you?" I asked. "You've gone into situations and places just as bad."

He groaned, throwing his head back again, and scrubbed both hands down his face where they now rested over his lips. He muttered something, and Rylla giggled.

"What now? Even fae with sensitive hearing didn't catch that," I said.

He jerked his hands away. "I hate you all." He stared off out the window. "I'm afraid of the dark."

Rylla giggled again, which was not helpful as he elbowed her off of him. Clove kept a straight face, and so did the wi—Innara. I'd accepted her as part of our team now.

"I am sure we can make a light," Clove said.

And as much as I wanted to poke at Dain, I knew it wouldn't be right. He'd admitted something he had managed to hide from all of us. I reached behind Rylla, gave her braid a sharp tug.

Then I clapped Dain on his shoulder and said, "I'm sorry we are hearing of this now, but I am glad you told us."

Rylla spoke into her glass a bit drunkenly. "So we can make fun of you."

I sent a glare her way, wishing my mental powers meant telepathic communication. But for now, the glare would have to do. "We'll think of something. A torch if we have to."

As I drew back my arm, Innara sipped at her glass, watching me over the rim, and did I dare think that approval was in her eyes? My stomach tightened at the thought she might see more of me than she initially did, might see the real me.

No, that thinking would only lead to entanglement.

Dain nodded. "I know it sounds silly, but it's debilitating." He rubbed his hands along his thighs. "But I'm in."

I leaned forward to shake his leg. "I won't let the darkness descend on you."

WE'D MADE THE DECISION. SO WHY COULDN'T I SLEEP? I WASN'T DWELLING on the Delves. Not entirely. I couldn't believe Dain had hidden that fact from us all these years, but when I thought of it, it was in front of our faces the entire time. Even in my hideaway, the light from the fire reached the loft. At home, he slept with a light on, not the brightest one. I'd asked him about it once, and he just ran a hand through his hair and said he fell asleep reading.

He was always the one saying to face our fears. There were times when he seemed like the bravest, or the stupidest depending on how one looked at it, always charging in to protect us. Yet, he always had a fear that, in his own words, was debilitating. Maybe when we had our full power it didn't affect him much. He could depend on that power to light his way.

No more.

It shook me. What were the others hiding? Everyone had secrets. Some big, some small.

With our powers lessening, we were all now keenly aware of our own weaknesses, especially ones we didn't have several years ago. But shouldn't I know theirs? Wasn't I supposed to be their leader?

One shared weakness was needing rest to restore our power more quickly. Everyone was in the living area. I was on the long couch. It made it easier to not have anyone bump into me. That thought alone would have kept me up. Rylla, Dain, and Clove spread their bedrolls on the floor between my couch and the short couch which held the sleeping form of Innara.

She rolled over, facing away from me. The firelight highlighted the deep reds in her normally chestnut-colored hair. Her bedroll slipped down to expose a mostly bare shoulder. Only a slim strap marred the expanse of her skin.

I wanted to stroke it and see how warm she was.

That line of thinking was no good. I rolled away to stare at the back of the couch and closed my eyes. I let my awareness focus inward until I felt like I was walking on a black plain. The stray thought of Dain hating this occurred to me. It never would have before today, but my mental ability would be his nightmare.

Focus.

Where would I like to go? I used the most basic ability of mine. I could visit places again and again. If I had been there and seen it, I could go and include all the details I had seen, even if unaware of it at the time. The book on the desk? I could come back like this and see the title. But if the book was in a drawer I never opened, the drawer would be empty.

And Wall save me, my mind went straight to the conversation with Innara at my hideaway.

It was sweet torture. I replayed our conversation until the part where she mentioned her boyfriend. And my jealousy boiled. Instead of the vitriol I had spewed, I let the words I had wanted to say come out. "And what if I told you your boyfriend wasn't here, and you can tell me anything you want."

A shimmer went through the vision.

Innara gaped at me. Did she know that, with the fire behind her, her silhouette showed through the shirt Clove gave her? I could move forward with this. My ability allowed me to replay and then bring things into a more dreamlike state where I could live out my fantasy.

But this was not the time or place for that. It was playing with fire.

I sighed as I relished the look of her mouth, her skin in the fire-light. In this state, I could allow myself a touch.

One small taste. I reached forward to stroke her cheek.

But she crawled out of her bedroll, wearing only her underthings. The shirt Clove gave her was gone.

My pulse sped up. This was not my doing. I wasn't thinking any of this.

She stopped right in front of me, between my legs, and rose up. Her hands went to my knees and glided along my thighs.

I wanted to push her off. I wanted to pull her in. This was too real, and I wasn't making this happen. Something else was going on, and the panic from her touching me was right at the surface.

"I'd say, 'He isn't my boyfriend anymore, though I never got much chance to make that clear to him' and..." She bit the side of her lower lip. The flesh popped back out, shiny and plump.

My mouth went dry, and blood rushed to places I was sure she would notice soon.

I should stop this. Whatever this was.

"If I was to tell you anything, I'd tell you how much I want to know what your skin feels like." She reached up, and I grabbed her wrist, causing her to let out a tiny squeak.

Our eyes met, and heat bloomed. No words came out of me.

In this vision, my bare hands held her wrist, and I hadn't died.

Realization hit.

How was she doing this? It had to be her. Because it wasn't me. Now my pulse hammered away at the possibility.

I let my hand loosen around her wrist and slide down her arm. Her skin was so smooth and warm that it made me shiver. How I craved this. She held my gaze. I wondered what she saw in mine. In hers was a woman taking power. Her pupils dilated and burned with heat and intensity.

Taking my release of her wrist as an invitation, Innara crawled up and straddled my legs.

Goosebumps peppered her skin, and I marveled at the feel of them under my fingers.

"Say something," she whispered as my hands coasted over her shoulders and up along the side of her neck. She curled into my touch, and I applied the slightest pressure to the back of her neck. There was no resistance, and our bodies gravitated toward one another.

My brain stalled, and I rapidly turned into a ball of need, craving touch.

A tentative press along my neck made me moan. A small smile curled her lips as she drew closer. I trailed my hand from the back of her neck down her spine, and she let out the softest sigh. As our lips barely touched and heat erupted inside of me, a harsh intake of breath startled me, and the woman in my arms vaporized.

My heart jolted, and I abruptly pulled out of my vision state. Across the room from me, Innara rustled to a seated position.

I rolled over. "Are you okay?"

Her hand went to her lips, and wide, frightened eyes locked with mine. A scent tickled my nose, and the musky scent of her arousal filled the room. Her hand trembled as she pulled it away from her mouth. She looked at me as if she'd seen a ghost. Could it be? Had she somehow used our bond to meet me in the alternate plane?

She stood, nearly naked, only in her underthings. I sucked in a breath as she fixed me in her sight.

"I have to use the bathroom," she said.

I only nodded as she passed me on her way out of the room, in too much shock to say more and not wanting to embarrass her. And glad my bedroll covered the evidence of what she had done to me.

CHAPTER 21
INNARA

What was *that*? I stared at myself in the mirror. My skin was paler than usual, and with the moonlight, my eyes nearly glowed.

That dream was so vivid, so real. When I woke and Kir saw me...

I groaned. It was like he knew. He knew I had woken up turned on, but it was like he knew just what—who—had turned me on. I could barely look at him.

I splashed cold water on my face before I sat on the closed toilet with my head in my hands. The butterfly touch of his lips on mine was still there, and his hand trailing down my back. Just the memory caused goosebumps to break out on my skin again.

Wall, I was in my underwear, and I'd walked right past him.

He didn't know who I'd dreamed of. He couldn't. How could he possibly?

But that look in his eyes when I managed a glance at him—it was heated yet concerned. And what kind of fool would I be if I actually thought he cared? He was a fae, for Wall's sake, and I knew what he was capable of.

I gripped my hair until my scalp tingled. The events of the dream weren't fading like they usually did. No, it lived in my mind in vivid detail. How I crawled across the floor to kneel between his knees, climbed up, and straddled his lap. Dreams had that ability. We all acted, *could* act on our most base instincts in them. Inhibitions gone. Because otherwise, how was that me?

But the pull between us in the dream had been relentless, like a siren's call. I hadn't been able to ignore it. His touch, his body. I had wanted to feel it all, and there had been no time to waste.

I squeezed my thighs together. Thinking on it wasn't helping.

I still felt the pull, not as strong, but it was there. It had been, ever since he had come to me in the lake, guiding me, helping me, telling me I could do it and that he had me. If I was honest, I'd felt something since I'd first met him. Faerie tricks, I had told myself, but now I wasn't so sure. Out of everyone, I wanted to talk to him, glance at him, be near him.

Touch him.

And something inside me told me he felt it too and fought it.

The sink dripped beside me. A constant reminder that seconds ticked by, morning on its way. I couldn't go back out there right now, not with Kir awake. At least he hadn't knocked on the door.

It had to have been a dream. He'd touched me, acted like he *wanted* to touch me, and he had asked me not to do that just the other day. So, there was no way. Maybe it was a trick. Maybe he sent me a dream to muddle my mind. He could enter minds.

I chewed my lip to the rhythmic *drip drip drip* of the sink.

Either way, his trick or my brain, it was a dream. A very vivid dream, but that was all it was. That was all it could be.

I stood and splashed more cool water on my face and washed my hands. My mind was clearer, and I straightened my shoulders. I couldn't hide in here forever. He had to be back asleep by now. The last thing I wanted was to wait too long and then have to prance in front of everyone in my underwear while they woke up.

Now or never. With a deep breath, I opened the door.

Kir lay on the other couch and didn't move as I passed by. But Dain, on the floor, did. I froze. He rolled over, and his chest rose as he breathed in deep.

After a moment, I crawled into my bedroll.

I laid there for an hour or more until the sun rose. Everyone began to stir. I swear these fae had some alarm clock with all their *we ride at first light* talk.

My muscles tightened as everyone woke, stirring about and then freezing. Silence reigned, and no one moved.

Dain sniffed the air. "Did someone have sex last night? I must have been tired because I slept through it."

No one said a word.

I couldn't help it—I glanced at Kir, who was watching me. My stomach plummeted, and I quickly looked away.

He didn't know. He didn't. It was a dream.

But he knew I woke up turned on. That was the only reason he was watching me.

"Everyone has sexual dreams from time to time," Kir said. "You, out of everyone should, know that, Dain."

Heat rose to my cheeks. I'd never been so mortified in my life—it wasn't as if the rest didn't know it was me. But Kir's comment at least normalized it.

Clove rose out of her bedroll. "Yeah, Dain, it's not as if we haven't all seen your morning wood."

She looked pointedly at his lap.

Dain only stretched out, giving a slight shrug, not a whisper of inhibition. And that was that.

We spent a few days in the haven. The fae rested. Dain and Rylla went stir crazy, but Kir and Clove were content to read. No one discussed the Delves. No one spoke of Dain's fear, and thankfully, Kir never said a word to me about that night.

The only thing I did notice was his watchfulness. The burn on my skin whenever he glanced my way happened more often. I tried to catch him at it, but he had a knack for knowing just when I was going to look up. But it was him. Only his gaze burned me like that, warmed me. Our eyes only met a few times, and though no words were exchanged, my stomach tightened every time.

Otherwise, he stayed away, spending more time in the small office room where he moved his bedroll. Clove argued with him about it, and he snapped up one of his sound barriers faster than I could grasp.

When we left, the landscape changed. Red striated rocks rose up on either side of us. Shades of pink and white undulated like waves through them. Without the trees, the utter silence was the only thing that gave away Faerie was suffocating. No birds screeched on their hunt. No wind howled down the canyon. Only our feet padding on rock and an occasional crumble of dirt from above. After the tree glitch from before, all I could think of was the rock cycle and what if these rock walls that towered above us spontaneously turned to dust.

It was Faerie; it could happen.

"According to Muriel, we should almost be there." Clove broke my train of thought.

For the past hour, we'd descended along the canyon, which made different muscles in my legs ache. After a bend in the rock and some narrow slots, the canyon opened into a flat area with a depressed oval in the center. Clove made her way straight there.

"This is it," she called back to the group.

The rock under us appeared smoothed by water. My feet slipped as I neared it.

Kir knelt and placed his hand on the center of the lowest point, a perfect oval. A pulse vibrated through my feet. His face formed into a scowl. Clove knelt and placed her hand where Kir's had been. Another vibration. She turned to me from her crouched position and waved me in.

I moved, my feet sliding as I came down to their level. My body swayed and Kir appeared to brace himself..

But Clove jumped up and steadied me. "Muriel said we would need you. How about you try with Kir?"

"Try what?"

Clove, already kneeling again, waved me down. "Just put your hand here." She placed her hand next to Kir's and then picked it back up. "Send a tendril of your magic in."

I knelt across from Kir and extended my hand. Grasping my magic came easier for me, especially when I was calm. But I made the mistake of meeting the gaze across from mine, and my breath hitched. His pupils dilated. I had to tear my gaze away. He was so close I could smell him, cedar and fresh snow.

Clove slowly stood and backed away.

I tried to focus on my hand. Looking at Kir was not helpful. I should be thinking of my mother or Nolan, even though I was going to break up with him right before he saved me. Technically, he and I were still together. No thinking things about a fae.

I squeezed my eyes shut. I was a mess.

"Breathe, Innara," Kir said in a low voice. It felt intimate, even though the others could hear, and I wanted to curl into the comfort of it. "There is nothing to worry about. A small tendril is all we need."

I don't know how he did it, but when he spoke to me like that, it exuded calm. I let a breath out slowly through my mouth. There wasn't much life energy around us, so I took from mine. It wouldn't make me too tired.

My tendril made its way out of my hand like a snake seeking the sun. I directed it straight down. A burst of color exploded before my eyes.

"I'll send mine in now," Kir murmured.

Warmth cocooned my tendril. I'd never felt the likes. My witchery conveyed information to me about the health of a person or the needs of a plant. But never anything like this. It was a caress. His magic swirled around mine in a dance before the two twirled together and dove into a dark tunnel. It was sensual and luscious. Something I could get lost in.

Then vertigo slammed into me, and I fell. A scream erupted out of my lips a second before I made impact. I was on the ground, splayed out on my back. Air stalled in my lungs. That had hurt.

From above, Kir peered at me through an oval with gray sky behind him.

"It worked!" He shifted, and a few pebbles fell, hitting my legs. Two feet hung down before he gracefully jumped down beside me.

"A warning would have been nice." I sat up, rubbing my head with a groan.

"I apologize. Are you okay? I hadn't realized it would be a drop down."

From above, Dain shouted, "Move, you two. We need to get in before this door decides to shut and cut one of us in half."

I scrambled away. It hadn't been a long fall, but it shocked me. All limbs and lungs worked properly now.

Clove dropped down and promptly checked me over. "If you have any soreness, I have that draught."

I grimaced, not really wanting any kind of tea from her, the last one helped, but like the witch hazel it had tasted awful.

By the time Rylla and Dain were in, I'd gotten a good look at our surroundings.

Dark was the best word. But the motes I had expected as typical of Faerie were here. I could only see them where the light from above glinted off them. The walls were made of earth and formed a circular room with two tunnels extending in opposite directions.

"Light, Clove," Dain said through clenched teeth.

"Right, sorry." A glowing orb popped up above Clove's extended hand and floated in front of her. It brightened the room and shone off what looked like water running down the inky black walls. The ceiling curved like an earthworm had carved the tunnels.

The light from Cirrelea cut out. The portal we'd fallen through was no longer there, and what remained was a rustic wooden-framed mirror attached to the ceiling. Dain heaved a sigh, and I had to agree. At least fae had better sight, but I suspected his anxiety was high with only one light source.

Clove crouched and searched around before rising. "Okay, let's see if this works." A stone in her hand glowed, making the flesh of her fingers turn pink. She giggled. "I haven't done that in a while, but it should work for a day or two."

She passed one off to Dain, who eagerly took it but then clearly had no idea where to put it. If anything were to happen, rocks in our hands would be replaced by weapons.

"Wait, I have an idea. Necklaces? Rings?" Clove said as she lifted a hand toward Rylla, who tugged something from inside her shirt: a small trinket on a chain. Before I knew it, it glowed with light. Kir unclasped something from around his neck, and Clove set her ring glowing. Dain, however, had nothing except the rock in his palm.

I hesitated but figured I was now a part of this group so I could aid our success. From my pocket, I fished out Nolan's necklace. "Here, wear this, but I want it back when we get out."

Dain's eyes darted from my hand to my face. "Uhhh..."

"Take mine." Kir handed Dain his necklace, which startled Dain even more.

"I can't," Dain said to Kir before his eyes drifted back to my necklace, and he held up his rock. "I have this."

I tried not to show that the rejection stung. I'd saved them. They'd saved me. What did it take to buy a little goodwill?

"Take it. I order it," Kir said before handing his necklace to Clove, who lit it up and gave it to Dain. Kir then held his hand out to me. "I'll wear that one."

Warmth spread through my chest, and I held it out.

Kir snatched the amulet, careful not to touch me. "If anyone takes the risk, it'll be me."

What a fool I was. I crossed my arms, the warmth I'd felt earlier turning into a kindling fire. "I crossed the Wall with a necklace simply in hopes that a fae would have to enchant it and then I could fool one of you into wearing it to murder you. I'm such a wily witch."

Kir stared me down as he took Nolan's now-glowing necklace and clasped it behind his neck. All the fae seemed to hold their breath. Nothing happened.

"Oh look, you're not dead," I said before I held out my arm with my bracelet for Clove to enchant.

Kir grunted as he let the stone fall to his chest, and Clove hummed as she let mine go with a quizzical look on her face.

"Which way?" Kir asked as he looked down the tunnels leading out of the room.

We all made a circle around the room. There were no signs or sigils anywhere.

All eyes fell to me.

"I have no idea," I said. "I'll probably be accused of setting you up."

"Just choose one, drama queen," Rylla said as she looked at her nails, which were now painted black as death.

Insufferable. But if that's how they wanted to play it, so be it.

I picked the one I stood closest to. "This one, then."

WALKING THROUGH DARK TUNNELS THAT HARDLY CHANGED FELT LIKE AN eternity. So far, there had been nothing. No noise, no wind. All had been still.

"I think the witch chose poorly," Dain said followed by an oomph. Kir was next to him, and I imagined he gave Dain an elbow to the side. They had asked me to choose, so it wasn't as if I was the only one at fault.

Funny though, how Kir would touch others but would shy from their touch. It struck me that perhaps it was not that he disliked physical touch. In my dream, he certainly had not. The mere thought of it sent heat flaming to my cheeks, and I cut off that line of thought right then. It was not the time or place.

Besides, my mind made it all up.

I revisited it often, however. Too often. I told myself it was Faerie playing tricks on me, but as much as I hated to admit it, with Nolan I had never felt the way the dream of Kir had made me feel. And I didn't know what to do with that.

Wind howled through the tunnel, cold and biting. This was new.

Everyone stopped, and swords slid out of their scabbards.

"I don't like it," Rylla said.

I hated to agree with her, but yeah, same.

No one handed me a weapon. To them, I *was* a weapon. The healer in me balked at that notion, but perhaps I needed to think more like they did. I was in Cirrelea. Think like the residents. I had attacked the baedour. But then the swirly feeling of *what if* hit me. What if, when I needed to, my magic was out of my grasp? The all-too-familiar feeling of my limbs tingling zinged through me.

Kir turned and raised a brow at me. "What just happened?"

At first, I wasn't sure he was speaking to me. So he repeated the question, tacking my name onto the end of it.

Innara.

I shivered at how he rolled the 'r.'

He waved a hand in front of my face. "Hello?"

I jerked. "What do you mean?"

"Your heart rate sped up, and your breathing went ragged."

"Do you monitor me?" I hated these reminders of how much they could read me. Knew when I was afraid, knew when I slept, knew when I was turned on.

"It was a little hard not to notice it. It's like you were part of the background noise and then came roaring to the front of it, demanding attention."

Dain grunted in agreement from off to the side.

"I was thinking how I should see myself more as a weapon. How you all see me. I'm not trained that way. I'm a healer. My instinct is to help, not to harm. I need to remember I can harm things, but I panicked when I thought about needing to use it to save myself or any of us. What if I can't grasp it?"

We continued walking down the endless and never-changing tunnel. Swords went back in their scabbards. Water dripped, echoing around us.

"What happened to you to make you fear your magic so?" Kir asked.

"I don't fear it."

"You do. Maybe you don't fear the magic itself, but every time you reach out for it, there is a layer of fear." Kir gravitated toward me, leaning in a bit as if he wished to give us privacy, and I tried to control my heart rate, lest I call attention to myself again.

But I didn't move away, even though I knew I should. "You're right. I don't fear the magic. It was the fear of being caught and having to run again if I used it when I shouldn't. There were so many rules. As a kid, it was hard to keep them all straight, and until I learned not to call it when angry or upset, I was always on edge. If I felt too much, I'd call it, and then Mom and I were running."

"And you still fear those things here?"

"Seriously?"

Kir looked ahead a bit of chagrin on his face. "I see how we have not made you feel safe, but I hope we are changing that."

Rylla cleared her throat from behind us.

"It's safe to use your magic here," Kir finished, stepping away.

"Then when I do things like hand my necklace over for any of you to use, it would be nice if it wasn't met with suspicion," I said. "You've gotten your answers on where I am from. It's time to fully trust me."

"Then exactly why did you lead us down this tunnel?" Rylla, who left no conversation to be private, asked.

"You asked me to choose. I chose the one I was near. I had no way of knowing more than any of you did."

"You know how the Delves work," Kir said to Rylla with authority in his voice. "We're in them now. All we can do is push on. Sometimes, all we can go on is our instincts."

"Sometimes, the Delves want to make you work for it." Dain pulled up the rear, his expression tight. This place had to be a certain kind of torture for him, but he had still taken the back of the group with no complaints.

"You make it sound like it's sentient," I said.

"Some theorize it is." He didn't say more.

The very idea made me shiver like we were in the belly of the beast. I tried not to think how long we had already been inside. If it was sentient, would it ever allow us to get to our goal?

No. I couldn't let my thoughts trend in that direction.

We would get there. We would find our way out.

The passageway bent, enough to make me feel like we were headed in the direction we had come from, but the floor pitched. We were headed down. Down into what, I had no idea.

"Are we underground?" I asked.

"No," Clove said. "Think of it like we are not in Cirrelea. We aren't on your side of the Wall. We aren't even on the planet we call home."

"I like that less than underground," I said.

Kir chuckled, and it caused goosebumps to flicker over my skin.

"So this is another dimension," I said. Scientists back home theorized on that. It wasn't a concept I could entirely wrap my head around. "How does time work?"

Clove grinned. "I'm impressed. Time exists here, but our time spent here is only a fraction of our time in Cirrelea. At least, we hope. Our loss of magical power—does it affect places like the Delves, places tethered to ours?" Her smile faded. "I guess we will find out."

CHAPTER 22
INNARA

Macachera hadn't shown himself, and no one mentioned his name. We studiously ignored the biggest worry in all of our minds—except for maybe Dain. I'd caught him pulling the rock out of his pocket a few times to check it still glowed, even though Kir's necklace lit the way in front of him. We all lapsed into silence.

"You should practice grasping your magic," Kir said, startling everyone.

"Do you think that wise?" Rylla spoke in a hushed, tense tone as she lengthened her stride to walk beside him.

"I've been thinking. She's right. We got our answers on where she is from. It's time we trust her. If anything were to happen and we are all drained of power"—he held a hand up as her mouth opened to object—"she is the only one who could do anything. Like the baedour. So, yes, I believe it is wise for her to practice. I'd prefer her to be able to harness her power quickly when needed."

"She's a witch."

"She is. Out of all of us, if I can manage to look beyond that, so can you." He glanced back to me. "Try. Perhaps we can help."

Rylla dropped back near Dain. I didn't like her eyes on my back. They felt like tiny daggers stabbing between my shoulder blades.

I drew in a deep breath, reaching out for Clove's arm as I closed my eyes. She'd guide me. At my touch, she pushed her elbow away from her body before pulling it in and slipping a warm hand over mine. But even though I couldn't see Dain and Rylla, I could feel how they tensed. My kneejerk reaction was anger that they thought I would do something, but then I tried to see it from their point-of-view. Clove was their friend, their partner.

"I won't harm her," I said, opening my eyes to grin at Clove.

Clove's face lit up. "She won't. I'm her favorite."

In front of us, Kir snorted.

Her lightheartedness was what I needed. I shut my eyes again and focused inward, sinking into myself, noticing my breath as I drew in and let it out. Walking was an additional challenge. I couldn't quite put all my focus on centering myself.

I called on my witchery, making my skin tingle. I opened myself to the life around me. There was a blip of green, and then it was gone as my toe caught on an uneven surface. "I almost had it."

"Sorry," Clove murmured.

"Not your fault."

"Try again," Kir said from ahead.

I pressed my lips into a line. Recentering myself, I reached out. My foot snagged again, and I gritted my teeth against the impulse to flail and open my eyes. Green wavered before me, flickering in then out and back in again. "I have it."

"Good. Now release it," Kir's voice was closer.

I did, and the green vanished.

"Do it again, but this time try to open your eyes once you have it."

I'd never opened my eyes before when under duress. Healing didn't really need it. I let my instincts and the feedback from the magic guide me. So much had to do with blood that magic just flowed through the circulatory system. An entire physical could be done in less than a minute. No eyesight needed, and I had become accustomed to closing my eyes and relying on all my other senses when I actually could use it. Because when it came to humans, it was the old-fashioned way.

"I can try." I closed my eyes. Centering came easier each time. That was an improvement, especially since the ground was not even. My ability to split my focus came along.

The green life of each of us popped into my dark vision.

And that was it. Nothing else.

I hung onto the witchery, not wanting to let it go. I'd never let myself just revel in it before. At home, it was grasp it if I could, use it, then release. Quick. It always had to be quick. We never wanted to hold it longer than we had to. It was too much of a risk.

But here, I could. These fae no longer thought I was going to unleash unholy death upon them and smite them with my will. Well, maybe Rylla did.

I let my witchery flow through me, felt the glorious tingle of it in my veins, and then I released it.

"Again," Kir said.

HOURS LATER, THE FLOOR WAS COLD AND HARD, AND I WRAPPED MY FUR-lined cloak tight around me. It wasn't that the Delves were cold like the Winter Court. In comparison, they were balmy, but we'd been in them for hours with no sun, not even the one clouded over by gray in Cirrelea.

The idea of no sun and being in some alternate dimension got to me. We needed to find this stone and get out of here.

Our group formed a circle, enough space between us to lay down. That position felt too vulnerable to me. Macachera lingered somewhere in this thing, and that wind blew through every now and again. Sometimes successively, sometimes an hour in between. It felt like he breathed down our neck as he watched, waiting to pounce.

"I have first watch," Kir said from across the small widening.

I sat with my back against the wall. The other three curled up on the floor, already listening to their lord's orders to sleep. Soft snores emanated from Dain almost immediately. Figured. Across the way, Kir watched me, so I slid down the wall a bit and closed my eyes. I reached for my witchery, and it was right there. The green lives of my companions glowed brilliantly. I released it. Kir shifted with some scraping.

"Sorry. I should have warned you," I said.

"It wasn't that. You should practice. But you should also sleep."

The order was apparent, but I opened my eyes anyway. He'd promised not to use his magic on me without my consent. He leaned against the wall, a sword across his lap—the scraping noise must have been taking it off his back. I hugged myself under the cloak. Ever since that dream, I hadn't been able to look at him the same way.

I swallowed my nerves. "Thank you for the practice earlier, for helping me. When you aren't a jerk, you're actually pretty nice."

He'd been looking down the tunnel, but now his gaze scalded me before the side of his mouth quirked. The silence stretched out, and I wasn't sure he was going to acknowledge that I'd spoken.

"You're welcome." He paused. "Sleep."

I let the back of my head rest on the wall and stared up into the blackness. Our small lights on our jewelry seemed to be eaten by the darkness. But I couldn't sleep. I was hyperaware of the fae man across from me. Something in me kept telling me to get up, sit by him.

But he wouldn't welcome that, Mr. No Touch.

I tried for my magic with my eyes open. I had been able to do it a few times earlier. Maybe staring into the blackness helped. It was like my eyes were closed. The green lit up, and so did that gray rope between my tattoo and Kir's.

I thinned a small amount of my life energy down to a thread, barely visible, and touched the rope. Across from me, Kir let out a hissing breath.

I dropped it all, a vice clamped around my heart.

A look at him told me he was fine. He rubbed his wrist.

"What did you do?" There was no anger in his words or his face.

Should I tell him? But wasn't he the one who'd helped me get out of that frozen lake? He knew that rope existed.

"The connection between us, between our tattoos—I touched it with my magic."

"Warn me next time. And sleep, for Wall's sake."

I let a smile cross my lips. "What is it?"

"What is what?"

"The connection. The rope I climbed—that you told me to climb —to get out of that lake."

He pulled his legs up and pointed his sword into the ground. "Clove told you what bargains entail, yes?"

I nodded, and he gestured with his hand like a magician when they finish a trick.

"But why can I see it?"

"Witch magic. Not my forte." He was hedging.

"Humor me. Speculate on why I can see it."

"You're not going to sleep, are you?"

I let out a soft snicker, not wanting to admit how his warm tone pleased me or how again I wanted to sit by him. This time I let my instinct win. His willingness to chat made me brave, bold. I picked my way around the sleeping forms. I chose a spot a foot away from him and sat down. "My mind is spinning. I can't sleep when I can't shut it down."

"I know the feeling." He turned his head and gave me a secret smile.

My heart skipped, and I chastised myself. Smiles like that could devastate someone, and my mind went back to that dream and how it felt for him to touch me. "Speculate, Lord Kir."

"Is that an order?" The humor in his tone nearly knocked me over.

"If you want it to be." Wall, was I flirting with him? I pressed a hand to my cheek.

He let out an amused snort but said nothing for a moment.

"Don't do that." His tone was now serious, quiet.

"Do what?" But I had a feeling about what he meant, and embarrassment rose to my cheeks.

He didn't respond but then finally said. "The rope is a tie, a bond. I won't speculate on why you can see it. Uneducated speculating gets us in trouble." He paused. "You really should sleep." Another deep breath. "I can smell your embarrassment. Don't be. I started it, and I know better."

His words weren't quite a balm, but they did take out some of the sting. If he was implying I shouldn't flirt, then he had admitted that he was flirting too. But what did it mean he should know better? My head still spun. I was never going to sleep now.

I cleared my throat. "Can you help me along? Just a smidge?"

"I have your permission?"

"Yes." At least in sleep, I wouldn't mortify myself.

A tingle on my forehead and my muscles relaxed, followed by a heaviness in my eyes. I slid them closed and into slumber.

CHAPTER 23
KIR

My watch was nearly over, though I was tempted to spell Dain to continue sleeping. He'd do his job, but his fear would make the watch hard on him. But that wasn't the entire truth. I wouldn't be able to sleep. Just like Innara, my mind spun, and sleep would be hard to find.

Why couldn't I help myself? Forget that she was my mate. I genuinely found myself liking her. She had a combination of vulnerability and backbone. All that laced with humor and a nice dose of snark. I had teased her—flirted, truly. She had stolen the air from my lungs when she suggested ordering me about.

And she knew of the bond the bargain created. Thankfully, that was the one she saw. But I suspected it existed so strongly due to our mate bond. Bargains tended to bring it out more, another way to tether. And if a tether already existed, the bargain would act as reinforcement.

Dain rolled over. I never knew how he did it. An internal clock or something, but it never failed.

"My turn," he said as he sat up and gripped his sword that lay next to him.

Innara was still next to me. I had gotten up and moved down the tunnel a few times, but I had always come back to the spot where I had been. We couldn't touch, but the nearness was pleasant.

Dain moved to where she had been across from me to start. He said nothing about how she had moved. Smart of him. Maybe he sensed how on edge I was.

With my sword near, I closed my eyes. I hadn't drifted to my mental place since that night when Innara had met me there. Fear kept me away. At least that was what I told myself. Having a mate upended my life. Keeping my mate would upend it more. Or completely end it.

But now, I needed it to still my mind.

I quickly found my black room, picturing my living room and the roaring fire, and they appeared. I sprawled out on the couch, where Innara and Clove had sat not long after I'd found out she was my mate. But I didn't want to think of Innara. I needed a distraction, something to cool my heels, remind me why I held her at arm's length.

So I went back to a time when Violet had been in the room with me.

She stood in the archway to the kitchen, a glass of water in her hand. Her flirty dress fell off her shoulder, and her red hair flowed loosely down her back. She was sensual with a note of wild woman to her, but now I knew how black her heart was.

How hadn't I seen through the ruse? Embarrassment threatened to throw me out of the vision-memory completely. How had I not suspected? How had I not seen that Gaelin threw someone who fulfilled my *type* right at me?

Violet smiled and padded barefoot across the lush carpet as I lay on the couch.

"Everything all right?" She brushed a few hairs away from my forehead.

I threw an arm behind my head and reached out to her with my other, threading our fingers. "Gaelin is up to his usual antics. Nothing to worry yourself over."

She leaned over to place her glass on the side table, giving me a cleavage shot, which I now realized was entirely calculated.

Violet sat on the edge of the couch, wiggling her hips to get me to move over and make way. I loved the move. And I did as intended. I moved to the back of the couch and rolled to my side, so she could be the little spoon.

"We're alone tonight, yes?" She twisted in my arms to speak.

I liked the sound of that. "Mmhmm." I nipped at her ear as my arms wrapped around her. "Both Rylla and Dain went to Fale Seren."

I paused, realizing I'd named the village.

She giggled. "Don't stop. If we have the place to ourselves, I have a number of surfaces I'd like to get to know you better on." She rolled over and placed her hand on my stomach as she bit her lip, before she trailed it down to gently rub over the ridge that told her I liked everything she said. My mind went blank as she leaned in and our lips met.

The vision did nothing for me now except mortify me. How had I been so stupid? I'd given her the village name. She knew it and immediately distracted me with sex before I could think better of it and send Haze.

The vision continued, and the kiss lengthened. But something changed. My embarrassment faded. I didn't want to stop. The frenzy that it began with calmed. Everything turned liquid and languid. I wanted to draw it out.

She moaned, stirring something in me.

But that wasn't right. Violet and I hadn't taken our time. Within moments, we had both stripped bare and made good on her suggestion.

And then the scent hit me. Jasmine and sage.

My eyes popped open. The red-haired witch was gone. Instead, Innara lay beside me. She had her hand on my cheek, stroking it ever so gently.

I pulled back to get my bearings. I didn't think.

The words flew out of my mouth. "You can't be here. Violet was just here."

"It's my dream. I think I can be here." Her voice was husky and drunk on our kiss. But then her face crumpled into a frown. "Violet?"

I sat up. I should leave the vision. Innara thought these were dreams, not real.

She followed my lead, so we could sit next to each other on the couch. "She's the witch you fell in love with."

Damn it, Clove. I ran a hand down my face. "Love is a strong term. Briefly enamored with is closer. Eternally mortified another."

Her hand reached out to touch my knee but pulled away, so I grabbed her hand and placed it there. I couldn't be sure, but I swore she whispered, "Just a dream."

Innara scooted closer, our hips and thighs pressing together. "Tell me about her."

In my head, alarm bells rang. I should leave. This was dangerous for me, for my heart.

She let out a small laugh. "This is weird, touching you. Not being allowed to must make me crave it. Taboo."

I ignored her comment and fisted my hands together in front of me. "She was enchanting. She was everything I wanted—thought I wanted. But there was a reason for all that."

I hesitated. If I told her these things, she'd figure out these weren't dreams. I'd be letting her in, but maybe she'd see me. This place seemed to drop her inhibitions, her prejudices. She followed her instincts more.

I leaned back. "Decades ago, Gaelin was my best friend. He knew me like no one else. And now, he uses that knowledge. He trained a witch in what he knew appealed to me.

"And you blame yourself for falling for her, for it." She craned her neck to glimpse my face.

"Of course I do. As Lord of the Winter Court, I don't have the luxury of flings. They can be too costly. And I learned that lesson."

She pursed her lips. "She was a fling?"

"Yes." She wasn't, even if I wished she had been, but I spoke with my mate. I couldn't tell her that I'd considered marrying Violet, even knowing that I supposedly had a mate out there. A mate who hadn't shown herself.

"What did she do?" Innara asked.

"She gained my trust. She was in my house for months, becoming a part of us. She respected when we had to meet and discuss protections of the Winter Court. She would leave and explore my property. I trusted her. All of us trusted her. She hunted with Rylla. Played board games with Dain. She insinuated herself into our lives. Until I slipped one day and mentioned the name of one of the villages where the majority of our people live. She distracted me immediately, so I didn't consider it too much. And before the distraction was over, she drugged me."

"How?"

I raised a brow at her.

"Sorry. I shouldn't ask that. This all makes it seem hopeless that you all will ever fully trust me." A look passed across her face before she met my eyes. "But this is a dream, isn't it?"

I clasped her hands in mine. Avoiding the truth did none of us any good.

A jolt ripped me from the vision. I gasped, my eyes popping open.

Dain was there, shaking my shoulder. Wind whipped around us. Innara, beside me, jumped up. Our eyes met, and I tried to tell her with our shared look what I wanted to say in the vision.

It was real, it was so very real.

But the wind ripped at our hair, at our cloaks. It pushed us back the way we came.

"We need to move." I tried to push forward the way we were headed before resting. The wind only increased. The fae in our group could push against it, one dogged step after another. But Innara couldn't. The wind pushed her backwards, her feet sliding and bumping along the uneven ground. Dain grabbed her before she slid past us.

An image of her flying backwards into the black made me shiver, but Dain had her. She was okay.

Every step we took increased the wind. My skin pushed along my skull like mush.

"This is no use. Turn around," I said. Instinct told me not to allow this wind to drive us, but we lacked the strength we once had.

As soon as everyone faced the other direction, the wind stopped.

"It's herding us," Rylla said.

I agreed. I didn't like it one bit, but we couldn't push forward.

"Backtrack?" Dain asked.

"Looks like it. But we know the Delves. It doesn't mean we'll traverse the same tunnel we walked before."

The wind had been a lot even for us fae. Dain gently put Innara's feet on the ground, and her arms slipped from around his neck. I wanted to roar at their touch, but he'd saved her.

Once she was steady, he backed away.

We didn't walk far past where we'd rested when a light appeared ahead.

Dain grumbled. I reached for my swords on my back, and the metallic scrape rang out as weapons came out of Rylla's and Dain's scabbards. Clove nocked an arrow, her smaller frame crouching low into a hunter's stance. Only Innara made no move. I selected a knife from my bandolier. Iron. She might need it.

I slowed my pace to hand it to her.

Rylla's eyes flashed, but at this point, we either trusted Innara or drugged her. There was no in-between.

The light led us to a room off the tunnel. It hadn't existed before. There was no way we'd missed a door like this, especially a large, open one.

We all squinted as we entered, hands up to shield our eyes. Mirrors surrounded a brazier in the center, the light reflecting around the room.

"What is this place?" Innara asked.

"A crossroads."

A question passed over her features. She didn't understand.

"The mirrors are roads within the Delves, within Cirrelea. This is what we have been searching for." I walked around the room. Macachera ages ago would lead you to these rooms and guide you through. He knew exactly where each one went. Now, just the thought of him made me fear I could conjure him.

"So which one do we take?" Innara's voice was tight, agitated.

"I believe this is where you come in. Muriel said you would be able to lead us, so..." Dain raised his arms, beckoning her into the center before he swept them past a few mirrors.

Her gaze flicked to mine. I nodded. Dain was right.

A wind blew through, lifting my hair. It felt teasing, less like wind blowing past my face and more like someone lifting my hair for fun.

"Spread out. Look for anything," I said as I headed toward a mirror. There had to be some way to tell where these went, and we needed to find it fast.

Everyone moved, all feeling the same urgency.

Clove shouted about symbols, Old Fae ones.

"Keep looking," I said.

Somehow, Old Fae didn't seem like what we needed.

"I have one that doesn't look fae," Rylla said from across the room. I crossed to where she stood, peering at the frame.

The mirrors didn't all reflect this world. Maybe that was a clue. The one I passed didn't show me in the room, though it did show the other mirrors. They were all different. Wood frames, metal frames. Some had vines twisting around the edge, while others had intricate metalwork like lace.

How much of all that was the code? At the top of the one Rylla stood by, there indeed was a symbol. A groan echoed through the room, causing us all to stop before refocusing. My heart clanged in my chest.

"Innara, come look at this one," I called.

She came immediately. At the top of the plain wooden frame was a sigil. She drew her fingers over it. "It's a witch symbol that means 'earth' or 'terra.'"

"Could it mean 'stone'?" I asked.

She screwed up her face and then nodded. "Yes, I think it could."

Next to us, the silver of the mirror bulged. I had to resist the urge to put my arm in front of Innara and lead her away. The surface snapped back, and what appeared to be iron filings poured forth.

Macachera.

"In the mirror," I shouted.

Dain and Clove ran across the room. Clove went right through the one Innara and Rylla identified.

Next to us, the iron filings formed into feet and building knees.

Time was short. He'd know which mirror we went through. I was sure of it.

I turned back, readying myself to jump through the mirror, but Innara stood there, staring in horror at Macachera. Rylla and Dain had gone through.

"Shit." I grabbed her arm with my gloved hands and heaved her through with me.

CHAPTER 24
INNARA

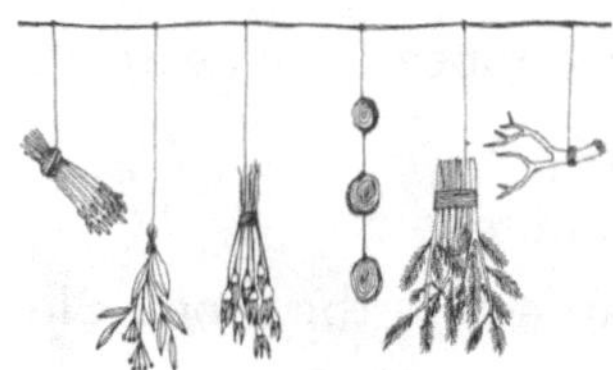

My back slammed against something hard and warm before we hurtled through the mirror. Cold slime and pressure and then I was out the other side, tumbling onto a rock floor. Kir rolled away before standing up, putting distance between us.

We hadn't entered a room. The mirror had spat us out into a tunnel. Rylla was right about being herded. There was nowhere to go but forward.

"Run!" Kir shouted before we all took off.

After a few minutes, my breath sawed through my lungs. Running had never been my thing. But these fae seemed as if they could run for hours. My legs burned and slowed. I couldn't match them.

From behind me, Rylla shouted, "The witch can't keep up. She's slowing down."

Kir glanced back over his shoulder. "Dain!"

"Move," Rylla said as she pushed past me.

Dain rushed me and grabbed my waist, throwing me over his shoulder. The position was terrible for trying to get my breath back, as my abdomen bounced against his shoulder again and again. If there was anything in my stomach, I was going to retch it up.

"Keep an eye behind us and tell me if you see it," he said as he flicked a finger behind us. A spark flew from his finger and sped down the tunnel until it grew large enough to light up the area we rapidly left behind. I didn't want to think what that cost him to use his precious magic to light an area we had left.

I tried to raise my head, but the bouncing made it near impossible.

"Steady yourself however you need to," he said. "I'll worry later how a human inappropriately touched me."

I rolled my eyes, but I sank my hands around his belt just above his butt to hold myself up. I couldn't do it indefinitely, but with small breaks, I could manage.

Behind us, something morphed into a cloud of a million pieces, bouncing back and forth down the passage. It was faster than us, but it was far back.

"I see something ahead," Kir shouted.

"It's behind us," I shouted out, which seemed to have the effect of each fae finding even more speed. Dain passed Rylla, who threw her arms out. The tunnel between us and Macachera filled with wall after wall of ice.

Dain ran into a room and dropped me unceremoniously on my feet next to Kir, who looked as if he might rip Dain's head off.

"Search again," Kir said. "A symbol you don't recognize or, for Innara, one you do."

We all spread out, moving from one to another with one eye on the icy entrance. The wind picked up, and the room groaned. Ice shattered.

Macachera was closing in.

I found the symbol quickly on a mirror with a similar frame as the last room. "Found it!"

But I was too late. Macachera flew into the room, effectively dividing Kir and me from the others.

Macachera's form appeared out of the cloud of iron filings, sifting into feet clad in boots with a spike on the toe. The skull of something like a cow was his head. A shifting cloak disguised his movements as it whipped in a nonexistent wind. Fingers like claws stretched out as he reached behind him and pulled a black sword out.

"Too late, Cursed One," he said.

Kir selected a knife from his bandolier and threw it at Macachera before shouting, "Run! Our lives are more important. Get out however you can."

The knife slung through Macachera's chest, and the iron filings burst out behind him like blood with a gunshot. What would have been Macachera's ribcage collapsed like a building under a controlled demolition.

Kir, beside me, made sure the others climbed through a mirror on the other side of the room as Macachera swung wildly at them, only temporarily and not fully incapacitated. Once the others were through, Kir said, "Let's go."

I jumped through the mirror with the witch symbol. I tumbled, falling to my knees.

Another room. Not a crossroads, an intersection. This one held a pedestal and two mirrors. I groaned, but as Kir tumbled in beside me, breathing hard, something moved on the other side of the room.

A fae man with curling, dark blond hair and icy blue eyes glanced over his shoulder at us. As handsome as what I had imagined the fae would be, so pretty it hurt. Something was in his pale-skinned hand. He grinned and held it up like he was toasting, taunting us.

It had to be the stone. Was this Gaelin?

I fisted my hands at my side, reaching for my magic. But it slipped through my fingers, blipping in then out.

Kir leapt to his feet and lunged.

The man stepped through the far mirror, casually, like he hadn't a care in the world and definitely not as if another fae was charging him from fifty feet away. A relaxed hand held the side of the mirror. That hand was clad in black leather.

Then he ducked his head and disappeared.

Kir's body slammed into the mirror and bounced backward. He sat up with a groan before slamming his gloved hands on the floor. "Fuck!"

I cringed as more curse words poured out of his mouth. Not that it offended my sensitive ears but I didn't know what to do. Our group was split, and now the stone had been stolen literally from right beneath our noses. That monster was likely to follow us into this room, and the way out was blocked. We were well and truly screwed.

Kir scrabbled to his feet.

"Get up." His breath came out short.

I sat on the floor, staring, hope draining from me.

"Get. Up."

"That man. He had the stone. We lost it." I babbled. He knew this, yet I still said it.

"Gaelin." He paced, running a hand through his hair before stopping in front of the pedestal. I knew what he saw. A small velvet pillow with a small indentation where something very recently had rested.

"That was Gaelin?" Why was I asking? Of course it was.

Kir didn't bother to answer me but kicked the mirror we had come through. It clattered to the ground but didn't shatter.

"The others better have made it out," he said. "We should break this."

"It's the only working mirror." The words rushed out of me as he drew one of the swords on his back.

"Macachera is on the other side." He looked at me like I was daft and raised the sword above his head.

"Stop. You'll strand us here

Kir lowered the sword. "Macachera is on the other side of that mirror, and if I know Gaelin, then *that* mirror"—he used his sword to point at the one he'd bounced off of— "won't be blocked forever. He'll let go of the magic that turned it solid. None of us can waste our magic longer than we need to. It has repercussions."

We had minutes, if not seconds, before Macachera tried to enter—Kir hadn't incapacitated him that badly—unless he'd followed the others. And I surprised myself as I hoped he didn't follow them. Somehow along the way, I had begun to feel as if this was Kir and me needing to find the stone and they were along for the ride.

"You're certain?" I asked.

"What in life is certain?" he replied with a shrug.

I sighed. "I don't need philosophy right now."

"I'm as certain as I can be. Besides, the Delves are not static. At some point, something would happen that would allow us to get out." He twirled his sword. "I think."

I ignored that last bit. It didn't help. "Or it allows Macachera to enter anyway."

This was not my idea of a fun adventure. The choice before us felt like damned if we did and damned if we didn't.

"Or that," he said before he raised the sword above his head again. "Yes?"

Our eyes locked, and I nodded.

"Do it." I turned my back and pressed my fingers into my ears, eyes squeezed shut.

From behind me, an almighty crash preceded glass tinkling.

We were safe for now.

"How long do you think we have to wait?" I drifted to the other mirror, touching the surface with one finger. Solid.

"A few minutes," Kir said.

A few minutes to stand here, wait, and think. My mind drifted directly to the dream. I'd had no time to consider it yet. We'd been up and running as soon as I'd woken from it.

Kir stared into the mirror and placed one gloved hand onto the side, propping himself up. When I'd woken, our eyes had met, and he'd seemed like he had been trying to tell me something. From sitting on the couch, talking, to being wrenched out of the dream to him looking at me, it was as if he was trying to finish what we had been speaking about.

"Was it real?" I asked.

"Was what real?" He turned his head to consider me, the light from the mirror dancing across his features.

He was so close. When had he stopped constantly backing away from me? My cheeks flashed hot. I didn't want to say it, but I needed to. I needed to know.

"The couch. Telling me about Violet. Was it real?" The blood in my cheeks grew hotter and ran down into my neck and chest, painting me in scalding red. "And the other night..."

I couldn't finish it.

I wanted to hate it, hate him, hate all the fae, but I didn't. Not anymore.

"It was real," he said, his voice tender and low, which somehow made it worse.

The words hit me like bullets, and I stared at the ground. My breath came and went quickly.

It was real. It was real. It was real.

My instinct was to run and hide, but there was nowhere to go. Probably a good thing we broke the other mirror. I might have considered throwing myself at Macachera's mercy.

His hand slid off the mirror as he straightened, body turning to face me. "I should apologize for allowing things to get as far as they did that one night."

I sensed him shifting and imagined him rubbing the back of his neck.

"Look at me," he whispered.

I couldn't, but I found words. "No need to apologize." Tears welled in my eyes, and I willed them not to fall. "I threw myself at you. I'm the one who should apologize."

Kir stepped closer, and my breath hitched as he reached a gloved hand out to tip my chin up, cool leather when I craved the warmth of his skin.

"No apology necessary. You didn't know what was happening,

but you should know you went from a spark to an inferno. Beautiful to behold."

I had so many questions.

He dropped his hand away and stepped back. He dragged a finger on the mirror, and it sank in.

It was time to go. He was already reaching a gloved hand out to me.

The coldness of the mirror cooled my inflamed cheeks, but I was barely steady on my feet before Kir pushed me to the side, followed by him hissing in pain and the echoing clank of metal on metal.

In front of me, multiple Kirs and multiple Macacheras were dueling. Macachera towered over Kir, but Kir appeared to hold his own, fending off cleaving attacks and forcing Macachera to dance as well. Hundreds of mirrors filled the room and hung from the ceiling. The light from the sconces peppered around, reflecting off some and devoured by others.

No sign of Gaelin.

Two more arms formed from Macachera. He raised them and swiftly heaved them toward the ground. A pulse of wind bellowed from him. My hair blew back from my face, but that was no regular wind. Every single mirror in the room winked out. Darkness descended.

A raspy, grave chuckle emanated from Macachera.

He'd cut off any way out we had. I frantically searched the room. All black. Only sconces lit the area.

But wait. There was one.

On the ceiling.

Now, in the dim light, Kir and Macachera were easy to find, particularly Kir, who wore Nolan's glowing necklace. Mirrors fell to the floor in their wake as they swung their swords and crashed through them. My heart squeezed to the sounds of tinkling glass and crunching wood.

Kir's leg twisted in the bent frame of one, and Macachera dove for the opening. Kir threw an arm out, and Macachera ricocheted off whatever shield Kir had put up.

"Innara, do something!" Kir roared.

"Can't you do something? Crush his mind?"

My yell attracted Macachera who turned and eyed me. His face was a skull, yet somehow, he was still able to express himself in the cock of his head, the balance of his shoulders.

I was an easy kill, and he was going to take it.

"I've been searching," Kir called. "His mind is not with him."

Macachera let out a maniacal laugh.

I stepped backwards, my shoulder bumping into something—a frame of a mirror. *Careful!* They may not be on now, but Macachera had demonstrated that he controlled them. I moved. Too risky to be too close.

Macachera lunged toward me, and so did Kir. He slid through shattered glass with an arm outstretched before he slammed into me, but he held his head at an awkward angle to keep it from bumping into the top of mine.

"We're shielded," Kir breathed. "For now."

Macachera paced in front of us like a caged beast.

Kir kept an arm around my waist and one up in front of us, pivoting us as Macachera got too far around one side.

"Do something," Kir whispered near my ear. "I can't shield us forever."

This was the situation I'd feared. But now I knew I could use my healing magic to hurt. What gave life could take it away.

Later, I'd think about how I really felt about that.

I reached for my magic, but nothing happened.

Kir's breath heaved in my ear and stirred my hair. He couldn't hold it for long, stretched too thin.

I tried again. Nothing. "I can't."

Kir slowly backed us up a step, glass crunching under our feet, as he whispered to me, "My shield is weakening. You can do this. Be the woman from the other night. Be an inferno. Fearless and bold, seizing what she wanted. It's within you."

His words bolstered me. I closed my eyes and reached out. I put my hands on his arm, with his clothes between us, and drew on the feel of his solidness. His life popped into my view.

But not Macachera's. Instead, Macachera was a cloud of sparkling gray.

"He's not alive," I whispered.

"I gathered, with the no-mind thing," Kir said, stepping us back again, creating space.

Macachera raised his sword and poked at the shield. The iron filings broke apart when it touched it and reformed into his sword as he pulled it away. His head tossed like a bug flew around it. The gray magic undulated and wove through him, around him.

Macachera twirled his sword, and I knew he wasn't going to let us go, whether we had the stone or not. He saw us as a threat to it either way.

I mentally grabbed a handful of the gray sparkles within him and tugged.

Macachera growled and staggered backwards as his sword evaporated.

I pulled with all my might, but he was so strong, matching me. I attempted to crush the sparkles. It only made him stamp his booted foot and snort the air.

I gritted my teeth, throwing my hands up before me.

The sparkly rope between Kir and me fluttered.

An idea formed as the mirror above twinkled. I still didn't know what magic the rope represented. But life magic could give life—and it could take life. A water witch needed only the smallest water thread of her own to control a river.

And whatever had made Macachera, I had my own right here in front of me, connecting me to Kir.

I thinned a thread of it and snaked it along the ground, hoping my pulling on Macachera distracted him enough. I poised my thin thread of our bond beneath his feet, directing it like a cobra strike, plunging into the heart of him.

Macachera let out an unholy gasp that threatened to explode my eardrums.

I reversed direction. Instead of pulling, I pushed. Kir dropped his shield and aided me with a lash of air.

Macachera wasn't ready for it, and we lifted him up, up, up and shoved him into the mirror. Instead of the usual syphoning of black particles, his entire being went through like a rock hitting water, circles emanating from where I had dropped him in the center of it.

As the last iron filing went through, the mirrors winked on, illuminating the room.

Kir whooped, and I breathed out. *I'd done it.* Kir watched me with an expression I couldn't place on his face.

"You did it," he said. A leather-clad finger grazed my cheek and pushed a few hairs behind my ear. He was so close. I wanted to clasp him to me as elation made me dizzy and a warmth stole over my body.

Kir's hand dropped as he grimaced, breaking the moment. He stepped away, and with one lash of air, he smashed the mirror. "We shouldn't waste any time."

He had been backing us up toward a mirror the entire time, choosing it out of all these others, his faith in me evident, or at least hopeful.

Together, we jumped.

CHAPTER 25
INNARA

We were out of the Delves.

Sunlight beat down on us, causing me to squint and shade my eyes as I heaved a breath out. "Will it...will he come out?"

Kir, face pale and sweaty, sprawled on the ground beside me. He shook his head. "He stays in the Delves. I only hope we drew him away from the others and they are out now."

"How will we find them?"

"We won't." He sat up with a groan, dusting dirt out of his hair. It was one of the few times I got a glimpse of his slightly pointed ears, which made me wonder if he kept his hair longer for a reason. "Haze will find us all soon enough and apprise of where the others are."

"And where are we?" The air was hot and dry as dust. Sweat beaded on my forehead and between my shoulder blades. I slipped my cloak off my shoulders.

"Summer." Kir grated out. "We need to be on our guard. Gaelin's forces have a tendency to shoot first and ask questions later."

"Could this be good luck? We could intercept Gaelin with the stone?" The stone was my key to leaving this place. It being in

Gaelin's hands did not sit well with me—or Kir. We had been so close to having it too. There had to be a way. We had to get it back. It's all I could see going forward.

Kir turned, eyeing me. "Perhaps. I don't like our odds. I'd feel better about that plan if the others were here. We should get our bearings. I know the latest intel of the area. It should be easy to figure out where we are, and then we can plan better."

I stood, wiping the dirt off my backside. Underneath my feet, detritus crunched. The area reminded me of a cornfield in autumn after the harvest.

Kir got to his feet. "Looks like Gaelin has been trying some things."

"What do you mean?"

He gestured. "This is recently dead. He was trying to grow crops. Or someone was, at least."

I reached my hand out to touch a stalk.

But Kir stopped me. "Don't."

"Don't what?"

"Don't use your magic on their land."

"I wasn't going to." I ripped a leaf off before cracking a stalk in half, examining it, parts of it crumbling into dust. "But why would I not want to?"

Kir's shoulders relaxed. "Gaelin has spies all over, watching. If you did something, that wouldn't go unnoticed. Let's head to that hill, where I can get a look."

The dead field sprawled around the hill. An army of brown. My fingers itched to heal some of it, but I heeded Kir's warning. Beside me, Kir panted up the hill with his hand inside his jacket.

"It's hot. Why don't you take the jacket off and your gloves," I said.

He ignored me.

"That's a good way to get heat exhaustion. But maybe you're not familiar with that, having had powers all these years."

"Centuries."

I glanced at him, wishing for the momentary tenderness back in the Delves and the dreams. "Whatever. I know I'm a puny human."

He chuckled, which made me smile. Who would have thought he had a sense of humor? Actually, I had known, but it was nice to have it directed my way.

"Well, the bad news is we are nowhere near our intended path," he said as he took in the view. Below us was the brown field. To the east was a rock cliff far in the distance, and behind us to the north lay towering mountains covered in snow. We hadn't seen those in the Autumn Court. It seemed odd to me that they would be in the Spring Court.

"And the good news?" I asked.

"The actual court is not that far." He pointed south, where I could just make out the glint of windows on the horizon.

Kir swayed.

"Whoa! Are you okay?" I reached for him, and he backed away.

"Don't touch me."

I groaned, hating this whole fear of being touched. He certainly hadn't minded it in the dreams. "Did Macachera hurt you?" I remembered a hiss coming out of Kir at some point during that fight. "Can't fae heal fast?"

But their powers were draining. He needed help. I stepped toward him again.

But he backed away. "Innara, you can *not* touch me."

"I have to touch you, to heal you. Let me see."

"Stay back." He flung out a hand, and I bounced off a shield.

"Are you kidding me? You won't let me touch you when you need help?"

"I don't let anyone touch me."

"Why is that?" I bit off, wanting to say something snarky about how he was too good for everyone. But now that I knew something was wrong, I could see the pain etched into his features. He was fae —he didn't sweat in this heat. He was sweating because of whatever wound he had. "Explain. Because you don't look good, and I can help. I'm a healer."

I remembered his story about Violet. He trusted me, yet he didn't. And I couldn't blame him for that.

"You're going to have to trust me. I haven't tried to kill you." I tried a soft smile.

"But you will if you touch me."

"I promise I won't."

He shook his head and made his way down the path. I followed, sensing he wanted to be less visible. We walked a path for a few minutes before he heaved a sigh and spoke. "That isn't what I mean."

I didn't get it.

"The witch called me Cursed One," he said, and I nodded not wanting to interrupt him. "That's because I *am* cursed. No one can touch me. I can't be physically touched by love."

I stopped dead. What in the world? "For how long?"

"Decades now."

Oh. *Ohhhhhh.*

"A touch can kill you?"

"It would kill me, yes."

"But you've grabbed me, touched me when you had to." I frowned as he raised his hand clad in black. "The gloves," I said, "so you don't accidentally touch anyone."

"I did, and I was...uncomfortable, but sometimes other instincts win out over the fear."

"But...I don't love you." Truth be told, I didn't know what it was to love someone.

Kir winced.

"I don't know you that well." I remembered his touch in the dreams and how he had seemed starved for it. The dreams brought heat to my cheeks. I had gotten to know him in those more than I thought I ever would. "Love...that just seems farfetched, no?"

"To heal me, you would have to touch me, yes?"

I allowed the change in conversation. "It's how I've always done it. But I could try without or with your gloves."

He kept walking, considering what I said. The sway in his body concerned me. "The wound is a graze," he said, "but Macachera's sword is poisoned. Do you know how to deal with that?"

I nodded. The graver the wound, the more exhausted I would be afterwards, as it required use of my life energy. Mortal injuries might require several life witches for healing lest we take our own lives in the process. But poisons were a different story. I would need to transfer the poison to another living being, preferably one we didn't want to live.

"We need to find an animal," I said.

Kir swayed. "The sooner, the better. If we get our full power back at some point, I swear I won't take it for granted."

He pointed to the edge of the cliff where the ground had a lot of loose rock.

"Ankle biters would be in there." He sank to his knees. "Try not to kill me, but I think if you don't heal me, I'll die anyway. If you do have a mission, then it will be complete."

"Holding on to that theory till the very end, I see. Stubborn." I smiled, knowing he didn't really believe it.

His breathing was harder as he sat back until he lay down.

I needed to move quickly. Nothing appeared as I scanned the rocks for movement. Ankle biters didn't sound like something I needed to mess with. Kir slid his hands out of his gloves and waved them at me. I took them, appreciating that I would have them if I had to catch a rodent...or worse.

"Open your shirt, so I can see the wound," I said. "I need to find an animal."

He undid his shirt, pulling it out from the waistband of his pants revealing a muscled, lean torso.

I tore my eyes away. *Focus. Not the time.*

"Try your magic?" he asked.

"Is it safe? I held off. You said Gaelin could detect it."

"He would certainly have his land monitored, but I doubt he is out searching for any witchery to be used." He groaned. "I may not be awake much longer." And then he gazed at me as though he wanted to tell me something.

I'd seen the look a few times: deathbed confession. "Don't. You will live. Whatever you are about to tell me, you keep it to yourself."

He let his head fall back and set his gaze to the sky as sweat beaded on his forehead. His skin was a ghastly pale.

With his reassurance and no time to waste, I cast out my life magic, allowing it to expand like a net in front of me. Life essences abounded beneath the rocks. I zeroed in on one I assumed would be large enough to hold the poison before succumbing to it. I didn't want to have to cast about and find another.

I squeezed like I had with the Trappers back at the wall and tugged, pulling it toward me.

I cringed when the rocks rolled away and revealed what I had caught. A snake. Ankle biter. I should have known. I hated snakes. Though perhaps I'd rather this die than a cute, fuzzy bunny. I would have to hold it with one hand, clamp its jaw shut. I had no idea if the triangular head detail was the same on this side of the Wall. Not to mention if it was some odd Faerie beast that would suck out my soul instead of injecting its venom.

Kir saw what I had. "Here," he flicked his hands. "I've immobilized it, but it won't last long."

I grabbed the snake, expecting slimy but receiving dry and scaly, and not entirely sure what was worse.

I set it beside us, not liking that it could wake up at any moment. All the more reason to work with haste. I slid Kir's gloves on, still warm from him, and examined his wound. It wasn't deep, but it oozed black puss. I'd never seen anything like it.

"I'm going to place my fingers on you," I said.

Kir held his breath.

Even I held my breath as I placed my leather-clad fingers on his skin on either side of the wound. But nothing happened. Kir tipped his head back with a sigh of relief. Leaving one hand with my fingers propped around the wound, I flicked the glove off my other, easy due to the size of Kir's hands. I placed that one on the snake, grabbing its head and securing the jaw just in case. The feel of it made me shiver, but wearing a too-large glove seemed too risky to me if it woke and struggled.

I closed my eyes and formed the connection, focusing on the pathway from Kir to the snake. I was a conduit between the two. With the connection established, I dove into Kir's wound with my magic, pulling on the poison, herding it down the pathway I created. Like with plants, my magic sent feedback: where the poison had traveled in his blood stream, how concentrated it was, and if it had already done damage. The poison was rancid and dark. It was almost like a void yet full of tiny black particles. I could only think that they were tiny parts of Macachera himself.

The thought of having Macachera in Kir made me shudder, but soon I had all the pieces out. The wound had been a graze, so there weren't too many but enough to do some damage. I sent some of my life energy and the snake's to patch Kir's heart. It seemed as though Macachera had gone straight there. But once I healed some, I could see Kir's body healing on its own.

I was about to pull my hands away and cut the pathway when a single tendril from Kir tentatively touched me, wrapping around my life magic. It reminded me of when he entered my mind. It was like a cat brushing up against me. My breath stilled as I popped open my eyes and cut the path from him, through me, to the snake.

Kir hissed in a breath, but he quickly glanced at my hand. Right. I took my hand off him and rocked back onto my heels.

Realizing I still held the snake, I dropped it a few feet away. It would be dead soon anyhow, but still, the less snake in my life, the better. I stood, brushing dirt off my legs before I removed his gloves and dropped them on the ground by his legs.

"I got it all and patched up some of the damage, and then your fae blood seemed to take over." Indeed, the wound was already closed.

He looked down at his chest before reaching to poke at it.

My head swam, and I sat down again.

"Easy there," Kir said as he sat up, buttoning his shirt and slipping his gloves on.

The snake twitched once, and its entire body began writhing. I had enough wits to know we needed to move, but my body was not cooperating.

I had used too much of my own energy to heal Kir.

Everything happened in slow motion—Kir reached for the snake, and the snake reared up and lurched toward him.

No, I just healed him.

An arrow pierced straight through the snake's head.

"Kir," someone called. "You grace me with your presence. To what do I owe the honor?"

I swiveled, my vision warping as my eyes threatened to close. It was the same man I had seen in the Delves.

Gaelin.

CHAPTER 26
KIR

"Interesting to find you here, Kir, with a human witch," Gaelin said as he approached on the path. His icy blue eyes, so pale they were nearly white, bore into me. His eyes, even when we had been friends, unnerved me. As the spawn of the Summer King, it seemed to me they should have a warmth to them. Instead, they were ice-cold.

Now he stood, a bow in his hands and a woman—a witch—clad in red beside him. She looked as calculating as he did, her raven's eyes taking me and Innara in. I felt fairly certain she had the lay of this situation.

If only I did.

My limbs were weak, my skin clammy even in this heat. It wasn't in me to respond, let alone fight back right now. Everything was an uphill battle lately.

"You are on my land, uninvited. I see you outlasted Macachera. I suppose I owe you my thanks for distracting him, but it's a pity he didn't finish you off." Gaelin rubbed at his chin, hiding his facial expression from me. "But once I saw you with this witch, I knew Macachera would be no match for the two of you."

He spoke with such authority and self-assurance while mine fled even further away as the shock of everything wore off and in its place a weight sank through my body.

This felt all too familiar to Violet. *This witch.*

Innara swayed next to me, and I wanted to reach out and stop her from falling sideways, the natural urge to protect a mate. Yet, the thought that she might have set me up was in the forefront of my mind. Had this always been the plan? Deliver me to Gaelin?

She fell sideways, toward me. I let her head hit my arm before I lowered her to the ground. Better for her not to be touching me.

Even as doubt filled my heart, I checked she was okay. Her chest rose and fell.

I couldn't leave her here with Gaelin. I couldn't leave on my own either. Gaelin would have me in less than a second. And the bastard knew it. My one course of action would be to go along with whatever scheme Gaelin cooked up and figure out my options from there.

Gaelin's attention was now on Innara, assessing. Always assessing and reassessing for every minor change in circumstances. But it allowed me my own opportunity to examine him, to look for weaknesses.

Would the stone be on him? Would he have used his rift? I certainly would have.

But who was I kidding? I was so low on power I was like a mewling kitten on his doorstep. If I suspected he still had the stone on him, I couldn't do anything about it at the moment.

My eyes snagged on his light cloak. There was a tear in it. It wasn't a clean slice either. No, this was blackened around the edges. It appeared Macachera had gotten close to him too. He, who always wanted to appear untouchable, was indeed touchable, and he would hate if I pointed it out. That was a tidbit to store away. I snorted and quickly rubbed a hand over my lips. The other witch—with her midnight-sky hair, pale skin, and red lips—raised a brow, but Gaelin's attention was still on Innara

I stole a look at her. In rest, she appeared so innocent. Suspicion rolled through me, all dark and greasy. We still had our bargain, a fairly open-ended one at that. It gave me more than enough leverage to keep her on my side or at the very least to do my bidding.

A wide and wild smile broke across Gaelin's face, his attention back on me.

"Since you did distract Macachera for me and since I'd love to hear how you knew to come to the Delves too, I'll forgive you for entering my lands uninvited." He proceeded to offer me a dramatic bow with a flourish. Upon straightening, his eyes wandered to Innara. If she was his or not, she would be of interest to him.

Doubts piled on top of each other. What if I'd delivered her to him? Served her up right on a platter? Fuck. The urge to protect welled up in me from the bond and from emotions I'd have to look at more closely later.

"Who defeated Macachera?" Gaelin raised a brow as he propped both hands on the bow, grinding the other end into the dirt.

I forced a sly smirk on my lips, denying how weak I was. With every ounce of energy I had left, I made myself stand. Let my extra inch on Gaelin speak for itself. His cloak billowed out with the breeze, and I seized my opportunity. I stuck my finger into the charred hole in the fabric.

"Looks like you owe me a bit more." It was my turn to raise a brow and ooze cockiness, if it meant he believed I, and not my mate, was the one to defeat Macachera.

Gaelin's eyes took in the hole, narrowing. Interesting. He most definitely had not known Macachera had been that close. The muscles in his jaws tensed and relaxed before he let out a soft huff, a chagrined smile playing with the corners of his mouth.

"I see. Well, then you shall be my guest of honor. I grant safe harbor to you." Gaelin's eyes zeroed in on Innara. "Is she special to you?"

I hadn't been expecting safe harbor, and his question threw me more. With a casual glance at her, I took the moment to gather my thoughts.

He could not know.

If he suspected, he could use his soul magic to pry further, find out she was my mate.

"Not special to me. Besides, I've had my use of her." I didn't know where the words were coming from or how I managed to utter them.

I'd lied. A mystery for later.

Gaelin gave a slow twirl to his bow in front of him, the dirt crunching beneath it, but then stopped, his attention caught on something. He stared at the necklace Innara had given me and Clove had enchanted with light. I didn't like it, the look in his eye, and reached up to tuck it under my shirt.

"I'd like for you both to stay for a bit, enjoy my...hospitality." He flicked a finger to his witch, who had stood silently beside him this entire time. "This is Alana."

Alana immediately reached into a satchel and rummaged around, if the clinking of small bottles said anything. She pulled one out to show him, and he nodded his approval.

"Of course, the witch"—Gaelin nodded toward Innara—"will need to earn her keep."

My stomach roiled at what he meant. But there was no way I could get us both out of here right now. There weren't many sane choices, but relative safety while I stayed near to him, near to my mate, to get that stone back seemed the better option, even if only relatively so.

I met his eyes. "Let us go then."

Gaelin lifted a finger and pointed to Innara, and Alana crouched to cradle Innara's head and help her drink whatever was in that bottle.

Alana was one of the ones he must have bargained with. A glance at her throat told me the truth of it: a tattooed collar of thorns adorned her slender neck. Her billowy cloak seemed as though she positioned it to hide it. A touch too high and a touch tighter than what I imagined was comfortable. Gaelin's throat, however, did not have the matching tattoo. Vain bastard probably glamoured it away, but I couldn't detect one.

Alana poured tiny amounts of liquid into Innara's mouth and then rubbed her throat. I worried for Innara, as much as it galled me at the moment. My emotions bounced between suspicion of her and worry that I'd led her to her demise.

Gaelin watched me, his eyes keen. "Have no fear. It is a concoction to rouse her, laced with witch hazel."

"And you just happened to have it with you." I hated that the words popped out of my mouth. They gave too much away.

Gaelin turned and began to walk. "I like to be prepared."

He liked to make sure everything he had was laced with witch hazel. One never knew when one would stumble upon an unsuspecting witch who could be threatened into a bargain. I didn't follow until Innara showed signs of waking, which was within moments.

She woke with a start when she came fully to. A ping of I don't know what—sorrow, guilt—zinged through me when she glanced to me for reassurance and I turned my back. She'd missed out on the earlier conversation, and I had to play the game. She might not like what she saw, but I could do nothing about that at the moment.

I kept an ear out as she stood and fell into step with Alana. Satisfied that she could walk and travel, I sped up to Gaelin.

The sun here was brutal as he led us down a well-trodden road. I rifted away all my extra outer items. Hopefully, Gaelin would think I had power remaining even though it used up my last drops. Innara, behind me, sweltered if the sweat on her brow was evidence, with her cloak slung over her arm. I wanted to take it from her and rift it away, but it was better if I showed no more concern than I already had, Besides, I couldn't do it again.

The trees, like those in the Autumn Court, had no leaves or a sparse few, and the land here looked no better than mine. Whatever this plague was, it affected our lands equally. I didn't ask about the field we had seen. He was clearly up to something, and it was something I could try to learn about during my stay.

Gaelin walked with his hands in his pockets, lord of his realm. But there was that tear in his cloak. It gave me hope. He wasn't as untouchable as he would like others to think.

"How did the witch come into your possession?" he asked.

It rankled me that he spoke of her in that way. *Possession. The witch.* It didn't escape me that I'd referred to her the same way only a few days ago, but the hobgoblin part of my brain knew she was my mate and reacted as such. Pure base instinct. If I listened to only it, it would have had me rutting with her in my house, curse be damned. That part of my brain wasn't to be trusted when it came to her.

But if Gaelin thought I did have some claim on her, perhaps I could offer her some protection until I figured out if she had set this rendezvous up or not.

"I saved her from a baedour, and now she is in my debt." He would get no more from me on that front. If he knew of our bargain, he'd use it against us, and Wall help me if he figured out she was my mate.

"Why did a witch need saving from a baedour?" He pointedly glanced at my gloves. "I bet you wondered the same thing. I bet you wondered if I sent her." He looked off into the distance, a smirk playing on his lips. "Didn't Violet need rescuing too? I'm sure you'll have a chance to reacquaint yourself with her in my court."

I fisted my hands and held my tongue.

Gaelin stole another look at my gloves. "Then again, maybe you won't want that, considering the dangers." He was entirely too pleased with himself. Safe harbor wouldn't save me from his verbal torture. "But back to *your* witch and the baedour."

I took a moment to breathe and released my clamped fists. "There is nothing more to say."

Gaelin put a hand to his chest in mock horror. "You don't say," he murmured before swiveling to look back at Innara, a finger tapping his lip. All my senses went on alert as he continued. He sniffed the air. "She does not smell of the witches from here. I happen to have a dungeon visitor that I think would interest you both. Similar odor."

"Who?" Innara blurted, and I wanted to drag her back and warn her to watch her tongue around Gaelin. But that act itself would give away too much to him.

Gaelin grinned as one did who held the surprise. "You will see."

No one spoke, and I hoped that was it for now. His court couldn't be that far. I scanned the sky in hopes of seeing Haze, but there was nothing. He'd find me. I cast out a searching thought, but my source fizzled. Later, hopefully in a safe room and once I gained back some power, I could contact him.

"You were in the Delves," Innara blurted again as her legs quickened to catch up to us.

"Alana," Gaelin said, irritation in his voice.

I forced myself not to react, not swing an arm out to hold her back, and not tell her to lock her lips.

Gaelin shot me an amused look before turning slightly to both acknowledge and dismiss her question. He flicked out a finger, and I tensed at whatever he was about to do to Innara, but it was merely another signal. Alana behaved like a dog on a leash, trained to her master's commands, both verbal and nonverbal. It sickened me. She slid her hand around Innara's bicep and indicated they should walk together.

I shuddered. Being trapped at his court and having to suffer, I had little good to look forward to, but his verbal sparring would allow me to find out what I could about the stone and keep an eye on Innara, figure out the truths behind her. He thought me too moral to do most things. I'd have to use that assumption to my advantage, play the game he'd been teaching me for years.

I glanced back at Innara, who widened her eyes. I could almost hear her saying, *What is going on?* But Gaelin needed to think she was my pawn, so I turned back with as stony a face as I could muster.

As much as I told myself I wanted Innara out of my life, the goodbye would cleave me in two. The only way to do it without driving myself mad would be to know she was safe.

And currently, she was not.

CHAPTER 27

INNARA

The Summer Court was a stone castle surrounded by what must have been gardens. Now the gardens seemed to be mostly hedges, but they were green and alive. It was a marked contrast to the desolate land we walked to get here, dirt so dry every step sent up a puff of dust. I felt covered in it.

Alana slashed out her arm, halting me, as Kir and Gaelin walked ahead. "We stay behind."

I couldn't get a read on her. As a fellow witch, I yearned for camaraderie, but it felt like barking up the wrong tree. My gaze fell to that tattoo around her neck. Perhaps her loyalty wasn't where I hoped.

The witch hazel sat sour in my stomach. Some of it may have been due to how little mind Kir paid me. I wasn't sure if it was an act or if something had happened while I lay unconscious. My gut, however, told me something had shifted. And I felt unmoored. His presence, as annoying and unwanted as it had been at times, had turned into a safety net. He'd sifted to save me from the baedour and dove in to shield me from Macachera. And then those dreams. Lately, I had wanted him near, and I thought it might be a mutual feeling.

Now this shift.

Kir and Gaelin spoke together for a minute before Gaelin called Alana to him. And off she trotted. I couldn't help pursing my lips.

I could run.

But I'd seen enough of Cirrelea to know I wouldn't survive. I might have my witchery, but I lacked all the knowledge of how things worked and the beasts that prowled.

Alana and Gaelin walked toward what had to be stables.

Kir stood alone, his back to me. His fists flexed once by his sides before he unclasped the necklace. He strode right to me, holding it out. "Thank you for the use of this, but considering we now have light, I no longer need it."

His face was a stone. Back to expressionless Kir.

I grasped the green gem. The leather strap slipped through his fingers until I had it all and tucked it under my arms as I crossed them.

"Did I do something wrong?" I asked.

His nostrils flared, but he didn't answer the direct question. "We'll both be staying here for the near future, but it appears Gaelin will exact his price from you. It'll be good for us both to have some space from one another."

Space? His price? "What about—"

"It's not done," he said curtly, his eyes hard.

"But—"

"What I need to save my court." He bit off each word.

I huffed out a breath before tucking Nolan's necklace into my pocket, and the realization of what I agreed to all the way back in his living room hit me with full force. I was definitely not off the hook with that bargain.

Gaelin approached, his eyes darting from me to Kir like he eagerly awaited the release of the latest movie on the wire. Kir hadn't noticed him. When he did, he pivoted, heading for the large arched doors into the castle.

"I suppose he'll figure out where his room is." Gaelin watched him go, a calculating look in his eye. He stood close, a little too close, with a finger tapping his lip. "Correct me if I am wrong. It sounded as if you two had a deal. Kir said you owed him a debt."

I pressed my lips together. I'd heard nothing good of this fae, and so far, nothing told me to trust him.

He *tsk*'d. "I see. Well, if you bargained with him, I would tell you that was a poor decision."

"Why is that?" This fae irked me more than Kir ever did.

Gaelin smiled. He was so beautiful, and I hated that it caused a tiny flip in my stomach. But I got the sense he knew that, in the way so many men gifted with looks used to their advantage. It quelled the flip instantly.

"Give me your hand." He held his palm out, waiting for me to obey. His skin was pale but olive in tone with a hint of blue veins on the soft side of his wrist.

I was so used to not being allowed to touch Kir that, at first, I balked, taking a tiny step backward. Gaelin impatiently waggled his fingers. I didn't see an alternative, so I placed my hand in his.

Warmth oozed off him, and my palms began to sweat. He placed his other hand on top and closed his eyes, humming.

"Life witch." His eyes popped open "And a strong one. Anything else?"

"You didn't answer my question." I wanted my hands back and gave a slight tug.

He chuckled as I wiped my palms on my thighs and glanced back in the direction of the arched doors into the castle. Kir was gone. "Your Lord of Winter can lie. He told me you were nothing special to him, and yet, I sense two pieces of your soul missing. If someone had a piece of my soul, they would certainly be special to me." He waved his hand in the air as if to flit the entire matter away from us. "Souls are my specialty. But don't worry your head on that. You had interest in who I had in my dungeon, did you not?"

His words sent me reeling. Fae supposedly couldn't lie, and yet, one of them did. I didn't want to think it was Kir, but the way he acted now sowed doubt.

I seized on Gaelin's offered topic change. Someone from the other side of the Wall was of definite interest to me. Maybe they knew how to get across. What if I could get back without Kir's help? Would a sliver of my soul be worth it? But I didn't want to say too much, not to this fae. I had gotten used to Kir and his crew. Guarding my tongue, especially with Kir seemingly leaving me to sink or swim, would be best. So, I merely nodded.

"I'll grant that request." An ingratiating smile crossed his lips, reminding me too much of the market sellers as they haggled you for the best price. "And then we will discuss your role here."

"My role? I want to get back across the Wall." I didn't want a role.

There was that smile again. It grated on me.

"Everything here has a price." He dragged a finger from my ear along my jawline. I jerked away. "Perhaps we can find a mutual agreement. Life witches are not easy to come by. But even so, you must pay too." He began to walk away before stopping. "I'll tell Alana no more witch hazel if you promise not to harm anyone in my court."

"And if I were to harm someone?" I shouldn't have said it, but it popped out.

"That visitor in the dungeon—the one I think you will be *most* interested in—their life will be forfeit."

Gaelin called for a will-o'-the-wisp to lead me to the dungeons.

The shimmering ball of light liked to whip around corners, so I had to rush to follow. But I swore it was purposefully trying to lose me, twinkling as if laughing when I finally found it.

As soon as we entered the dungeon, it winked out of existence.

As far as dungeons went. This one didn't seem so bad. I always imagined a strong smell of urine and feces with an overlay of body odor would permeate this sort of place. But the scent was clean, sterile in fact. A fae guard asked me what I wanted and led me down a blank hallway, pure white. At the end, he touched a door, and I couldn't decipher what he had done. Behind the door we entered was more white but lined with muted gray doors. But it wasn't silver metal; it was iron.

The guard slipped gloves on and opened the first door on the right with a simple key. The door wasn't into the cell itself. Iron bars greeted me, but there was space for several people to visit whomever was being kept.

A man lifted his head from his hands as he sat on a simple bed, and my heart caught in my throat.

"Nolan," I said as I stepped forward, wrapping my hands around the bars.

He stood, and his face lit up as he approached the bars. "Innara. You're here."

My heart thumped. Someone I knew, someone I recognized. It was like I had found a slice of home.

"I don't …" I shook my head, trying to get my wits. I had hoped for my mom, but Nolan here was wonderful. I pushed aside the guilt that rose that it wasn't my mother's life on the chopping block if I stepped over a gray line. Nolan's life mattered too, but he wasn't my mom.

"I'll be outside the door," the guard said, leaving us alone.

I stepped close to the bars. I had so many questions. "I can't believe you're here. Are you okay? Did you fall through after me? How did this happen?" Nolan shoving me through the Wall flashed in my memory. Or was I pulled? Never mind that. "Is my mother okay? What happened?"

Nolan stood just on the other side of the bars. I reached through, and he clasped my hands. Our fingers laced, and he used his index fingers to rub against my palm. It felt so good to be touched by someone I knew who cared. Even if…even if I had been trying to break up with him when my life had turned upside down.

"Your mom is okay. She's safe or was when I last saw her. I found her after… She had to heal my neck. You ripped my necklace off." He let one of my hands go to rub the back of his neck. His cheeks reddened. "I hate to ask if you have it. It was important to me."

I pulled my hands away, happy to have one thing accomplished, although small. "I do." Reaching into my pocket, I held it up, and it glowed with the light from Clove. "Sorry, that was necessary. It should go away in a bit."

I dangled it through the bars.

He held it before clasping it around his neck and tucking it into his shirt.

I took the opportunity to look him over. He didn't look bad off. A bit tired with bags under his eyes. What had he been through? How did he get here? I hesitated. Maybe he had been through even more than I had.

I was about to ask more questions when shuffling behind me caught my attention. Kir walked through the door.

"Kir. What are you doing here?" This was awkward. I never imagined being in the same room with my boyfriend—I wasn't sure if Nolan was technically my ex, since I didn't finish breaking up with him—and the fae I had most recently dream-kissed.

Kir leaned against the doorjamb. "Gaelin sent me a message that if I wanted to see the human that came through the Wall, I could come now. So here I am, a bit late, as the wisp took me through a tour of the castle. Carry on. It appears you know each other?"

His face was bland, almost bored. Or was there a touch of hurt in his eyes as his gaze passed over me? He and I would need to talk soon.

Nolan squeezed my hand, bringing my attention back to him.

"I..." I didn't know what to say.

We had an audience, and Kir acted so indifferent, like he had when we first met. But I couldn't let that or Kir's presence stop me from speaking with Nolan.

"What happened...after?" I rubbed my thumb on his hand. "Your hand! It's okay." In my memory, it had turned black, and he had screamed in pain.

He slipped it from mine and turned it over, flexing his fingers. "It got shocked, but your mother was able to heal it for me."

"Your hand smoked and charred black."

"You already fell through the Wall. It burned me, but it was minor."

I curled my fingers around the bars. Maybe Faerie was messing with my head. Maybe the Wall showed me something that wasn't the truth, like how I now suspected Kir could lie. But I couldn't let myself get thrown by every tiny detail. "Is my mom okay?"

Nolan carefully reached through the bars and rubbed my arms before fishing my hands over to his side. "I had hoped you'd walk through those doors, but I guess there was a better likelihood of that for me. You probably had no idea who you would see in here. But you're here. Safe. Whole." His eyes darted to Kir. "You had help?"

"Yes. Seems like we've both had adventures. But my mother, Nolan." I needed to know.

He looked down, chagrin written all over his face. "Sorry, it's just a shock. You fell through the Wall. It was like you got sucked in once you touched it."

I frowned. He had shoved me. Or was that another Faerie falsehood?

"The Trappers left me alone. They were after you, not me. Even though I interfered, they dropped me and went after your mom. Luckily, I knew the area better than them and took a shortcut through the woods when they took the main road. I got to your mom and got her out of the house after she grabbed some essentials and a few of your—wards, I think she called them? I hid her in a cabin I found north of the village. She healed me. Then we traveled south for days, and she helped me cross the Wall so I could find you."

I released his hands and backed up. "She helped you cross? How? Why south?"

Nolan shrugged, his boyish curls bouncing. "We came south to get away from your father. His men were crawling like ants in the north. She handed me what she said was an enchanted stone. I think it was one of the wards she took from your house. It allowed me to cross."

This could be it. A way home!

I gripped the bars. "Do you have it still?"

Nolan plopped onto the small cot in the room, shaking his head. "It disintegrated as I passed through the Wall."

I banged my head onto the bars. Just when I thought I had a way out.

Nolan jumped up and placed a kiss to my forehead.

Kir pushed off the wall. "I've seen enough."

I lifted my head, having almost forgotten Kir was there. Nolan still thought we were together. Kir's footsteps echoed down the hall-way. I wanted to call him back. To explain. I couldn't help but feel he left because Nolan kissed me.

"Nolan," I started, "there's something you should know."

"Later." His eyes darted to the door. "With that fae gone, we need to talk about how to get out of here. I haven't had visitors, but I doubt the guards will allow you to stay much longer. Gaelin has questioned me a few times. He's very interested in your father. I couldn't answer a lot of his questions, but I bet you could. We can use that. Get me out of this dungeon and then both of us back to the Eastlands."

He hadn't let me finish what I was going to say. But this was Nolan, someone I knew. Someone who wanted to get back home as much as I did. Maybe telling him I had wanted to break up with him back at the Wall just before he aided my escape wasn't the nicest thing to do to a guy who had found his way across the Wall to rescue me.

"I'll do my best to get you out of here," I said.

"Promise? This place is maddening."

I squeezed his hand. "Promise."

"Don't trust that fae," he said as parting words.

CHAPTER 28

INNARA

The wisp reappeared as soon as I exited the dungeons. It moved quickly, like it was in a rush. A few times as I ran to follow it around the corner, it waited, fading in and out like someone tapping their foot.

Finally, it stopped in front of a door. Lush smells of herbs and baked bread wafted from inside. We'd eaten in the Delves, but not knowing how long we would be in them, we had rationed our food. My stomach gurgled, and I pushed the door open.

Several tiny flying creatures hovered in the air. All of them stared at me. A twig-like man with dark skin and leaf green hair approached.

"Would Gaelin's guest like some food?" His words were polite, but the purse of his lips and the way his eyes trailed from my feet to my face told me what he really thought.

"Yes, please." I was already salivating.

He sniffed and turned, clapping his hands. The flying creatures began buzzing about, and before I knew it, a small plate with freshly baked bread and some cheese was placed on a small table with benches on either side. A large, paned window stood behind it. The twig man waved to me to sit.

My stomach grumbled again, so I wasted no time diving in. The twig man carried on about his business but kept throwing me sidelong looks and heavy sniffs. I ignored it. He didn't like my smell; he didn't like me. Well, likewise.

Outside, the light was growing dim. A smaller, humanish creature with hooved legs like a deer placed logs within a circle of rocks. They had tufted ears on the top of their head. Some fables from home described creatures like this. Maybe it was a faun or perhaps a satyr?

Tables appeared out of thin air in small groups throughout the courtyard as small, twinkling lights flickered, hovering in the air. The effect was bewitching. Upholstered chairs and large pillows emerged one by one around the area. Some were in large groupings, others off on their own and somewhat hidden.

"What's going on?" I asked no one in particular, hoping the twig man or the flying creatures—pixies, perhaps—would answer. Was it some sort of celebration or ceremony?

The twig man came over, and I got a good look at him now that I had been able to take in more of the room and everything in it. His legs were spindly, and his tailored pants ended in bare feet. Narrow toes tapped against the floor as he made his way to me. His skin had the rough appearance of bark. Iridescent but clear wings sprouted out of his white, pressed shirt, and were tucked tightly to his back. He turned, noticing how I stared. They vibrated in what I interpreted as annoyance.

He stood with his hands clasped behind his back as he observed the preparations outside. "The master must have called for a party tonight."

"Does that happen often?"

The twig man cocked his head in an unnatural way. "One does not question the ways of the master. It is for his *pleasure* and the pleasure of his people."

Hmm. I didn't like how he kept saying "master," and his attitude could definitely use some work. I hadn't questioned the reason for a party. It seemed like, in the Winter Court, there was little cause for parties, and yet Gaelin potentially threw them regularly. But how were all these creatures here? I saw none of them in the Winter Court. Up there, I'd only seen Kir and his friends and the baedour. Kir said they were in hidden villages, but he might be able to lie.

Platters appeared on the tables. Fountains sat in the center, with pink wine pouring out of them. Crystal glasses popped in all around.

My mouth watered. The plate in front of me now seemed meager. "Can anyone attend?"

The twig man eyed me, looking from my half-finished plate to my face. A mischievous twinkle passed over his face as he looked me over, head to toe once again. "You'd prefer the food out there?"

Now I'd gone and offended him. "This fresh bread is delicious, but it looks like there are meals out there."

His beady eyes, narrowed in a cruel slant. A vine shot out from his hand, snatching my plate.

"Hey!" I said.

"If you prefer that food, best go get it. Off with you. Drink up," he said. The plate disappeared before he opened the door, shooing me outside.

Fae and Faerie creatures gathered, many with outfits that raised my brows. Sheer fabrics and revealing cuts. So far, I hadn't seen many fae, but the ones I had seen wore leathers or uniforms. All relatively normal clothing.

A witch strolled up beside me. Her slinky, black dress left little to the imagination, the fabric hugging her curves. Smoky makeup set off her green eyes, and a sprinkling of freckles across her nose and cheeks made her features almost girl-nextdoorish, despite bright red hair that hung loose and wild around her shoulders. A scent wafted off her that was utterly delicious. Just before I asked what perfume she wore, her tattoo caught my eye. One just like Alana's circled her throat, but this witch left hers on display, judging by the low drape of her dress and lack of any jewelry.

"Gaelin's new guest from the Eastlands?" she asked." This must be all so new to you."

Another humanish creature with hooved feet drew my attention when it strummed a small guitar. I nodded my answer.

"Satyr," she said before leaning in and indicating the other hooved creature I had seen before. "Faun." Then she pointed out a twiggy creature who flicked a finger at a pile of logs and lit them on fire. "Sprite. Watch out for them. They are prickly."

I chuckled, and her eyes lit up.

One of the small flying creatures from the kitchen zipped by, and the mysterious witch said, "Ah, and there we have a pixie."

As she pointed out and named creatures for me, fae and their ilk winked in from who knew where. Sifting. All around me, they greeted each other with lingering hugs, kisses on the cheeks, but all with an amount of touching that struck me as overly friendly. Perhaps this was how Faerie was. I hadn't seen such a large gathering in Kir's court.

Alana entered from a large door on the other side of the courtyard. She looked my way, and I waved. Her eyes nearly bulged out of her head before she gripped her skirt to lift it up, revealing a lot of naked thigh, and hurried over to us.

The woman next to me muttered under her breath, "Here we go."

She shifted her stance, jutting a hip out and crossing her arms.

Alana reached us, glaring at the other woman before she grabbed my arm and turned me away from the other woman. "You should not be here."

I had no idea what was going on. "I was trying to get some food before finding my room. The sprite in the kitchen wasn't very friendly."

Alana sighed.

The other woman said, "Relax. Let her eat."

"Mind your own business, Violet. I told you to leave this one alone. You disobeyed a direct order."

Violet? *The* Violet? My gaze shot to her, surveying her. *This* was Kir's type?

She noticed. A feral smile grew on her lips before she clicked her teeth at me. To Alana, she said, "You know as well as I do that I don't need to take orders from you." Her gaze slowly dropped to my feet and back up again. "I wanted to see the new witch for myself. She doesn't look like much."

I choked back a gasp, my hand gripping in a fist.

"Go bother someone else," Alana gritted out as she wrapped her fingers around my wrist.

Violet, for what it was worth, left without another snide word. She sashayed away, picking up a glass of the pink wine and sipping at it. She reminded me of the models in the big cities of the East-lands, outrageous clothes and bright lights with more makeup on than I even owned, strutting the catwalks.

And I hated how the one thing I couldn't get my mind off was how Kir had fallen for her.

Alana turned back to me. "I'm so sorry. I knew you'd meet her eventually, but I had hoped to delay it."

Alana tugged at her dress. It was red and made of feathers. Or was it wings? I grimaced. Surely, those were not real wings. The grotesqueness was then accentuated by a sweetheart neckline.

"The dress is not my choice." Alana said, catching my perusal. "It's barbaric."

"And whose choice was it?" Yet I feared I knew the answer, my gaze drifting over to the sprites carrying in a sedan chair to a dais overlooking the festivities.

She glanced at me from the side of her eye. "We should chat. You should know what this party is."

What this party was? A party was a party.

Several more witches appeared in the door Alana had come in.

"Shoot, I need to talk to them. They're always late. I'll be back.

Don't go anywhere." She gathered the skirts of her dress again and bustled over.

Alone and with nothing to do, I made my way toward a table, picking up a small plate and filling it with pastries both sweet and savory. I crunched into the flaky crust of one. Warmth cascaded over my tongue, and I moaned. This hit the spot.

Music thrummed as more fae filled the space. Laughter rolled out as bodies began to move rhythmically to the tune. Some alone, others together, their bodies moving as one, pressed close as a head leaned back in abandon. My belly heated, and I felt like I should avert my eyes but found I couldn't.

Gathering myself, I refocused on what I was here for. Food. I ate another pastry and another. A faun jostled me as she reached for the wine. It was the one thing every creature, every witch, every fae picked up.

The wine.

And wine was what I needed next. The warmth on my tongue from the food turned hotter, begging to be quenched.

I grabbed a crystal glass and held it under the pink stream of the fountain as the satyr played a sensual tune. Around me, fae and Faerie's creatures danced. Violet rounded the bonfire, her flame-red hair flying behind her as her hands licentiously roamed her body from hips to breasts to neck.

Gaelin appeared, and the revelers hushed, many bowing or taking a knee. He barely noticed them and made a beeline for me, hands held out as my eyes widened.

"You came. Oh, I am so glad." He took in my empty plate, speckled with crumbs, and my glass of wine. "Drink up. I have a lively night full of merriment planned."

"I think I'll just be having a bite to eat and finding where I should stay." I stifled a yawn. Even though this party was waking me up, whatever Alana had given me to rouse me back outside the Delves exit had worn off hours ago. The Delves and healing Kir had taken its toll.

Gaelin's face fell. "Of course, of course. When you are ready, the wisp will take you to it. Just head in those doors there." He indicated an arched door into a different part of the castle than what I had already seen. His eyes gained a twinkle. "But I do hope you'll decide to stay for a bit. Ah, look. Here is your friend, Kir."

Kir strolled up beside me, took one look at what was in my hands, and grabbed the wine glass. "Don't drink the wine."

"Whyever not?" My tongue burned after all. I moved to grab it back, but he held it out of my reach.

Gaelin grabbed another glass and filled it, handing it to me. "Whyever not is certainly the question. Drink up. It's delicious."

He leaned forward and winked, causing his shirt to gape at the neck. A hint of green caught my eye. Could that be Nolan's necklace? The green disappeared as he pulled back and readjusted his collar, revealing an amulet with a citrine gem. Perhaps it was the light.

Kir dropped my wine. Shattering glass and a spray of something wet along my legs had me taking a step back but not before he took the new glass as well. "Trust me. Don't drink it."

"Kir, the lady is thirsty." Gaelin tilted his head as he held up his hand and another glass filled with pink appeared.

This felt like some weird game between them with me in the middle. I could almost hear Kir's teeth grinding.

He leaned in, turning away from Gaelin. "Can I talk to you?"

The way he left me on the way in, and now he wanted to talk?

"I thought you wanted space?" I asked.

The flicker across his face was gratifying. I couldn't put my finger on what exactly that flash was, but it wasn't a positive emotion. Alana, in her beautifully ghastly dress, slid in beside Gaelin. She said nothing, but Kir took all of her in.

Something ugly rose inside me. My fingers tightened around the glass until I told myself to calm down before I smashed it.

Gaelin's arm slid around my waist. "How about a dance?"

I glanced to Kir, who mouthed, *Don't.*

What right did he have to tell me what to do? He needed his space after all. Then space he would get.

"I'd love to," I said before I sipped the wine. Cool, silky liquid poured down my throat, and it was oh so sweet. The ripest berries burst forth on my tongue, and I took another sip, watching Kir over the rim of my glass.

His face paled.

"Dance," Gaelin said as bodies writhed to the music behind him.

And so I did.

Colors whirled past. The song faded, and a new one commenced. On the outskirts of the bonfire dancing, some of Faerie's creatures fell to the pillows on the ground, mouths and tongues everywhere, stirring a warmth in my belly. Sparks from the bonfire turned into shooting stars.

My mind was delirious with the lusciousness of all of it. I could taste the smells of Faerie from the barest hints of lavender to the decadence of smooth, milky chocolate.

And I wanted more.

Gaelin whirled me in his arms. "Are you having fun, little witch?"

I leaned in, laughing. The velvet of his jacket was intoxicating. I fought the urge to rub against it as a small voice in my head reminded me, *This is Gaelin.*

"You shouldn't feel this good." I staggered backward because another voice in my head said, *Who cares?* "More wine."

Gaelin's icy blue eyes crinkled with amusement, but he allowed me to pull away, trailing a single finger along my palm as I left. He was so familiar with me, and my body reveled in it. Tonight, he felt like an old friend.

This is Gaelin.

Yes, it was, and other than right now, he'd only given me a tight, strained feeling in my belly. How could someone so detestable feel familiar to me?

I glanced to Kir, who stood just outside of the dancing circle. A fae couple occupied the couch a few feet from him. My eyes bulged as the male eased up the dress of the female, his hand sliding between her thighs.

Kir didn't look their way. His eyes followed me like a hawk.

Maybe that was it. After two weeks of being not entirely welcomed—sidelined, even—the change was nice, and I found myself wishing I was that female with Kir behind me.

The thought liquefied my insides, so I quashed it as I made my way to a table but found a wall of chest in my way.

"You've had enough to drink. Go to bed." Kir peered down at me, arms crossed.

I frowned. Mr. Serious. "You and your orders."

He sighed, jamming a hand through his hair. "The wine is enchanted. Trust me. You do not want to experience the effects."

"The effects? Like how I feel glorious?" I stepped toward him, my chin a mere inch from his arms across his chest. He'd changed his clothes since we'd arrived. The sleeves of his shirt were tight, showing off his forearms, as he still had them crossed. I wanted to sink my teeth into one of them, trace the veins I knew were just beneath the layer of cloth. I didn't want to mention how even being near him right now made parts of me throb.

"You do not understand what game you are playing." He slid his arms to his sides and leaned forward, whispering yet somehow biting off each word. "Go to bed."

A bed was certainly a place I wanted to be right now, and I was about to tell him when a slim arm slipped right in between us, holding a glass filled nearly to the brim with more delicious pink wine.

"Drink," Alana said. She had a glass of her own and brought it to her lips with a wink.

"Innara," Kir warned as I took the offered drink.

I sipped it. "Make me stop, Lord Kir."

As glorious as I felt, it felt even better to watch his jaw clench. I wanted to place my lips right where the muscles flexed and feel the movement and then move slowly down his neck, his chest...

The couple I'd seen earlier were now splayed out on the couch, clothes gone. She straddled his lap, her head thrown back in pleasure.

I froze as I brought the glass to my lips. Perhaps I should heed his warning. Perhaps what he said was true.

No, he could lie. He'd probably been lying to me this entire time.

I gulped the wine.

Delectable warmth spread to my toes and fingertips . I found myself watching the couple. How his hands gripped her hips, how she ground into him, how her moan rang out. My fingers tightened around the glass as more groans and sighs echoed.

The world around me spun of its own accord. Kir and Alana's faces twisted together as they watched me. But then the feeling eased, and a warm haze settled in.

"What were we talking about?" I asked.

Alana drew close as she downed the remainder in her glass before she dropped it to the ground at her side. Behind her, fae and witches danced, grinding into one another. Gaelin had moved to the throne on the dais, watching everyone writhe around the bonfire. But his eyes kept flicking back to me and then to Violet, who danced with another witch. Their bodies twisted with each other, their mouths seemingly everywhere.

My head swam, and the world swayed. The beat of the music thrummed in my chest, pulling me along with it. I wanted to dance. I wanted to be the music.

Alana ran a hand up my arm and placed it on my shoulder before she brought her other hand up. Slowly, she began to move her hips, pulling in close. She leaned in, her lips a whisper on the shell of my ear.

"Have some more wine. Then dance with me. I need to tell you something." Teeth lightly clamped down on my lobe, and I sucked in a breath.

Over her shoulder, I locked eyes with Kir, who was the vision of a storm held in check.

What would make the chains around him break? I so desperately wanted to find out.

But Alana seductively ran her fingers along my neck and collarbone and down my arms, and it felt so incredibly good, like tiny fireworks going off along my skin. I gulped the remainder of the wine and dropped it at my side too. Glass shattered, and the shards pelted my ankles. Without my leathers, I'd be bleeding, but one must have hit just right, cutting through the leather to my skin. The pain only heightened the pleasure of her hands caressing my skin.

Alana closed the distance between us, pressing our bodies together. I didn't have to do anything. She moved both of us in time to the beat.

"I don't have much time, judging by how much you just downed at once. I wasn't expecting that." She laughed, the air hitting my ear, and I moaned as I ran my hands up her back.

My body was on fire, and her touch, the feel of her clothes, her skin, somehow cooled it.

She turned her face, kissing and sucking a line up the side of my neck before speaking again. "I'll get to the point. You must not make a bargain with Gaelin. Do you hear me?"

I nodded, but I wanted more friction. My hips moved with hers, to satisfy a need I felt building.

"Listen to me." She bit my neck hard, and I let out a yelp that turned into a groan. My body acted of its own will, grinding against her. "You can not make a bargain with Gaelin. No matter who he threatens, no matter who he says he will kill because if you do…"

She gagged.

Her words sobered me enough to stop my incessant grinding. "Because if I do?"

Her breathing sounded labored. "Because if you do…"

She gagged again before she stomped with a frustrated groan. A sprite glided by with a tray of drinks on it. Alana grabbed one and drained it, letting out an *ahhh* when she was done. She shook her head, her midnight-black hair tickling my hands, and my nipples throbbed.

When she met my eyes, hers were glassy. "If you do, it won't help any of us. You, me"—she cast her gaze behind her—"Kir. It will only benefit *him*. Do not fall for it. Any control over your soul is a big deal and his more than others. It's his proficiency." She backed away, grabbing my hands, and led me to Kir. "Get her out of here."

Kir stood before me with open disgust all over his face before something in me tugged, like a rubber band snapping.

CHAPTER 29
KIR

Innara let out a small, throaty gasp. Her body swayed before she turned to me, eyes wide. Her hands came up, reaching.

Oh no. I grabbed them with my gloved ones. While it prevented her from touching me, the main effect it had was to pull her closer. What the hell was I going to do? Her body ached for release, and she would seek it out with or without me. The wine would drive her nearly mad until she found it. I knew. Too many parties with Gaelin when we were friends. He had always loved to ply unsuspecting humans and lesser fae with his wine. But then we always drank it and let it drive us wild too.

"Kir," she whispered. "Is this a dream?"

She tried to free her hands, and something pulsed within me. A deep, aching want. I wasn't sure if it came from her or from me. The pulse came again, and it nearly took me to my knees. She was so close. She finally tugged and wiggled a hand free before bringing it up to touch my face, and I ducked away.

Shit.

My ability to resist was decreasing. I was so tired. So tired of wanting and not being able to ever satisfy it. Some days, all I wanted was to have someone I cared about touch me, hold my hand, lay their head on my shoulder. So much I had taken for granted through the years. Simple pleasures now gone. Larger pleasures too.

And Innara tugged on all the strings attached to both. What I would give to just hold her.

I croaked out, "Not a dream. I am so sorry."

Her hand paused in midair, and her face screwed up like she was about to cry.

Double shit.

I grabbed her hand and brought hers and mine down between us, pulling her close. I wanted to whisper things to her. Tell her I didn't want to push her away. And when she looked up, the hurt in her eyes nearly made me forget my curse. She made me want to let it all out.

"And what do we have here?" Gaelin slithered in beside us like the snake he was. He took in our hands tucked between us and raised a brow. "Looks like maybe we found a way to satisfy some needs."

I rolled my eyes. "What do you want?"

The smirk on his lips faded, turning into a hard line. "You would do well not to test me, Kir." He slipped behind Innara, capturing her between us. "Your friends are in the Autumn Court."

Point taken. Information along with a veiled threat.

But I didn't have time to react.

Innara apparently heard what Gaelin had commented on and took it to heart. She pressed her hips in, smashing our hands between us. Fuck.

"I could give you what you need, Innara." Gaelin slid both his hands down her arms, and she shivered, her eyes rolling up in pleasure at the touch.

Her body began to lean away from mine. Toward his.

In the state she was in, the effects of the wine flowing in her blood, she had no inhibition—her hips ground against our hands. Her body was on fire with an ache that wouldn't stop for hours. Her emotions were heightened.

If I didn't help her, she'd find it somewhere else.

Fae gyrated all around us. Many had already found chairs or the ground, depending on how desperate the wine made them. The couple on the couch off to the side had wasted no time at all. Others with higher tolerance liked to toy with potential partners and draw it out, while others preferred taking their parties back to their personal quarters.

All of it meant she'd soon realize I was not needed.

She would go with Gaelin.

And I couldn't let that happen.

I freed a hand to push Gaelin back before settling it on her shoulder and letting the tiniest tendril of my magic snake along her skin to put her to sleep. Her weight fell into me, and I propped her up with a prayer that she didn't touch my skin. She might hate me in the morning for doing exactly what she had asked me not to, but I'd argue that she violated her end of the deal too.

Gaelin, however, only gave me a shit-eating grin before barking out a howl of laughter.

My stomach plummeted. I'd walked straight into something.

Once he finished his last chuckle at my expense, he said. "Take this witch that you care nothing for and get her to bed. I have a task for her in the morning, and she needs some rest."

I leaned down to hook my arm around her legs to pick her up and wove a light blanket of air to wrap her in for my own peace of mind. I'd already given away I cared for her.

Gaelin made to turn away, but I spoke first. "What is it you want her for?"

He stuffed his hands in his pockets. His shirt was undone midway down. Violet sidled up beside him, sliding her hand against his chest.

The sight of her filled me with fury, with revulsion, with seething hate. She whispered into his ear before tilting her head slightly to eye me and take in the witch passed out in my arms. She didn't speak, only a soft snort came from her before she leaned in to Gaelin again, whispering and biting his ear.

The sight nearly caused me to gag, but this time it was revulsion with myself. How had I been so blind?

"Let's go," she whispered, trying to turn him.

But Gaelin lifted a finger to her arm, stilling her. "Lord of Winter, here, had a question." The bastard knew the sight of Violet had thrown me. The twinkle in his eye told me so. "What was it again?"

I adjusted Innara in my arms, hating that he would make me repeat myself. And in front of *her*. Leaving was an option, but I wanted to know for Innara's sake. "What is it you need her for?"

Violet had gone back to nibbling his ear, down his neck, down his chest...stomach. I did not need to see this.

Gaelin's eyes went hooded with pleasure but, like a cat who had found the milk, looked at me. "For what life witches are best at."

It was all the answer I was going to get. My worry had been for his personal pleasure, though Violet clearly had that job.

The feelings that bombarded me were muddled and confused. There was hate of her. Of him. And jealousy but not that Gaelin had her. The two of them could bang like banshees, for all I cared. No, it was jealousy that they could have that and I couldn't.

Because of them.

I found myself almost glad that this entire debacle of finding the stone and finding Innara had led me here. Perhaps I could end this all. End them.

Or end myself.

Fuck, I'd never had these thoughts before. But it all became too much. Before now, I'd thought I could handle this curse, and I had been handling it right up until my mate finally showed herself. This was cruel to both of us.

The wisp zoomed around the corner, almost hitting my face but knocking me out of my morose thoughts. It backed up, blinking in a question.

Where to go? I looked down at Innara in my arms. I wanted her in my suite, but that way lay temptation. I could let her touch me. End my curse with a finality. But that would leave her thinking she caused it.

"Bring me to her room," I said.

The wisp blinked twice and zoomed off. Blasted thing didn't care I carried an entire other person with me. It led me to a wing that I had never personally stayed in. Dozens of doorways indicated small rooms. Not quite barracks but perhaps where another court's help stayed back when we did those things.

The wisp stopped in front of an open door. Once I stepped inside and laid Innara on the bed, it zoomed down the hall. Will-o'-the-wisps following orders and actually leading you where you need to go will never not feel bizarre.

Innara still wore her leathers from the Winter Court. She had at least stripped down to the strappy undershirt, which I would be happy to watch her parade around in all the time, but...

I scratched my head.

Where to begin. I'd help her with her shoes. As I slid her heel out of one, she muttered. I froze, the ache in my heart swelling. She wasn't Violet. Gaelin may have gotten something out of tonight, but so had I. Innara wasn't his, and she hadn't brought me here. But for now, it would be best if she stayed asleep. There was a chance she could sleep through the rest of the wine's effects. I slid her other shoe off.

"Kir?" she murmured.

Shit. I stood near the edge of her bed. I didn't want to be a jerk to her anymore. She needed me in this court, whether she realized it or not. And I...I needed her too and not just for figuring out what the hell Gaelin was up to. No, she'd already shown me that she understood my isolation.

"I'm here. You should sleep." It was a wishful thought.

Her breath hitched, eyes fluttering open. I held my breath, unsure of the hold the wine would still have on her. Sometimes the effects were acute and wore off quickly. But sometimes they were not.

Her gaze met mine. Neither of us said a word, but the room filled with the scent of her, nearly overpowering me.

I needed to leave. But my feet refused to move. My pulse thrummed, waiting.

The moment strung out, and my breath was heavy. I wanted her to do something but also knew I should leave, lock the door behind me and get to the safety of my room. Something held me there. Her intoxicating smell or the knowledge that I really shouldn't leave this room for her safety? The other Summer Court fae might be busy, but that didn't mean some weren't wandering around looking for mischief.

Right. I would stay, but distance would be good.

A chair sat next to her bedside table. It looked comfortable enough. She'd sleep in the bed, and I'd be in the chair. It'd be fine. No worse than any of the places we'd been so far. I removed my swords and worked on unfastening the bandolier of daggers on my chest. I'd leave one tied to my thigh for easy use if needed.

All the while, I felt her scalding gaze on my back. It had me feeling as if I was stripping in front of her, which didn't help the heat of the room. I ignored what I knew would happen, ignored that the effects of the wine wouldn't stop until she orgasmed and prayed that some infinitesimal amount of my magic came back and I could put her to sleep again.

Her smell grew more intense, and my cock twitched.

"Kir," she said breathily. A question, a plea.

I closed my eyes, trying to convince my body not to react to what I heard in her voice.

"You should sleep." I knew it would be impossible for her.

"Always with the sleep."

I smiled at her remark but refused to turn around. Eye contact and being able to see her made everything worse. The bed creaked, and her feet made a soft thud on the floor. A zipper came undone. My body shuddered, and my hands at the bandolier buckle stilled. I dared a quick glance over my shoulder.

She was behind me, pushing the Winter Court leathers down her hips.

"What are you doing?" I asked before I thought better of engaging her further.

Innara stepped out of the leathers, standing behind me in her underthings. "You said I should sleep. I can't sleep in those."

I stifled a groan. She had jumped up in front of me nights ago in only her underthings, but the difference was that time she ran like she had been scalded. This time, she knew exactly what she was doing. She stood now with confidence, looking me dead in the eye. I focused on my buckle, my resolve cratered.

Hopefully, she'd take the opportunity to get in the bed.

The bed where I would love to do all sorts of things to her.

I slipped the bandolier over my head. Now there was nothing for me to do but sit, but my legs were frozen to the spot. Fear and excitement swirled in me, and I drew in a deep breath.

"Kir." Her voice was directly behind me. She hadn't moved. Her hands came up on either side of my hips. I tensed out of panic, out of want. "Look at me."

I hung my head. Desire coursed through me. She was right there, my mate.

But it was the wine. The wine laid this bane, this gift upon my doorstep.

"No. Get in the bed," I forced myself to say.

She slid around my side, her hand sliding from my hip, grazing the top of my ass and along my side until she stood in front of me. I couldn't resist the shiver that shook my body, the sway into her touch. Her fingers hooked into the top of my leathers, and my breath rattled.

"I know you crave touch." She ran her hands up my chest. "So do I. My body..."

I clenched my fists at my side. This couldn't happen, but

yearning coursed through my veins. Touch had been denied to me now for years. What I would do to feel skin on skin again. I rocked into her hands as she ran them up to my shoulders.

"We're playing with fire." My voice came out rougher than I expected it to.

"I'm already burning," she said as she ran a hand down my arm, clasping my hand and then bringing it to her breast. At the touch, we both moaned, and I couldn't help but sweep my gloved thumb over her taut nipple.

"You're drunk on wine. You'll regret this." My senses were rapidly leaving me.

But I knew what the wine did to her, the ache it created that turned into pain. She said she was already burning—she wasn't far from the pain. And my magic was gone. I didn't even have a drop to help her sleep through it.

She stepped closer, her hips pushing into me, her thigh slipping between mine.

"Kir," her voice this time was needy and laced with the first beginnings of discomfort. Her hips moved against mine.

A primal urge flared up within me. The pain had set in for her, and I couldn't bear to see her go through that. Her fingers were already going for my belt. I grabbed her hands, holding them together.

She looked up at me, her eyes wide and bright.

"I need," she whispered.

My body or my heart made the choice for me.

"Shh. I know what you need," I whispered as I backed her up till her knees hit the chair behind her and buckled.

Above her was a sconce, and an idea formed. I released her hands, but as soon as I did, she was going for my chest, trying to find a way in.

No. I needed her in my control.

I stepped back, pushing a gloved hand to her sternum. "Stay."

Innara whimpered. I undid the buckle on my belt and slid it out of the loops. In front of me, she squirmed. Her hands flexed on the armrests.

With my belt out, I said, "Give me your hands."

I made quick work of wrapping my belt around them and then raising them above her head to tie them to the sconce. I doubted she'd have the strength to pull it off the wall.

I took one second to enjoy the picture of her—arms up, chest out, and legs slightly spread. Her dark hair was a tousled mess falling around her shoulders, and her eyes gleamed. I took some comfort in that. They were hazy with lust from the wine. She knew who stood in front of her, and I hoped she wanted this too. That it wasn't only the wine.

Her chest heaved from excitement. I tugged on the belt to make sure it was secure, and she groaned. My witch might like this, but then came the slightest scent of acrid fear.

That wouldn't do.

I propped one hand on the wall above her head and placed my other one at her throat. She gazed up at me, and I was lost as I ran my gloved hand from her throat to a breast. When I reached it, her eyes fluttered shut, and a breathy moan left her lips.

What I would do to taste them right now. "I'll take care of you. There is nothing to fear."

Then I slowly ran my hand down her stomach. Her breath hitched, and her hips bucked, demanding.

My own heart raced, and my cock throbbed, begging for release. I moved my hand down just enough that my gloved fingers rested right where she needed me.

She moaned and her hips bucked up into my hand.

The sound was nearly my undoing, and I was desperate to shuck the gloves and feel how wet she was.

I moved my hand, the gloves and thin layer of her underthings my only protection. We stared at one another, her pupils dilated all the way, and then her eyes rolled up into her head as my hand and her hips fell into a rhythm. Her head twisted to the side, her nose pressing into her arm as she rode my hand, and I gave into temptation, dropping down and biting her aching nipples through her shirt and then soothing them with my tongue.

Her moans came closer and closer, and the speed of her hips picked up. I took one last nip at her breasts and got up.

This was something I needed to see.

She was beautiful. The light reflected off a dewy sheen all over her pale skin. Her mouth was opened in an O, and a piece of her hair was caught in her mouth. She was more wild mountain witch than I'd ever seen her.

She threw her head back with a throaty moan, and her hips jerked against my hand.

The bond between us pulled me in. I couldn't take my eyes off her. My mate. It took everything in me not to capture what I knew was coming with my mouth on hers.

Her entire body tensed, and I kept moving my hand as her orgasm pulsed through her.

My balls tightened, and I nearly came in my pants. It was as if, for a split second, I felt her pleasure.

I eased my other hand down to pull the strand of hair out of her mouth. The bond relaxed.

Her eyes lazily opened, fully satiated.

"Good girl," I said as I drew my finger back to her lips. She bit down gently on my finger, and I closed my eyes, trying to savor every sensation.

But then she released me.

Her eyes shifted down. I sighed. With orgasm came the end of the effects of the wine. I reached to release her from the sconce. If we ever had the chance again, that was something I would certainly be doing.

If not, tied up like that, she painted a picture I'd never forget.

The belt came undone, and I rubbed along her arms, massaging the muscles. She pulled her arms in, away from my touch. Unease spread through me. I crouched in front of her, forcing her to look me in the eye again.

"What's wrong?"

She shrugged, her head tilting to the side. "I don't know if I should..."

"Should what?"

"Return the favor." She cleared her throat as she avoided looking at me directly.

The idea of that had my cock throbbing, but alarm bells went off in my head too. Somehow, me touching her felt under control. Her touching me, even with clothes in between, was another story.

I gathered her hands in my gloved ones.

"I'll be fine." I'd been dealing with that issue on my own now for years.

A sad smile spread on her lips, and my heart broke a little. The last thing I wanted was for her to feel shame from this, but I also didn't want to hint at my feelings. Feelings would tangle us all up. Muddle everything in my world, and in hers.

"You were just helping me out because I stupidly drank the wine you told me not to?" she asked.

"Something like that." I pulled her up. She needed to get in bed.

"Not because you wanted to, right?" Her eyes darted down to my crotch, making her point clear.

I pulled the sheets back on the bed, motioning for her to slip in. "I think it's pretty clear that I was willing."

She sat down, lifting her legs and sliding them under the covers. "It's not like you care for me or anything."

I paused. She always went straight for the heart of it with me. But the less she knew, the better. It was safer for both of us that way. I grabbed the covers and pulled them up to her neck, refusing to answer.

"What is this pull between us?" She shifted underneath the blankets, and I longed to climb in beside her, feel her warmth, tell her everything she wanted to hear.

I stepped away from the bed, closer to the chair, dragging a hand along the back of my neck. "You know there is a bond between us. The bargain."

She said nothing for a moment, her eyes holding disappointment in them. "Is that all?"

I sat down, dragging my hand down my face, the smell of her on my glove tantalizing. What could I say to that? I couldn't tell her there was more. So, I went to the oldest Faerie trick in the book.

"What more could there be between us?" In the dark, I grimaced, hating myself for it.

She didn't respond, and I leaned back, letting my head rest against the wall. We would fulfill our bargains with each other, and she would go be with her people.

Minutes passed, and I figured she had fallen asleep when she whispered, "Gaelin said you can lie. Tell me you can't lie. Tell me you haven't been lying to me this entire time."

CHAPTER 30
INNARA

My body was loose and languid, ready for sleep, but my heart pounded. Kir lounged in that blasted chair, leaning forward, elbows on his knees. His gaze bored into me. I couldn't look at him. The blasted pull was still there, even after what we'd done. Silly of me to think that maybe it would go away. I'd only want more, and here I was, unsure if I should allow his gravity to pull me in. I was already orbiting.

Gaelin said Kir could lie. I feared it was true. Nolan told me in the dungeon not to trust a fae. It was all too much. My head swam, and to top it off there was the wine.

I squeezed my eyes shut. Mortification at what I had done with Kir flowed through me. I'd wantonly ridden his hand.

And if I could do it again, I would.

He was like the sun and I a meager planet flying around him. It threatened to overwhelm me. This didn't happen with Dain, who was arguably as attractive, or even Gaelin. What was it? Was it some fae trick of his, designed to make me trust him or fall for him? He'd been so cold since the Delves.

But that wine... I would have allowed any of them to have their way with me.

Kir *had* tried to warn me.

I drove my hand into my hair and squeezed. I'd done what I had done. Let him help me. While I wasn't sure I could look Kir in the eye again, I was glad it was him instead of anyone else.

But what if Kir lied when I asked if he cared for me?

His silence was an answer.

I swallowed my embarrassment. What had I been thinking? I was a human plaything to him, nothing special. A means to an end.

I let out a long breath. Why was he still here?

He'd taken care of my need, taken care of his asset.

"You should go," I whispered. The tentative hold I had on my emotions threatened to break.

The seat creaked as he adjusted.

"I can't lie, generally speaking," he said.

I turned my head toward the window, not sure if I wanted to continue the conversation or make him leave. "But you have?"

"I did but not to you."

I waited. He needed to say more. That was what scared me—I always wanted more from him. More time together, more conversations, more shared visions.

"I'm not sure how I did it," he finally said.

Tears welled in my eyes. Was I supposed to believe that?

Rustling came from the chair before he stood and gingerly sat down on the bed beside me. "You remember how I wanted to see your memory?"

How could I forget?

"Let me show you one of mine. You need to sleep first. On your own. I don't have enough magic in me to bring you to that spot. You have to come to me."

I held his gaze for a moment. His memory could answer things, and it would be interesting to see it from his eyes. So much to learn.

An opportunity like this to observe a fae's thoughts couldn't be passed up. I nodded and closed my eyes.

I focused on my breathing, trying to settle my emotions. Soon, exhaustion pulled me under, and a light flared to life.

Kir stood in front of me, wearing only his leather pants. The muscled chest I saw when I'd healed him was on full display. A tattoo swirled on his left pec and around his shoulder and another full of symbols right over his heart.

I had to stop myself from moving to him.

He'd admitted to lying. He wouldn't tell me what this pull was between us. It rankled me. Most of my life, pertinent information had been withheld. First by my mother, now him. I couldn't let this primal instinct inside of me take over.

The light flickered over his features, beckoning me to trace his face, his lush lips.

I flexed my fingers at my sides. "I'm here."

His eyes flicked to my fingers then back to my face. His body seemed to sway toward me. In these visions, he always struck me as starved.

"Entering my memories will make you dizzy. Are you ready?" His voice was low as he took a cautious step forward, and I followed suit.

He raised his gloveless hands to my neck.

When his rough skin coasted over mine, fingers sinking into my hair, thumbs resting in front of my ears, a pained sigh rose from him, and his eyes fluttered closed.

"Ready?

I nodded. Instinctively, I gripped his wrists as I closed my eyes. Electricity flared between us, and then I tumbled. Vertigo bloomed as I catapulted and careened until all was still and I saw myself lying on the ground near where I had healed Kir. My view was Kir's perspective. Gaelin stood in front of me—in front of Kir—as my body lay on the ground on that hill near the Delves exit.

This was Kir's memory. I swore I felt doubt co-mingled with

protectiveness of me, the witch. The feeling bloomed and was quickly quashed.

"Who defeated Macachera?" Gaelin asked.

I—Kir—gritted my teeth as I stood, not wanting to show my weakness. I pointed out a charred spot on Gaelin's cloak, a smug satisfaction blooming in my chest as I realized Gaelin hadn't been aware. But Gaelin countered with granting me safe harbor, which both surprised me and shook me. Safe harbor was good. It meant he couldn't attack me, but it also meant I was at his mercy and stuck in his court.

Thoughts and considerations flicked through my mind before I settled on accepting it. It bought me time. Then Gaelin looked at the witch sprawled on the ground. He asked if she was special to me.

Without a thought, I lied.

I lied, and I realized it.

It was like an electric shock to the system, and I warred with my body not to show it, not to reveal it to Gaelin. But I didn't have the luxury of mulling it over. I filed it away to examine later. Gaelin's eyes caught on my necklace, and the memory faded.

Coming out of the memory was easier than going in.

I stood there, myself again, in the dream place.

Kir stroked my face with his thumbs, his forehead pressed to mine. "I don't know how I lied, I swear it to you."

"I believe you," I whispered.

I did. In that memory, he was mystified by it.

He'd lied about me being special to him to protect me. So, what was this? *How* was I special to him?

He was so close, his lips right there.

In these visions, I could do what I wanted. But he refused to tell me what this was between us.

Still, my body called to his. The heat of him warmed me. So much naked skin, begging to be touched. I flexed my hands on his wrists.

Both our breaths hitched. Time strung out.

"Innara." It was a plea.

I almost lost my will. But this was Faerie. The doubt that had badgered me on the way here roared back. He was toying with me. This was a fae game.

I had to focus on my goal, getting home.

I pulled my head back and forced my hands to drop. Confusion clouded his eyes as his hands hung there before he dropped them to his sides.

I steeled myself. "You should go. Go to your room. I'll be fine."

Kir had saved me. Who knew what would have happened if he hadn't been there to tell me not to drink the wine and then to help me after I stubbornly did anyway.

"And thank you for the …" I swallowed the bloom of heat. "For the help. But I'm fine now. You should go."

His head gave the slightest jerk, his eyes widening, his head dropping to stare at his bare feet. "I see."

My body swayed, a physical manifestation of wanting to suck my words back into my mouth.

He looked up, and his eyes flashed in the flickering light. "I won't leave while you rest. It's not safe. But I won't bother you here."

Kir snapped his fingers and then nothing but the blissful void of sleep.

I JERKED AWAKE. LIGHT STREAMED IN THE WINDOW. SWEAT BEADED ON MY brow, between my breasts. I threw the sheet and blanket off me with a groan. I was in my underwear, and the night before screamed back into my brain.

The chair was empty, but above it was the sconce where a leather belt hung.

An image of how I must have looked, arms up, chest out, legs spread, as Kir got me off, bloomed in my mind, and I clenched my thighs together. Had he enjoyed it? No, he must have thought me a fool after he'd warned me not to drink the wine.

Fools, however, could be manipulated. I sighed.

The door burst open, and Alana glided in with a glass in one hand and what looked like a basket of clothes under the other.

"I have something for you." She held out the glass. "This should help with the hangover from the wine."

In my head, I saw her tongue flicking out and tasting my collarbone, heard the moan that left my throat. I stared at the tattoo encircling her neck because her eyes were too intimidating.

She wiggled the glass. "Hello?" She paused, pulling the drink back, leaning down to look me directly in the eye. "Are you freaking out?"

Kir's belt on the sconce mocked me. Heat bloomed everywhere, and the room spun.

Alana grabbed my shoulders and led me to the bed until I sat. After sprinkling two powders into the glass, she shoved it at me "Drink this. It'll help."

"So you say. What is it?" It smelled funny, not appetizing at all.

"It's a mixture of Strangler's Fig and Shamewort. The 'wort tells the strangler fig what to focus on. In this case, your shame."

I finally met her eyes. Those plant names meant nothing to me, but she'd told me what they were. "Last time I drank something in this court, I found myself coming on to everyone around me."

She laughed. "Yes, well, welcome to the party. If you're freaking out about our dance, don't worry about it. The wine gave me the excuse to speak to you." She spun, with a clap of her hands. "But enough of that. We need to get you ready."

I eyed the glass. It wasn't the pink wine from last night. And if she was fine with everything, I resolved to be too. I shrugged. Bottoms up.

It tasted ghastly, but my head cleared. The anxiety I'd felt over her, over Kir, became lighter, manageable.

Wow. That was a recipe I needed to get. Alana was already

throwing clothes at me to change into.

"Where are we going?"

"Gaelin will take us out to the field," she said as she held a pair of leggings to my waist to make sure they'd fit.

"For what?"

She opened her mouth, coughed, and shrugged. "You'll see."

Alana spent the next few minutes getting food and pulling out various clothes for me for proper fit. The entire time I thought about how she tried to tell me not to bargain with Gaelin but gagged in the process.

When we met Gaelin, we left without so much as a word. He led us a different way than yesterday. Near the edge of the enormous, dead field, we dismounted, leaving Alana behind. One time when my mother and I lived in the city, we had gone to a sporting event. The field was at least four of those. Maybe more. Without any discussion, Gaelin led me into the desiccated plants.

When we got to the heart of the field, the harsh sun beat down on me, and I wished for more of Alana's concoction.

Gaelin smirked as if he'd read my thoughts. "Enjoyable party, was it not?" He looked me over from head to toe. "I see the effects of the wine wore off."

I stiffened. Holding my gaze, he reached down, slid his hand over mine, grasping it. I resisted, but his grip tightened.

He brought my hand up, dragged his nose across it as he breathed in deeply. "Didn't help yourself, I see."

I took in a harsh breath and ripped my hand away.

"I would have been happy to help you."

How dare he. I huffed and strode away. "What am I doing here?"

"Heal it," Gaelin said.

"All of it?" My head throbbed. There was no way I could do the entire thing. I'd never healed something this large all at once. Back home, it had to be tiny amounts so as not to arouse suspicion. We had our wards, but there was always the paranoia about them failing. "Right now?"

"Is that a problem?" His tone knocked me off kilter, and his ice blue eyes narrowed.

This sounded like a bargain, and I was done with them. I had two with Kir, and Alana had warned me not to bargain with Gaelin. Out of all of them I was inclined to take her advice, a fellow witch who had seemed to take a risk to give that advice. "I won't be part of more bargains."

Gaelin's eyes lit with victory, and I realized what I admitted.

"I'm not sure I can do it all at once." I hated how my voice caught.

"I understand. No bargains." He patted my arm. "Instead, I'll grant a boon commensurate with what you heal. What is it you humans say? We can shake on it."

I forced my face to not show anything as I gazed over his shoulder, taking in the brown, crinkly leaves.

"Anything you want." Gaelin's voice rang out but filtered, like the wind snatched at his words.

Anything I wanted.

I *wanted* to go home.

But everything here had a price. Besides, if I asked Gaelin to help me go home, I'd leave a sliver of my soul here with Kir. That idea didn't bother me as much as I thought it should. What I hated more was the pang that went through me as I considered leaving without so much as a goodbye.

But a boon...

Well, perhaps I could at least fulfill my promise to Nolan.

Gaelin wanted the field healed. I'd heal it.

I kneeled and dug my fingers into the soil. In the greenhouse, I always liked to have my hands in the dirt. With my eyes closed, I felt for my life magic. Every single dead plant out here held a kernel of life. In my mind, I let my magic flow out, mapping the field.

I slowly breathed out, letting my life energy float out like puffs on the breeze, landing on the field. It sank into the soil, each bit attaching to the kernels I found. Merging, morphing. I encouraged them to grow roots, deep roots. That would be best. Deep as they could to find water and nutrients, though this soil lacked both. When my arms shook and my legs trembled, I stopped. Pulling my hands out of the dry dirt, I released my magic.

The surrounding field was a vibrant green, full of corn-like plants. My healing didn't go the entire way to the edges, but it went most of the way.

I had done this. Me.

I'd always let it out so slowly, so carefully, that I didn't know what I could do. How much could I heal at home?

"I've done what I can," I said. "Earth and water witches should come and see what they can do, or my work won't matter for long."

Gaelin stood silent. His feet ground in the dirt as he spun, taking it in. When he finally made it full circle, he laughed, hearty and full. "Your boon. What is it you ask for?"

My awe at my ability faded. By now, I'd learned Faerie would reward something like going home only if I did something equally as big.

"You consider your options carefully," Gaelin said as he lifted a finger, a signal for Alana to approach with the horses. He studied a hill at the edge of the field.

Alana rode near and twirled her fingers. Water seeped from the air, the plants. The plants in our immediate vicinity drooped and withered.

Thankfully, her control meant it didn't come from us.

Death by desiccation didn't sound fun. But what was the point of my healing? I wanted to say something.

Thousands of tiny droplets zoomed together and spread like an oil sheen, creating a dome above Gaelin and me. The walls dripped from the top of the dome to the earth, enclosing us in its capsule.

Ignoring how she ruined my work, I grabbed the pommel of the saddle and hoisted myself up. Testing, I asked, "What did you want the stone for?"

"If you're considering asking me for the stone as your boon, think again. You could heal all my land and not earn that." Already astride, Gaelin peered down at me from his larger horse and height.

I shook my head. It was as I thought.

He watched me and seemed satisfied with my reaction. "I didn't want it falling into the wrong hands."

Kir's hands. Kir, who wanted to tear down the Wall.

"Do you know how fae gain power?" Gaelin pursed his lips, tilted his hands to gently lead his horse down the curved path. His other hand, gloved, sat on his thigh. He darted his gaze back to me, catching me staring at his hand. "Kir didn't tell you? We can gain power if we kill another fae. The power transfers from one to the other."

I gripped the reins. What was his point?

"And who is the most powerful fae?" He gave me a moment to come to the obvious answer. "Curious, don't you think?"

I stared straight ahead.

"Did you see any of his precious people while in the Winter Court?"

My mind raced. We'd gone through several abandoned villages, but I didn't see the people. Kir had mentioned hidden villages. I slid my gaze to Gaelin. He looked almost gleeful. He was enjoying this. My breath quickened, and I knew he heard it, just like my racing heart. I averted my gaze back to the road ahead.

"You've put a lot of faith in a fae who can lie," Gaelin said. "He so conveniently found you. He always loved rescuing damsels in distress. I'm sure you've heard of Violet, the cause of his curse. He likes to say I sent her, but she wasn't in my debt yet."

"Stop. Please." I was going to be sick. It couldn't be true.

But Kir had admitted he could lie.

"All right. I'll drop it." His leg bumped mine as his horse drew near. "You've seen my court. You've seen my people. I take care of them. We have food. My witches make sure of it."

"What of it?" I gritted my teeth, wanting to be anywhere but here. I needed time to think, to consider everything.

"I can help you. The Wall. There is a way through."

"How?" My heart leapt. I'd free Nolan, and we could go. Be away from this place where I didn't know up from down.

He lifted a finger. "Patience. First, what is the boon you wish for?"

I slowed my horse. Gaelin had effectively told me going home was more than a simple boon. And if I couldn't go home yet and the stone wasn't an option, there was only one thing I wanted from Gaelin.

"Release Nolan," I said.

"You care about this other human? He is your lover?"

I squirmed, not wanting to answer. "I care for him, but no."

"You'll both be moved into rooms near each other. You've earned much nicer quarters." Gaelin studied me before slapping a hand on his thigh. "Now for what I need. Did you know life witches are some of the most dangerous in this realm? And we have so few. They were hunted. Much too powerful. And they weren't nearly as strong as you are."

I didn't like his implications.

"You see, life witches have an ability to steal a fae source. The stronger the fae, the stronger the life witch needed."

I pulled on the reins, stopping my horse, and Gaelin did the same.

"No," I said as realization hit me. I doubted Kir. But stealing his fae source? I didn't think I could do it.

Gaelin didn't smile. "Yes."

"I'm a healer."

"If you do, I can get you home. Isn't that what you wanted? Look at how he's manipulated you."

"What stops me from taking yours?"

Gaelin threw his head back in a laugh. "Simple. I'll kill that friend of yours."

CHAPTER 31
KIR

The whiskey slid down my throat, smooth yet hot. The burn helped me feel alive. Numbness overtook me when Innara told me to go. I hadn't slept since inside the Delves, and I'd slipped out of her room as soon as the sun broke the horizon. But rest still eluded me.

I slammed the glass down on the side table. I had shown her everything of that moment. She'd said she believed me yet still told me to leave. My fingers tightened on the glass tumbler, and I ran my fingers over my lips, catching the scent of her.

I hated being in this place. We hadn't been here a day before Gaelin had sunk his hands into our heads and mucked around. Now all I could think about was keeping her safe. The stone and saving my people was secondary.

Fuck!

I hurled the tumbler at the fireplace. The glass smashed and shattered. Razor-sharp shards tinkled to the ground as my breath bellowed. I flexed my hand into a fist over and over.

This sort of complication was exactly what I had tried to avoid. These sorts of emotions. They clouded my head. I had to stay focused. If she continued with our bargain, that would guarantee our proximity and my ability to keep her safe. I could kill two banshees with one stone, especially since I was incapable of staying away.

I was mad to think I could ignore the bond. Listening to Rylla and sending Innara on her way would have been the smart thing to do. But even thinking that made my heart ache. I already knew that, once the time came for us to say goodbye, I would be reliving all the moments with her in my visions until my final fae breath.

I scrubbed a hand down my face. She didn't trust me. That much was obvious, even after I had shared my memory. I ran my hand over my mouth again before ripping it away.

I had to stop doing that. The emotions, the yearning it stirred, were too much.

A picture of her trembling formed in my mind. She had been both the lioness in our dreams yet shy in person. Could it be? Could she be inexperienced?

I sat with the thought for a moment. Were humans, even with their short lifespans, less promiscuous? How much of that was the cause of last night's reaction?

How much of it was because I wouldn't tell her she was my mate? I wanted to, but Gaelin's strength in soul magic was too dangerous. As far as I knew, he hadn't looked. It was such a rare thing I doubted he'd checked for it, but if she slipped, said the wrong thing...

A thump sounded on my balcony, followed by a querying meow.

Haze's front paws pressed to the glass of the balcony door, and I sprinted over to unlatch it.

"Took you long enough," I said as he pranced in and nuzzled my bare foot. Immediately, I put up a soundproof dome. Haze didn't talk, but I sometimes did.

Haze nipped at my ankle. He hated flying in the summer court. Too hot, too dry. I poured some cool water into a glass. As much as I champed at the bit to get information, he needed a few minutes to recuperate.

Haze crouched over the glass, lapping up the water. His beak made tiny tinking noises on the glass. As he drank his fill, I found the tray of food I had called for after I'd left Innara. Choosing several meats, breads, and cheeses, I placed them all on a small plate and laid it down on the floor near the water. Haze dug in. I frowned. He usually wasn't this bad off.

After a few minutes, the plate was empty. Haze sat, licking a paw and wiping it behind his tufted ear. A blend of images came to me: The Autumn Court. Rylla, Dain, and Clove sitting in front of a fire, grave concern written on their faces.

The rope that had been tied around my chest since I'd watched them go through one of those mirrors loosened.

They were okay. They survived.

Haze hopped to my leg and curled up in my lap, a soft purr emanating from him as a vision of flying through the sky came to me. Apparently, Haze had found them and then headed in exactly the wrong direction to find me as he sent me images of the muted white landscape of home.

I stroked his head. "I'm sorry, my boy. I tried to send you a flare. I didn't have enough power left in me." He opened his beak and placed it on my wrist. Clearly, I had interrupted him. "Okay, okay, go ahead. I'll shut up."

Another stream of images: treetops flying by under him, the snow of my court. My heart gripped in the cage of my ribs. A steady stream of the Wild Hunt crossed from snow to brown leaves. An arrow loosed, zipping right by Haze's head. He screeched, banking his flight to the left. Then the sound of more being loosed. Haze was adept at dodging in flight, but that was a lot. One nicked his side, and the pain seared through him.

My free hand dug into his feathery fur, searching for the wound. It was there. Thankfully not deep and not infected. I wanted to get up and get an ointment, but his beak on my other wrist clamped down.

There was more to show me.

Now he kept his distance, tracking the Hunt from an altitude where their arrows couldn't reach him. They hiked not on any path or road. They unerringly headed in one direction. Haze picked up speed, following the same bearing, but my stomach already roiled. I suspected where they went. Haze's imagery skipped ahead, and the castle of the Autumn Court rose in the distance.

Haze released my wrist and chirped mournfully. If the Wild Hunt stayed on that trajectory, they were at the Autumn Court, and what exactly did that mean? Clove would have set wards. They would have warning. I had to believe that.

I curled my fingers into Haze's fur as he purred. He was exhausted, and that injury needed to be seen. And the one person who could tell me what the Wild Hunt intended was in this very castle.

I scooped up Haze and placed him on my bed. "Sleep, buddy. I'll get you more water and food and an ointment for that injury."

True to my word, I called for more food and poured him a large bowl of water. He was already fast asleep by the time I slipped into the hallway in search of Gaelin.

AFTER HALF AN HOUR, MY SEARCH PROVED FRUITLESS. GAELIN WASN'T IN ANY of the usual spots, so I found myself in the halls I had been in last night. Alana emerged from Innara's room. I hesitated, but Alana looked up and saw me.

"She's fine," she said, "if a bit mortified."

I nodded, shoving my hands into my pockets. Perhaps my earlier assumption was correct.

Alana sidestepped away from the door. "Don't let me stop you from seeing her yourself if that is what you want."

"Actually, it's fortuitous that I ran into you." I waved away her concern.

"Oh?" She raised her brow.

I didn't want to let on that Haze was here. He'd be safe enough in my room for the time being. I gripped my side. "The wound I suffered in the Delves takes longer to heal fully. Would you have an ointment I could use?"

She studied me for a second before reaching into the pouch looped to the belt at her waist. "Of course," She pulled out a small container and began to twist the top off. "Lift your shirt."

I stepped back. This was a first that my cursed worked in my favor. It gave me an excuse.

"I think I need to apply it. Would you mind if I just took the container?" I reached out.

She held the small jar, considering it. "Sure. I have more anyway. I'll grab it before we go out."

I cocked my head "Before we go out?"

She shook her head in chagrin. "Gaelin has plans for Innara."

A pang went through me. What type of plans did he have? "Oh? And what is that?" It was a feat that I kept a straight face.

"Not information I can share."

Of course, he had effectively muzzled all the witches in his court. I'd get no further with questions in that direction. "Gaelin was my second question. I need to talk to him. Do you know where he is?"

Her eyes narrowed. "He's currently busy. We won't be back till this evening. You can find him then."

"It's urgent."

With what seemed like a touch of sympathy, she said, "He won't care."

She left me standing in the hall, holding a jar of ointment. From inside Innara's room came the sound of a spoon scraping a bowl.

I could go in. Speak with her.

No. She wouldn't want to see me. Alana had said she was mortified.

I returned to my room and aided Haze while I decided on my next course of action.

If I couldn't talk to Gaelin until this evening, I'd make use of the time. The spot where Gaelin found had us and I had lied. I needed to figure out if there was a disturbance there or not. Eliminate at least one reason I was able to lie. If I had to, I'd bring Innara there. She needed to know I hadn't been lying this entire time.

THE SUN CRESTED IN THE SKY AS I CLIMBED THE HILL FROM THE DAY BEFORE. Heat prickled on my head, and a dry wind blew past. Below me, a pressure wave rippled through the fields, like a stone thrown into still water.

I crouched, watching. The crops straightened, life bled into them, turning them green and healthy.

Innara. It had to be her.

The blast wave made it easy to pinpoint. People were in the center. Only she would be able to bring life back to these fields. And Alana had mentioned they were heading out.

I slowly rose, entranced by the sheer strength of Innara's witchery. She didn't even know. She'd barely scraped the surface of that strength when attacking Macachera, but using her practiced talent she displayed it without a second thought.

A witch like that...a *life* witch like that could—

My stomach roiled.

I knew exactly what Gaelin sought to do. The oracle had said there would be a life witch strong enough to take a fae source.

And I'd delivered her to him.

How long would he wait before he twisted her to do as he wanted? How long did I have under his safe harbor? Oh, he was smart. Safe harbor protected me from him and his court. But she was not of his court. He'd played us from the very moment of killing that ankle biter. And I walked straight into it.

I turned, surveying the area, my feet grinding in the stoney earth.

The wind whipped around me, whistling through the newly verdant field.

I could leave this place. Right now.

Break safe harbor, find a safe space, and figure out a way to get Innara back to safety with me. But how long would that take? How long before Faerie exacted its own price for breaking its rule? Faerie was never easier than the fae.

Clove and the others were surrounded by the Wild Hunt, but surrounded didn't mean they had been attacked. Yet. If they were aware of the Hunt, they'd make sure they had enough power to sift away, but knowing them, they'd bide their time, waiting to hear from me, putting their faith in Haze.

If I left now, I'd be feeding Haze and Innara to the literal wolf of Gaelin. I'd be on my own. And there was no guarantee I'd find the others quickly.

I couldn't do that to either of them.

But Faerie wouldn't be kind for breaking safe harbor. There was a good chance it would take my life.

The sun neared the horizon. How long had I been here contemplating what to do? So much time wasted when I could have been figuring out how I'd lied.

Now it was even more imperative to convince Innara she could trust me. I paced the area, found the spot I believed I was in when Gaelin asked me if she was special.

No weather disturbance present.

But what if not all disturbances were weather related? What if some bent the rules of Faerie?

"What exactly are you doing?" someone asked.

I spun.

Gaelin stood just down the sloping path so that only his head was visible.

Fuck. "What do you want?"

He sauntered up the rest of the way. I glanced behind him—alone. I let my gaze wander out across the fields.

"Alana is riding home with Innara." He paused as he stepped closer. "Quite the witch, isn't she?" He cast his gaze out to the healthy field, bursting now with a ripe crop.

I knew he'd gotten at her strength and what that meant. Veiled threats were his specialty.

All I could do was grunt as my mind raced with what I could do. What options were open to me? What leverage did I have? I grasped at fucking straws. Threatening my mind power on him was useless unless I was serious about breaking safe harbor.

Gaelin circled me as he gave an amused sniff. He surveyed the area, a grim smile forming on his lips. "Trying to figure out how you were able to lie? Innara asked you about it, didn't she? She was quite distraught. Moreso than someone who only owes you a debt."

My fists clenched. "So what was it? What is special about here?"

He shrugged. "Your guess is as good as mine."

"Have you experienced it?"

Gaelin watched me out of the side of his eye. "I can give her what she wants, you know."

I swallowed the primal instinct to shred my competition, shred *him*. He may not mean anything sexual, but no one else should give her what she wanted or needed, except me and herself.

"And what is it *you* want?" I asked. He always exacted a price.

"Maybe I'll keep her drunk on my wine and give her exactly what she'll want. And it won't only be my hand." He reached out for my wrist, but I yanked it away as he sniffed the air. "She smells luscious. I'd love to taste her."

I snapped. More than emotion drove me. A primal need to protect my mate. I lunged forward and gripped his throat. "She's mine."

Gaelin's eyes lit up despite being choked. "We'll see about that. You should be more concerned about what price I will ask of *you*."

He lifted his hand and rifted an eye into it. It was large, easily three times the size of a normal fae's. The iris was black with striations of bluish white through it like lightning bolts.

The huntsman.

Gaelin would have had to best him to control the Wild Hunt, and now he held his eye as proof of that.

I still gripped Gaelin's throat. His face turned a satisfying shade of red. Veins bulged in his forehead.

"I'd let go if I were you." His free hand came up and gripped mine, trying to pull me off. "My huntsman has orders. If something were to happen to me, he'd act on them."

If Gaelin died, any bargain would mean the huntsman's soul fragment would return.

Unless...unless it wasn't a bargain but a soul trade.

My fingers tightened around Gaelin's throat before I shoved him backward. Such a piece of shit.

If the huntsman had sacrificed his soul for his life, upon Gaelin's death, the huntsman's soul would die too. The huntsman would act on whatever orders he had been given. A slab of meat with no conscience. No will, no soul. He'd follow the orders relentlessly until his physical body perished.

Gaelin coughed, smoothed down his shirt. He lifted his hand, the eye floating an inch above. The eye swiveled in his hand until it focused on me. "Look into the huntsman's eye. You'll see what he sees."

A sick feeling floated in my stomach. I already knew where he was, and I didn't want confirmation. I dreaded it, but I had to know. As risky as it was to allow myself to be so vulnerable in front of Gaelin, I did it anyway. Rylla, Dain, and Clove were depending on me. I gazed into the eye of the huntsman, felt myself drawn in, floating, flying until I saw what he saw.

He stood on a cliff, looking down toward the Autumn Court.

Glowing runes appeared, drawn in the air. The huntsman could see wards, an ability I had not known he possessed. Had he always, or had Gaelin gifted it to him? Perhaps the witches had.

That was the moment I realized exactly how formidable Gaelin had become. He'd painstakingly built an army over the years.

And I'd let him.

I hadn't wanted to sacrifice a single soul of my people to defeat him, blind to the absolute threat he would become, always thinking that, as long as I remained the strongest in fae power, he would be unable to beat me.

And I let him continue chipping away.

The huntsman deliberately showed me the wards. The Wild Hunt stopped just shy of them to not trip the triggers. Rylla, Dain, and Clove had no idea what sat on the cliff. And like the huntsman could read my thoughts, he cast his gaze back behind him, where miles of the dead stood, motionless, awaiting orders.

I'd seen enough.

I ripped myself out of the vision with a jerk of my head, eyes squeezed shut. And the way the huntsman seemed to almost know my thoughts frightened me.

And I had seen something I hoped I hadn't given away.

The Wild Hunt sat on the wrong side of the castle.

The other side held an escape route. If I could get Haze back to them, he could get in and out without detection.

I would give anything to protect them if needed. "What is it that you want?"

Silence greeted me.

Gaelin had sifted away.

CHAPTER 32
INNARA

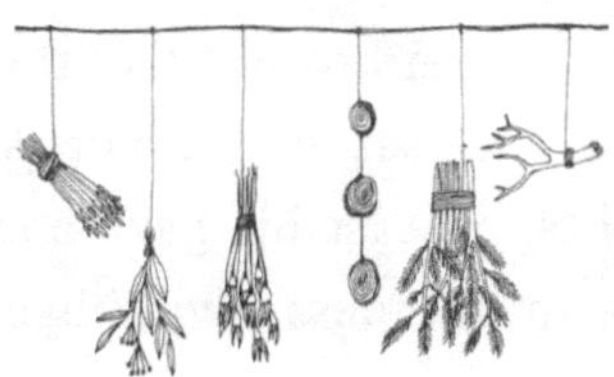

My new room was luxurious. The bed alone was so much better than any I had ever slept in. I felt cradled. My body craved more rest, but I had things to do. Gaelin had all but bargained with me to take Kir's fae source.

A way home. The question was if I could do it—and if I *should*.

Gaelin had worked hard to sow doubt in me about Kir. It worked, but Gaelin hadn't made me feel like I could trust him either. Gaelin was out for himself. Was Kir? Did he play up the whole "my people" thing to make himself seem unselfish? And what if helping Gaelin was my only way home?

I didn't know who to trust. There was only one person from this side of the Wall who seemed like I could trust them.

Muriel.

A witch, who had led us to the stone. A witch who was untethered to Gaelin. Who had provided aid when it was needed with no strings attached.

Muriel was exiled, but the witches here had to know how to find her. I needed to speak with Alana. Muriel had been in the Autumn Court, and there was no way I could go back there now.

I splashed water on my face and put on my Summer Court clothes: light leggings and a tank top under a gauzy shirt. With the extended winters at home and the Winter Court, the clothes here felt like wearing nothing at all.

Nolan stood outside with his hand raised to knock, a boyish grin on his face when I opened the door.

"You're awake."

I stepped forward, my arms sliding around him and feeling his familiar warmth. "You're out of the dungeon. Did they treat you okay?"

"It was a dungeon, but it was clean, and I was well cared for. Honestly, I'd rather stay there than an Eastlands jail any day." He laughed at his joke before his face grew serious. "I owe you my thanks." He cupped my cheek and pushed my hair behind my ear. My body shivered, followed by an unwelcome roil of guilt. "Can we talk?"

I glanced back into my empty room, pulled the door shut behind me. "Ah, I was on my way somewhere. I've been summoned."

I pasted a smile on my face, hoping he'd believe it. As much as I wanted to talk with him, now was the time to find Muriel, and I didn't know how much time I would have before Gaelin demanded action from me.

His eyes lost some of their gleam. "Of course. Later, then?"

"Definitely," I said.

He pulled back. "One thing. I wanted to apologize for how I acted the day you fell through. I wasn't myself that day—stress, lack of sleep." He shook his head as if clearing his thoughts. "None of that really matters. What matters is I was dismissive, and I never meant to treat you like that."

My heart warmed. "I'm so glad you said something. It was an odd day, so let's say you're forgiven."

He'd apologized. I should have been elated. Everything that had annoyed me that fateful day had bothered him too.

We could go back to being happy. Find our way out of here.

Nolan tilted my chin up, slid his hands to either side of my face, and placed a butterfly-light kiss on my lips.

My eyes shut, and I swallowed down how I wished it had been Kir's lips.

His tongue slid over mine as he pressed his hips into me. In the Eastlands, we'd shared a similar kiss. The door behind my back had been a tree, and we'd fired each other up until we were both bundles of want.

But now?

I felt nothing.

A door slammed, and I pushed Nolan away before using my thumb to wipe at my mouth.

The side of my face burned. Down the hall, Kir's face was a mask of fury. I slid my gaze back to Nolan, who was turning back to me too, a smirk on his face.

I needed to get out of here. "I should go, or I'll be late. Stop by later?"

"Sure." He leaned forward, pressing a chaste kiss to my cheek.

THE WITCH WING OF GAELIN'S COURT HAD A LARGE COMMON AREA. Rectangular tables filled the center. Several seating areas for conversations filled in around the sides, with bookcases used as dividers. All around the exterior were doors to what must have been private rooms.

Alana sat at one of the tables, a plain white dish with crumbs in front of her. Her crossed legs were swung off to the side as she read a book. Oblivious to my approach, she took a sip from a teacup.

I stopped on the other side of her table. Once she noticed me, she closed the book, not even marking her spot.

"What brings you here?" she asked.

"Muriel. Do you know of her? I need to know how I can speak with her."

Alana set her cup down with a clatter and shot me a glare. Several witches occupied the room, but most of them were farther away. Soft laughter and whispers. It reminded me of a library.

"Sit," Alana said as she flicked her finger to send a trickle of water from the pitcher into the air. Once it was a foot or more above our head, it spread out like it did the other day with Gaelin, oozing over an unseen dome until it reached the floor. "There are witches here who would be more than interested to report to Gaelin on what we speak of."

"And Muriel would be of interest to him?"

"She's a powerful witch, even more than me, but she's exiled. He never found anything to bribe her with. He has nothing she wants. But you could prove to be that missing link for him if he knows you have interest in her."

"I met her in the Autumn Court. She helped save me from..." I shook my head, clasped my hands. "Kir said it was a disturbance. She said I would know a time when I needed her again. But I don't see how I can go see her in the Autumn Court right now."

Alana tapped her nail on the teacup. It made a barely audible *tink tink tink*. "The coven could help you too."

I pulled my chin back. Muriel was the one I trusted.

She continued. "Join the coven. You'd have every witch in Cirrelea at your back. Including Muriel."

"But she's exiled." How could she be in the coven?

"She is, but exile is physical. Once one is part of the coven, one can never be fully removed from it."

Those words did little to ease my mind. "I need to talk to Muriel first."

Alana sighed. And her finger *tink tink tink*'d again. "I know what Gaelin wants of you. I didn't hear it. But there is only one reason why he would want a life witch who is so powerful."

I didn't respond.

"Will you do it? Is going home that important to you?" She paused, casting her gaze down the room. "You need us."

"And why is that?"

"Do you know how to do what he requests?" She leaned forward and ran a finger over my bracelet.

"Muriel first."

She glanced around the room again, chewing her lip. "All right, I can communicate with her. It'll take a bit of work to reach out, but I'll convince her to meet you on the border of the Summer Court. But for you to go, I'll have to create a distraction. I'll only take that risk if you'll join our coven."

I narrowed my eyes. I was tired of being pushed around. Playing some pawn on the chessboard while everyone spoke of how powerful I was. If I was as powerful as they said, I would play to that, seize it. "What is in it for you? Why do you want me in the coven so badly?"

Alana smiled, but it didn't meet her eyes. Half feral, half sad. "I crave a sisterly bond with you." She leaned in again as if to tell me a secret. "We can teach you to take a fae source."

I leaned in, reaching for my witchery, letting it lift my hair, lift hers. It swirled inside the dome she had created. "Tell me why you want me in the coven."

Her eyes lit from within. "With a witch as powerful as you, the coven could reclaim—"

She gagged.

I narrowed my eyes. She'd done that while she danced with me too. "The bargain prevents you from speaking of things, doesn't it?"

Alana didn't respond, but it was in her eyes. The truth of it still glistened in them.

"Help me meet with Muriel, and we'll see about the coven. Otherwise, I'll figure out how to take his source and leave this dying land behind. And every single last one of you can rot with it." It made no difference if what I said was true or not. Unlike fae, I could lie.

Alana's eyes flared as I let my life magic press in on her, squeeze her ever so slightly. Her eyes lit with shock and discomfort.

My strength frightened her.

It scared me too, but I needed to embrace it.

"I'll send a message when it is set up," she finally said, "but you need to be ready at a moment's notice. The distraction can only last for so long, and Gaelin wants you healing our fields every day."

Alana was right. Gaelin sent me to another field that afternoon and the next morning too. Luckily, how much I slept after the initial field meant he didn't expect me to expend myself. Besides, he wanted me to take Kir's source, and using all my magic on healing his fields would mean I wouldn't be able to do that.

I took comfort in that. The more time that passed, the more I realized any thought of taking Kir's source was a false bravado. It went against something in me. I told myself it was because I was a healer at heart, but I knew something else was preventing me. My feelings were muddled.

I rested in my room. I hadn't spoken to Kir since *that* night. The memory of it still brought heat to my cheeks, a flush to my skin.

A knock sounded at my door, and my treacherous heart leapt at the thought of Kir.

Nolan leaned, one arm propped up against the doorjamb, when I opened it. I stifled the betrayal of my disappointment and smiled.

"You're a hard woman to find." He pulled a rose from behind his back, sniffed it, and handed it to me.

Before, this would have had me melting. The sight of Nolan used to set my stomach alight with butterflies. A lick of anger at myself whipped up my spine.

The rose smelled sweet, not like a rose at all. I moved into the room to find a vase. "I was here yesterday evening."

Warm hands slid over my shoulders, a gentle massage. My body swayed backwards into it. I hadn't felt someone's real touch like this since home.

"Sorry. I wound up with my own summons." His fingers worked their way up the back of my neck.

But I stiffened at his words. "Who summoned you?"

"Gaelin."

Cold ran through my veins. I pulled away and sat in one of the chairs in the receiving area of my suite.

Nolan sat across from me, concern in his eyes. "What's wrong?"

"What did he want?" The other day in the field, Gaelin had seemed to gauge how much I cared for Nolan.

He leaned back into his chair, a picture of relaxation. "He told me he offered you a way home and that he wasn't sure you would do it."

Our eyes met. Somewhere in the castle, a clock struck the hour.

"So, he was right. You may not do it." Nolan walked to the balcony doors to look out. A muscle in his jaw clenched.

"It's not so simple. I don't know how to do what he asks."

"Someone must know. The witches?" He turned his face to reveal his profile. His eyes darkened, and his stance no longer held the casual relaxation it had earlier.

"I'm working on it."

"But?"

I clasped my hands in my lap as my insides twisted. "I'm a healer."

"It's our way home." He turned, with his hands shoved in his pockets. The light of the setting sun behind him caused his hair to glow a bronzed gold.

"I know, but..." I pinched my nose. The thought of taking Kir's source felt like I'd be ripping my heart out. "It feels wrong."

"Wrong? Who cares? He's fae. They mess with your head." He strode forward, dropped to his knees. "We could go home. You could see your mom. We could be together." He slid his hands around mine. "Start a family."

We shared a moment, silently speaking to one another. How could I tell him I didn't want to do it because there was something between Kir and me?

I must have shown too much on my face because his went stony.

He dropped my hands and stood up. "Don't be naive. Did you fall for that fae? Tell me you didn't."

Naive.

Last time that word caused a world of self-doubt, but this time only rage simmered. I couldn't meet his eyes.

"I'll find another way," I said as I stared unseeing out the balcony doors.

"Oh? And would that be with that other fae?"

I didn't respond.

"He's using you. Did you bargain with him? Did he rope you into an eternity of helping him?"

I swallowed. It was too close to the mark. Kir had tricked me into more than I'd realized.

"I'll find another way," I said again. Maybe it would be with Kir. Maybe it wouldn't. Gaelin's way seemed straightforward, but I doubted it was.

Nolan threw up his hands. "I can't talk to you right now about this. You won't take the easy way home for both of us, and I get the feeling that making a life with me is no longer remotely close to what you want. Naive doesn't even begin to describe you."

CHAPTER 33

INNARA

Three days passed. I healed fields. Nolan was off to who knew what. He never came back after our last chat. I'd kept my word and gotten him out of the dungeon, so that was off my conscience. I'd only seen Kir once since the hallway, as he spoke with Alana and handed a jar of ointment back to her. There was so much I wanted to ask him, all those things Gaelin had mentioned, but I feared the answers.

Instead, I bided my time and waited for Alana's signal. I'd packed a bag and taken it with me each day, slung over my shoulder.

Today, I was in that original field again. My work didn't hold as well as I liked, but there was only so much the water and earth witches could do. Just now, an earth witch dug her hand into the dirt. After a few minutes, she nearly passed out from the exertion of finding minerals in the dead soil.

Alana rode up on horseback, out of breath. She reached out a hand to bring me up on to the horse behind her. "It's time. I hope you have nothing in your room you wouldn't want Gaelin to know about."

"Why?"

"He's searching the rooms. Seems he misplaced something of great import." She smirked.

"And what is that?"

She shook her head. Ah, yes, she wouldn't be able to tell me. Hope flared that maybe she had gotten her hands on the stone.

"How did you get it?" I asked.

"You really don't want to know," she shouted over her shoulder as her horse galloped back to the court. "Don't worry. It wasn't the first time, and it won't be the last."

We pulled into the court, and Alana brought me towards the dungeons. We turned a corner, and Kir stood there.

"What's he doing here?" I frowned, but my heart picked up speed.

"I told him about it. He has his own reasons to go to the edge of the Summer Court." She glanced at me. "Don't be mad. I took a hefty risk, and it may as well help as many people as possible."

I couldn't argue with that logic.

Even from the halls leading to the dungeon, an uproar met us—furniture scraping the floor, drawers opening—overall, a general cacophony.

Alana drew up a tapestry on one wall and unscrewed a bottle at her hip. Water poured forth, and she wove her magic. I studied her weavings. The way she thinned and threaded. I wondered if the same technique would be useful with life magic and healing.

The stone wall behind the tapestry disappeared and turned into a slim crack in the stones.

Kir took a moment to unstrap his swords so he'd fit. As it was, we'd have to turn sideways. Behind us, the tapestry fell against the wall, hiding us from view. Alana ushered us in farther.

A tunnel lay ahead, dark, dirty, and musty smelling. Kir flicked his hand up, and a ball of light appeared, not too bright. Enough for us to see one another but not attract attention from anyone in the hall.

Alana's elegant hand twirled. Water hovered in the air. She

twisted and molded it, forming it into the thinnest sheet, and flung it in front of us. "The tunnel will lead you several miles into the Summer Court. I cleared the illusions that hid the directional marks. It's a warren down here." She tapped the wall where a white circle now appeared. "So you need to follow these marks. They appear every so often. If for some reason you get turned around, white leads out. If you're heading into the court, they are green. It will take you far enough to get you past any of his guards on patrol."

She turned away, but I grabbed her arm.

"Thank you," I said. "I don't want this to cost you."

"I've covered my tracks. I never should have made the bargain with him to begin with, but I fell for his tricks. Only a curse by him could be worse." As she realized what she'd said, she whipped her head up to gauge Kir's reaction. He showed none, merely peered off down the tunnel.

"Why did you?" It wasn't the time for this discussion, but the words popped out anyway.

"He made many promises before the actual bargain. By the time I figured it out he had too many of my sisters. I couldn't leave them to him." She looked down the tunnel. "Go. I'd think he will find what he seeks today, but then there will be questions. You have two days at most."

Kir grabbed my arm with his gloved hand, giving me a quick tug.

Together, we double-timed it down the inky black tunnel with Kir's light to guide us and reveal the white blazes. Soon, Alana was gone. We were alone.

The tunnel had offshoots every ten feet. Without the blazes, we would have never found our way out. Neither of us talked as we navigated each turn. Eventually, the maze slowed.

I finally had the courage to break our silence. "What are you hoping to find out here?"

"The others. I've had Haze ferrying messages. When Alana mentioned this, it seemed like the perfect opportunity." Kir glanced down at me. "You'll see Muriel?"

"Yes." I wrapped my arms around me, the air chilly, as we turned left and the tunnel pitched down. "Where have you been? I saw you in the hall..." I stopped speaking as I realized he had seen Nolan and me.

A tense silence strung out. I picked at my nail, debating if I should say something else, but Kir spoke first.

"Yes, the hallway. I take it you are back together with..." He waved his hand in the air.

"Nolan? No. What you saw was..." I dared a glance at him. He stared straight ahead with a tense jaw. "I don't know what it was."

His eyes shot down to me. "Oh?"

I wasn't sure why I kept going. "We are not in agreement right now."

"What is it that you need to agree on?"

Could I tell him that? I bit my lip.

Kir stopped walking, turned to me with a raised brow and studied me. "Ah, it's about whatever Gaelin wants you to do."

My mouth went dry. Nerves stole my voice. I so badly wanted to tell him but froze in indecision.

"What will he give you for my fae source?"

My eyes widened as shock licked over me. "How did you know that?"

"They say a strong life witch will be able to take a fae source. What else could it be? I'm irritated I didn't think of it sooner." Then with a soft voice, not quite a whisper. "The way home?"

"Yes." My voice stuck in my throat.

Kir stuffed his hands into his pockets and began walking again.

I reached out and snagged his arm. "He mentioned other things, like how you are the one with the most power."

"What about it?" He kept walking but allowed my hand on his covered arm.

"He said you killed your people. That when a fae kills another fae, they inherit their power."

Kir pulled up short. "He said those exact words?"

"He alluded to it."

Shaking his head, he began walking again. "That's different. He was trying to make you doubt me. My people are well hidden in the Winter Court so Gaelin can't find them. But I did kill someone to inherit all this power. I didn't want to."

"Who was it?" I swallowed, dreading the answer.

"My uncle. Our power already faded. Gaelin had already killed fae and was gaining power. We saw what was coming. *My uncle* saw what was coming. He had an illness, and while he had many years left, he saw what should be done to fortify the Winter Court. He asked me to kill him in order for me to inherit the court and double my power. I didn't want to, but when the wards tripped, when we knew Gaelin was in our house." Kir's voice cut off.

I heard what he didn't say. So much pain caused by one fae.

"And so your boyfriend wants you to take my source to get you both home. Maybe you should."

I didn't have time to respond. The tunnel spit us out into the blazing sun of the Summer Court with no warning. Behind us was a tree with a thick trunk, and in front of us was a bridge.

Muriel stood with a straight back, looking toward the Summer Court. Her posture seemed almost regal, even if I detected a note of resignation.

The bridge was made of wood, now gray and dry from baking in the sun.

"It'll hold," Kir said, erasing my worries. "Enchanted."

A chalk boundary separated Muriel from us. The boundary between courts.

Clasping her hands behind her back, a small smile graced her lips once she saw us. Her hair hung down her back, reaching her thighs. Braids in the front kept it out of her face as the barest of breezes blew in from the Autumn Court. The cooler air felt luscious.

"You came," I said as Kir and I walked down the creaking bridge.

She nodded, her eyes closing a touch. "I knew we would meet

again, though I had not seen this." She unclasped her hands and gestured to the ground. "Mindful of the boundary, hmm?"

Kir and I came to halt in front of her, keeping to our side of the line.

"My companions?" he asked.

Muriel held up a hand. "They are on their way. Let me talk to the witch."

She stared at him until he backed away, wandering back toward the Summer Court to give us privacy.

Muriel looked to me. "Now, tell me why you have had me summoned here."

"I...I..." Suddenly, I felt silly. I'd taken this woman from her daily life, all to ask her who I should trust.

"Out with it."

"I came for your thoughts. You aided us in the past. I don't know who to trust."

She pointedly glanced to Kir. "It seems you do. Look who is here with you. And who helped you summon me?"

"But—" I leaned in, dared a peek back. Kir had his arms propped on the rail of the bridge, gazing down the dry riverbed, the picture of casual. But he could hear.

Muriel raised a finger. My hair moved in a slight breeze before my ears popped. "Speak freely now."

"I can't help but think his interest in me is protecting an asset. I bargained with him to get me home, but he tricked me and made what I agreed to quite open-ended."

"Sounds like a fae thing to do. This bargain was before you met me?"

"Days before," I said.

She nodded along. "In other words, during the time he didn't know if he should trust you?"

My stomach sank. I hadn't thought of it that way. "It's just...there is this thing between us. It's like we're magnets. There is this pull, and I can't be sure if it is real or something he is doing to me."

Muriel's eyes twinkled. "He has not told you?"

I shook my head. "One of the reasons I find it hard to trust him."

Kindness lit her eyes. "It's not my place to tell."

"But you know?"

She sighed, studying Kir before focusing back on me. "Last time, I told Kir that there would come a time when the witches would have to choose Kir or Gaelin. We can not sit on the fence forever. At that time, I told Kir I believed they would choose him. I still believe that. Does that answer your other question?"

I pressed my lips. Her change of topic was answer enough. She knew, and she wasn't going to tell me. It was infuriating not to know when others did.

But I came here wanting to know what to do, who to trust. I wanted something concrete. "And the other witches? Alana? Should I trust them?"

"You should never trust all of them."

I sighed. This was going nowhere.

Muriel adjusted her weight, shifting her feet. "You must listen to your instinct. Hone that. It won't lead you wrong. Who do you trust? Right now."

"You," I said.

"Why?"

"I don't know. I just know it."

She smiled. "That is your instinct. Who else?"

"Nolan."

"Why?"

"He is from home. He came here to save me, even if we are currently in a disagreement."

"Home. This Nolan is human? A witch?"

"Human, yes. Not a witch."

She frowned and rubbed a hand on her temple. "I do not see a human near you that is not a witch in my coven. Them and fae. But do you think those reasons you stated are good enough to trust him?"

I nodded. "We have the same goal: to go back across the Wall, to go home. We just don't agree on how to do that."

Muriel glanced to Kir and back to me. "That does not sound like instinct to me. It sounds like reasoning."

"Is that bad?"

She tilted her head, pouted a bit in thought. "Sometimes. Sometimes not. I am more mystified why I have not seen him."

"Maybe because he is from the other side of the Wall?"

"Perhaps. Anything else I can help you with?"

"You mentioned the coven. Alana asked me to join."

"You should. Witches are not meant to be covenless. It is a shame your mother never brought you into hers. If she had, there is a chance that getting back across the Wall would have been easier for you."

The mention of my mother brought a sting to my heart. I didn't believe she had purposely made things harder for me. She had done what she thought was best.

I stared at the worn board beneath my feet. Through a crack, I could see the rocks of the riverbed below. My mother had said I would be safe on this side of the Wall, yet she was the one who'd taught me of the Fell Fae. Going through the Wall took me away from my father, so safer in relative terms. Or maybe she knew witches existed on this side too. That had been a revelation to me. Not once had she even breathed that suggestion. I knew she was in a coven. She'd said it was dangerous for me to be in it. Much like what Alana said about theirs. There were always witches who would do what was best for themselves and only themselves.

"Everything in Faerie has a price, a reason," I said. "What does my joining the coven do for you?"

"The coven would benefit. A witch of your strength coming in would strengthen all of us. Anything else?"

There was one last thing. I glanced back toward Kir. "Do you know how to take a fae source?"

Muriel's eyes widened, and her gaze flicked to Kir. "This is what is being asked of you?"

I nodded.

She clasped her hands in front of her as she pressed her lips together. "I do not, but even if I did, I would not share the information. Witches stealing sources is an act that causes imbalance."

A belch sounded out, and three figures stood on the rolling hill just behind Muriel.

Muriel rolled her eyes. "That one could try my patience. Him and the haughty one."

I laughed, a burble of happiness forming in my belly at the sight of Kir's friends.

CHAPTER 34
KIR

Dain strolled down the hill, taking his time, while Rylla let out a whoop and Clove screeched in happiness as she ran. Not to be outdone, Haze swooped down to land on my shoulder and nibble on my ear.

From my rift, I got one of his favorite morsels.

"Well done, boy, very well done," I said as I scratched behind his ears.

They clambered onto the bridge, and Muriel shot out an arm before pointing to the white line. "He will know if you cross it."

I raised a brow. That was new. "How…"

"It is one of the many ways he utilizes the witches in his power."

I took heart that she clearly felt that as distasteful as I did. But my heart fell as Clove dropped the arms she'd been holding open for Innara. They all knew not to hug me.

Clove, however, immediately got to the point. "Okay. We found the pages. It took all of us stumbling along the Wall in one area for an entire day and someone may or may not have lost their eyebrows." She rifted pages into her hand and waved them at me. "But we have them." She shuffled through them, her gaze darting over the words. "I've been translating them as we travelled. As far as I can tell, these aren't telling us much. The Winter Court ones said the stone could tear down the Wall and hinted that those who built the Wall planned that it would need to come down. These Autumn Court pages confirm that the Wall was never meant to be in place indefinitely. It mentions the stone has a cavern, which I don't yet understand what that means. I keep seeing words like cavern and even source." Clove reached up and scratched her head as she brought the papers closer to her face. She let them down to her thigh with a swoop. "We need the Spring Court pages, which I hope tells us how to use the stone. I doubt it is as simple as sending magic into the stone."

"It's never that simple if fae were involved in the making of it," Muriel said.

Clove nodded.

"Then we go get the other pages," I said, drinking in the sight of the three of them. I didn't want them to leave so soon, but we didn't know how much time we had left. And I still had no idea how to get the stone from Gaelin.

Clove's gaze darted to Innara, but it was Rylla who spoke. "We should take Innara with us. We could be there this evening and back by tomorrow morning with her help."

"Absolutely not," I said.

Everyone gaped, including Innara, who said, "But I can help. We only have so much time with the distraction Alana created, and hopefully, that distraction might mean he won't notice I cross the boundary. I don't think we can get back out here again."

I didn't want to admit it was the protectiveness rearing its head. But there was a logical reason. "We're both under safe harbor. We can't leave. Leaving would give Gaelin a reason to punish her or, by proxy, me."

Dain pinched his brow. "Then we go and hope we find it faster this time."

"Now hold on," Clove said. "You're positive it applies to both of you? Because you of all fae know how tricky the language can be."

And I did. I'd already realized how safe harbor protected me from his court but not from Innara. I tapped a finger on my hip, allowing the memory to pour into my mind. I had been exhausted, just healed, and filling with doubt if Innara had led me there. Gaelin being tricky with words and intent was more than possible.

But I needed a second opinion. "Clove, I know you hate this, but let me share a memory."

She sighed, rifting the pages away and closing her eyes. "If I vomit after, no one is allowed to laugh. I hate that swirly feeling. But if it might mean we find the cave right away, fine."

With her consent, I focused on her forehead, finding her mind and tentatively tapping on it to let her know I was there before entering. Invading the minds of my friends, even for something like this always, felt a bit distasteful. They were so vulnerable—I could read any stray thought if I wanted to. I waited for her to relax, or it would be worse for her.

Finally, a hand rose up out of the darkness. I grabbed it and brought her with me to mind. I pulled up the memory and let it run. We'd been out of the Delves, I'd pointed out the tear in Gaelin's cloak. He granted safe harbor. When he did so, he didn't glance once toward Innara. And then he asked me about how special she was to me, and I lied.

May as well show her that too, as that was something we needed to discuss at some point. The only explanation to me was the rules of Faerie faded as Faerie died.

And that was a depressing thought. Chaos would ensue.

Slowly, I pulled her out of the memory. But I kept the mind-to-mind connection. *What do you think?*

He wasn't ambiguous. He flat out didn't include her, but you were too out of it to notice, she said. I didn't release her. *And you let the memory keep going to show me—*

I lied.

You did. How? Clove asked.

I have no idea. I was hoping you could figure it out. It's disturbing.

I'll think on it.

And with that, I exited her mind, slowly, to let her adjust.

Within moments, we were both mentally back with everyone else.

As much as I hated what it meant, I knew Innara would leave. All of them would. Leaving me alone even more than usual.

"Safe harbor only applied to me." I met Innara's eyes. "So go with them."

"But he'll know I left when I come back?"

"We'll deal with it. Considering what he needs you for, you're likely to be forgiven, but we'll need a decent excuse." I focused my attention on the other three. "You know your orders. What I expect." To protect her with their lives.

Dain and Clove nodded, while Rylla looked like she had a sour taste in her mouth before she also nodded begrudgingly.

Without a word to me, Innara crossed the boundary. Neither of us were sure of the other at the moment.

Clove embraced her. "Come. Our horses are tied to trees just over the hill. You can ride with me."

"Horses?" I asked.

Dain rubbed the back of his head. "Muriel helped us find a few."

I stuffed my hands in my pockets as anxiety crept and twisted around my ribs. "Did the Wild Hunt see you all leave?"

Dain shook his head. "Not that we know of."

"It'll only be a matter of time before Gaelin realizes you all escaped. Ride fast, my friend."

The four of them clamored back up the hill. Innara turned around once to look back, and hope surged in my heart.

Soon, it was Muriel and me.

She watched me with a keen eye. "You have not told her yet."

It was a statement.

"No. She is not used to how Gaelin can trap you into saying

things you do not wish to reveal. It is better for her, safer for her, not to know."

"This is what you tell yourself?"

"What's that supposed to mean?"

"Telling her would gain her trust."

I laughed. "Yes, learning she is the fated mate of a fae who can't be touched by those who love him would certainly gain her trust. If I was a human and learned that, I'd think they manipulated me."

Muriel pressed her lips together. "You underestimate your mate. She feels it, wonders what it is. She fights it. It's like an unseen enemy to her right now. She can't trust what she feels. She can't trust her gut because she constantly wonders if *you*"—the word struck me like she poked a finger straight into my chest—"are playing fae games with her."

I swallowed and rubbed at my chest.

"But for that dose of reality, I offer something else, a balm for the pain. There is no way for me to know this for certain, but it is possible that a witch adept with unraveling curses lives on the human side of the Wall. Our numbers here have dwindled. And while witches there are hunted, their numbers are greater. Greater chance for a witch adept with curses to exist."

That was interesting indeed.

But I couldn't leave my court. I was needed here. "I'm afraid that will have to remain something I never know about. Unless we succeed in tearing down the Wall."

"We never know what Faerie will throw at us. It's information all the same." She was silent for a moment. "Has Gaelin made known what he wants from you?"

I felt the same wavering as Innara. Should I trust this witch? I knew Muriel wasn't beholden to Gaelin. In some senses, she wasn't as beholden to the witches of Cirrelea either. But she had her own motivations. "Last time we met, you mentioned you hoped the witches would choose me to ally with. Why do you think that?"

She walked to the rail of the bridge and leaned against it. This river had been such a beautiful blue at one time. And now it was nothing.

"You have not done much for the witches of Cirrelea."

I scoffed. "I gave them a place to stay in safety."

"But why did you do that, for their safety or to twist a blade into Gaelin?" She tilted her head, watching me like a bird would. "You know as well as I do it was prompted by your hatred of Gaelin. But you have never tried to use witches for your own purposes. And when you have asked for assistance, you have always found ways to repay them. Gaelin on the other hand..." She twisted her hand around her throat to make her point. "Only the witches drunk on power would side with him, but that number is not small. I fear it grows."

I moved to the rail as well, standing a foot away from Muriel. Her chalk boundary split the space between us. I needed to make overtures of an alliance with Alana. Wall knew when I would see Matriarch Verna again in the Winter Court.

But Muriel had asked me about what Gaelin wanted. All my talk had been to stall answering. But Innara put her faith in this witch...

"Gaelin wants Innara to steal my fae source. He controls the Wild Hunt. If we don't do what he asks, I'm sure he'll give the huntsman orders to ravage the Winter Court and to look again for my people." I scrubbed a hand down my face. I didn't even want to think of Innara refusing him. "I think, if it comes down to it, she should do it."

"Why?" Muriel's voice was a whisper.

I turned my head sharply to her. "She's my mate. I fear if she doesn't, Gaelin will threaten her life."

"Hm. There is power sometimes in doing the expected when you do so with your eyes open. But I have faith. I think together the two of you will find a way. You are a lord of three courts with his fated mate. Mates have a power all their own. Don't underestimate it." She pushed off the rail. "But it is time for me to get back."

Muriel trudged up the hill and disappeared down the other side, and only then did I make my way back to the soil of the Summer

Court. I found a sheltered area and got comfortable. It would be a long evening and night.

But sleep eluded me, even though nothing came this way. Maybe whatever distraction Alana set up had made Gaelin pull his patrols closer to the court.

Innara was away from me and in danger. Everything, physical and emotional, was in a knot. It was becoming all too clear that the force of the mate bond was not something I could fight.

The stars above me twinkled, and I focused on my breathing.

I chided myself. The Wild Hunt was in the Autumn Court, and the baedour was hopefully further north too. She had the others.

They would protect her. They knew their duty.

Seeing the others had been a balm for my soul. I rubbed my chest. Muriel's words gave me hope. Perhaps we could figure out a way.

A pang of dread went through me, a lick of panic.

Something was wrong. Sweat broke out on my temple, and I sat up. I didn't know how I knew it—I just did. I rose to my feet as silent as could be. Had someone found me? I picked my swords up off the ground and held them in my hands.

A scream erupted in my mind. Fear. Blinding fear.

My heart rate spiked, and I spun in a circle.

This is how I die. But it wasn't my thought in my mind. It was Innara's.

My chest constricted, and something tugged me, begged me to come. I didn't even think. I didn't consider consequences.

I sifted to where I was beckoned.

In a flash, I was in the Spring Court. The air was heavy with the scent of ozone. A spring storm brewed, and that was never good news. In front of me was the backside of a wyvern, its spiked tail lashing the ground. It had something pinned against the rocks that rose straight up out of the ground.

A female scream erupted.

Innara. I couldn't see her, but she was definitely the one pinned. Where were the others?

I scanned the area quickly—only the one wyvern, and I had the element of surprise, always the best advantage. I sifted right onto its back and stabbed down into its neck.

The beast let out an almighty roar and bucked me off before I could attempt to do more damage. In an attempt to confuse it, I sifted again to land on my feet on the other side of it. All this sifting would cost me. My legs were already trembling.

In the distance, thunder rumbled. This needed to be done before the storm hit.

Just as I hoped, the wyvern searched for where it thought I would land, giving me another chance to attack. I raised my swords and slammed them down again in a scissoring motion. The head fell to the ground with a thud, hot blood spurting as the body took one step forward and fell. I kicked the head away.

Blasting pain seared through me. I doubled over. My breath stuck in my lungs, and I gasped like a fish out of water.

This was no attack but another power loss when I was already so low.

My head swam, and my muscles turned to jelly. Innara crouched against the Wall. Her eyes were huge and glassy in the moonlight, her skin ghostly pale. She wouldn't understand what happened.

"You're safe," I said. Why hadn't she used her magic? I took a step toward her, but the world twisted and turned. My legs gave out, and I crumbled to the ground. The last thing I heard was Innara shouting my name.

CHAPTER 35
INNARA

"Kir!" I scrambled over to him, ready to check for a pulse, but pulled back when I remembered not to touch. His chest rose and fell, unlabored, so I knew he was alive. A quick scan of his body with my witchery didn't show any wounds.

It must have been the sifting, and I could do nothing about that. He'd depleted his power and overdone it.

To save me.

I rocked back onto my heels. He'd broken safe harbor.

A wind blew through the trees, making them creak and groan. A looming dread filled me as dried leaves scattered and danced, while the coppery, putrid smell of the beast's blood made me gag. The sky lit up in a flash, illuminating the weeping branches, followed by a roll of thunder. The storm blew in fast.

Considering the state of Faerie, I didn't know what to expect. I'd seen the snow in the Winter Court, the absolute desiccation of the Summer Court. I couldn't imagine the rain in the Spring Court being anything but a deluge.

Kir lay on the ground before me. The stars above winked out one by one as cloud cover billowed in. I had to get him out of here. But where?

The sky burst with light again, and I barely made out what might be an opening in the rock wall. I grabbed Kir underneath his armpits and dragged him toward the rocks. His shirt would have to keep him safe from me.

He was heavy, but I would manage it. I had to.

If the opening I saw wasn't a cave, maybe there would be an overhang. I couldn't take him far, in any case, my breath already labored with the effort of moving him.

Light flashed, and there was the opening. It had to be a cave. Hopefully, nothing lived in it. Hopefully, it was the dead wyvern's home, and it had no mates. It wouldn't smell nice, but it would be shelter.

Sweat broke on my brow as I backed into the opening. Kir's feet ground through the gravel, carving two trails as I went.

But we were inside, safe, and just in time.

Outside, the skies opened, and rain poured down. Thunder shook the ground. I moved us farther in. Bones crunched and rolled under my feet. This was indeed the wyvern's den. I found the nest, free of any carnage, and pulled us into it.

Woven leaves and grasses made a round bowl of a bed. It was surprisingly soft and warmer than the rock beneath it. I sat down with my back resting on an edge of the nest, pulling Kir so that he lay on me, his back to my stomach and between my legs. My energy to move him slipped away.

And then just like him, I passed out.

KIR MOVED WITH A JERK, AND MY EYES FLEW OPEN.

My legs were on either side of his hips, making the moment seem surprisingly intimate. But he moved away to create space.

I shivered with the loss of his warmth. "Sorry. I didn't have the energy once I got us in here. I fell asleep."

"Where are we?" He stood up and put a hand to his temple then sat back down again. "We lost power last night."

"Spring Court. The dead wyvern is just outside this cave. What do you mean you lost power?" The entrance glowed with rosy light from outside.

"After I killed the wyvern, a power loss occurred. I didn't think I was that low until that happened." Kir slowly rose and stretched. "I should thank you for finding shelter. There was a storm coming."

"No. I should thank you. I don't know how you found me, but..."

"Why didn't you use your magic?"

Rising to my feet, I shrugged with embarrassment. I'd been working hard not to be in the very situation I'd found myself in last night. "I panicked. I couldn't think. It all happened so fast. One minute, I was on the back of Clove's horse. Then I was in the air." I shuddered at the memory of the talons around me, my feet dangling just above the treetops. "And when it dropped me outside this cave. I knew I had minutes left."

"Then I am glad I came." Kir took a step forward, arms out as if to embrace me. But he stopped, dropping his arms. "Are you okay now?"

"You broke safe harbor."

He scrubbed a hand down his face. "Indeed."

"What now?"

"I'll need to receive my punishment. If I don't face it, Faerie will mete one out." He dropped his chin, staring at the ground. "I'd rather face Gaelin."

"What would Faerie do?" I resisted the urge to move to him, comfort him. This was a special kind of torture. Wanting to be near someone and not being able to. This must have been how it was for him. Only he'd dealt with it now for years.

He cast a searching gaze around the cave. "Take my life? Halve it?" His search ended on me. "It tends to be vicious to those who try to escape the rules. Circumventing them is one thing."

"So what do we do?"

"We go back to the Summer Court and face the music." He looked about again. "How do we get out of here?"

"The entrance is over there." I pointed before carrying on. "What about Gaelin telling me to take your source?"

Kir sighed and muttered something about Muriel before sitting on the edge of the nest and jamming his hands into his hair. "I don't see a way out. Running means I'd be subject to safe harbor punishment. I have to go back. But I think we could find a way. And if we don't, then take my source, find your way home."

"You can't be serious," I said as I sat down a few feet away. Any closer and it was hard not to touch him.

I still had no idea how he'd come to be here just as I needed him.

"I can't do it," I whispered as my eyes began to sting. I paused, swallowing the lump in my throat. That wasn't how I'd get out of this mess. I wanted to go home but not like that. Ripping his source out and leaving him at the mercy of Gaelin was selfish. Steel formed in my spine, and my eyes ceased their sting. "I won't."

"Why not?" Kir closed the distance between us. "You have no idea what he will threaten you with. He'll have something. If we can't find a way, you must because..."

He cut himself off, averted his eyes.

"Because?" I allowed myself one inch closer to him.

He turned back, his eyes dark and hard. "We play his game. Let him see what we want him to see and hide everything else. The more we surprise him, the better."

"I don't even know how to take a source. I'd take his, except he threatened Nolan's life if I did."

"He'll set the Wild Hunt on the others too."

"How do you know that?"

"He showed me. He may not know where they are right now, but the huntsman can be relentless. And Gaelin already told me the huntsman has orders to follow through in the event of his death."

An army with orders if he died. Gaelin truly was a conniving bastard.

Kir tapped his thighs as he thought. "If we could do something about the huntsman and the witches, defeating him might be easier. Don't take a straight-on tactic. Fight the things he'll lord over us."

We needed Clove. Maybe she could think of something with the huntsman and the witches.

Faint voices outside heartened me. Female and then a deep, masculine one. Dain.

They'd found us.

I dashed outside. Dain, Rylla, and Clove held their horses by their reins. All three stared at the wyvern. Dain kicked its head, setting it to roll down a small hill.

"I didn't know life magic could decapitate things," Dain said.

They all turned at the sound of my feet in the dirt. Clove whooped and ran to give me a hug.

"How?" Dain gestured to the head.

"That was me." Kir walked out of the cave, making the other three gasp.

"You broke safe harbor!" Clove released me. Kir's only response was to nod as he ran a hand through his hair.

"Okay. But how did you get here, and where did you both come from?" Rylla asked as she tied her horse's reins to a tree.

I wanted to know the answer to the first part of her question, but Kir walked near them and murmured something. Blast my human hearing. I knew it had to do with this pull between us and he wouldn't tell me.

But then they all looked to me for the second part to Rylla's question.

"There's a cave," I said as I hooked my thumb over my shoulder.

Rylla asked, "What cave?"

Clove squealed and clapped then grabbed my arm, tugging me. "Show me. This is like the others. We can't see it, but you can."

From behind me, Dain said to Kir, "You'll be in a lot of shit."

"I had to do it. You know that," Kir said.

As much as I wanted to stay and listen, Clove kept tugging me till I led her to the entrance, and she walked inside with me. Inside, she illuminated the cave with several balls of light she allowed to float around.

"You slept here?" She eyed me up and down. "Explains the smell."

"Not much of a choice with that storm," I said. "Where did you stay?"

She sighed as she looked about, shining her light on the walls. "Dain tracked the wyvern until that storm hit. Luckily, we found a hut to stay in and rest. Once the storm was over, we got back out here." She whooped. "Look! I knew it."

On a rock ledge above the nest and out of our sight in the dark, a box corner peeked out. Before I knew it, Clove found holds in the rock and climbed up. She pulled the box and handed it to me while she held on with one hand.

"Do your thing, witchy woman," she said, waggling her brows at me.

I laughed, remembering how fun it was to be around Clove. I sent out a tendril of magic, and the lock evaporated in a thousand tiny, sparkly motes.

Clove took the box and opened it. Inside lay a few pages, just like the original box. Her gaze darted across the pages.

"You know..." She stopped and looked at the bracelet I wore. "Do you mind?"

I let her pick it up off my wrist as she closed her eyes.

"Yes, I remember this," she muttered. Her eyes popped open. "Curious. This one and the one you lent Kir." She shook the journal pages, making them rustle. "These mention the stone having an inner well. So did the Autumn Court pages, but this makes it clearer.

It seems the stone needs a power source. But from the description here, it seems like your bracelet has one too, at least the well bit. I can sense a cavity on the inside of it, but it's not carved out like someone scooped it out. That would be impossible. It's more like a void. It wants something."

I screwed my face up. "You make it sound alive."

That was an unsettling thought, since I'd worn this bracelet from a very young age.

She laughed. "No, not alive, but something should be there. I sensed it when I put the light spell on this one and the other one in the Delves. There was this sensation of it drinking up my magic, but I didn't have time to think on it. And the feeling I got from it didn't seem dangerous or nefarious."

"So what do you think it is?"

Clove looked back to the pages. "I don't know. Let me keep reading. Where is the other one?"

"It was Nolan's. I gave it back to him."

Her gaze flew back to me, so I explained how he was in the Summer Court. All of it made her very thoughtful.

The two of us left the cave. Outside, Kir was arguing with Dain and Rylla.

"Oh Wall," Clove said. "I'm going back inside to read. They'll have to figure out whatever this is without me." She turned and felt her way in.

Behind me, Rylla said, "We are going back with you."

It appeared Kir had told them things they didn't like.

"You will go back to the Winter Court. That is an order." Kir slashed an arm through the now heavy air. As long as I had been around, he had been loath to issue direct orders. Allowing for others' thoughts and opinions was a hallmark of his.

I slowly moved into place among them as the silence thickened.

Kir stood, hands on hips, one finger tapping. He brought the other hand up to rub the back of his neck. "Nothing good is coming. I need you all in the Winter Court to help there. You cannot be in the

Summer Court. Gaelin will use your lives to force either my hand or Innara's. It puts you needlessly in harm's way."

Rylla scoffed and kicked a rock on the ground. It flew away and thunked into the side of the dead wyvern.

I glared at her. Did she disagree, or was she making light of his concern?

"You have no plan. We're all here. We go. Now," Dain said.

Kir growled. "I must go back for breaking safe harbor. He has me backed into a corner. Innara and I will have to find a way." He held his arms out to his sides before letting them slap back on his thighs.

Rylla looked to me. "And if you don't, will you take his source?"

"I don't want to," I said.

"But will you?"

I swallowed. "Kir thinks I should, but I'd rather take Gaelin's if it comes to it."

Kir opened his mouth, I assumed in protest.

But I cut him off. "If I take a fae source, it will be my choice whose it is."

"I'm beginning to like her more," Rylla said.

"And what will we do?" Dain asked, grinding his toe into the dirt.

"Protect the people up there. Know that the Wild Hunt may be coming. If you need to get everyone moved, do it," Kir said.

Clove exited the cave. "I think I could be reading this wrong, but it's not that the stone needs a power source." She pinched her nose. "Well, it does. The power source is a fae source."

Kir and my eyes met.

"But also, I think I am picking up on some language here that makes it sound like the one Gaelin took from the Delves isn't the only one."

"What do you mean?" Kir asked.

Clove paced, shaking the pages as she went. "I'm not sure. I need time. I need my books. I've seen it in each journal set, but I recall that in Old Fae, one of the words I keep seeing has a few meanings. And —" She stopped her pacing, pinching her nose again before she looked up, appearing fully defeated. "I need my books to be sure. I don't want to lead anyone wrong."

Kir's voice softened. "It's okay. We understand. But say there was more than one stone, what does any of this mean? Do we need all of them? And once they have a fae source, what would they do? Tear down the Wall?"

Clove groaned. "I don't know. I suspect the Summer pages would tell us, which Gaelin must have. But like the other pages, these hint at things that are distinct in the following set. The stone doesn't just tear down the Wall. There are other uses."

"Like what?" I asked.

"I don't know," she whispered. From the look on her face, I knew she thought she was letting us all down. I placed my arm around her shoulder and squeezed.

"Well, we know why he wants my source," Kir said.

I had thought the same thing when Clove mentioned that. "But couldn't he have any fae's source?"

"Size of the source likely matters. The stone was created before any of our loss of power occurred, so Kir's or Gaelin's would be the best bet to do something that large. But the bigger question is if he's looking to use the stone for one of its other unknown uses."

Yes, and what would that be? But something tickled the back of my mind as we said our goodbyes. Like a puzzle where I had all the pieces—I just needed to know how to put them together.

CHAPTER 36

INNARA

Kir made the other three figure out a location to sift to that he didn't know about. None of them looked happy about it, but their lord had spoken.

I only hoped, when all was said and done, this wasn't the last time I ever saw them.

We took a horse they left and rode back toward the Summer Court. Kir held himself rigid, and I did my best not to lean back into him. This sort of proximity was torture. The ability of clothes to protect him was a double-edged sword. The more I did touch him, the more I wanted to and the more unaware I'd be in a casual manner. It lulled us into a false sense of security.

As we crossed into the Summer Court, Kir said, "We'll be questioned when we get back. What story do you want to tell?"

I sighed. He wouldn't be able to lie, so we had to stick as close to the truth as possible. I barely had time to think on how I'd accepted his memory as the truth. "I left of my own accord. A wyvern cornered me, and you tracked me."

Kir scratched at his chin. "I think that works. It'll have to do.

Omission is best. I don't want him knowing about the others being here. Better he thinks he has them cornered in the Autumn Court. I worry it reveals too much, but I don't know what other story to tell him. Hopefully, he'll be more fixated on wanting to punish me than the why of you leaving."

Hours passed, and my limbs began to unwind from the heat, the rocking of the horse, the security I felt with Kir there with me, and the lack of guards appearing to lock us away. I stewed on what Kir wanted me to do and, how at this very moment, just like he proposed, we walked straight back into the belly of the beast.

Perhaps Gaelin had been so preoccupied with whatever Alana had done that he didn't notice we had left. Maybe that explained why we hadn't yet been waylaid.

But my hopeful thinking was only that. A troop of Gaelin's men rode toward us on horses not far from the Summer Court.

"Breaker of safe harbor!" one of them shouted. "Do you come here to receive your punishment, or do you trespass?"

Kir handed me the reins before he held his hands up. "I come for my punishment."

One of the smallest fae jumped off their horse. She looked to be the youngest, but it was hard to tell. All these fae had appearances that could belie their true age.

She approached Kir like she'd approach a predator. Steady and slow. Once she reached him, she motioned to see his hands before she slapped iron bracelets on him.

His skin sizzled, and he let out a low hiss. Otherwise, he didn't complain.

I swallowed a lump in my throat as another guard came toward me. Was it to be iron? Witch hazel? Some other drug? But no, he lifted me off our horse and brought me to his, where he had me sit in front of him.

I missed the feel of Kir behind me. The safety was gone. I wondered if this fae had only done it to drive Kir mad. They'd let Kir stay on his horse, attached the reins to their horse, and surrounded him. I rode ahead unable to see him.

Once we arrived at Gaelin's castle, they escorted us to the dungeon. They threw me into one of the first cells, but they took Kir down the hall until I could no longer see where he went.

My stomach sank. I was in the for-show cells.

What was Gaelin hiding deeper within?

My room was much like what Nolan had been in—white, clean, with only a cot—but without the outer visitation area. The bright white hurt my eyes, so I sat with my head in my hands for I didn't know how long.

What were they doing to Kir? What would they do to me?

The sliver of sunlight that hit my face eventually traversed the room.

Footsteps echoed, and then Nolan grabbed the bars. "What did you do? How did this happen?"

I jumped up. A familiar face warmed me, even if it wasn't the one I was desperate to see. But maybe Nolan knew something. He'd learned I was here.

"What have you heard?" I asked. "What are they going to do?"

He shook his head, and the look on his face was disappointment. "What were you doing? Was it just you and Kir?"

A warning bell rang in my mind. He hadn't asked if I was okay. My mouth gaped open like a fish out of water.

Muriel's words came to me. *I only see witches and fae near you.*

But this was Nolan, right down to the scar beside his eye. He knew me, knew my mother.

Still, I narrowed my eyes. There was a way to be sure. "How did you ask me out the first time?"

His chin lurched back. "What are you on about? Perhaps we can fix this, but you need to tell me what you were doing."

"Humor me," I said, "I've lived in the land of the Fell Fae for a while now. How did you ask me out?"

He sighed and rubbed his temple before he reached between the rungs to grab my hand, slipping his index finger between to stroke my palm. "I brought an injured Wall Walker to you and your mother for healing, and I stayed around longer than I should so I could ask if I could see you sometime."

His lips curled in that boyish smile he had given me that day.

It was him.

I breathed a sigh of relief, but I'd agreed with Kir to tell everyone our story full of omissions. That included Nolan. It was too dangerous for everyone else. If Nolan knew the truth, he'd be in danger. And I couldn't have that, even if I was still irritated about his parting words several nights ago.

"I ran." I cringed to be somewhat convincing, as well as hide my lie. "I'm so sorry, Nolan. It was cowardly of me to leave you here. You were right in how naive I am." I spoke to his hands that still clasped mine. "Gaelin... What he has asked me to do... I just don't think I can. So I ran. How will I tell him no?"

"You ran? Alone?"

"Yes." I pressed my forehead to his hands. If he saw my eyes, he'd know.

"So how did you wind up with Kir?"

If I didn't know better, I'd have thought he sounded jealous, which meant he believed me.

I pulled my hands away, and I dared look him in the eye. "Running was stupid." That I could say with a straight face. "I'm no match for the fae beasts out there. A wyvern cornered me. Kir found me in the nick of time."

All truth.

"So Kir tracked you?"

"I guess." I shrugged. Better to say as little as possible, but again it wasn't a lie.

Nolan stared at me for a moment, his gaze going hard. My stomach roiled. Something was not right. He'd never looked at me in such a manner. "You promise you are telling me the truth?"

Instinct roared to life. He had to believe me. Him believing me was critical. It was time to make him feel I trusted him, even if I didn't anymore. I cared for him—enough to not want him in danger. I could omit something from what I told him just as Kir did to me.

The comparison nearly sucked the breath out of my lungs.

I grabbed Nolan's hands again, forcing myself closer. I looked up into his face, into his eyes, willing him to believe me, trying to bring back how I used to look at him when I had been so enamored. "I swear to you."

The hardness left his face, and he smiled. "Good. I know you don't like what Gaelin asked, but I hope running and being cornered has taught you that this is our only way out."

I dipped my chin down. My emotions flared hot. Had he always been this way, or was this a new side of him? I thought I knew who he was, but the doe showed me that maybe he was hiding something.

But I couldn't show I suspected anything. He had, after all, been summoned to Gaelin in an effort to sway me. I wanted to push him away.

Instead, I nodded, playing up how properly chastised I was, and managed to squeak out, "I know."

He kissed the top of my head. "Good girl."

I boiled inside, but I didn't look up. His words lit an entirely different fire in me than when Kir had said them to me, making me want to burn it all down.

"I have to go. I'll come back as soon as I can," he said before he turned and left me there.

I reeled.

That was Nolan, but something was off.

The only conclusion I could come to was Gaelin got to him. I nearly laughed. How naive of me to think Nolan would rely on me to get us out of here and not also work his own angle. Definitely not the man who wouldn't even give me a moment to try to heal a hurt doe.

I plopped on the cot to berate myself. I had trusted him. Fully. Up until moments ago.

Now, I wasn't sure how much I should trust him at all. Had I ever known him in the Eastlands? We'd only known each other a few weeks. He'd come here to save me, and for that, I had believed in him. Now, I was learning there were people here I relied on. They weren't who I had expected to trust.

My mind drifted to Kir. I worried Gaelin was torturing him.

A guard appeared at my door, breaking me out of my thoughts. The beam of sunlight was now long gone. He pulled out a key and, with grating gear noise, unlocked the door and swung it open.

"Gaelin gave orders for you to be released. Our mistake. You should have never been in here." His voice was cold, stilted.

I didn't stand right away. This felt too good to be true. "Where is Kir?"

The guard ignored my questions and made his way away from the cell and up the stairs leading out. The door hung open, so I followed. But I couldn't go up the stairs. Not yet. I turned so I faced down the hall where they had taken Kir earlier that day.

"I wouldn't think about doing that, miss." The guard paused on the stone steps, his body slightly turned with one leg on the step above.

"Why not?"

"I'll be forced to put you back in that cell."

I didn't move a muscle. Fae had the element of speed over me. Even a mad dash would get me only a few cell doors down. It wasn't worth the risk. And I had more potential to find things out if I wasn't in the dungeon.

So I forced myself to follow the guard out.

On the main level he said, "You're free to go."

Then he took up position just outside the dungeon stairs in a silent message: *don't even think about it.*

Since no one had said my room had changed, I headed back to the last place I had slept in this court. The day had been long. Rest was sorely needed.

It felt like I had only fallen asleep when a sprite in my room pestered me to wake up.

"The master needs you to get ready," the female sprite said. Her entire being was pale, translucent, and her wings beat so fast it lifted her hair as her feet floated off the ground. She must be an air sprite. She clapped her tiny hands. "He sent a dress for you."

"A dress? What am I being summoned to?"

"Everyone is invited. It's quite the to-do." Her voice was pitched high and excited.

She spread the gown on my bed. It was flesh colored on top and a vaguely see-through white on the bottom. Sparkly white beads were embroidered in it to look as if branches climbed up my chest and my arms. I'd never had anything so beautiful. I ran my hands over it, the beads digging into my palms.

I couldn't take my eyes off the dress. "What is this gathering for?"

"A celebration." The sprite flitted across my room and into the bathroom, where I heard the tub begin to fill.

"A celebration of what?"

The sprite tugged me. "Time to get you out of these clothes."

I pulled back. "Answer me."

"A celebration of Gaelin, of course." Her eyes were wide, as if I should have known the answer.

My stomach lurched. I had a sick feeling I knew exactly what this was.

Kir's punishment and his demand for me to take Kir's source.

Our time had run out.

The sprite tugged me to the bathroom and fussed with my clothes.

She nearly pushed me into the tub. "Soak for a bit then bathe. I'll be back soon to help you out and then prep your hair and makeup while you have a bite to eat."

Before she left, she spread out several items and canisters on the shelf near the tub.

I sank into the water. There had to be a way.

I slid my eyes shut, trying to calm myself. My witchery eased into me, which was galling. Why was it so easy all of a sudden? It had been no use to me with the wyvern.

The faintest blue lit up before me. What was this? Even fainter was a flicker of red.

My hands trembled in the warm water. There had been a fae power drop last night. When it happened during the baedour attack, I saw the bond for our bargain for the first time. Blue for the water in the tub. Red for the candle lit across the room.

As I submerged my hands. The blue and red wavered, coming in and out of focus. I pulled my hands out. It did it again.

I sat up, sloshing water out of the tub. It couldn't be.

I put one hand in. Nothing. I put the other hand in. Again.

I focused on the red of the candle in the other room and held my bracelet away from my skin and out of the water. The candle came into focus more strongly, the red brighter.

My heart thudded, and my breath shook. I wrapped my fingers around the stone. The red of the candle dimmed. I gripped it hard as tears welled in my eyes. This was for protection, or so my mother had said.

But for me or for others? What else had she hidden from me?

I gave an almighty yank to the cord. It was leather, and she had spelled it to make it one continuous piece. It pulled on my wrist, burning my skin with the friction. I let out a moan of pain but didn't let up.

But it was no use. I leaned back into the tub. A flicker of light off silver caught my eye.

Scissors from the sprite.

I grabbed them and cut the leather of my bracelet. It slid from my wrist and into the water as a wave of energy washed over me.

I sucked in a breath, dropping the scissors and gripping the sides of the tub.

Wave after wave went through me, pounding my lungs, my

heart. And then all ceased. Ragged breaths sawed through my chest. The parts of me out of the water felt clammy and cold.

What in the Wall?

I reached for my witchery, and every single elemental color bloomed into my vision. My body froze. This could not be.

My mother had hidden from me that I had ability with all the elements.

THE AIR SPRITE HELPED ME READY. INTRICATE BRAIDS PULLED MY HAIR AWAY from my face. She wove flowers throughout and allowed tendrils to be free. Smoky eyes and rosy cheeks completed the look. I'd never felt so glamorous before, but that didn't stop the warning bells of what I was being led into.

The sprite led me to the courtyard from my first night here. The memory brought Kir to the front of my mind. He had to be here. This was Gaelin's spectacle, and there was no doubt Kir and I would be highlights.

As we approached a set of double doors, the air sprite flitted away, and two others opened them for me. Harp music drifted in, along with laughter and the murmurings of a large crowd.

Everyone turned.

The crowd, made up of every type of fae I had seen so far and then some, parted. Their dress was every color imaginable. The cacophony it created was disconcerting: silks and leaves, glittery and nature-based, modest and sensual. My gaze jumped about, taking it in until it rested on Gaelin, dressed in clean leathers, lounging on his throne.

My heart beat out a staccato as I made my way in.

Where was Kir? Alana?

The fae peered at me as I passed. Some had frowning brows as if they worried for me. Others appeared almost giddy. But one thing they all had in common was they wanted this spectacle, whether they were on my side or not.

I was the lamb led to the slaughter. I was the entertainment.

A familiar set of stony-blue eyes looked back, and my chest relaxed. Kir stood near the end, whole and healthy. His wavy, brown hair fell across his brow, and though his face was serious, when our eyes met, a quick smile whispered across his lips.

Violet stepped out from beside him. Her gaze flicked from Kir to me, a satisfied cat. His face went blank, devoid of any emotion.

My breath came quicker as Gaelin stood from his throne.

"My guest of honor is here. Let us begin our celebrations!" He stepped off the dais to reach for my hand, pressing a kiss to the back of it. I had to force myself not to pull away. He leaned down to whisper in my ear. "We have much to celebrate by the end of this night. I have so much planned for you." He backed away, waved his arm as if to introduce me to someone. "But for now, dance now with your friend."

Nolan stood there, looking wholly uncomfortable. The usual air of confidence he carried was nowhere to be seen. He held one hand out, while the other remained behind his ramrod-straight back. Utterly formal.

My gaze strayed to Kir, where Violet curled a hand around his bicep, tugging him deep into the crowd. Before he disappeared, he lifted his hand to brush hair out of his face. The movement revealed his wrists with iron bracelets.

Nolan cleared his throat, pulling my attention back to him. His offered hand beckoned with a twitch of his fingers. My thoughts were in a muddle, but I gave him my hand.

Play the game.

I could control all the elements, and no one else knew, a clear advantage.

Nolan pulled me close but not too close. His arms around me

were stiff, like he didn't want to touch me. We began to move, to spin with the music and the other dancing couples, but instead of graceful, his movements felt constrained, begrudging.

It felt wrong. *He* felt wrong. Ever since he came to see me in the dungeon.

I tilted my head up, but he was focused on others. We swirled past the dais where Gaelin sat again on his throne, watching everyone, watching us.

Nolan swallowed, and his hand on my waist tightened. "You know tonight is the night Gaelin will ask you to do it." He looked over my head at the crowd. "You must."

When I didn't answer right away, he finally looked down at me, and his grip on my hand clamped down, his steps slowing.

"You're hurting my fingers." I wriggled my hand until he loosened his grip.

"Say something." His eyes pierced me like daggers. There was hate behind them, and something cold sank in my stomach. When I didn't speak, he swirled us through the crowd and into an alcove with a stone bench, setting me down forcefully. "You have to do it. It's the only way."

"What has gotten into you?" I asked.

This didn't feel like Nolan—even when he had had killed the doe, even when we argued. The collar of his shirt splayed open. Bare skin.

"Your necklace," I said as I reached up to touch where it used to lie.

His hand went up, batting mine away. "Why does it matter?"

Had he used it as some sort of payment? I shifted away from him, not liking how he was behaving. "You said it was important to you. Where is it?"

"It's nothing. What is important is you doing what Gaelin wants to get us out of here."

Nothing? I'd kept that necklace safe, brought it back to him. He had asked for it as soon as I'd seen him in the dungeon. "What is going on? You aren't acting like yourself."

Nolan grabbed me by the shoulders and shook me before getting in my face and grating out, "You will do it, human."

He froze. I froze.

His eyes widened, and a look of stark fear passed over his features. Then he released me and sped out of the alcove, pushing through the crowd.

Human? He was human too.

My skin went clammy and cold. I sat there, too shellshocked to do anything else, rubbing my temples. I should find Kir. Nolan wasn't on my side. Gaelin must have turned him. Perhaps had turned him long before I'd arrived in his court. And I had trusted him.

I stood, smoothing my hands down my dress and taking a deep breath.

Outside the alcove, Gaelin greeted me with extended hand. "I saw your friend leave rather emotional. Shall we dance? Perhaps I can offer comfort."

For once, he didn't smile, but there was a tension to his brow.

Comfort from Gaelin was the last thing I wanted, but rejecting him wasn't an option.

Play the game. I had an ace in my back pocket.

I let him take my hand and guide me to the dance floor. He held me closer than Nolan had and leaned down.

"What happened to get you both so upset?" His finger slipped between our clasped hands, and he stroked my palm once then twice.

I stiffened as my mouth went dry.

"N-nothing," I stammered.

His finger stroked a third time, and the world around me wavered as my head grew light. This couldn't be. Nolan always did that with my hand, and when we danced, he hadn't done that.

Breathe. But the tightness of my dress wouldn't allow it.

Gaelin kept us spinning on the dance floor. The laughter and casual banter of others stung my ears. Now was not the time to freak out. I had to keep a level head. I had to play the game. Gaelin would know something was off.

Faces whirled by, garish and animalistic. Where was Kir? I couldn't find him. Cackles pierced my soul, colors flashed by, and blood whooshed through my ears.

"Don't lie. Your friend looked positively furious." Gaelin leaned in closer, to the point where my nose was near the base of his throat. "Did you tell him you fell for a fae?"

I took in tiny, sipping breaths, focusing on his throat. He was baiting me. My racing heart would give me away.

Breathe.

Kir's face appeared in the crowd. We locked eyes. As we whirled, I kept coming back to him. He steadied me, keeping his sight set on me too. I saw his chest rise and fall slowly. He was coaching me. I matched the pattern and calmed.

I was a witch, a powerful one with ability no one here knew of. I could use it.

I seized my witchery. Let it steel my spine.

The world lit up in Technicolor.

I began to work my threads. I'd never used water magic before, but I'd seen Alana weave it to remove glamour in the tunnel. I had to try. What was he hiding?

Thin. It had to be the thinnest I could make it. One of the witches here was Violet. And the others? Best to be careful. Loyalties could be tricky things.

So thin, thin, thin. They could not know what I could do.

With all the elements in my vision, colors melded and morphed. It was almost more information than my brain could handle. I blinked. In front of me, shadows wavered like a shifting cloak. Illusion. Glamour. All around Gaelin's neck and where a necklace would lie along his collarbone and chest.

My hands grew sweaty. *Play the game.*

"And what fae would I be falling for?" I added lightness to my voice. "No human would fall for a Fell Fae."

I wove the water threads thinner than spider silk, allowed instinct to guide me. Small changes to reveal, not to remove. I didn't want to expose; I only wanted to see.

"You're lying again," Gaelin said. "I can hear your heart race, feel the sweat on your palm."

His throat shimmered before the veil fell away, revealing a thick band of tattoos. Dozens of inky lines matching the ones that the witches wore, one on top of the other. His skin appeared raised to the touch, thickened from all the ink. The band was wide, a solid black with branches sticking off the edges. A few strayed farther up his neck and down towards his chest and shoulders. But it wasn't the tattoos that struck a white-hot dread.

"It is only my nerves. I know what this celebration is," I said as I stared at Nolan's necklace on Gaelin.

No.

I stumbled in our dance, tripping him. His arms strained to bring us back from making a spectacle. I shook my head, forcing myself to look at him and not the necklace, forcing myself to smile, forcing myself to speak.

"I'm so sorry," I said. "I'm a terrible dancer."

Kir stood in the crowd past Gaelin's shoulder. Our gazes met. He still coached me. I slowed my breath.

I could not let Gaelin see the panic on my face as things fell into place in my mind like pieces of a jigsaw puzzle. He'd note my heart rate, my faster breathing, but a stumble and embarrassment could disguise that. I'd already mentioned nerves.

But none of that really mattered, since the necklace he wore was the one I had handed Nolan. It was the one Kir wore in the Delves. And I think I knew how Kir had lied, which, if true, meant Gaelin could lie. But the thing that sent alarm bells through my head was the question of why Nolan would have had a necklace that would allow him to lie when he was human, when he was the Eastlands.

Gaelin's arms relaxed, and we continued our dance.

My thoughts raced. Muriel said she'd only seen fae around me, and Gaelin did the same finger touch on my palm as Nolan did.

I stumbled again, using it as an excuse to let him go. "I need a moment."

The crowd blocked me.

Kir appeared. His eyes held me up, chased off my panic. Gaelin, behind me, curled a hand over my shoulder. Kir's pupils dilated before he looked at the man who had caused all his pain.

A lump formed in my throat, and my skin crawled as Gaelin's other hand curled over my other shoulder. Pressure, the hint of a massage. It all felt familiar.

An idea formed in my head, and I wanted to deny it. How would it be possible? If the idea was correct, I had been thoroughly manipulated. Faerie tricks indeed. And they'd begun long before I'd entered Cirrelea.

Gaelin was Nolan. Nolan was Gaelin.

We'd kissed in the Eastlands. I'd nearly fallen in love with him. And oh Wall, what had I told him these past days while I thought I could trust him? What had I revealed?

"I think your presence bothers my life witch," Gaelin said to Kir.

The damned dress wouldn't allow me to breathe properly. Kir's eyes flashed at Gaelin's words or my state, I didn't know.

"I broke safe harbor," Kir said. "I come to receive whatever punishment you deem fit."

I stiffened. He was doing this now?

I pulled away from Gaelin's grip, to better see them both and get his hands off me.

Gaelin's eyes narrowed before they morphed back to his usual penetrating stare. "In due course."

He turned his back to us, made his way through the crowd as he headed for the dais.

"You deny me my punishment?" Kir raised his voice, projected it. It rang around the courtyard. "Faerie rules demand you do so once requested."

The crowd froze, dancing ceased, and dissonant notes rang out as fingers stopped plucking strings. Gaelin slowly turned, one foot on the first step up to the dais. He twirled his hand, and a crown of thin green branches appeared above his brow.

"And I will. When I deem it time," he said.

CHAPTER 37

KIR

"Are you mad?" Innara said before her eyes flicked to the side and her face hardened.

Beside me, Violet shifted into my view. "Thought you lost me?"

I hadn't been trying. I'd seen the panic on Innara's face as Gaelin swirled her around, and I'd spared zero thoughts for Violet.

"Why is she here?" Innara's voice held a note of irritation. "I have things to tell you."

"I'm afraid she is my watchdog for the time being."

Innara let out an irritated sigh as Gaelin strutted across the dais. Doors opened off to the side. The crowd in that area let out harsh gasps. We both craned our necks to see who it was. Innara's hand went to her throat.

Alana came out, escorted by guards. She was clad in chains and wearing a flimsy, hole-filled sack of a shirt.

"Since some felt they deserved attention, I decided to begin my lineup of entertainment." Gaelin's voice projected around the courtyard like mine had only moments ago.

Those in the crowd who hadn't been watching all turned now. A general tittering rose. They loved this sort of stuff.

"Some"—Gaelin sought me out in the crowd, and our eyes met—"need to learn patience. But what say you on beginning with the appetizer I have planned?"

He raised his arms to the cheers of the gathered fae.

Gaelin was in his element with a crowd of blood-thirsty onlookers egging him on. He'd invited his entire court to this, but only the ones who loved the show were here.

"What's he doing?" Innara asked.

I hadn't seen Alana since the tunnel. She looked awful, with knotted hair and days-old makeup running down her cheeks.

"Making an example of her," I said.

Innara stared with a creased brow as Alana moved up the steps, all the while struggling with the guard, fighting the entire way.

"This woman is a traitor to my court." Gaelin's voice ricocheted off the stone walls. Somewhere in the back, a vase crashed to the ground, and a few of the gathered fae covered their ears. Gaelin paced along the front of the dais as he gazed at the crowd, making everyone present feel like he was addressing every single one of them. His eyes fell on me and Innara with a glimmer of twisted glee.

The guards forced Alana to her knees once they had her in front of him.

Gaelin lowered his voice. "Traitor."

Alana looked up at him with rage in her eyes. "I'm not the traitor. You are, betraying all of Faerie for what? More power? A true ruler would look after more than his court. You don't even look after all your people."

"She's going to get herself killed," Innara murmured beside me.

Violet, beside us, snorted in a pleased way, making Innara glare at her.

"I think she's aware of that and does not care." I said.

On the dais, Gaelin backhanded Alana. Her head whipped back, but she composed herself, bringing her chained hands up to catch the blood flowing from her now-broken lip. He crouched in front of her, whispering something for only her ears as he dragged a finger down her neck and then her chest. Alana shied away.

Gaelin took a few steps. "You are charged with defying your bargain. You stole from me and tried to frame another witch." He stalked away, throwing an arm out to point at her. "You betrayed me. You betrayed your sisterhood."

"Let my sisters have me then." She spit blood on the floor of the dais.

"I don't think so. You stole from *me,* defied *me.* I can't have anyone else getting that idea, can I?"

"So kill me. I dare you."

"We should do something." Innara clutched my arm, and I didn't move away. My attention was glued to Gaelin and Alana.

I curtly jerked my head. As much as it pained me, helping Alana right now would only make everything worse on us. He was doing this to scare us, scare the other witches.

Gaelin crouched in front of Alana, one finger tilting her chin up. She jerked away, and he grabbed her chin, his fingertips white. Spittle flew out of Alana's mouth as her head thrashed to get out of his grip. Her eyes raged at him, while her arms flexed and pulled, trying to get out of her binds.

"I curse you to lose thirteen minutes of your life for every time you consider lying, double if it is to me," he said. "Thirteen minutes for every second you wield your water witchery. And because I'm not a monster, for every morsel of information you bring me that I deem useful, you'll gain back thirteen minutes." He shoved her face back, but by then, she'd stopped fighting, the horror of his curse settling in.

She screamed, and Gaelin grabbed the front of her shirt, exposing a portion of her chest. A tattoo bloomed over her heart, similar to mine. I pressed my lips together at the memory of the pain of that etching. Nothing at all like the bargain tattoos. Curse tattoos felt more like someone carving your skin out.

Gaelin hadn't released her from his service. He'd make her use her water witchery, and as she used it, the fear of death would force her to spy on her witches to gain some of it back.

He'd turn her into everything she didn't want to be.

"Get her out of here. She is to live in the dungeon for now. No contacts unless approved by me," Gaelin said before guards dragged Alana from the dais, her body limp and her face listless.

But this display had its intended effect. His treatment of Alana shook me. The words he had said to me on that hill days ago echoed in my mind. *You should be more concerned about what I will ask of you.*

Guards appeared beside us, and the surrounding crowd, even Violet, gave us space.

It was our turn. A path parted among the fae, leading to the dais. The guards didn't ask us to move, but one cleared his throat. Gaelin wanted us to come of our own free will. Little would it matter that coercion stood right next to me.

I allowed my arm to brush Innara's. She needed the comfort. Or perhaps I did. As we approached, Gaelin's gaze was like a hawk. Anticipatory. Predatory. He brought clasped hands to his lips as we closed the distance.

On my last step up, I flicked my hand, revealing my crown: inter-twined branches similar to Gaelin's but with elements from my three courts. Antlers for Winter, bright green buds for Spring, and gems in shades of orange and red for Autumn.

A display of my power.

Even with iron bracelets on, I could still wield my magic if it only affected me.

Gaelin's eyes narrowed when the crown appeared, but he composed himself and plastered his ever-present smile on his lips. "You're here. How wonderful."

We approached, and as we did, Nolan and Violet stepped up near several guards behind Gaelin.

"My punishment?" I asked before he could say more.

His eyes slid to me. "Patience. First, I would like to show you something." With a flick of his hand, he rifted the huntsman's eye so that it floated just above his palm.

Innara, beside me, stiffened.

"The huntsman," he said theatrically. "Let me show you where he is. Don't be shy, Kir. Have a look."

The crowd shifted and murmured. They had loved what happened to Alana. Now they wanted more.

Gaelin raised his arm and a white curtain dropped down behind him. "I've magicked the eye so that what the huntsman sees, all can see once you've made the connection."

I hesitated, but I knew I had to look. He brought the eye closer to me. I gazed into the inky black iris and allowed myself to be swept away.

It wasn't the detritus of the Autumn Court that greeted me but the barren wasteland of the Winter Court. My heart thudded. It was as if Gaelin and the huntsman had choreographed this. The huntsman ran along the column of undead warriors, which gave me time to get my bearings, let the dread seep in.

First, I saw crossroads then in the distance the Hibernal Shore. The direction this column pointed was one I knew well. It was where I had sent Rylla, Dain, and Clove to prepare our people, the majority of which were in the hidden village this army pointed towards. My friends may not have even arrived yet. I had no idea where they had sifted to. There was only so far they could go without draining themselves.

Seeing more wouldn't do me any good. He'd made his point. But as I pulled back, the vision went hazy. I saw what looked like a cord, like the vascular system behind the eye, extending as far as I could see. I ripped my vision away. Gaelin's screen might reveal it to all, to him.

The crowd cheered as my sight and hearing came back to my body.

Innara's face was pulled tight. "Kir," she breathed.

"Had enough?" Gaelin asked.

"What do you want?"

"What will you give me?"

The conversation with Muriel played in my head. There was power in doing expected things with our eyes open. When Violet had brought me here years ago, Gaelin wanted me to cede my power. It hadn't worked. Would it now?

Gaelin expected the fight, defiance. Playing the game sometimes meant knowing when to bluff. He wanted his crowd to see me fold. I hung my head and breathed in.

I plucked my crown off my head and held it out to him. "I cede my power."

Greed flashed across Gaelin's face as he considered what I held before him. The huntsman's eye still floated above his hand. He grabbed it between his fingers and dropped it to a pillow upon a pedestal as he moved closer to me. He laughed, eyes alight.

"How easy! You roll over like a dog." He pranced to the side, putting on his show. "Lord of Winter, everyone, ready to give it all up. He'll hand over his people at a mere threat."

He held his hands toward me and clapped. The crowd jeered.

"I'll do what is needed to keep my people alive," I said. "I'd sacrifice my power for their benefit."

Gaelin lunged toward me, spittle flying out of his mouth. "But it's not that easy. I want more than that this time."

The crown flickered out of my hands and settled on my head.

"You and I know that doesn't work," he said. "I want something else. Try again."

My stomach dropped. What more could he want? Whatever my face showed, he embraced. His magic dove into me and plucked at the mate bond. Next to me, Innara sucked in a breath at the same time I did.

"I want you to trade me your soul," he whispered, and the crowd went wild.

The wind went out of my lungs. I'd been prepared to hand over my power, but this was something else entirely. My soul?

"With your soul, you would be under my control. Your courts, your bargains, your *bonds*. All of them. I would decide if you keep them or not."

"Never." I said it with such vehemence the blood rushed into my face. He had threatened my mate bond, my people, everything I'd ever cared about.

"I knew you would say that. Allow me to illuminate what you will lose if you don't. Bring it in."

Nolan moved to Innara, slipping an arm around her waist and pulling her away. Gaelin stepped back, and the floor where he had been faded away. A *clank* brought something up.

I should kill him now, consequences be damned. But the damned iron bracelets prevented me. I breathed in deeply, holding it, preparing myself for what he had planned next.

A cage rose through the dais with a woman inside. She turned around, her head tilting up. Her skeletal face became apparent. Sluagh. Her body appeared young and nubile, but her clothes hugged her rotting flesh to her bones. Fingers long and encrusted with blood and grime curled around the bars.

Innara struggled, but Nolan held her there. I ignored her, steeling myself for the vision. Sluaghs were adept at finding your worst nightmare or your best dream to entice you into their lair.

Gaelin spoke a word, and I found myself in my court, cooking breakfast in my underthings.

His voice stole into my head. "If you trade your soul, you could have this. I'd let you keep your bond."

A warm feeling settled in my chest. I was happy. Scrambled eggs sizzled on the stove as I prepared two cups of coffee.

Behind me, Haze jumped onto the counter, prancing close to rub against my shoulder.

"Haze, you know better than to be on the counter," a familiar voice said. Innara strode into the room, a small child with slightly pointed ears on her hip. She leaned in to me, tilting her head. I wrapped my arms around the two of them, kissing them both.

Dain walked in, swiping the coffee I made. "Gross. Get a room."

Rylla and Clove followed with their arms wrapped around each other's waists. Clove reached out for the child—*my* child—and snuggled him close.

"We brought a present for our favorite nephew," Rylla cooed at him.

My heart was full to bursting as Innara rested a hand on my chest and enjoyed the presence of our friends.

The picture swirled and fades. I grasped for it, wanting to bring it back. It felt so real, so right. I ached for what had been before my eyes.

Gaelin's voice enters my mind. "If you don't trade your soul, I'd settle for you giving up your mate bond."

A new image formed. Innara in bed, writhing. Pure ecstasy written on her face. At first, the vision had me above her, in her, there with her in the ecstasy. A mirror glimmered into reality behind the bed, and the face looking back was not me.

It was Gaelin. My heart stammered, and I wanted to get up.

Innara moaned out his name, and pure rage, molten and hot, slithered up my spine.

I had no control over my body, his body, in the vision. He forced me to watch her, what he did to her. He made me look into the mirror again, and his face morphed from Gaelin to Nolan.

The vision changed again, and the whiplash of it nearly had me vomiting.

The Wild Hunt plundered a village, my Winter Court village. I was the huntsman, running, jumping over burning beams, slamming my axe into anything that moved. The reek of death and smoke was nearly overpowering, but it only fed me. I reveled in it. It was what I was made to do. My axe slammed into another body, and hot blood splattered in an arc across my face. I carried on, looking for my next target. Rylla. My pace slowed. I watched as undead warriors overwhelmed her, and my hands went to the buckle of my pants.

The vision cut out.

I found myself on my knees, retching the contents of my stomach onto the dais. That vision was too real.

He'd given me the terms. Gaelin would have Innara, or he would have my soul.

I had been ready to give him power over my courts. It would have allowed me to continue fighting. But he wanted it all. There was no guarantee he would allow me to keep the mate bond with her.

No, she would be his. And it tore me apart. The image seared itself in my mind, and I couldn't make myself stop seeing it. My lungs bellowed. Everything had been so real. It was as if I was there. Making love to Innara and then wielding the axe that split my people in two. I could still feel the thud that went through the axe handle as it cleaved their bodies and the spray of hot, coppery blood.

I retched again.

"Kir!" Innara dropped to her knees beside me. Nolan must have let her go.

This couldn't be happening. This was so much worse than ceding my power.

Gaelin's chuckle rang out, and I wiped at my lips. He stood where the sluagh had been, her cage already lowered.

"Don't like what you saw?" he asked.

"I'd rather die."

He strode forward, eating the space between us in two steps. "I'm afraid that isn't an option." He leaned forward to whisper in my ear, a tactic that meant Innara didn't hear him but all the fae would. "If you die, your friends die, and I'll be the one comfort-fucking your mate. Nolan doesn't exist, but I'll be sure he does for her."

He stood and walked away, picking a wine glass up off a tray and sipping at it.

I roared, leaping to my feet and lunging after him. But it was no use. Without my power, I only had physical strength. We grappled for a moment, knocking into the pedestal with the huntsman's eye on it. Gaelin wrapped me in air and tossed me away.

But I got in one good punch, as his bloody lip attested.

I landed in a heap back near where I had been. My soul or my mate bond? Off to the side, Nolan held Innara by her elbows. Could I give her up to save my people?

Something curled around my wrists, caresses of air. They wove and wrapped around my bracelets, keeping them from my skin.

Someone gave me my power back. Plus the element of surprise.

Immediately, I reached out to Innara.

CHAPTER 38
INNARA

"It appears you need some time to consider your options. How about we add more clarity," Gaelin said.

Kir lay in a heap, and I completed the air wrappings around his iron bracelets. I hoped it was enough.

The huntsman's eye rested right by his hand. The huntsman and the witches were what Kir and I had spoken of—take care of them, and we stripped him of power.

"Innara, take his source," Gaelin ordered. "Let him see that the more he wastes time, the more he will lose."

Nolan squeezed my arms slightly. I needed Kir to talk to me. I'd hoped the air would work.

"No." My voice was barely above a whisper.

"No? You need more convincing than going home?"

"You've never told me how it is possible."

Kir stared at the huntsman's eye with a thoughtful look to his eyes. I tore my gaze away, focused on Gaelin who rifted the stone into his hand.

"It's simple," he said. "A fae source goes inside this, and you can go through the Wall."

The stone flickered away.

My heart thudded. That lined up with what Clove had said, what she had read in the journal pages. Gaelin *did* have a way for me to get home, but now I didn't want to go.

From his spot on the floor, Kir glared at Gaelin, but the huntsman's eye was gone.

His gaze flicked to me.

His presence roared into my mind. *I can take out the huntsman. Have you figured out anything with the witches?*

No. I'd been too caught up in what Gaelin demanded of Kir.

Gaelin got in my face. "His source. Take it."

I seized my witchery, hoping for anything. With the full spectrum of elemental colors blooming before my eyes, I saw it—within each fae in the room, a glowing ball of power.

The prophecy they all adhered to had nothing to do with life witches. It wasn't a life witch that could take a source. It was a witch that wielded everything.

It was me.

Nolan released me and shifted, revealing his fae source too. I was right about him not being the same tonight, and I would have bet I was right too about Gaelin being him. The man beside me was a stranger.

Focus on the witches, Kir said into my mind.

The witches. Gaelin's source was right there for the taking, but I knew Kir was right. Taking Gaelin's source would get rid of him but not the huntsman. That wasn't something I wanted to risk.

Gaelin grabbed my arm and dragged me away from Nolan. "It feels as if you need some motivation."

He turned me to face Nolan. All the while, I searched.

How could I deal with the witches? Joining their coven wouldn't help me now. And then I saw dark threads emanating from Gaelin's tattoos. Bonds just like I had with Kir.

"You want to go home? Your friend here crossed the Wall to save you." Gaelin rifted a rapier into his hand and struck out, the blade whistling in the air before stabbing straight into Nolan's chest.

I screamed as whoever wore Nolan's face crumpled to the ground, grasping at the gaping wound.

"Take Kir's source, and his death won't be on your conscience," Gaelin said.

I stared at Nolan as his mouth opened and shut before looking Gaelin dead in the eye. I knew exactly what to do. Just like the baedour.

To Kir, I said, *I know what to do. Kill the huntsman.*

And to Gaelin, I whispered, "I'll never do what you say."

Gaelin's eyes hardened, and I pulled on my witchery, focused on those bond threads spiraling out of him like tentacles and thought, *Snip them all.*

As one, the threaded bonds whipped back to him, smoking and recoiling into his flesh.

Gaelin pushed away from me, grabbing at his throat. His face was beet red, and he fought for air. "What did you do?"

Violet, near the huntsman's pillow, fell to her knees, grabbing at her neck as well, clawing. Her fingers stilled, and her gaze darted to me. Pure hatred seethed from her. "You know not what you do!"

But I had no time to respond. Kir held the huntsman's eye in front of his face. Within moments, the eye burst, a yellow, viscous ooze bubbling out of it before the entire thing blackened and turned into a pile of dust. His arm dropped, the ashes he grasped falling to the floor. His head lolled to the side like his body had the life drained out of it.

The crowd surged and screamed, fear thick in the air. Fae trampled one another to get out, pushing and shoving, and I swore the snapping of limbs cracked through the air.

Gaelin still scratched at his throat, thrashing violently. Violet only suffered once, but he suffered for every witch he'd bargained with.

Fitting. But it wasn't enough.

Gaelin's source was right there. The huntsman was no longer a threat, and neither were the witches. I reached to rip out his source.

But my vision blackened. I tried to breathe in but only succeeded in a high-pitched, pained wheeze as my hands reached for my throat too, trying to ease the pain.

Violet moved into my view, her face lit with a sick glee.

"Ah, ah, ah," she said as she wagged her finger at me.

Of course she was a threat. She didn't need the bargain to hold her to Gaelin.

My blood thudded in my head, ringing began in my ears, and my vision went hazy as my hands fell to my sides.

CHAPTER 39

KIR

I retracted from Innara's mind immediately, knowing it would be unpleasant for her, but there was nothing I could do about that. Then I focused on the huntsman and slid into his mind.

I had been right that first time I'd looked through his eye. There was a connection when I viewed through him, a tenuous thread from the vast space between this eye and the rest of his body. But it was enough, and with the iron bracelets not affecting me, I saw the path.

The huntsman, who was never a bright fellow, didn't notice me. Didn't see how I traveled the path of light from his eye to his person. But once I was there in his mind, he felt me. Shields went up, but they were weak, pathetic really.

I knocked them aside, diving down until I found the core of his mind.

Its kernel was black, rotting, and putrid. Death was all he thought of, all he wanted to taste. He wanted me to kill Gaelin. He wanted to act on his orders. The vision Gaelin had forced on me swam into my mind. I knew how the huntsman wanted it, could feel it in my veins.

I let the rage I felt during the vision fuel me and extended my fingers like talons, encircling that kernel, letting him feel the scrape. He thrashed and tried to squirm away, but it was futile. My fingers stilled for a split-second before the shell of the mind cracked.

My hatred for my ability nearly choked me.

But no, this was right. Cirrelea was better off without this creature in it. I could wield this ability if it meant ridding Faerie of creatures like this. The huntsman's seething hate poured out of him. His hatred for me, his hatred for the living—I took it all in, hardened my resolve.

I wouldn't enjoy it, but Faerie didn't need me to. Faerie needed me to bear it.

I squeezed and ground the kernel of his mind, the yoke oozing between my fingers.

Then I ran. Sprinting back down that thread, lest I lose myself too.

But it faded too fast, the distance too great. My path disappeared. Behind me, the huntsman's mindscape crumbled. A thread extended from me, from my chest. It lit up once, bright. I followed it.

It lit again but dimmer.

Again. In a pattern. Like a heartbeat.

I seized that light and ran each time it lit up. But every time, it faded a little more. I had to get back. I dove into the lighted cord, became one with it, travelled at blinding speed.

And then I was there. Home.

Innara.

"Kir," she breathed. "Violet."

I ripped out of her mind. My power dwindled, but I didn't need it. Violet faced Innara. I grabbed a metal candlestick within my reach and whacked her in the head. She crumbled to the ground with a satisfying thud.

Innara's body lay in a heap right where Gaelin had brought her. She breathed. One hand went to her neck as she sat up.

Gaelin kneeled near her, gasping for air.

With Innara alive, I didn't waste a second. Surprise was on my side.

I jammed myself into Gaelin's mind, oily and rancid. I waded through the muck and commanded him to summon the stone, kick it toward Innara. I saw through his eyes that he did as I commanded. But he pushed back on me. Black oil solidified, bulged.

No.

Crushing his mind would take power I no longer had. Not after the huntsman.

"Cede your power to me." Never in a thousand years would I want his soul, but freeing his people—that, I could do.

Gaelin chuckled. "I see you finally left your morals behind."

"My morals are just fine if I am ridding the world of scum like the huntsman and you."

The black, solid sheen wall of his mind pushed harder.

"Cede your power. I killed your huntsman. The witches are no longer under your control. Cede." I scraped my mental talons over the walls of his mind. I let them sink in, but my power was dwindling.

And he knew it. He laughed. "You'll have to find me for that."

Then the black walls shoved with a force I'd suspected was coming but could do nothing against. Our powers were too well matched, and he had more in reserve than I did. He flung me back to my mind in time for me to watch him sift away.

But where he'd stood, a hand mirror rattled on the ground until it stilled.

CHAPTER 40
INNARA

I roused and Kir was there, whole and healthy. Violet lay in a heap, a candlestick on the ground next to her and her temple oozing blood. Kir grabbed his head with a curse. I wanted to go to him, but I was still lightheaded, my witchery not quite there.

Where Gaelin had stood, something clattered to the ground.

It was familiar.

It had rested in my bedroom for twenty-two years. It was one of the things my mom had told me to always pack when we ran. The handle had that familiar loop at the bottom, the filigree at the top. I crawled to it, picked it up.

It was my mirror. Why did Gaelin have it?

I flipped it over, and the mirror reflected my mussed hair. Bits hung down, while some still remained in the intricate braids. The kohl around my eyes ran down my cheeks.

The mirror's surface undulated. A new picture formed. I couldn't look away.

It was my mother. She looked thinner, older. She sat at a table, sipping from a spoon over a bowl. Behind her was a nondescript wall with a plasmavision hanging on it. She sighed and pushed at hair that looked grayer than when I'd last seen her. I turned the mirror, turned my head, trying to get the view to change, to show me the rest of the room.

But nothing worked. It was only this view.

She looked up. A shadow flickered, and a line formed between her eyes. Someone was in the room with her. She tracked them. Strained creases formed on her face as she tried to smile for whoever it was. But I knew her. Her eyes told me that what she felt was fear.

Fingers appeared, sliding along the table toward her. An arm—a man's arm—formed as he drew closer to her.

My pulse raced, and dread coiled in my stomach as the cufflink came into view.

A cross consumed in flames.

My father was there. He had my mother.

I threw the mirror away from me as panic seized me.

I had to get back home. The stone warmed in my hand. If what Gaelin had said was true, I held the means to get there now. But it needed a source.

Kir crouched beside me, panting like he was in pain. "What is it?"

"My mother. The mirror. It showed me she is with my father." The mirror now lay cast off a few feet from me. I wanted to kick it farther away, but Kir reached for it.

It looked so small in his large hands. Dainty. He twirled it until he could look in the mirror. With a frown, he said, "I see nothing."

"It was there. I swear it. It was my mother's. Mine, actually."

He lifted the mirror and sniffed. "It has fae magic on it."

I got to my feet, smoothing out my dress, not that it mattered. The crowd was gone, leaving a storm-swept courtyard in its wake. Goblets and trays were spread everywhere. Food littered the tile like detritus. A path of destruction had trampled the greenery. And the worst of it was here and there, bodies were strewn about like a child casting their dolls around. I turned away from the devastation.

"I can't leave my mom with him," I said as I swept the hair out of my face.

Kir dropped the mirror to his side as he looked out across the courtyard, his horror incrementally growing as he took it all in. Nodding, he swept his free hand through his hair and rubbed the back of his neck. "I'll go with you."

"No. You can't do that. You're still lord of three courts here. They need you."

Before he could reply, we both hissed in a breath. Pain lanced across my chest, etching and carving. A voice rang in my head, a female I didn't recognize. *Your lives are tied. If one dies, so does the other.*

The pain ebbed, but the whisper of its searing remained.

I panted. My skin over my heart itched.

Kir undid his buttons to stare at his chest. A new tattoo lay near his heart, intertwining with the one he already had, but this one was gold, not black.

A matching one painted my skin. I looked up at him, eyes wide.

"Faerie exacted its punishment for breaking safe harbor. It was lenient." He stared off at the courtyard. "Gaelin didn't punish me when I asked for one." But his eyes darkened when he turned back to me.

"But why..." I started.

He pivoted back to me, crowded me, then tilted my chin up with a glove-clad finger. His eyes held an intensity, and the muscles in his jaw tensed. Something flickered across his face, a slight tension before coming to a decision. "You want to know what is between us? You're my mate, and there is no way I'll let you go back to the East-lands alone."

Mate. It sucked all the air out of my lungs.

He nodded as if encouraging me to process it all, what it meant.

"That's this pull?" I whispered.

"It'll only get worse. We need to be near each other. I tried to keep you away. Had hoped distance at the start would delay this. Give you time to get away from me. Give me time to not..."

"Not what?"

"You're my mate, and our lives are linked. In more than one way now, thanks to Faerie." He clenched his jaw. "I can't have you risking yourself over there without a fae bodyguard."

I pressed my eyes shut. He needed to be here with his people, no matter how much I wanted to take him with me.

"Clove could come," I said. "Or Dain." But not Rylla. We'd kill one another.

"Not going to happen. I'll trust no one else to protect my mate or our conjoined lives."

Mate.

It explained so much, but I still had so many questions.

Kir cast about. Violet still lay there, but her foot twitched.

"We need to get out of here," he said. "Who knows where Gaelin went."

A rattling breath drew in from behind me. Nolan. Or whoever it was.

"Not yet," I said. "Watch Violet. I need to do something."

Nolan lay there crumpled over, his back resting against a pedestal. His eyes flicked to me as I approached, and red saliva frothed at his lips.

"I can heal you," I said.

He shook his head, so I reached for his wrist. With what must have been some of the last amounts of his energy, he pulled away. I sighed. The stone was still in my grip. With my witchery, I could still see his power source.

"You want to die?" I asked.

He nodded. These fae and their hatred for witches. I turned the stone over in my hands. The cavity or void that Clove described was there. An idea formed.

"Gaelin made you do this? Made you wear a human's face? Then he killed you," I said. His breathing increased, and he groaned. "Allow me to give you your face back, the dignity of passing as yourself."

His face lost some of its tension, and he nodded assent. I knew all this questioning cost him. I pulled water from some spilled on the ground and washed away the glamour he wore. I'd briefly considered that it wouldn't work if it was all fae magic, but some witch must have helped Gaelin do this. It had been tied off so it would last quite some time. This poor fae would have been buried with a human's face.

With the glamour gone, a fae man looked back at me. Raven black hair, almost white eyes, and rosy lips. His skin, however, was ghastly gray.

"You are you now," I said.

He slow-blinked, showing his thanks.

"You still don't want me to heal you?"

He shook his head.

Kir came over, positioned himself so he could see Violet. "She's rousing. A few minutes, I think."

He looked down, took in the fae, and crouched, placing one hand on the fae's shoulder.

"He doesn't want me to heal him," I said and looked directly at the fae man. "But I can offer you the ability to not allow Gaelin to inherit your power. He forced you into this and callously slaughtered you. There is a way he won't get your source."

It didn't take him much time to consider. His breathing was labored, but he ground out, "Do it."

Doors flew open, and Alana rushed in. "You're here."

Gaelin had sent her to the dungeons.

"No time to explain," I said.

"Do you have witch hazel? Can you deal with Violet?" Kir nodded to the other witch's body.

Alana scurried over and dropped to her knees, her fingers going for the pouch at Violet's waist.

"Do it," Kir said to me. "He's fading, and then you won't be able to." He bent his head over the fae man, grasping his hand and uttering foreign words I'd never heard any of them speak. It was beautiful, mournful.

I reached in and pulled his source out.

The fae had reason to be frightened of someone like me.

With the stone in front of me—I made sure the man could see—I placed his source within the stone. Like Clove had said, it felt like a magnet as soon as I got the source close enough. It snapped together, causing the stone to emit a warm glow from inside.

"Thank you," I said. "Gaelin won't have it now, and this will help all the fae of Cirrelea."

The man's eyes glistened. He blinked once and stilled.

"She's fully dosed with witch hazel," Alana said. "With the amount I gave her, she'll wake with such a brain fog she won't know which direction is up for the next eight hours." She looked from us to the now dead fae. "Rowan." She took his free hand, bringing it to her lips. "He could be an ass, but when it came down to it, he knew right from wrong."

"He didn't want me to heal him because I am a witch," I said.

"No, he was one of very few fae who found their mates. She died." Alana looked to me as she placed his hand down and closed his eyes. "You took his source?"

"So Gaelin wouldn't have it."

She chuckled. "Rowan would've loved that. As much as he wanted to be with Arden again, he wouldn't have wanted to be sacrificed by Gaelin."

I nodded, feeling as if I had been able to do something to make this horrible mess somewhat better for someone.

Kir stood, rifting his bandolier and swords to him, and then shoved the mirror through a loop. "We need to go. Alana?"

She shook her head. "I need to find the witches that will follow me."

"Gather them and head to the Winter Court," Kir told her.

Alana glanced to me. "You cut our bargains from him. All my sisters, I know, offer their thanks." She glanced to Violet. "Well, most of them." She grimaced like she didn't want to say the next part. "But you didn't undo them. He still has our soul slivers. You cut the tethers that connected them to us."

My stomach sank. Of course, and that must have been what Violet shouted about. Maybe even she hadn't wanted Gaelin to own a part of her soul. "How do I fix it?"

"I don't know. But in a year and a day, he will own them permanently."

I had caused this. "Where can I find out how to undo it?"

She glanced down at the stone. "You're heading to the Eastlands? The witches there might have better ideas than we do."

Another reason to go. I looked to Kir. He nodded.

"Yes, we're going," I said.

Violet groaned.

"We need to go," Kir said. "The Winter Court," he repeated to Alana.

She nodded and dashed out of the Courtyard.

Kir grabbed my arm, and we sifted as far as his power would take us.

THE WALL, THE CAVE WHERE I HAD FIRST ENTERED CIRRELEA, LOOMED IN front of me as the dead branches of trees behind us creaked in the wind. I couldn't help the agitation I felt. A mixture of anticipation, eagerness to go, dread, and sadness at the inevitable goodbyes. People here were now dear to me. Clove, Dain, and even Rylla. Alana and Muriel.

Kir and I spent the past week getting to the Winter Court and setting as many things to right as we could.

Alana and the witches loyal to her headed to the Winter Court. Kir notified Verna and offered for them to move into the hidden village. Since Gaelin knew the most recent location due to the Huntsman, Kir assigned Rylla, Dain and Clove to oversee the move.

"They don't like it, do they?" I asked Kir as I led him into the cave.

"No, but they'll do their duty — rule in my absence, hunt what remains of the Wild Hunt. Protect my court."

Protect his court because he was leaving to protect *me*, his mate.

We took the same path we'd both taken out of this cave so many weeks ago. So much had changed.

Mate.

The tunnel opened to the cavern, the box that held those first journal pages lay discarded off to the side. My feet crunched over ice as I walked to where Kir had held me in those air bonds.

"Speak, witch," Kir whispered from behind me. His breath tickled my ear, and his voice held a note of humor. He remembered our first encounter too.

Mate.

He came closer. The heat of him radiated, warming me from behind. How I longed to sway back to feel his support. Turn and rest my head on his chest.

But I couldn't.

Mate.

"You knew since the time you invaded my mind." It was a statement. It was a question.

"Yes," he said, somehow knowing that I referred to the word that kept repeating in my mind. His voice rumbled more than usual as if emotions clogged his throat.

We hadn't talked about it at all since he announced it after Gaelin sifted to who knows where. It had been a shock, yet also not. If I was honest, I'd known something bonded us, something more than our bargains. It'd been there since we met in this very cave. If he hadn't been my mate, would I have thought following to ask for his help was a good idea after he tied me up? Would he have warmed the bonds? Would he have rescued me from the baedour?

"And you didn't tell me because?" I asked.

"Look at me." His voice was low and gruff.

I paused, not wanting to. If I did, a well of emotion I didn't think I could stopper would break open.

When I wouldn't, he moved around me, feet sliding over ice. Somewhere a drip echoed. He lifted my chin and ducked to meet my gaze. His steel-blue eyes swelled with something I couldn't name. They were full of wonder and yearning, but behind it I still saw the sadness, the ache he must feel every day. It stabbed me in the heart.

"Perhaps I was an idiot to ever think you wouldn't find out. I didn't say anything because I didn't want to hurt you. I didn't want to hurt myself. And then I did it to protect you from Gaelin finding out." He smoothed his thumb over my chin. The cold leather made me shiver. "Some fated mates don't like each other all that much. I had hoped—maybe." He shrugged. "It would be easier that way given" — he waggled his leather-clad fingers. But then he pocketed his hands, his eyes shuttering. "I can't be your mate in the ways I want to."

I closed my eyes, letting his words sink in. It felt like a rejection, but as I repeated it in my mind, it wasn't. He wanted to be my mate in all the ways. A tear trickled over my cheek, freezing as it slid. "I don't accept that."

Silence.

"What do you mean?" he finally asked and with what I thought was a tinge of hope.

I opened my eyes, gazing at him. That serious and rugged face that had irritated me so much was now my home. "I don't accept that it sounds like you still want to put space between us."

He stepped back. "I'm cursed. It's not a choice I'm making because I want to."

"Then we figure out how to undo the curse. Add it to our list of things to do in the Eastlands."

His face was aghast before it morphed. Wonder and hope spread into his smile. "Muriel mentioned the witches there might be able to help me. Do you think it's possible?"

"Balance." I smiled, putting as much confidence into it as I could.

"What was done can be undone. There is always a way to achieve balance." I took heart in the core belief my mother taught me. We had to figure out his curse. Kir had said the pull between us will only grow. If we didn't figure out a way, then we would have to part. Doubts wanted to rise up, but I pushed them all down. I had thought getting away from Gaelin was impossible and we'd managed that.

Kir studied me for a moment before he nodded, a slight quirk to his eyes. He rummaged in a pocket of his cloak and pulled something out. "I have something for you." A pair of black gloves, sized to fit me. "Contact always feels safe—controlled—if I initiate. But I miss.." His eyes slid shut as a flexion of pain crossed his features.

I slid them on. The fit was perfect, like the gloved was magicked to be a second-skin that covered past my wrist. I had a niggling feeling that Clove had a part in it. If not the magic, the idea.

Kir moved closer, an invitation. His next breath hitched as I slowly raised my hand. His eyes slid shut as my fingers coasted into his beard and across his cheek. He leaned into it with a sigh.

Warmth bloomed through me, and his eyes snapped open, nostrils flaring.

Damn his senses.

He wrapped his fingers around my wrist. "We're going to have to be careful of that or we might drive ourselves mad." As he pulled my hand away, he paused. His finger slid under the edge of my glove, examining the tattoos that he revealed. After a moment like he'd come to a decision he pushed the material back. "I release you from our bargains." Then he brought my wrist to his lips, pressing a kiss to the material, as he held my gaze. Even with my new glove, I could feel the heat of his lips as the burn of the tattoos disappearing sang along my skin. And the combination was heady: his releasing me, his lips so close to my skin, and the tiny bite of pain of the tattoo.

I let out a tiny moan, making his eyes dilate.

His curse most definitely needed to go.

"We should get going," I whispered. The sooner in the Eastlands, the sooner we could figure a lot of things out. I hoped.

I pulled the stone out of my cloak. Clove had said I needed to touch it to use it. Kir grasped my other hand, giving it a squeeze. And we stepped through.

Kir and Innara's journey will continue in So Wicked Are the Witches.
Release date TBA.
Until then, stay up to date on all my news.
Visit www.katkeenanbooks.com and sign up for my newsletter.

Acknowledgments

First and foremost, thank you to my husband, Andrew, who has been a constant source of support of my dream to be an author. (I did it, my love!) And thank you to my kids who have most-of-the-time respected when the door was shut so I could get some writing done. I love you to the last planet and back.

This book wouldn't be what it was without my critique partner. Jenn Lessmann, you know this book as well as I do, from the worldbuilding, to the blurb, to the book cover. You called me on all my writerly B.S. and this story is stronger for you having read it and commented (probably a zillion times) "but why?" Thank you, thank you, thank you. I'm truly grateful for your story knowledge, your willingness to delve into brainstorming with me, and your friendship.

To Carrie, my BFF. You've understood my need to write for ages. In some ways, we might be polar opposites, but in so many others, we just make sense. Thank you for the EWWWW's and for always being honest. I love you.

Sarah, Vee, Beth, Kristen, Holly, Elena and Mariel. Thank you for your support and friendship. You've all believed in me when I had little belief in myself and helped me in so many ways, from reading Never Go Home to being a Dain stan or just brainstorming and chatting about the writing life. I couldn't have done this without you.

Thank you to Sara, my friend and proofreader. You always have a listening ear for me and jumped at the chance to help. I'm so grateful you approached me at the playground to say hi. Thank you for your friendship.

This story began as a vibe as I listened to Breathe by Fleurie in the midst of mourning the loss of my dad. It took a bit to find my footing, but I hope you've enjoyed the result. So lastly, thank you to the readers. Your votes, notes, and love keep me going.

About the Author

Kat grew up in the US and now lives in the Great White North with her husband, three children, and family cat. Since she moved around a few times, her accent is kind of wonky, a little southern drawl with an 'eh' attached.

She's always wanted to be an author, but discovered her love for fantasy and romance in college at the used bookstore. Now she loves writing fantastical worlds with swoony romances just as much as she loves reading them.